Charisma

Tor Books by Steven Barnes

Achilles' Choice (with Larry Niven)
Beowulf's Children
Blood Brothers
Charisma
The Descent of Anansi (with Larry Niven)
Firedance
Gorgon Child
The Kundalini Equation
Streetlethal

Charisma

STEVEN BARNES

A Tom Doherty Associates Book
TOR® New York

CHARISMA

Copyright © 2002 by Steven Barnes

This book is printed on acid-free paper.

Edited by Beth Meacham

Book design by Jane Adele Regina

A Tor Book
Published by Tom Doherty Associates, LLC
175 Fifth Avenue
New York, NY 10010

www.tor.com

Tor® is a registered trademark of Tom Doherty Associates, LLC.

ISBN 0-312-87004-3

First Edition: June 2002

Printed in the United States of America

0   9   8   7   6   5   4   3   2   1

For Steven and Sharlene:
you make your uncle proud

ACKNOWLEDGMENTS

Arson *maestro* Noel Petansu, Dave LaFave, Jamie Charles, the staff and counselors of Wondercamp: Jennifer, Ocean, Deb and all the rest. The Wonderkids themselves, especially Lizzy, Michael, Jessica, Ryan, Jacob and the unforgettable Molly. And a special thanks to Dr. Al Siebert for his insights into both the psychopathic and survivor personalities.

The Nine Principles:

1) Do not think dishonestly
2) The Way is in Training
3) Become acquainted with every art
4) Know the Ways of all professions
5) Distinguish between gain and loss in worldly matters
6) Develop intuitive judgment and understanding for everything
7) Perceive those things that cannot be seen
8) Pay attention even to little things
9) Do nothing that is of no use

—Musashi Miyamoto, 1645

A choice, once made, creates its own path.

—Alexander Marcus, 1984

Charisma

Prologue

Perversely, the closing minutes of Tanesha Evans's life were among the happiest she had ever known. Her new Schwinn Aerostar was the color of strawberry lemonade, as responsive as a circus pony. The sidewalks were still damp from the pre-dawn shower that had scrubbed the air as clean as her face and hair. The sun had emerged from the clouds, warming the crisp morning air with a promise of summer days to come.

She wheeled down Washington Boulevard past the deserted white two-story husk of an abandoned Ralph's Grocery store. Three years ago it had been a living maze of shelves and bins, a forest of tastes and aromas. Tanesha had held her mother's hand while they shopped, gazed wonderingly up at the vast shelves as if they were the jagged walls of the Grand Canyon. Now the windows were patched with weatherworn boards, the signs that once offered *Charmin tissue two for four dollars* or *Oranges forty cents a pound* were concealed by posters for the latest hip-hop album or gangsta film. In just thirty-six short months Tanesha had watched the neighborhood shrivel like that fabled raisin in the sun, hope draining away as commerce fled west to Culver City and north toward Hollywood and the Wilshire district.

Washington was a major artery, a four-lane east-west conduit stretching from East L.A. through downtown and all the way to Santa Monica beach. Right through here, through Central L.A., it was starting to look like a scenic route through a war zone: the Disney Autopia, maybe, skirting the border of Ghetto World and Barrio Land. (Tanesha imagined happy Mouse-signs reading: *don't feed the natives!*)

She laughed at the thought, and focused enough attention to avoid a six-year-old girl lugging a brown paper bag of groceries half her own size. Tanesha zigged and then zagged without slowing down. Perfect timing. She was about two minutes from Mrs. Johnson's shoe-repair shop when she spotted Jesse "Wizard" Cambridge running the shell game over by the number ten bus line. She braked up short enough to sniff rubber. Jesse was six-foot-five of knobby black knees and elbows, gifted with a loose-limbed grace that had, once upon a time, made him the lightning-fast power forward for the L.A. Romans high school basketball team. He was the golden boy then, swooping off to the University of North Carolina on a full athletic scholarship. Even with the generous leeway afforded athletes of his caliber, academic pressure had folded Jesse Cambridge in two short years. "Wizard" left the neighborhood with a parade, but snuck back under silent cover of night.

Now here he was, wearing a satin vest with vertical rainbow stripes, bustin' moves behind a little red folding table at the number ten, deep in the fleece when Tanesha rolled up. She watched with narrow, intensely interested eyes.

Tanesha was thirteen years old, slender and dark-skinned with almond eyes and Asiatic cheekbones. Her hair was bound smartly with a red ribbon. The cheekbones were a gift from her mother, whose grandmother had been Korean. The bicycle was a gift from her stepfather Floyd, a reward for maintaining a 4.0 average. Tanesha could laugh. As if anyone would have to motivate her to study, or work hard, or turn her schoolwork in on time. For longer than she could remember, the urge to excel was as much a part of her as her bones. *The Way is in Training*.

She could no more be satisfied with a mere "C" than she could levitate. As Tanesha often said, "Grades are a way of understandin' thatcha understand, getting thatcha got it." Too many of her contemporaries seemed to think they earned grades to make their parents happy, or worse still, to pave the road for college. What crap! You do it because you do it. But since Tanesha was only thirteen, and maintaining those grades meant kick-ass perks, she wasn't about to tell Floyd (who was a little slow, even if he *did* own a chain of dry cleaning shops) that she would have done it for zip.

"Hey hey hey, it's time to get paid!" Bullion flashed in Jesse's mouth. He grinned blindingly, switching the little red plastic shells around more swiftly than the eye could follow. Faster than *most* eyes could follow. Tanesha's followed just fine, thank you ladies and gents. More important than seeing, she *observed,* and as she did she remembered something very important indeed:

Jesse's brother Mickey attended Mt. Vernon, her junior high school. Three months ago, on Career Day, Jesse had, at his little brother's request, brought his magic act to fourth period class. She didn't believe for a minute that he could ever make it as a professional magician. Oh, "Wizard" could do some kick-ass card tricks, and some scarf magic that had the other kids *ooh*-ing and *ahh*-ing, but what she remembered most was the way that he made coins and handkerchiefs, a basketball and even a little stuffed canary disappear.

Perceive those things that cannot be seen.

It took about eight minutes for Tanesha to detect Jesse's shell-game pattern. It was like bim-bam-*boom*. He would lose and lose, and then win. Then he'd lose some more. He didn't do this rigidly, either: his win-loss ratio was keyed to his audience, calculated to keep pedestrian interest and gullibility high, suspicion low. When the foot traffic began to drift away, he would lose a dollar or three. When the pot got weighty, *what do you know!*, his luck magically improved.

In the middle of his *hey-hey-hey* spiel, Jesse winked at her. Just idle flirtation, sure. He didn't recognize her. She thought he was cute, though, in a roughneck kind of way.

That made her decision more difficult.

On the one hand, there was the money. God, there was so much money on the table, such a crazy cluster of ones and fives and silver coins. She knew she could take it all, because she knew just what Jesse was doing. Tanesha knew that when the money got high enough, he just palmed that little ball right off the table, using the same quick hand trick he'd used that day at Mt. Vernon.

But if she dropped the dime, exposed Jesse as a cheat, something way nasty could happen. Her grandmother had told her about an old schoolmate, a man named Beaumont, Rudy Beaumont, a local thug who got *shot* in his own pool hall, caught cheating at cards. Shot through the chest and laid there on the floor and bled out before an ambulance could arrive. *"Blood fanned out around him like a big old valentine heart."* Grammy had said it with a bland, distracted kitchen-talk voice, just something to do as she pried hot buttermilk biscuits up out of the pan. *"Boy wasn't never no good, no how,"* she added philosophically. *"Biscuit, baby?"*

Tanesha didn't want Jesse to get *shot* or anything. She just wanted to print a little paper. So the girl fussed, and figured, and found herself an answer.

All she needed was the nerve to bet Mama's ten bucks. That particular pair of Lincolns had been heading for Johnson's shoe-repair shop, to pay for new soles and heels on two pairs of her mom's nursing shoes. If she were wrong, a whipping would be the very *least* of the consequences. But if she were right, if she won, and brought all that money home (and there had to be at least fifty dollars on that table!), maybe Mom would reconsider about summer camp in Arizona, let her miss the stupid old reunion in Kalamazoo or wherever.

"Hey hey hey. Time to get paid!" Jesse chanted again, golden teeth gleaming. The crowd was thick, and the money heavy. Her heart pounded in her chest. She just *knew* that this would be it.

Jesse's hands were a feathery blur, juggling those red cups around and around, slowing and then speeding, deliberately letting the ball "accidentally" show. Then a disarming aw-shucks of a Fort Knox grin, followed by another burst of speed. Then he leaned back, the lean bundles of muscles flexing in the long black neck, his smile a dolphin's smile, fixed and meaningless. He searched the crowd, seeking a challenge. . . .

Tanesha slammed her money down.

Jesse's answering smile was brotherly. "This ain't for you, little lady." Jesse spoke the words out of the side of his mouth, almost stage-whispering. Those eight syllables represented, for a hustler like Jesse, an almost saintly gesture.

"Whassa matter?" She deliberately drawled the words, trying to make herself seem slower, and younger. And dumber. " 'Fraid I might break your bank?" He glared at her, and looked around, as if seeking a way to avoid the confrontation. The crowd had swelled, murmuring its appreciation of her bravado, and wishing her luck.

For a long beat nothing happened, just the sound of cars cruising the Boulevard.

Then some silent communication passed between the two of them, and Jesse nodded. *You want the whole load, little sister? You got it.*

His hands blurred. Jesse chattered like a chimp, rattling his rap at a pace designed to dazzle, hypnotize, and intimidate. "Round and round it goes, watch the hands, not the toes. Under one's the fun, and under two is what's for fools. Choose right, set tight. Pick wrong, sad song." Her eyes glued to the shells as they slipped and slid, glided and jittered. Then the shells stopped, as if pausing to catch their breath.

"All right, little lady," Jesse the wizard said. "Where is it?"

The crowd was silent, waiting, some of the older kids elbowing each other. Somebody was about to lose, but who would it be? The con man or the cocky kid? And when it came right down, as long as it wasn't *their* money, nobody gave a rat's furry behind which it was.

"I tell you what," she said finally. "I tell you rock solid where it *ain't*." And tapped the two outer shells.

Before he could protest, she flipped both over. Both were empty.

Tanesha pressed her finger against the top of the middle shell. "So it must be here, right, Jesse?"

His smile was bronzed into place. An ugly whisper crept through the crowd. Bad juju. Somebody was about to put two and two together and get .22.

Then Jesse swept the shells off the table. He jammed the cash into her hand. His eyes and the line of his mouth were as cold and sharp as a straight razor.

The red and white number ten MTA bus was trundling toward them. He swept the little red table up, folded it until it fit snug under his arm. "I see you again, Little Bit."

"Hope so," she said, and gave him a little curtsey. The crowd roared.

But as he got on the bus, Jesse swept his vest back, exposing the butt of a gleaming little steel-handled automatic. She couldn't tear her eyes from its dark, ugly weight. It was the first time that she had seen a real gun, and she knew its reality without examining it, without counting bullets or peering down the barrel's single cold eye. Something about Jesse, something about the way that the gun, tucked into the side of his belt, seemed to be the center of his body. She knew, could *feel*, that Jesse was angry enough to hurt her right now, hurt her bad.

It would be good not to encounter Jesse while she was alone. For a while. Say, like the next twenty years.

Then the closing doors cut him off from view.

Tanesha pocketed her loot and jumped back on her bike, weaving through the crowd of backslapping well-wishers. A light touch on the Aerostar's handlebars was all she required to maintain balance. The Schwinn was a part of her body, rubber-tread feet and spoke-wire legs streaking the sidewalk like a wheeled breeze. Its basket was stacked with library books: Tony Rothman's *Instant Physics,* Sun Tsu's *The Art of War,* Twain's *Huckleberry Finn.* Each would occupy her for about two days. Then, next week, she would dig back into Shakespeare. Maybe *Antony and Cleopatra.* She liked love stories.

The other kids called her a brainiac when they thought she wasn't listening, and sometimes when she was. Hell with it: she could dance circles around the best of them, and found it ridiculously easy to get elected to any student office she chose. She knew what people wanted to hear, but didn't say it unless it was true and suited her purposes.

She knew who they really were, but didn't reveal her knowledge, and never used it against them. While the other kids struggled to be popular, to be *noticed,* Tanesha just settled for being herself, and seemed to generate a crowd wherever she went.

She could feel it in her bones, heard the voices whispering in her ear: She was *special,* she was *different,* and the rosy red glow of a future waiting just beyond the horizon was hers for the taking.

She felt a twinge of anxiety as she wheeled away. That curtsey had been kinda stupid, a deliberate rubbing of Jesse's nose. *Do nothing that is of no use,* she thought. Making money was business. Making enemies was stupidity.

A little snatch of music plucked at Tanesha from an open shop door. Not top forty. Some bluesy jazz: Oscar Brown Junior, she thought. She bobbed her head to *Dime Away from a Hot Dog* as she rolled past, keeping perfect time.

She zipped down Washington Boulevard toward Rimpau. She passed a thrift store, a blacked-out storefront, then O-Jaye's Barbershop, where the scent of hair oil and the sound of Marvin Gaye drifted out to the sidewalk.

Poor dead Marvin was crooning something about sexual healing. Tanesha was certainly aware of sexual issues. Lessons from her Human Development classes had been supplemented with library trips to dig into the Kinsey report, and a fascinating series of Scientific American articles. That had led her to questions of pregnancy and communicable diseases, which in turn had led her to the World Wide Web, and the page hosted by the National Institute of Health.

Her classmates had had more visceral and personal reactions to the lectures. Already, the most persuasive boys and the ripest girls clung to each other in dark after-school hallways, in latchkey homes, in the echoey, damp spaces beneath the stadium steps. She understood what happened there, knew who played what games with whom, watched as children became ensnared in the ancient game of man and woman. Which was predator? Which prey? She wasn't sure, knew only that the entire issue had teeth, could bite and trap and tear. Tanesha felt a deep and not entirely explicable uneasiness when the matter came to mind.

The plaintive sound of a popular girl group's hit song drifted out of the doorway of a little beauty salon. Ironic, she thought to herself. (*Irony* was a new concept for Tanesha, one she had acquired from a critical analysis of O. Henry's short stories.) She applied the concept not to the song's crazy-cool lyrics, which warned of the dangers of AIDS (she actually found the lyrics naively rhymed and *puerile,* another new word), but rather to the fact that one of the three singers had subsequently tested positive for HIV.

Musician, heal thyself, she thought. She brayed laughter, then frowned, momentarily saddened by the realization that there was no one, absolutely no one at all down here in L.A., who would groove to that particularly nasty piece of humor. Once, she had had friends who would understand, especially Patrick, who had given Tanesha her first, and still sweetest, kisses. But those kisses, and her friends, were now many months gone, and a thousand miles north.

As she zipped along her mind went to more serious thoughts connected with HIV. Without volition, a strain of music accompanied those thoughts, almost like a carrier tone. The music playing in her mind wasn't the moderately harmonious sound of the girl group. Nor was it Marvin Gaye. Rather, it was Mozart's *Piano Concerto No. 20 in D minor,* the version played by Stephen Bishop Kovacevich. Its subtleties were a deep and calming river. Her thoughts on HIV drifted in its currents, melding and fluxing in melodic geometries. It often resulted in strangely, illogically juxtaposed combinations. Sometimes the results were startling and apparently original: her art teacher told her she resolved perspectives as if they were algebraic equations. Her math teacher told her her proofs didn't work, but she produced the right answers anyway. Weird. She didn't understand why other people didn't see and hear the patterns that had coursed through her veins for as long as she could remember.

Simple, really: certain strains of serious thought spontaneously triggered one of perhaps three dozen pieces of classical music, ranging from the current Mozart to Handel's largo from *Xerxes* to Vivaldi's allegro from *The Fall.*

Let's see . . . she might cross-reference medical and cultural views of the various factors involved in the spread of the disease. Boys gave it to girls, and boys gave it to boys, and dopers passed it around on their needles. That pattern felt right. But regardless of what was taught in health class, girls didn't seem to give it to boys hardly at *all.* No matter what the doctors said, they never had the actual numbers to back it up, and the crystalline symbolic structure in her mind refused to come into focus. . . .

Her thoughts drifted, intense but tranquil, gripping at her with sinewy arms, drawing her into a world of pure speculation, most of her mind seeking pattern and counter-pattern while a small, barely conscious portion concerned itself with the tricky business of navigation. That small part guided as she bumped down from the curb, planning to roll up on the sidewalk right into the shoe-repair store. The rest of her broke free to full awareness barely in time to hear old Mrs. Johnson's warning screams.

Finally, too late, she looked up in time to see the metal-gray juggernaut of a Chrysler bearing down on her.

Oh God! *It's Jesse . . . !* she thought, then registered that there were *two* people in the front seat. A black man with short white hair, too thick of face to be Jesse, drove. A Caucasian in his early fifties hunched in the passenger seat beside him. She had time to register their drawn mouths and dead eyes. There was no surprise in either face. And no anger. Perhaps . . . regret.

She had time to think: *They're not even* trying *to stop—*

Tanesha experienced the impact more as light than pain. Then flying, a negation of gravity. Dimes, quarters and crumpled bills exploded from her pockets in a spray. A second impact as her neck thudded against the window of a parked Volkswagen Jetta.

Darkness.

Dancing speckles of dim light. She heard change jangle to the ground, coins spinning like little silver tops.

Final moments: splayed broken on the ground, deaf to the growing screams around her, ears filled with the sound of her own wet and tortured breathing. Things were shattered and torn inside her, and her arms and legs wouldn't respond to her mind's commands. Oddly, she could *feel* but not *hear* her killers' Chrysler as it accelerated away.

She couldn't feel herself breathe. Couldn't move her neck. Distantly, she heard the Aerostar's front wheel rotate. Fast at first, and then winding down, grinding slow. She knew by the sound that the wheel was bent. She hoped that stepfather Floyd would be able to straighten it out.

Tanesha felt no pain. Absurdly, blessedly, the sound of Kovacevich's dancing fingers still floated through her mind.

It's not so bad, she thought. Not nearly as bad as people always seemed to fear. She wished she could tell her mother. Mommy was always so afraid of everything. Tanesha was sorry about the bike. She wanted to apologize to Floyd for spoiling it.

The music grew softer, blended with the breeze, devolving into an inaudible murmur. With a final shush, the Aerostar's wheel stopped.

Moments afterward, so did Tanesha's fluttering heart.

1

Renny Sand drove south along I-5 from Vancouver, British Columbia to Vancouver, Washington, taking a little side trip to Claremont. His intention was to visit the town where his conscience had last been sighted, lurching through the foggy northwest landscape like Bigfoot.

The trip takes about eight hours, a straight shot down the Five, an emerald explosion of evergreens and brush and lush grasses. He'd driven four hours, stopped off in a tiny single-offramp hamlet in the middle of a thousand rolling acres of farm land, and found a motel next to a right-wing Uncle Sam billboard blasting left-wing politics in general and dose ol' debbo liberal Democrats in particular.

He woke at six the next morning and hit the freeway again, grabbing coffee and a breakfast bagel sandwich from one of the countless espresso stands sprouting like toadstools in the Washington rain. The radio blared enough country music to make him want to Uzi a line dance.

Renny's stomach felt raw and tight and sour. He punched the buttons on his rental Saab's radio, looking for something to listen to that didn't make him feel like a long-haul trucker or a holy roller, and finally settled on a sports station. Forty minutes of talk-show chatter about the Seahawks' latest draft acquisition dissolved in a sea of static. A few more twists of the dial found some pre-programmed top forty presented by a cloned disk jockey, resulting in twenty miles of rap, grunge, and annoying teenybop. Finally, he gave up and turned the damned thing off.

The last trip along this interstate had been six years earlier, in February of '95. He was just another one of a dozen big-town reporters descending on the town of Claremont, a lumber town of twenty thousand set thirty minutes north of Portland. There they sat, in a poorly ventilated courtroom watching a parade of children testifying in the most infamous day-care scandal since McMartin.

Live testimony, deposition, videotape . . . one piece after another in a bizarre and heartbreaking jigsaw puzzle assembled painstakingly for judge and jury.

He recalled his first impression of the courtroom: bad lighting, cold air, packed house. There was one empty seat, next to a big red-faced farm girl with a phenomenal chest and crystal-blue eyes almost intense enough to pull attention from the trial.

The kid talking on video was a little straw-haired boy named Darnell Whittaker. Darnell looked clean, neat and frightened, about eleven years old, with rings under his eyes that suggested that he hadn't had a full night's sleep in months.

"And do you remember any of the other games they played with you?" asked the unseen inquisitor.

Darnell's eyes darted around like an animal seeking escape from a trap. "Bad games," his video image replied in a low, shaky voice. "Naked lady games."

That was all he would say. Darnell hadn't looked at the questioner again. The tape ended, and the monitor was rolled out of the room. The first of the live witnesses took the stand. This child was black, a remarkable kid named Tanesha Evans. At only eight years old, she had true star presence, reminded Renny of that spooky-smart little girl on the old Cosby show. Tanesha's skin and eyes fairly radiated health. The courtroom couldn't pry its collective eyes from the girl, from the moment she walked through the door until she laid her left hand on the Bible and raised her right.

The D.A. was a middle-aged Seattleite named Betty Ann Welles. Betty affected a rather grandmotherly air today, but once upon a time Renny had watched her grind a crack dealer into splinters, her Miss Marple demeanor transformed into a damned fine impression of Jaws. "Tanesha?"

"Yes, ma'am."

"When did you begin to have the nightmares?"

Tanesha paused only a moment before speaking. "About a year ago. Maybe longer, but that was when I first began to remember them."

Pretty impressive phrasing for a girl her age. Renny looked around the courtroom, wondering where her parents were. There were several candidates, the most promising being a heavy woman with black and Asian features in a floral muumuu. She sat on the far side of the courtroom and leaned forward slightly, hanging on Tanesha's words, lips curled tightly with satisfaction and encouragement.

"And can you tell us what these dreams were about?"

Normally you would have expected Tanesha to hesitate for a minute, as if she were a child of a younger, perhaps more innocent time.

But then Renny often felt trapped in a generation gap, suspended half-way between Aretha Franklin and Lil' Kim.

Not exactly progress.

"Sex," Tanesha said positively. "Bad sex. Hurting women." She had looked out at the courtroom, not down at her shoes. She wasn't ashamed. She was just telling Betty Ann Welles what the D.A. needed to hear. For some reason, the sight of this brave little girl, her face so dark and clean, her eyes so filled with intelligence, filled him with both shame and a fluid, corrosive anger.

"Were there children in the dream?"

Tanesha had shaken her head. "No." She paused. "Well, I was there."

"You were there. And was anyone else in the courtroom there?"

She hesitated, and then pointed. "Mrs. Coffee was there. She was the woman." And she pointed to the owner of the preschool, a small, pale, frightened woman who looked as if she had not the faintest idea why and how her world had suddenly imploded on her.

Bad sex. What in hell had Tanesha meant by that?

Renny Sand took the first Claremont exit, turning off onto Allan Street. The freeway had dumped him into Allantown, a tiny low-rent burg connected to Claremont by proximity and a two-lane bridge. Heading west, he passed through a town straining to be cosmopolitan (huge electronic sign above the Claremont Mall announcing a carnival, posters proclaiming the near-future erection of a new bridge) but reminding Renny of a fifties-era midwestern town: mom-and-pop bakeries, corner shoe-repair shops, feed stores, horse-tackle emporiums complete with hitching posts.

Across a narrow bridge was Claremont proper. Claremont and Allantown were both settled by mill workers, but Claremont budded off from the older, poorer town. That's where the executives and business owners lived, and where the tax money went. He couldn't drive a block without noticing that Claremont's streets were in better repair. There were fewer boarded-up windows, fewer taverns, more smiling faces. Money makes a difference.

There weren't too many cars on the street, but he did notice one kid on a bike. White kid, pasty-pale, maybe twelve, he wore a pea-green jacket with that Army-Navy look, and had dark short-cropped hair and wire-rimmed glasses. He glided along like a ghost, not seeming to pay any attention to the traffic. When it was time to turn left on River Front Drive, Renny stopped for him. Without looking at the reporter, the boy paused as well. Neither of them moved for a good five seconds, and then the kid turned and stared at Renny incuriously, waving him on.

River Front parallels the Cowlitz river, and Renny marked three miles of winding road, past happy signs for neighborhood auto repair and used appliance dealers, to the site of the Claremont Daycare.

The faded blue building sat a Frisbee-throw from the river. It was empty now, but walking its overgrown periphery, he could easily imagine the excited babble of children's voices. Claremont Daycare had been abandoned for six years now. The building was still empty; a weatherbeaten real estate sign erected in the front yard suggested that no one had made serious efforts to sell it in a very long time. Its walls were stenciled with faded bootleg silhouettes of Daffy and Bugs and Luke Skywalker. It was almost impossible to believe that anything more scandalous than a little copyright infringement had ever occurred in the vicinity.

But according to duly noted testimony, between January and September of '93, *something* had indeed occurred, something which gave the forty children entrusted to Claremont Daycare grotesque and recurrent nightmares of sexual abuse, intercourse, violence, death, and torture.

A chain-link fence separated the school from a trailer park to the north. On the far side, a pale, fleshy woman was hanging laundry, pretending not to watch him. Curiosity is a two-edged sword. Renny approached her smiling his friendliest smile and walking his very best newsman walk, the one that said he was the eyes and ears and conscience of the people.

The clouds were high and bright, the sun shining with that almost unnatural clarity sometimes found in the northwest, rendering shadows so sharp and black they seemed painted on the ground.

"I'm Renny Sand," he said. "Marcus News Services. I was here six years back, covering the trial." Even after all this time, he didn't have to say *which* trial.

She nodded without speaking, continuing her labors, pinning another sheet up on the line. Her eyes were very bright violet, the color of a morning glory petal. They were almost childlike in their directness. There seemed a penetrating bafflement about her, as if she awakened every morning, wondering exactly how an eleven-year-old's heart had become trapped within such a tired and doughy prison.

"You were here at the time?"

"Nowhere else," she said.

"Must have gotten pretty sick of it all. The same questions, over and over again."

She turned, her colorless lips studiedly neutral. "You got that right."

"Tell me . . . of all the stuff you've read in the papers, all the things said on television, all the things that people asked you, whether or not you think they listened to the answers—what is the one thing that you wish someone had asked you? The one thing that no one ever thought to say?"

Now she stopped. Her small bright eyes glittered at Sand as if she wondered if perhaps he wasn't quite as dim as the others. She lowered her gaze, hiding her reactions. Without meeting his eyes, she pinned a blue and red striped sweatshirt with cutoff sleeves onto the line, and then turned back.

"School was good to those kids," she said. "I don't know what might have happened later, but everybody forgets that they was problem kids."

"All of them?"

She nodded. "If somebody in the neighborhood got into a fight, you could bet it was with one of those kids." She met his gaze then, defiantly, as if daring him to try to contradict her. "Child-care folks seemed to go out of their way to find troublemakers. Bad families." She paused, her little blue eyes searching for the right words. "Mister, I don't mean this wrong, but they was trash. All of them—even that little Emory scamp, still lives right here in this park."

"So . . . the family still lives here?" He pretended to search his memory. "Vivian and Otis and little Patrick?"

"Her old man moved out, but she and the kid are still there."

Something like electricity ran along his spine, a sensation that made a mockery of his pretended calm.

"Anyway," she continued blithely, "I don't believe what people said about that school. Maybe they were just scaring Jesus into them."

"So you're glad they got off? Not everyone is."

Her lips twisted from neutrality into her very finest *look-at-the-idiot-big-town-reporter* sneer. "Maybe you call it 'getting off.' Look at that dump."

The challenge in her gaze had him hammerlocked, and Renny looked back at the shell of the old preschool. Maybe it was just a trick of the light, but the abandoned building seemed even shabbier, somehow hollow and husked. More than shelves and furnishings were gone: its soul was dead.

"That case ruined the Coffees. They lost their houses, the school, pumped out their credit cards, and probably had their wages garnished for the next million years. Old lady Coffee's health went bust. I hear she died last year. Broken heart, most likely. Losing the school, that no-account son of hers . . ."

"Her son?"

The laundress made a bitter coughing sound, but didn't answer the implied question. " 'Getting off.' Look, mister. I don't know much, but I know that those kids were brats when they started, and after a few months they weren't trouble no more."

Shrugging, she turned back to her laundry. There was something so sad about her, so heavy and tired, that he felt almost guilty for asking her to resurrect her painful memories. Feeling somewhat depressed, Renny returned to his rented car and headed back to the freeway.

2

Renny Sand sat at his desk in the sprawling Columbia River DoubleTree Hotel, smoking too many cigarettes in a designated non-smoking room. Maybe he'd hoped that consideration for the next guest's allergies or asthma might serve as sufficient leverage against a raging nicotine addiction. Wrong.

Deep down inside he wanted to take another whack at it, try one more goddamn time to pry himself away from the weeds, just take it one day at a time. Yeah, right. And ten minutes after dragging his luggage into the non-smoking room, he poured an inch of water into the bottom of a plastic cup, and had himself a makeshift ashtray.

Let's hear it for American ingenuity.

He stared at the wall mirror, the laptop just out of focus in his peripheral vision. The little Olympus micro-recorder was close to his lips, but so far its little red eye hadn't blinked.

The mirror reflected a middle-aged black man who stood about an inch and a half under six feet tall. Was thirty-five middle aged? His father died of liver cancer at sixty-nine, so maybe so. Light skin, the tone that used to be called high yellow. The man in the mirror could use more sleep. Still had his hair, still had the boyish smile, but it betrayed fatigue more and more often. Still hopeful, but tinged with anxiety. Gathering his energy to make one more (last?) leap for the golden ring. As fit as four weekly treadmill sessions could make a man, but the huffing and the puffing warred with each other. At this point, it was a toss-up whether sweat or Camel Filters would win.

The last time Sand stayed at the DoubleTree, it had been called the Red Lion Inn. Six years before, when he met the boy, Patrick Emory, and his father, Otis, and . . .

And his mother, Vivian.

An invisible fist knotted in his chest.

Oh, yes, Sand remembered the boy, who had testified right after scintillant little Tanesha. He'd been overwhelmed with the urge to speak with Patrick, and maybe his mother. Perhaps they would talk, give up a lead, a slant, an angle on a story already drilled to death.

Pat Emory was small, even for his age, which at the time Sand estimated to be around seven or eight. His posture was almost military. Unlike a lot of kids who testify in court, stress hadn't contorted him into knots. He wasn't fidgety, eager, cocky or servile. Instead, and greatly to his credit, he just seemed to be there to do a job. The kid radiated *class,* and everyone in the courtroom could sense it. His cheeks were plump, like two halves of a black peach. His eyes seemed to shine brighter than the dim overheads. His teeth were brighter still. The kid had a fortune waiting for him in toothpaste commercials.

"Patrick Emory," the bailiff intoned. "Do you swear to tell the truth, the whole truth, and nothing but the truth, so help you God?"

"I do," the boy replied.

Then the questioning began, virtually identical to the series Tanesha Evans and the others had fielded. Renny's attention drifted, gaze roaming across a sea of faces, finally zeroing in on a single, slender, very female form. Her skin was a perfect light caramel, her head exquisitely balanced on the long arc of her neck. Some men like breasts, some hips, and some legs. Renny saw that throat, the intelligent face and perceptive eyes, and a sensation that he could best describe as *electric ice cream* began melting down his spine.

He'd felt sexual electricity before, certainly, but this wasn't merely erotic, an urge to touch and taste, to see perspiration ruin the perfectly applied makeup, to reveal what the modest clothing concealed. This was a sudden, stabbing yearning, something that brought him into shocking awareness of his own empty bed. And life. He didn't *like* this, but couldn't turn off the clamor in his head once it had commenced.

Just as Tanesha's mother was recognizable on sight, he didn't guess or suppose, but *knew* that woman was Patrick Emory's mother. As Renny stared at her, an utterly alien thought tumbled into his head: *Would our child be so beautiful?*

His face burned.

Oh dear God. Sand, you're in trouble.

Mrs. Emory watched the boy intently. *Mrs. Emory? Miss Emory?* He was suddenly completely flustered, and excused himself from the courtroom before he found some new and imaginative way to make a complete ass of himself.

Outside the door he slammed his back against the wall and took one hell of a deep breath. What had *that* been all about?

"Who lit your britches, boy?" The voice was a Texas twang overlaid with maybe twenty years of Chicago. Renny looked up and saw a familiar face, a fifty-year-old AP stringer named Alfie Connors. Alfie had all the personality of a cucumber, resembled a hairy stork and could type 120 words a minute without a misstroke for hours at a time, a talent that had served him well in the dinosaur days before laptops and PDAs. The last Renny heard, Alfie was working out of Spokane.

"Alfie, I need some information. This kid, Patrick Emory?"

"Yeah." Alfie was a family man. Six kids, last he heard. Renny guessed that the whole trial made Alfie want to puke. "Good kid."

"Is that his mom in there? Second row."

"Good looking woman? Name's Vivian Emory. Big bruising husband next to her? That's Otis. Yeah. Why?"

Renny groaned. He hadn't even noticed. Some reporter. "Well, husband, huh?"

Alfie grinned, world-class radar homing in on the disappointment behind the inquiry. "Yeah. Purely dotes on her. Loves that kid. Good guy. Mill worker, I think."

Visions of romancing a single mother evaporated. *All the good ones are gone.* "Oh, all right. Listen. If I wanted to get a couple of words with that kid—" Alfie grimaced, and Renny raced on. "Strictly off the record, of course."

"And why should I help you?" Alfie said cheerily.

"Oh, come on. I gave you a few pieces at the Montoya trial. One hand washes the other?"

"Still have dirt under my nails. What else you got?"

Renny paused, then plunged onward. "I've got SuperSonic tickets. Good ones, for the playoffs. They're calling your name."

Alfie narrowed his eyes, but not before Renny caught the gleam therein. "Look, all I can tell you is that the kids go out the back of the courthouse, and that there's a connecting door through the cafeteria."

Which was how, after an exchange of addresses, Renny found himself at an EMPLOYEES ONLY corridor at the back of the building. He purchased a latté from a coffee machine, and was sipping it through a molecule-wide plastic straw when the first people began to trickle from the courtroom. Third out was Patrick's mother. She headed directly toward him.

Vivian Emory was shorter than he thought, no more than five-foot-six, but carried herself so gracefully you'd guess her three inches taller. Her hair was pulled back from a high forehead and perfect unlined face. She had almond, almost feline eyes. He could imagine her in the robes of an Egyptian queen, an Abyssinian cat curled in her lap. Her dress was cut to resemble a man's gray suit. Probably hand-sewn, one of a kind, Renny thought. She walked as if she had modeled. Her feet were sheathed in open-toed leather sandals that would have seemed excessively informal on another woman.

Her face was very sober. Sand gave her his best smile, and she inclined her head fractionally. Something terrible lurked behind the almost porcelain exterior, and he felt a sudden, chilling flood of shame.

She was married, probably happily, probably to a terrific guy. Renny Sand was only here to dip his quill in her pain, her embarrassment, and scrawl a message of implicit condemnation across the front page of a hundred papers. The big-town reporter had arrived to invade her home and privacy, to make accusations of the most inflammatory and embarrassing kind. It was his job to imply that Vivian Emory had entrusted her only child to monsters.

He'd momentarily considered pretending to be a Child Welfare officer, maybe get her to say something in an unguarded moment. But all thoughts of duplicity vanished the instant he opened his mouth to speak. It was absurd, but his only thought was to give her something, some token, a touch that might, for however brief a time, brush away the shadows darkening her face.

"Renny Sand, Marcus News Services." She stiffened, and he went on quickly, before she could turn away. "There will be no mention of you or your child in my article, nor do I want to interview either of you." There. It was out, and damned if he knew quite what to say next.

Luckily, she was taken aback as well. "I don't understand," she said.

"Neither do I." Damned if he didn't shuffle his feet. "I'm here to write a story, and I've just decided that you're not a part of it. Latté?"

She paused, and then nodded watchfully. He dropped coins into the slot, and watched her reflection in the polished steel strip at the top. Her complexion was flawless, except for a tiny heart-shaped mole just below her jaw on the left side of her neck. Her pores were so incredibly fine that her skin seemed almost plastic, a solid sheen any fashion model would have killed for. By firelight, it would have been the color of molten copper.

Standing that close, her pain baked off her like waves of heat from a fever victim. It required a physical act of will not to touch her.

"What *do* you want?" she asked.

A raft of half-clever answers floated through his mind. For once, nothing would do but the truth. "I want to do my job," he said. "I want to turn in a great story. I want a corner office on the twentieth floor, to slay social dragons and win a Pulitzer."

"And you don't think talking to my son would help?"

"Yes, it would. But I'd rather see you smile."

At that moment, it didn't take a psychic to read her mind. *I want to be anywhere but here,* she said without speaking. *I wouldn't have thought anything could make me enjoy this place, this day. But you are a nice man.*

Then her eyes dropped away. They were brimming, but not a drop spilled. Her cheeks shone in the dim light. Shone.

The machine finally dispensed her coffee. As she took it from his hand, their fingertips brushed.

Small lightnings.

Damn it, this is just getting worse and worse.

From the slight widening of her eyes, he knew that she felt the tug as well, and her armor, momentarily thinned, grew thicker. She took a step back, and broke eye contact as she sipped. He cursed the impossibly bad timing. Sand opened his mouth, but before he could make an utter and complete fool of himself, they were interrupted by the approach of a bear in a striped Sears suit.

Sand was just under six feet, and a fairly solid 210. But the bear's shoulders came up to his chin.

If not for the fierce protectiveness in his eyes, it might have been possible to dismiss the man as a mere brute. But the guy with one outfielder's glove of a hand on little Patrick's shoulder was so obviously kind and loving, so clearly devoted to boy and mother, that only a cretin wouldn't have understood why she was with him. Hell, it was not only natural, it was *right.*

That realization brought Renny back to earth, numbed the pain a bit. When he looked back at the lady, Mr. Emory had noticed his reaction. She had, too. For the first time, her eyes seemed to sparkle.

Ah, well . . .

Seen up close, Patrick was smaller than he'd thought, his chocolate skin so smooth and alive it seemed almost burnished. His eyes shone with the kind of love a child reserves for the parent of the opposite gender. Perfect, possessive, adoring.

She bent and took him in her arms, handing the latté to her husband. The boy wrapped his arms around her and nestled his head against her chest as tightly as he could, as if seeking the safety of the womb.

The courtroom ordeal had probably drained the boy's last drop of maturity. Now that the inquisition was complete, he could be a child again.

"Did I do good?" Kisses in reply. "Can we go now?"

His father nodded, but his eyes were on the reporter. Renny bet that Otis Emory knew *exactly* how he had reacted to his wife, had seen it many times, in many other men. That he had weighed Renny, taken his measure in an instant, and in some odd way accepted his admiration as good and natural.

Renny wanted to dislike the bastard, to see him smirk or taunt, but the moon face just seemed tired, and proud, and sad.

This is my family, it said. *I'm building it with my hands. There is pain here, but there is beauty. You're all right, buddy. You see both, and you're all right.*

Damn it, Renny liked the big lug. He smiled back, hoisting his latté an inch in silent toast. He knelt down to the boy's level. Patrick's gaze was deep and cool, chambers within bolted tight, closed to outsiders. Intelligence and confidence ran so deep that they struck Renny like a bomb. He'd never seen such eyes. He had an immediate, absurd sense that he'd take a bullet for the kid, and was startled by the thought. Jesus. What *was* it with this family?

When you've worked as many beats as Renny had, and kept your eyes open, you've seen the faces of abused children in Chicago divorce courts, Miami immigration trials, the dark narrowed streets of inner cities or the spotlights of Hollywood's Walk of Fame. In every case, there is something fearful, or brittle and challenging, or hopeful in their eyes. Something has been broken or bruised, burned out or prematurely awakened in them. Later in life they might seek abusive relationships, snarl themselves in a morass of hypersexuality or assume a monastic quasi-existence. Drug abuse, alcoholism, dysfunctional relationships, anorexia or morbid obesity lurked in their future. The weakest and sickest might become abusers themselves. He'd seen all these responses, and been horrified. What lived in Patrick Emory's eyes was something unsettling, but different.

In Patrick Emory's eyes was *control,* stark and solid as two inches of Plexiglas, a barrier erected between the random cruelties of the world and this child's emotions. He needed permission. Patrick's father looked down at him with the relaxed confidence of a sleepy t-rex, and nodded almost imperceptibly. Renny extended his hand. "Hello, Patrick. My name is Renny Sand."

The boy's small hand was as fragile as a sparrow's wing, his clasp cool and polite. "You're a reporter."

"Yeah. How did you know?"

"The way you looked at me," he said. "You broke me into little pieces, put me back together into different shapes. Reporters do that."

"How do you know that?"

" *'Know the Ways of all Professions,' "* Patrick Emory said. *What?*

Vivian Emory just shrugged. "He talks like that sometimes."

The boy was quiet and watchful.

"And when people do that," Renny asked, "does it bother you?"

"Wouldn't it bother you?" he asked.

Renny Sand found the kid utterly unnerving. "No," he lied.

And the boy knew it. The small warmth in Patrick's eyes died. "I don't want to talk to you."

A deep breath. Renny was off-balance, and needed to get back to true. "I don't blame you. If I were you, I wouldn't talk to me, either."

For the first time, Patrick's expression was uncalculated, unguarded. A bit confused, perhaps. Vivian and Otis Emory had watched the entire exchange. Renny had the sense it was something they'd seen before. "Take care of him. He's a good kid."

The big man nodded. "Count on it." And they moved on by, out the door. Otis Emory rested his enormous hand on his son's back. From wrist to fingertip, it stretched damned near shoulder to shoulder. At the last second the boy looked back at the reporter, his face changed yet again. That innocent, guileless child was gone, and in its place was something far older, and fierce, as if for a moment that transparent shield had dropped.

Then the three of them walked out of the corridor, the blaze of the midday sun transforming them into ghosts.

Renny was shaken. *There* was that quality he had noted before, in other children; although here it assumed an unfamiliar aspect. Patrick had lost something essential, but even the boy himself might not realize what it was. Something was both right and terribly *wrong* about the kid, at the exact same time.

He blinked, and they were gone. The sun-glare had bleached all detail from the parking lot. There was an emptiness, a vacuum in the pit of Renny's stomach. He'd never experienced anything quite like it, and had no idea how to fill it up again.

So there he was, lost in thought at the DoubleTree Hotel, the hotel that had been a Red Lion seven years before, when he had been another, better man. Feet up on a chair, CNN flickering soundlessly on the television, sipping halfheartedly at rotten in-room coffee. Thoughts of that previous encounter still rocked him. *Christ.* There was no logical reason for his reaction to the Emory clan.

It had just been a story, like other stories. And nobody had said anything to him that had to be kept off the record. There were a hundred ways he could have used impressions, comments, and visual color to deep-background a story, or create a composite character without violating privacy, or portray a hypothetical child in a way that no one would recognize. . . .

And in an instance like this, every one of those techniques was journalistic vampirism.

And what would he call his present thoughts? Investigative necrophilia? That old case was dead and gone, and here thoughts of resurrection danced in his head. He was seriously pondering ways to sell it to his higher-ups at Marcus Communications, folks who, in all probability, didn't care if, for a few weeks in '94, the Claremont Daycare case had been the biggest story in the nation.

Despite an acquittal due to lack of material evidence, the laundry lady had been correct: the owners' lives had been trashed. Had the parents hoped to sue? Was that it? Was the whole thing some kind of national psychosis, the guilt of single and working mothers imploding? He bet that Dr. Laura would be happy to offer a quote on *that*.

How about the possibility that there was abuse, but might it have been the . . . should he say *homegrown* variety? Women were often blind to the fact that step-daddies and boyfriends went a-creeping at night. Had Emory Senior's grotesque hand rested on the boy's shoulder a little too intimately? His own father never touched *him* like that. Certainly there was reason to suspect something wrong. . . .

Another cup of Columbian river-muck was perked and consumed. His hands were trembling, and not just from the caffeine. *Shit.* It was only a story, like other stories. But seven years ago his whole life had lain before him like the yellow brick road, the goodies he'd dreamed of since childhood dangling like golden apples, ripe for the plucking.

Tomorrow he'd be back in Los Angeles. But instead of the twentieth floor of the Marcus Communications towers, he would report to the thirteenth. Instead of one of Marcus's prestige publications—*Webwatch, J.P.G* or *Quanta*—it would be *Eyeful,* a high-circulation pulp-paper weekly available at quality AM/PM Minimart checkout counters nationwide.

The twentieth floor was impossibly far away now. It would be the third floor until he found something better.

He didn't want to think about it. But there was still life in Claremont. It tingled in the air. There was a story there somewhere. Maybe he could catch one last ride on the golden pony, snag an editor's eye, earn a few points.

He closed his mental door on further desperate speculation, and opened his Compaq Presario laptop.

It was just standard follow-up procedure to research on the Emorys after the trial, to learn that Vivian Emory ran a costume shop. And just happenstance that he'd kept tabs, and noticed when she went on the web, posting pictures of herself in her period costumes. Everything from Marie Antoinette to an Easter bunny. She was exquisite, so damned talented, that even the cheap digital pictures on her web page broke his heart every time.

And it was just good record-keeping to keep track of her e-mail address.

Maybe he could dash off a note. Just a way of saying "hi." Vivian probably wouldn't remember him, but since he'd passed through her neck of the woods, it would be polite to send greetings. Since he intended to pitch a news story related, however distantly, to the things that had happened to her family, it would only be courtesy.

It might be neighborly to let her know that someone thought kindly of her. Just in case she was feeling depressed. And maybe needed a friend.

You're a scavenger, Renny, and even worse, you're making a fool of yourself. But even that brief flash of fear didn't take the silly-assed grin off his face, and there, in the hotel room that smelled of cigarettes and bad coffee, Renny Sand started typing, happier than he had been in weeks.

3

Journal entry #302, Aristotle Project. RE: GENERAL BONDING.

One of the x-factors necessitating a wider test is the influence of the peer group. Most of the research on imprintation and role-model implantation deals with the reactions of single adult subjects. But group dynamics are a separate and powerful factor of their own, and must be accounted for. The test groups, ideally, will be carefully chosen and monitored, balanced for gender, race, and ethnicity, and allowed to evolve like mini-societies. Therefore, in no case will the test grouping consist of fewer than fifteen children . . .

Thirteen-year-old Patrick Emory lay in his bed, trying to decide whether to listen to The Artist Formerly Known As Prince's *Pussy Control* (a paean to self-control and redirection of sexual energy) or Mozart's *Violin Sonata in E-flat*. Not that he would place Prince on the same level as Mozart. There really wasn't *anybody* today who functioned at Amadeus's level. But he would certainly put The Artist on a par with any living composer. Trouble was, Mozart or Beethoven were great if you wanted to study or calm your mind. But if you wanted to boogie, forget it.

He rolled up and grabbed his art pad. That was easy, because his room was almost obsessively neat. It had the usual load of male teen-aged paraphernalia: mattress on the floor, stacks of books and magazines, baseball bats and balls, football and soccer ball, computer disks. Wall posters: Bruce Lee, actor Vin Diesel, publisher Alexander Marcus (one of his idols) and Halle Berry as Storm in *X-Men*. Everything was neatly in its place, indexed, referenced, instantly available.

Patrick closed his eyes to remember, then began to draw. The image was simple, untutored, but clear: a boy riding a bumblebee. He'd been watching an old monster movie called *Mysterious Island,* and some of the imagery had crept into his dreams. He laughed at it, and stuck it into a manila folder already crammed with dream images. Once a month he culled the best, chucked the rest.

Jeans, T-shirt, socks, shoes.

Patrick grabbed the Mozart from a rack of cassettes on his wall, popped a tape into his Walkman and slipped the headphones over his ears. He washed his face (managing to do a decent job without removing his 'phones), brushed his teeth, and stepped on the scale: 125 pounds of fighting muscle.

He said goodbye to his mom, who barely noticed, buried in some last-minute repairs on a Cinderella. He picked his way out through the living room. No easy trick. The entire room was stuffed, from one edge to the other, with potted plants, scraps and remnants of cloth, clothing dummies, hanging vines, books and videos on costumes from around the world and all different eras, windowsill flowers, and a sewing machine that had earned roughly two-thirds of the family income since Patrick was in diapers. Oddly enough, Patrick's bedroom was actually the cleanest and most organized part of the house.

Not that his father didn't work, and work hard—when he could get it. But Otis Emory was hanging on to his job by his teeth. Too many problems, too many missed days, so many arguments and fights he was lucky to get twenty hours a week these days. His dad pushed lumber at the mill: long, grueling, dangerous work. Alternating exhaustion and depression drained his dad so thoroughly that when he visited them, he often had no energy to enjoy himself (although always enough energy to hug his boy, and tease Mom). It was Vivian Emory's magic fingers that brought comfort and even a touch of elegance into their lives. His most pervasive image of his mother was of her bent over some scrap of cloth as she wrought it artfully into a wood sprite or a Rambo, the old Singer humming busily away for countless hours a week. Sometimes she didn't go to bed for two nights in a row, until she was raccoon-eyed but satisfied with some set of theatrical frillies. A sign over her disaster of a desk read: *Creativity is not a pretty sight.*

His mom, however, was. When he looked at her, he saw only her warm, tired smile, her effortless grace, the rich dark hair, and the loving heart that seemed to express itself in everything she did or said.

She watched Oprah on a thirteen-inch color screen as she stitched.

Her fingers seemed to have eyes of their own. A soft bluesy wail wafted from the radio in the background, Koko Taylor sassily warning women that they needed to watch their friends, not their enemies. Vivian Emory sang along, and listened, and watched, and stitched, lost in a blissful, busy glow all her own.

Patrick stepped past the sliding glass door onto the wooden deck of the double-wide trailer that was their home. The Claremont paper mill a mile south belched endless clouds of blue-white smoke into the sky. As a consequence, when the wind blew north the air outside went pretty foul. In the trailer it was almost always breathable, but only because Vivian Emory had a magic touch with plants. She kept every inch festooned with vines and little flowering things that made their little corner of the park its own woodsy world.

His bicycle leaned against the wooden steps leading to the porch. He slid his hands over its chipped green paint, greeting an old friend. There was some part of him that always looked forward to this moment, to the time of day when he could get home from school, or wake up late on a Saturday, and take his bike for a long ride along the River Front Highway beside the Cowlitz. Sometimes he could look down on its sparkling blue ribbon and watch the little fishing boats puttering around. He would wave to the people. Often they waved back. They rode the tide or the wind. He pumped his pedals. Sometimes he raced them and won, and when he did, he felt like he was king of the world.

They had more money than he did, but they weren't having any more fun.

The Riverside trailer park was home. He knew almost everyone on the south end of the park, the good end. It was a neighborhood. Most tenants had occupied their spaces for over a decade. Retired couples, welfare cases, single mothers with three or five kids crammed into two bustling bedrooms, young marrieds barely out of high school. Although some of them were only five or six years older than Patrick, they lived in an entirely different world. Sometimes on weekends the husbands would play football or baseball or soccer with Patrick and his friends. For a while they were all just kids, but eventually their chubby, sun-haired wives would call them to painting, or shopping, or weeding, and the game would break up.

It was a good place to live . . . or it used to be. A safe place, a trick-or-treating without needing a parent or guard dog kind of place. Or had been, once upon a time.

But Riverside had changed owners three years ago. What passed for the local CCRs had been thrown out the window. Recently, people were renting slots or homes to anyone with first-and-security. As a result, the neighborhood was falling apart.

Take, for instance, the two big Fleetwood trailers furthest north, with the boarded side windows and unkempt grass. The ones at the L he navigated daily. There was always a motorcycle or two parked out in front, and almost always someone lounging around on one porch or the other. Maybe one of the big men in tight T-shirts, or one of the pale young fleshy women who seemed to belong to no one and everyone. The women ignored him as he wheeled past. A year ago he had come to their front door, trying to sell Christmas cards. A big-bellied unwashed white man had rubbed Patrick's head, chanting, "Wish I had a watermelon." The boy had blinked at him, uncomprehending. The man and his friends howled as if that was the funniest thing in the world. Face burning, Patrick retreated, and never approached them again.

They smelled funny sometimes, too, a smell that sometimes reminded him of insecticide, and sometimes window cleaner or, odder still, a cat box. There was something about them that made his stomach crawl, and Patrick liked almost everyone. The one he liked the least was called Cappy. Cappy Swenson was a huge man, bigger than Dad, the kind of man who made sidewalk crowds part, that decent people instinctively avoided in movie theaters and parks. People gave Cappy elbow room. Cappy sported a wild mat of red beard, and a flat shelf of a face that looked like it had been hammered onto his skull. His eyes were little bright hot marbles, his swollen chest and shoulders disproportionate to his bowed legs. Cappy scared him.

Cappy had only arrived about six months ago, but the others acted like they had known him for years. When he was around the chaos over at the Fleetwood became a little more organized. He had been away, maybe in jail, and the others were glad to have him home. The first time he saw Patrick, the boy was pretty sure Cappy'd said, "Goddamn, how many jungle bunnies you got hopping around here?"

Nasty, enthusiastic laughter had followed. Patrick, little legs working frantically, had pedaled the hell out of range.

Of course, he'd heard language like that before. His mother told him that it used to be fairly common, but not here. Not around here. Claremont was *his* town, and he loved it.

He knew every inch of Claremont and its poorer sister, Allantown. In fact, he'd rarely been outside it. To Portland maybe three times,

Seattle once. It lay nestled in hills cradling the interstate, a community spiraling outward from the mill that birthed and sustained it. A saltwater inlet snaked in from the Pacific, usually loaded with freighters. Railroad tracks split the town east and west. Passenger cars and box cars trundled north and south through the hills, stopping at the Amtrak station east of the river, and the mill a little further south.

Patrick remembered when some of the housing developments were just green grass, scrub and trees, but slowly and steadily houses and apartment buildings and offices sprouted everywhere in little clusters, grew together, pushed the green back toward the hills.

The real estate developers and mill executives lived up in the hills: there were some beautiful homes up there. Patrick had accompanied his mom delivering costumes to a hill party, and had gaped with awe.

There were middle-class homes for the mill workers who lived over to the southwest: some of those neighborhoods were good, some bad. The difference was often just a street or two. Poorer folks lived over in Allantown, south next to the river, or in the hills north: unincorporated land without city services, folks who hauled their own garbage to the dump once a month in stinking Chevy pickup trucks with battered panels and peeled paint.

And at every point of the compass were the trailer parks, through which short-timers flowed and old-timers sank their withering roots, and people like Patrick and his family held on, and hoped for better days.

But in the town between the hills, split by the interstate and the river, Patrick knew every video store and park and used-bookshop, every gas station that provided free air (the Arco on 5th), every bakery that gave free samples (the Dutchman with his incredible doughnuts on Thursdays, Marco's Marketplace with their little toothpicked squares of pizza on Monday and Wednesday) and of course the bookshops. Not a lot of bookshops, mostly just the big one at the Twin Rivers Mall, and then there was one built into the Inside Edge coffee shop downtown. But there were a lot of secondhand shops, and in some of them you could find interesting stuff.

He wasn't thinking about the copy of *Huckleberry Finn* he had bought last month, or even remembering the warm smile from Rowan Matthews, the seriously retro owner of the Inside Edge, or remembering her saying that Patrick must be *such* a smart boy to appreciate a book like that.

Today he was much more interested in just getting to his weekly meeting place. So he went north, out of the trailer park and along the river for two miles, then crossed the road and entered the woods. He had to stand up and stroke with the big muscles in his thighs now. Grit and loose rock ground against his bike tread as he worked his way up the old logging road.

As he did, he experienced a strange sensation he'd known many times in the past: the illusion that he was standing still, the rest of the world flowing around him. He reveled in the cooling pressure of air against his face, but if he closed his eyes how could he tell whether he was moving, or merely enjoying an afternoon breeze?

The road jounced against his tires, but he'd been in the motion simulator at the Portland Museum of Arts and Sciences, and it felt much the same way, and he never moved a meter. A strange sensation, that much was certain. In physics they talked about *relative frames of motion.* His mind probed and poked at that, savoring it like candy. Then he let it float away. The sun was shining, and he was about to see his friends. And sometimes, that was enough.

A green scrap of cloth fluttered from a three-meter pine sapling on the left. He took the turn, then the first right turn, and pumped his way down a straggly path, until the paved road behind him disappeared. He hopped off the bike, and began to walk it up the mountain. The sun filtered down through a canopy of yellow-green leaves and cedars, alders, and Douglas firs quilting the ground with shadows. Distantly, water trickled, snowmelt runoff rivulets twining into streams that would flow to the Cowlitz and Columbia and eventually the glittering Pacific, thirty-five miles to the west.

He no longer followed a path, just a shallow rut in the ground. Only a few bent twigs suggested that human beings had ever passed this way. He didn't need the signs. Even without the ribbon on the tree, he would have known where to turn, could almost have found this spot in his sleep.

The brush grew heavier, then abruptly opened, and he entered a clearing.

He could smell the smoke even as he approached, but felt no alarm: spring had been drenching, so the fire hazard was low. And at any rate, he knew that the fire would be banked with stones, that there would be a bucket of water nearby, and that those who had started and maintained it were very cautious indeed. Watchful. That was their nature.

"Pat!" The tallest of the three kids in the clearing called. His name was Lee Wallace, a distant relation of the former Governor of Alabama, something that caused his parents both pride and embarrassment. Lee was five-ten, with pale hair and about two zillion freckles. He should have been gangly, but instead moved with a strange and almost insectile grace on the soccer field. "Didn't think you'd make it, man."

Lee had only attended the preschool for a year. Then his dad had opened a computerized print shop next to city hall, and they had all moved from Allantown to Claremont. He no longer lived in the neighborhood, but managed to stay in touch with them.

The shortest of them was Sherman Sevujian, Hermie Shermie to the Group, who had once been a little Lebanese butterball. He had always seemed to have a falafel or chunk of gyro sandwich stuck in his mouth. His father managed—and now owned—a sandwich shop over at the mall. A few years ago Patrick was afraid they would have to roll Hermie down the street to school every day. Lately the weight problem had resolved itself: he was biking everywhere instead of begging his mom or his older brother for rides. He played soccer and paid his own way into tae kwon do classes at Trask Matthews's Master Academy. These days, his mouth was more likely filled by a pear or orange than a Payday bar.

The last member of their quad was Destiny Valdez. Destiny was cocoa-colored, about five-four, with a trace of her old baby fat still gracing her waist. But that, and all traces of her childhood save her fiendish energy, were vanishing fast. When she wore her long dark hair back, and the light hit her just right, she looked a little like a cross between Jennifer Lopez and Janet Jackson, and that was very fine indeed.

Her budding breasts and hips *did* cause Patrick a problem now and then. Things had changed big time since the times out on Claremont Daycare's activity field. The tomboy still lived in Destiny, but there was something else, too, something that made Patrick feel uneasy. Boys were discovering Destiny, and Destiny had discovered them right back, specifically one tall, muscular ninth grader named Billy "Deep Blue" Kumer. Destiny and Deep Blue held hands, but rumor said that Destiny had never actually kissed him. She said that good Catholic girls didn't do that, but he suspected that they did, sooner or later, just that with Destiny and Deep Blue it was going to be later, or maybe never at all.

Not a *real* kiss, anyway, the kind of kisses that Patrick had seen in movies but never actually tried, the turbocharged ones with wet, open mouths and saxophones wailing in the background. Those spit-swapping marathons were dizzying just to *watch*. God only knew what it would feel like to actually *try* one.

He hadn't, and Lee and Sherman hadn't, and neither had Destiny. Billy was a bare-chest basketball, cap turned backwards, white wanna-be hip-hop gangsta, and not the type to be satisfied with pursed lips for long. Either Destiny would give up the tongue, or Deep Blue would find his jollies elsewhere. And wouldn't *that* be a pity?

Patrick was confused by his own reactions to her. Heck, it was just Destiny, after all.

Was it sex? Well, he knew about sex—more about it than his mom did, he sometimes thought. Heck, she couldn't even help him with his homework. He had Human Development classes in sixth grade, and stole glimpses at his father's magazines when nobody was looking. The hot-eyed, heavy-breasted women with staples in their navels siz-zled with secret, tantalizing knowledge.

"Can we bring the club to order?" Destiny asked.

"I dunno—*can* you?" Lee leaned back to avoid a swat.

"Hear, hear," Hermie Shermie said. "The first order of business is a report from the Pat-man."

Patrick leaned his bicycle against a tree and sat, his breathing already beginning to slow. The four friends formed a square. Patrick exhaled harshly, his heart beginning to slow. "First, the lawn-cutting business is doing just great. We've got two more customers."

"Will they pay in advance?" Hermie Sevujian asked.

"One will, and that's gas money. Five bucks a pop. We've got more lawns than we have people to cut 'em. I think we should hire Raff Slocum and his brother Chili."

"Chili's a dumbass."

"Right. We don't want him smart—he might undercut us and take our customers. But he's honest, and works hard—and he works cheap."

"You got *my* vote," Destiny said cheerfully.

"Let's talk to them, then. Kick-ass. What else?"

"We're getting about twelve hundred hits a day, and just got linked by Kidslife dot-com."

There was a round of cheers. With studied delicacy Destiny opened her vinyl notebook, and withdrew a sheaf of papers. She handed them around. "Here," she said. They all examined the drawings, passing them around as if they were leafs of the Dead Sea scrolls.

They were beautifully rendered drawings of warriors. Egalitarianly rendered in both male and female form, they wielded improbably heavy swords and staffs. And if they looked a bit too reminiscent of *Xena, Warrior Princess,* or heroic images on *Magic: the Gathering* trading cards, so be it.

They passed them around in a circle, marveling, regarding Destiny herself with awe. Hermie spoke first. "I couldn't ever draw like that," he said.

"It's just practice," Destiny said.

"The Way is in Training," Patrick said. The others nodded sagely.

Destiny dimpled prettily. "When can you scan them in?"

Lee chewed on his lower lip, thinking hard. "Well, tonight, maybe. Dad's usually pretty cool after six o'clock." That was true, and no wonder. Mr. Wallace's print shop owed much to Lee, who had coaxed his alcoholic father into A.A., and then helped him to save the money to open a computer printing shop in a vacant cubbyhole next to City Hall. The first May and most of June had been disastrous, then the city contract for the annual Independence Day celebration paid July's bills, and within a year, Wallace Printing was a resounding success. Despite (or perhaps because of) that framed photo in the lobby of infant Emmett Wallace sitting on Governor George's knee at a family picnic.

Their web page was just a lark, the Warriorkids dot-com page that they branched off Patrick's AOL account, scanning in drawings and posting stories. It wasn't until Destiny posted some of her mushroom cartoons that something else had happened:

The first week, they got seventy e-mails telling them how cool the little mushroom drawings were: Barbie 'Shroom, and Pterodactyl 'Shroom, and Hockey 'Shroom, and Xena 'Shroom, each snazzy little caricature dressing up the fantasian fungi in a rainbow of guises.

Progressing from there, they used Lee's dad's shop to make computer-generated T-shirt transfers, and sold them around the school. Before they knew what was happening, a local craze had resulted, every kid in the school needing a genuine, authentic, autographed Destiny Valdez Mushroom. They had been kept hopping ironing, sorting and managing a business that was now bringing in almost a hundred dollars in profit a week, a mind-boggling sum to thirteen-year-olds.

What to do with the money? With a startling lack of disagreement, they decided on ten cents of every dollar to charity, twenty cents into long-term banking, and sixty cents into a general expense fund. The remaining ten cents went into the chow-downs at their weekly meet-ings. Mr. Sevujian, for whom they distributed advertising flyers, often underwrote the scarfing sessions.

Hermie Shermie passed around bottles of apple juice and gyro sand-wiches, and they munched enthusiastically. The beef was crisp and flavorful. *Tzadziki* garlic-and-yogurt sauce ran with every bite.

They were mostly pretty quiet while munching, just enjoying the low crackle of the fire and the quiet of the woods. There were distant traffic sounds, and from somewhere to the north, the cough of a mo-torcycle.

Hermie seemed pensive, studying his half-eaten sandwich as if he expected it to reveal cosmic secrets. Then, somewhat clumsily, he blurted: "I don't know why they chose Destiny for the camp."

"Maybe they just liked my drawings."

"Yeah, well . . . we helped with those too. It's not fair."

She gazed at Shermie. It was true: the 'Shrooms had been his idea, but Shermie had all the artistic talent of a rock. He just couldn't see the images in his head the way Destiny could. To put it in Sherm-speak, he couldn't draw a line with a straightedge.

Destiny touched his arm fondly. "Hey, man. We're just going to split the bucks anyway."

"It's a savings bond. Won't mature until college." He sniffed, but squinted at her. "I'll bet they just want you to show 'em your panties, anyway."

"Jesus!" she exploded. "You asshole." And bounced a wax paper ball off his nose.

Lee stopped his chewing, and gazed out at the woods. He did that sometimes, just forgot anyone else was there and seemed to drift off. That was good when he was working at the computer, but sometimes it could mean other thoughts. Bad thoughts.

Destiny finally noticed his distraction. "Are you all right, Lee?"

"I was just thinking," he said.

"What?"

"You know, thoughts just bounce around some time. Shermie says 'panties,' and the next thing I know . . ." his voice trailed off.

"You're back there again?" Patrick asked.

He nodded. "We said nothing happened to us." He took a bite, and chewed slowly. "And the shrinks and stuff finally agreed." He didn't have to be more specific than that. Everyone knew exactly what he referred to.

Voice rising defensively, Pat said: "Well, it's true, isn't it? Nothing ever happened."

There was a chorus of "no's," followed by silence. "Then why do I still have nightmares?" Destiny asked.

Patrick stared at her. "You don't talk to your parents about them, do you?"

"Are you crazy? If they hear me at night . . ." she shifted uncomfortably. "If I'm making noise, you know? I'll just tell them I was watching *Scream* over at a friend's house, and dreamed I was being chased by a big guy with a knife."

"And they buy that?"

"They don't really care," she said, and looked down. "They just tell me to shut up and go to sleep." She glanced up at them, and then away, as if she couldn't tolerate the eye contact.

Pat looked at Lee. "When was the last time you had a nightmare? One of *those*."

"I mostly don't remember. Mostly." He was chewing more slowly now, as if the gyro had lost its appeal.

Shermie nodded slowly, then looked away. He hadn't been asked a question, hadn't really given an answer, but they all knew exactly what he meant.

"What is this shit?" Pat said. "Why the hell won't it go away?" He didn't have nightmares—or at least didn't remember them, more than a couple of times a month now. Fire and blood and women. Dying, in torment. Naked, bleeding. *Christ.*

The sick thing was that Destiny had them too.

"I don't think it was the school," Lee said soberly. "That's been over for a long time. I think it's *us*. We see each other twenty-four seven. I think we remind each other, you know?"

"But it wasn't just us. Tanesha had the same problems."

Destiny spoke, but her voice was hushed and low. "That was her uncle," she said. "I know. She told me that he used to grab her. That's why her mom kicked his ass out of the house. Moved them all to California."

For a time, there was no sound in the circle except the distant keen of a log boat cruising south on the Cowlitz.

"So it's just going to be you and Crazy Frankie out in the desert."

"High desert. They say it looks a lot like this. Anyway, Frankie's not so bad."

Lee lowered his voice. "Did I ever tell you about the time he blew up the mice? I swear to God."

"You're lying," Patrick said.

Hermie Shermie shook his head. "No, its true. I remember once Frankie went to the Triangle Mall pet shop, and bought some white mice. Said they were for his snake, only he didn't have a snake."

Destiny was fascinated in spite of herself. "So what did he do with them?"

"It was like July tenth last year, and he'd saved a couple of M-80s from the Fourth." Shermie lowered his voice to a conspiratorial whisper. "He threw a mouse and an M-80 into a brown bag together. I saw it, man." His eyes were huge. "I seriously saw him do that."

They were all silent, struggling to envision the unimaginable.

"Jesus," Destiny finally said. "He's messed up." They murmured agreement.

Patrick was the one to shake free of their spell. "Listen," he said. "I don't have any answers. I don't know why just you two got chosen, but Frankie's smart as hell, and I guess he deserves it. It's not real useful to bitch about it. Let's talk about something that we can do something about."

"The Compaq?"

Destiny seemed to shake herself out of her trance. "I talked to that guy at Office Max. The system'll be on sale again at the end of the month."

"How much?"

"Fourteen hundred."

"And how much do we have?"

Destiny opened her little book. It was dog-eared and wrinkled, but otherwise spotless, despite the fact that she carried it everywhere. "We have eleven hundred bucks."

The kids laughed and high-fived each other. "Pretty good, huh?"

Hermie Shermie said, "We could have done better than that if we hadn't had that rule about family."

"No," Patrick said firmly. "Remember what Marcus said." His voice became older, gruffer as he recited words culled from an interview article. " 'Anybody can sell to his own family. To develop your skills, you have to convert strangers into customers.' This isn't about raising money. It's about *practice*. We've gotta get good at this, or we'll never get out of this pissant town."

"Shit, yeah," Lee said, and as they nodded, some of the residual tension eased away.

They sat there in the woods, the four friends, listening to Lee's tape recorder. It was good stuff, Liszt's *Les Preludes*. Patrick could just about see the notes drifting up over the tree line down toward the river beneath them, fluttering out to sea like drowsy gulls.

It was quiet, except for a distant sound of . . . what was it? A chainsaw? No, it was another motorcycle starting up, somewhere to the . . . south this time? A slow feather of alarm brushed his spine, and then vanished. He had heard that sound before, and although it was far too distant for him to be certain, he could have sworn that was Cap's bike.

Nobody else noticed. None of them exactly *knew* Cap, but they saw him around town, and around the trailer park. He was impossible to miss: a red-haired giant lounging out on the deck of his trailer, smoking Shermans, his great meaty forearms propped on the railing, running his fingers through a tangled growth of crimson beard. He smiled speculatively at them, as Patrick might have smiled at a carton of night crawlers before setting the hook. Cap made his skin creep.

Cap worked a shift at the mill, but there were rumors that he had other business concerns as well, concerns that had more to do with pharmaceuticals than plywood.

"What are you thinking?" Destiny asked.

Patrick, who wasn't ready to share his musings, just shook his head carefully. "I was thinking that I need to get to my mom's shop," he said.

"Kinda nifty with the needle," Shermie said. "Be flying the fag flag next."

"Sit on my sausage, asshole. Real men patch their own socks." Patrick looked at Destiny, and their eyes locked. He was shocked by the intensity of the contact. Maybe he was reading too much into her expression, or maybe it was just having known her for over half his life. Perhaps the bond of shared experience, of Claremont Preschool and the trial and its aftermath: endless hours of psychiatrists and legal officials peering down their emotional throats, asking them:

Did anyone touch you? Hurt you? Did anyone expose himself? Where did you get the idea of hurting women?

Damn it, he didn't know what dark inner cave had spawned that filth, endless twilight dreams of mutilation, dreams that refused to die at dawn, that crawled into his waking hours like rotting corpses clawing free of the grave. Waking, half-asleep in the middle of the night, afraid, tiptoeing to his mother's room and easing the door open to see her mutilated body sprawled across the bed, her breasts ripped off, the sheets clotted with blood, and then looking down at his own hands to see the dripping knife—

Then waking again, knowing it was just a dream within a dream, and sitting awake till dawn, clutching the blankets to his chest, loathing the erection that pulsed insistently between his thighs, that forced him to fondle it until his fear and shame exploded into a galaxy of dying stars.

The next day he might be angry dawn to dusk, consumed with an unfocused, disorienting rage, wanting to rip the heart out of the world. He knew that those terrible daymares boiled up from somewhere deep inside him, someplace where the iron bands of control were rusting, rotting away.

And what would happen when they went? He didn't know, but did know that one day, they would. That thought scared the piss out of him.

Now.

But there was another, more deeply disturbing voice inside him that said, *Don't be afraid. When that day comes, when you turn me loose, you won't mind at all. Just wait for it, Patrick, old boy. Wait until I'm ripe, so ripe, bright and shiny and almost bursting to come out and play. Wait until the town has stopped watching you. Until they've forgotten that you're special.*

Then you and I will have real fun.

Even more, when he heard those things about Frankie, the puréed mice, he understood.

While drawing the line at warm-blooded animals, Patrick had burned plenty of bugs with magnifying glasses and matches, had poured salt on slugs and laughed as they contorted and bubbled green. But that was just a kid thing, wasn't it? And when his mother caught him doing it, and had taken his hands gently but firmly, and held the magnifying glass so that its bright hot point of light singed his skin, he had jerked away, more startled and scared than injured. She had made him look her in the eye, and told him that *animals feel pain, too, Patrick.*

He lay awake that night, thinking about it, thinking that animals had feelings, just like him, realizing that until then he had thought of them more like some kind of little meat puppets.

He was disgusted with himself, but . . . but kind of excited too. He didn't know what to do, what it all meant, but that night he had had the first wet dream he could remember. He woke up in the middle of the night, and found his underpants all gummy, had stripped them off in horror, and thrown them into the corner of his room, staring after them as if they might crawl back under the covers and into his lap.

In the morning he woke up, wondering if it had been just another dream, but when he'd reached under the covers, he had been naked. And when he'd crawled over to the corner of the room, and picked up his soiled underwear, they had been covered with fat, black, hungry ants.

Was it real? Another terrible dream?

It was real.

He had spent half that morning with his magnifying glass, in the back yard searching for ants, chasing and killing, chasing and killing, until his mother had caught him and took him to his father, who just laughed and said: *boys do things like that,* while she glared at him in disbelief.

So she spanked Patrick and sent him to his room. An hour later she came to him and looked him in the eye and said, *Do you understand now? Understand that they hurt, and feel fear, and want to live?*

And he cried and clung to her, confused as he had never been in his life. Confused that his mother was so angry with him. Confused that he was glad that ants could feel. He had *wanted* them to feel what he was doing to them.

And decided that until he could sort through his feelings, he would stop the small cruelties. He had wrestled with that part of himself, and the tortures had not continued . . .

So far.

He *had* drawn a line, and Frankie hadn't. Sometimes the voice inside his head said that Frankie was having more fun.

No. He couldn't think like that. Those thoughts were real, but they were *wrong.* He had so much, and his bond to these three meant so much. Whenever he and Destiny looked at each other, it was as if a current ran between them. It was similar to the current between Patrick and his mother, but different. Dizzying. Without her saying a word, he knew that Destiny was thinking: *real men don't need to patch their own socks. They don't need to blow up mice. I'm here, Patrick. See me. I'm here. I would patch up your socks for you. That, and other things. Things I won't do for Billy.*

Then suddenly, as if the intensity of the moment had grown entirely too powerful, she turned her head. Patrick blinked rapidly. He felt thick-tongued and light-headed.

Girls, most girls, triggered a strange anger in him. They flaunted themselves, got off on how boys watched them, mocked and ridiculed, whispered to each other as if circulating a dirty secret. But not Destiny. Of course, she wasn't a woman yet. She never wore makeup, and rarely anything frilly, and didn't play Barbies or crap like that. She could run, and catch, and hit, and climb better than most of the guys. Her breasts had yet to develop, although the swellings were beginning to push at her blouse. He didn't feel dirty when he looked at her, the way he felt when he looked at most women. He felt something else, something that he couldn't put a word to.

"Ah . . . Destiny? Want to ride down to Mom's shop?"

Her mild smile suggested that she was mirroring his thoughts. She nodded.

She rubbed Shermie and Lee's hair, and grabbed her bicycle, pacing Patrick as he headed down the mountain. "See you guys later!"

And of course, the inevitable reply: "Not if we see you first!"

Patrick and Destiny bumped their bikes down the path, sharing focus and effort in a comfortable silence. He let her get a little ahead of him, eyes narrowed as he watched her. Something about the way she bounced her hair confused him, but it was a *good* confusion. Sun and shadow played on her, filtering down from the trees like green netting. People complained about the rain, especially visiting Californians. But then, they always loved how green everything was. Jeez. As if you could have the one without the other!

Then they hit a long level stretch and she had to pump the pedals. She stood up, and he had a chance to look at the long, strong muscles along her spine stroking and pumping smoothly and evenly. The skin exposed by her halter-top was darkened by genetics as well as sun, smooth and lovely.

He just couldn't seem to tear his eyes from that single square foot of bare skin. He stared until he almost missed the branch coming at his face, slid sideways in a frantic attempt to avoid it, and tumbled off his bike. Destiny stopped, and looked back at him. Before she did it, she tossed her hair over her shoulder. Again, his eyes were riveted, the pain in his skinned shin forgotten.

"Why don't you watch where you're going?" She jumped off her bike. Destiny walked it up to him, and stared down.

Strange. She had always seemed so familiar, and now she was like something alien, as if she were branching off to become another species.

He began to phrase an awkward explanation, when another sound cut him off. That bike sound, from the southeast now. They looked at each other, and wondered.

This was private property. In all probability, that motorcycle was driven by someone who knew the landlord. The kids, on the other hand, were trespassing.

Was it Cappy? There were lots of motorcycles in the Claremont area, but only two real clubs. There was a bunch called Senior Cycles, in their fifties and sixties but still road masters.

Then there were the others, most pointedly Cappy Swenson and his scurvy crew. And although he felt a secret fear at the possibility that Cappy was nearby, he was uncertain if the trill down his back was fear or curiosity.

But there was another instinct that said, *Don't go down that path,* and said it loudly enough to surprise him.

"Come on," he said. "I don't like it here."

Maybe it *was* time for their club to relocate. Something was wrong here, and he wasn't interested in finding out exactly what it was.

He had the sense that they were being watched, and that sense, bubbling inside him like a cauldron, drove him on.

They hit River View Road a moment later, skewing out to the border of the yellow-marked bike lane, risking a brush with traffic. He pedaled like a fiend, chest thundering. Without realizing it, he had left Destiny behind him. Her bike chains rattled and whined as she fought to keep up. Finally, he slowed down, and she pulled up next to him. He planted his feet firmly on the pavement, and stopped.

"Hey, idiot," she panted. "What was *that* all about?"

"I don't know," he said. "I just felt something . . ." As the temporary flash of panic faded, his sense of absurdity increased, followed by shame.

Patrick hiked himself back up on his bike. Without another word they continued to pedal down River Front toward town. To their left, across the road, the blue-green waters of the Cowlitz sparkled at them through the trees. Adrenaline still seared his chest and stomach, but at least he was finally back in control. The embarrassment began to erode his sense of self-preservation, his deepest instincts, and even as he pedaled south along River Front, he chuckled ruefully to himself, already beginning to wonder what all the freaking nerves had been about, anyway.

What a wuss you are, Emory. Glad that it was only Destiny who saw that one.

4

Costumes, Period was set on the ground floor of a two-story mini-mall at the eastern edge of Claremont's downtown business district. If you hadn't seen the Yellow Pages ad, heard the word of mouth, surfed its web page or read a flyer jammed under your windshield wiper, you would probably never find it.

The nearest landmark was the Beefhouse steak joint just across the road. Patrick had stuffed countless flyers under the windshield wipers of cars parked there in front of the Beefhouse, soliciting customers for his mother's shop.

In fact, in recent months he had been buzzing with different techniques for increasing her business. They'd instituted Coupons, and Twofers, and Bargain Clubs, and convinced other neighborhood businesses to advertise cooperatively. He'd had those, and so many other ideas that finally his mother threw up her hands in exasperation, asking him how in the world he had concocted such a bewildering profusion of ideas, and would he *please* give her a minute to think?

Patrick and Destiny parked their bicycles at the back of the shop, next to the beat-up Ford station wagon with the *Back Off, I'm a Goddess* bumper sticker. He chained his bike to its bumper, while Destiny attached hers to a cyclone fence separating the mall from a humming, truck-sized electrical power transformer.

They shucked backpacks before reaching Costumes, Period's front door. "Knock knock," he called, and then pushed it open. The bell tinkled, announcing him.

Costumes, Period was crammed to the rafters with clothing and costuming of all types and descriptions: hats, masks, props ranging from witch's brooms to chrome steel samurai swords. Vivian Emory carried every kind of foot apparel from glass slippers to brogans, oil and water-based makeup, patterns and assorted do-it-yourself kits, tuxedos and other formal rentals, signs and sign-up sheets for sewing classes, and anything else that a fertile mind could cram into 1500 square feet of storage space.

He knew better than to disturb his mother, who was currently seated on a low stool, pinning a dishwater blonde customer into a Morticia Addams outfit. The costume was pure black down to the roots, and the blonde reminded Patrick of a black-handled bottle-brush. He whispered the observation to Destiny, and she made her famous piggy face in return: front teeth bared, nose flattened, snuffling for truffles. He managed to suppress his giggles: strange as Mom's customers sometimes seemed, they paid the biggest chunk of the rent. When you came right down to it, that was what really mattered.

He waited patiently for her to look up, and when she did, he chirped: "Hey, Mom!" She sighed and smiled at the same time. In the shop's flat overhead light, the bones seemed too prominent in Vivian Emory's mocha-latté oval of a face. Responsibility and woe were grinding her down. He could already see how his mother would look when she was old. That image seemed to hover around her, translucent but visible, like a ghost trying her bones on for size.

There were too many nights when she was up until three working at her Singer on some piece of costuming needed by nine in the morning. The extra double and triple-time money was just too useful. Those extra dollars paid for Christmas, and birthday presents, and holiday vacations.

Most of the year was kind of slow, but New Year's and Halloween were spectacular. December and October Patrick was lucky to have dinner with his mother twice a week.

Nobody said much about it, but he sometimes suspected that she had really started hiding in the costumes when things went to hell with the marriage, when Dad started hitting the booze too heavy, and having job troubles at the mill. Sometimes Dad's hours got cut back. When that happened, Otis Emory could get mad. He had yet to take it out on his son or wife. Dad loved them both far too much, but some nights he tiptoed back through the door with bruised knuckles and sometimes a black eye, and at least twice Vivian had bailed him out of jail. The arguments had grown horrific the weeks before she finally asked his father to move out.

When the Morticia clone minced back to the fitting room, Vivian Emory sighed and gave both the children bone-creaking hugs. Patrick leaned deeply into her. She smelled of perfume and dust.

"How's business, Mrs. Emory?"

"Need two more arms, Destiny." She cast a worried glance at the street-front window. "Or a way to make my new cashier a little prompter."

"Got the new flyers?" he asked.

Vivian Emory reached under the desk and brought out a box marked Qwik-Copy, five hundred Xeroxes of the new advertising stuff. She divided them between the kids. "Now, you be careful. And I don't want you hanging around that coffee shop."

She took a closer look at the girl. When Destiny shifted her eyes away, Vivian seemed to guess that something was wrong. Mom radar. "Destiny? What's the problem?"

"No problem," she said.

"Have you been over to the Inside Edge recently?"

"Not for weeks, Mrs. Emory."

"There's some kind of trouble going on over there, and I don't want you involved."

"Trouble?" Patrick asked. "What's going on?"

Vivian busied her hands with folding and hanging, but her eyes were worried and distant. "Just a story I heard. Your friend over there—"

"Manny? Rowan Matthews's kid?"

She nodded. "Yes. Manny got hurt last night. He's over at Mercy." Queen of Mercy was Claremont's town hospital, built by the mill owners back in the thirties.

"What happened?" Manny went to Cowlitz High, competed state-wide on the wrestling team, and was karate whiz Trask Matthews's younger brother. Manny was tough, and good-looking in a toothy, Jake Busey kind of way. He was a Baja Bug racer, always good for a short loan or a dirty limerick.

"Some kind of accident. Maybe." She seemed doubtful. "People are being kind of quiet." A racing accident? The stripped-down, balloon-wheeled Volkswagens called "Baja Bugs" could flip out on the beach where the older kids raced every weekend. It wouldn't be the first time . . . but something in his mother's face told him he was thinking in the wrong direction. "You aren't passing out flyers for them, are you?"

"Not right now," he said. Two months before, a once-famous folk singer had played a little gig at the Edge. Patrick and his friends had earned a few dollars stuffing leaflets under windshield wipers, and helped the coffee house pack the room.

"I don't want to have to worry about you. All right?"

"I won't go anywhere near it," he said.

Vivian looked at him, and then at Destiny. For a moment it looked as if she wanted to challenge him, and then she nodded. "Good. Well, back to work. Say 'Hi' to your mother, Destiny."

"I will, Mrs. Emory." Under Vivian Emory's doubtful eye, they scooted out the door, carrying a load of leaflets.

Out in the parking lot, Destiny pressed her handful of flyers against her chest and challenged Patrick. "Do you think we should have lied to your mother?" Her voice said that she already had an answer to the question.

He shrugged. *"Do nothing which is of no use,"* he said.

"Do not think dishonestly," she countered.

"I wasn't thinking dishonestly," he said defensively. "I knew I was lying. Just seemed the right thing to do."

"You're such a shit sometimes." Destiny twirled her bike's combination. She tossed her hair at him in a way that made him want to hit her and kiss her all at the same time. Honestly, she was just a girl, after all. There wasn't anything to get all excited about.

Before anything could be said that couldn't be unsaid, Destiny hiked herself up on her bike and zipped past him. "Tag!" she said. "You're it!"

And they went whooping off together, down the concrete walkway between the shops.

5

Vivian Emory's client was Mrs. Lolly Schmeer, a middle-aged lady with a fine, unlined face, a head of unbleached blond hair and a Tae-Bo body. Her husband Kiefer taught history at the junior high school, and was generally considered the dullest human being still sufficiently animated to draw breath. Vivian's husband Otis had never warmed to Kiefer, but Lolly was one of Vivian's best friends.

Lolly returned from behind the slatted white dressing room door with the Morticia costume on a hanger. "I like this costume, but could you raise the neckline a bit?"

"I'm sure I can," Vivian replied, and immediately began to plan her modification. The Addams costume was one of her favorites, a slinky, delicate piece of work, jet-black silk and cotton with fur trim at wrists and throat, fully fit for either Halloween or Friday the 13th. Neither was looming on the horizon, and she had an instinct about the aerobicized Lolly Schmeer.

She ran her fingers along the costume's neckline. Yes, she knew just the scrap of fabric. "No problem. You want this by Thursday?" She jotted the note on a scrap of paper. "Costume party?"

Mrs. Schmeer giggled. "No. Sometimes I just like to surprise Kiefer. Our therapist said it would put some spice back into our marriage." She was turning a lovely beet red as she said it.

"The plural of spouse," Vivian offered.

Lolly stared at her blankly. "What?"

"Spice. The plural of spouse." Lolly blinked, and then gave the horselaugh Vivian found disconcerting and endearing at the same time. "Never mind. You go on there, girl," Vivian said. "You might try the Teknique makeup base, though," she said, and put a bit of a growl into her voice. "It's edible."

There was a bit more girlish giggling, and some negotiations, after which money changed hands.

Vivian Emory sighed heavily. She was thirty-three years old, looked five years younger and felt ten years older. She loved her son, and her work, but every month it seemed harder to repress the sense that life was passing her by, like a train pulling out of a station. Moving slowly at first but gaining momentum with every empty day, rocketing along immovable rails toward a predetermined future.

There was the shop, which she had purchased from Mrs. Weatherly after six years' hard apprenticeship, performing the lion's share of the needlework. Mrs. Weatherly's retirement had been perfect timing, really. Vivian had always loved sewing, had learned it from her mother and aunt and grandfather (a master tailor), who had bought dolls for her to dress and collect for every birthday from her third to sixteenth.

And there was her very nearly ex-husband Otis, once the best right tackle Claremont High had ever seen. So her husband had earned his varsity letter, and the hand of the lightest-skinned black girl in Claremont. Pretty enough to turn heads in any part of town, and light-skinned enough that her own mother, who was similarly colored, had once whispered to her that she was lucky not to have to make "the worst decision in the whole damned world," namely, whether or not to *pass for white*.

The glory days of Claremont High varsity pigskin were far behind Otis now. When high school ended he had been forced to choose between a small midwestern college (the only scholarship offered), and a job at the mill. Kansas meant the academic grind, maybe a degree in Phys. Ed., and a teaching job down the road. There would be no pro ball: bad knees were an Emory family curse. And leaving Claremont meant leaving Vivian.

Working the mill meant floating his kidneys at Brogan's bar after work, still seeing his friends every day. Maybe landing a cushy desk job somewhere down the line.

The mill won by a length. Claremont Mill, built at the turn of the century by a man with the unlikely name of Enobarbus Claremont, was a place where half the old football team still hung together, remembering the glory days, still trying to pretend that time had not moved on, as it had. As it always did.

If Vivian was satisfied to live in the trailer park, satisfied to live the life that had thrilled her when she was a young girl just out of high school, everything might have been fine. But she wasn't, and it wasn't. There was more to life than that.

And that yearning for something more had eventually destroyed their marriage. She had to confess: there'd been no real feelings of love for Otis for almost two years, although for Patrick's sake she hadn't quite admitted the truth until just four months ago, when Otis's drinking went from bad to worse, and she finally had an excuse to kick him out.

Some day soon, just as soon as she could work up the courage, she was going to demand a divorce.

She examined the costume dropped off by a twenty-something Beefhouse waitress. It was a fine thing, a bangled and tassled Sheena Queen of the Jungle miracle of thrift-store ingenuity. Part zebra, part lion, and part Raquel Welch One Million B.C. peep show. One might easily have thought it a custom piece designed by Broadway wizards with all of the resources of a major theater company.

Vivian Emory had a gift, and upon that foundation she had built her life. When she first worked for the Weatherlys, she was a shy, fragile junior high school girl, with nimble fingers and a mind surpassing theirs in agility. She had cleaned shop for her employers, sewn repairs for them, and in time they had let her construct minor pieces. Once that threshold was passed, she was on her way. Because if there was a single area where Vivian's genius manifested most completely, it was in the minor miracle of turning trash into treasures.

Vivian had intimate knowledge of every secondhand shop within fifty miles. She ranged from Woodland to Battleground on her bicycle when the weather was good, begging rides from parents or friends on rainy days. She found every yard sale, Goodwill store and fabric overstock sale in the entire area. She could look at a scrap of nothing, destined for the trash heap, and see within it the seed of a formal gown, peacock-feather hat or shaggy-dog costume. She simply had the knack, developed back when she would costume and clothe and reclothe her Barbies in endlessly varied raiment.

The skills served her well. With material costs minimal, the only limitations were her skill, ambition and energy, and those were boundless. Soon, the Weatherlys, who had operated their little costume rental shop mostly selling Halloween items and New Year's party favors, who stocked helium gas and novelty hats and Mylar balloons intended for the odd office shebang, discovered that little Vivian's custom costume sideline was their most popular and profitable service.

When she graduated high school, they gave her a little apartment above their shop, paid for her B.A. degree in Theater Arts at Portland State, and provided opportunity after opportunity to invest in the store, with the hope that Vivian would eventually buy them out.

At the age of eighteen she had married her high school sweetheart, the solid and dependable (if occasionally uninspiring) Otis Emory, and labored to keep their life together, to create a happy family of three. They knew that the store would eventually pay off, and two years later she did buy the Weatherlys out, with a combination of cash and a percentage of net over the next five years.

And so at twenty, when most of her friends were happy with jobs at the mill or in secretarial or food service positions in the surrounding small towns, Vivian Emory owned her own business.

In those early days, in a *good* week she worked only sixty hours.

Sometimes, though, she wondered. Occasionally she caught a mirrored glimpse of the slender, caramel-skinned woman with the dark, straight hair, and wondered at the choices she had made. But a choice, once made, creates its own path. She had learned that from Patrick. It was something that his hero, Alexander Marcus, had said a thousand times.

Vivian had Patrick, and her husband, and her work. By sheer force of will she turned herself into the kind of woman who could *decide* to be content, and usually was. She could make the choice. Create the path.

This was her dream. And if there was anything wrong with having a dream, it was the fear that one day it might turn into a nightmare. She didn't call her own private fear a nightmare, exactly. To Vivian, it was the darkness beyond the dream, something amorphous, like a cloud of squid ink floating in murky water. Something that wasn't alive, wasn't conscious, but had a sense of direction. Perhaps it was something primordial and shapeless that sought heat and nourishment. In her heart of hearts, she dreaded that if she aspired to too much or held her head too high the darkness might find her.

And if she occasionally, too often perhaps, thought back to the events six years previous, when the men in the dark suits had asked her so many questions, when they had taken her son for questioning, when the darkness had awakened, fumbled blindly toward her and her family . . .

If there was order in the universe, any future disaster might well be attracted by her own secret shame, fear that she had once made a terrible, unforgivable mistake, that she should somehow have known that Claremont Daycare would prove a disastrous choice.

Customers came and went, one picking up an altered dress, another selecting a few pieces of costume jewelry for layaway. After the last sale Vivian closed the register and sat back on her stool, sighing. There were so many choices to make. Each closed another door, pared away another option in a life that already felt too damned constrained.

Power ran into Vivian's shop computer, a strawberry iMac, at all times, but its screen darkened when not in use. She touched the space-bar, and the CRT glowed to life.

A couple of clicks put her on-line. She had no dedicated phone line, but her modem program dialed *70 when she went on, so that she wouldn't get booted off by an incoming call.

The familiar series of AOL screens passed, irritating ads (no, she wasn't interested in a computerized gardening blueprint), and then the welcoming "You've got mail!" voice, followed by the sight of the little box with a yellow envelope protruding from its door.

Double-clicking, she took a quick look at a list of messages. Setting up the web page had been a lark. She hadn't anticipated much of a benefit, but America Online offered free web space, so she'd gone for it. Within six months she had received orders totaling over eight thousand dollars. At that point she realized that she'd better take cyberspace more seriously, moved her web page to Earthlink, and slowly began to put her stock on-line. Now there was hardly a day that an order from New York or Arkansas or Florida didn't fatten her till.

Patrick and his friends had made this possible. She didn't know how or where they came up with all their moneymaking schemes, but was certainly grateful for their help.

She clicked through the messages, looking at them one at a time, deleting the advertisements for porn or gambling, saving the business notes, and crafting swift replies for the few personal ones.

Then she came to one that surprised her. The e-mail address was RSAND@Marcus1.com. Something at the very back of her head felt a little warm and dizzy when she saw that. She clicked it, watching the screen with narrowed eyes.

It read:

Dear Mrs. Emory. What a pleasure to stumble across your web page, and see that you and your family are doing well. You may not remember me. My name is Renny Sand, and I introduced myself at the courthouse six years ago. I was driving from Vancouver B.C. to Portland today, passed through Claremont, and thought of you. Hoping that this note finds you all in the very best of health, and that your boy is thriving.

Best wishes, Renny Sand.

Vivian stared at the screen for a long time. She certainly did remember the tall, handsome reporter, and in fact had gone out of her way to look up some of his news stories. He was good, wrote simply and to the point, with a touch of poetry to balance what she guessed to be a deep and protective vein of cynicism. Most important, Renny Sand had kept his word and never written about Claremont Preschool.

The real question was: Why in the world did his promise matter? Why had she *really* looked up those stories? Why had she remembered him so quickly after six years, and why did she feel more than a little light-headed?

If she was honest with herself (and she always tried to be) she knew that the answer had to do with the way he smiled, the fact that he had conveyed a little light into her life on a day when trouble seemed to have swallowed the sun.

Perhaps it also had something to do with the choice that she had already made, the choice to divorce Otis, the fact that this man, the only man in ten years that she had responded to at all, had touched her life again. This was more than merely fortune. It seemed like an omen.

The e-mail jolted her like two cups of double-shot espresso. Vivian saved the letter and signed off. Then she stretched her arms, enjoying the good feeling of under and over-used muscles responding to the torsion, and began to devise her answer.

6

Patrick and Destiny were making good time on their bikes, tooling east along Ocean Way, Claremont's main drag. They passed out flyers to passersby, stuffed them under the windshield wipers of parked cars. A typical flyer read: *"Bring a Friend! 50% off the second costume at Costumes, Period."* It then continued with a glowing list of Vivian Emory's products and services.

Weeks before, Patrick had said, "Hey, Mom, if you don't blow your horn, who will?" Vivian shook her head in bashful exasperation, and conceded defeat.

Patrick and Destiny competed to see who could cover his side of the street fastest, laughing and enjoying the game no matter who won.

In the hills above Ocean Way, perched too high for the mill's endless clouds of blue smoke to trouble them, lived Claremont's wealthiest citizens. Without exception, the roads leading up to these expansive, landed homes were steep and curvy, but the worst of them was Angel Avenue. Its incline was almost impassable in icy weather, and its western drop-off claimed a car every eighteen months or so. Depending on the severity of the wounds and the social standing of the victim, there generally followed a brief series of editorials and public-access cable speeches, as a concerned citizen or city father debated the closing of so-called Suicide Hill.

The hilltop gentry invariably beat any such proposal down: *their* sports cars and jeeps had no trouble with the turns. *Their* moneyed children didn't lose limbs or lives. And the furor died down, for another eighteen months or so.

Generations of teenagers had made (and broken) their bones racing skateboards and bicycles top to bottom on Suicide Hill. It was socially disapproved, technically illegal and hazardous as hell, but adolescent ego is an insanely powerful evolutionary force. It was a rare day when some teen bravo didn't weave his way down, screaming or hunched grimly over his handlebars, waiting until the very last second before applying brakes and sizzling off to the left, toward the comparative safety of Ronny Falco's Mobil station.

Waiting a half-second too long meant sliding straight out into traffic and a grisly, glorious death as a Plymouth hood ornament. Or spill right and plunge over the side, a nasty drop to the concrete apron of Claremont reservoir. For this reason, most Suicide Hill challengers waited until the early-morning hours, when traffic was lighter, and the margin of fatal error comfortably wide.

But halfway through the distribution of Vivian Emory's flyers, a bright red ten-speed zipped down Angel Avenue, brakes screaming, turned left through the gas station, and almost collided with Patrick.

Patrick wrenched his bike to the side, grazed only by the maniacal laughter from the bespectacled kamikaze on the tenner. Patrick grimaced, trying to find a spot of anger, but the best he could work up was irritation. "Frankie! You could have killed me!"

Frankie flashed his trademark banana-sized grin, chockablock with braces and Chiclet teeth. He wore a battered green navy coat that made him look twice his size. "Be a lot more fun than I've been having today. Whatcha up to?" He snatched a flyer, pushing his glasses back up on his nose to read it. "Oh, for your mom, huh? Can I help?"

A little voice warned Patrick that *this could be trouble,* but Patrick rarely paid attention to that particular voice. He actually liked Frankie, despite (or maybe because of) the fact that trouble often seemed to follow him about. Frankie had an odd and interesting way of thinking. Never a dull moment. Still, Patrick hesitated. "Well, I don't know . . ."

Frankie clucked. His arms were all bone under his coat. In summer, his neck and back peeled in the sun. No matter how much time he spent outdoors, he never seemed to tan. "I know, this is all something for that club of yours."

"What club?" Patrick said blandly.

Frankie's smile was cold. "You know, the club you've never asked me to join. I don't hate you for it. Maybe I should. Whattayathink?"

That last was rhetorical, a mere Frankieism. Patrick knew better than to answer.

Destiny waited for the cars to clear out of the street, and then scooted her bicycle across Angel Avenue, pedaling like hell. She hopped her bike up over the curb and came to an abrupt stop. "Hey, Frankie."

"Dez." He acknowledged her with a nod. "Well, listen, I'm not trying to get into your stupid club. Just looking for something to do, and this looks like as much fun as anything."

Destiny and Patrick glanced at each other, and her mouth twisted into her "why not?" expression. Patrick's shoulders hunched in acquiescence. Pat gave Frankie a fat pack of flyers.

As Frankie thumbed them, he said, "Hey, did you hear what happened to Manny?"

Patrick and Destiny exchanged another cautious expression. "Yeah," Patrick said. "What did you hear?"

"Four ribs. Says hit-and-run. I say it's bullshit. What do you think?"

Patrick felt a little trill of warning. "If not hit-and-run, then what?"

"Got stomped. He was leaving a party over near the junior college, ran into the wrong guys, mouthed off. He won't talk, but that's what happened."

"How do you know?"

"Keep an ear out, and you hear things."

Frankie was probably right. You could take an early-morning trip to the airport to pick up a cousin, and see Frankie pedaling his bicycle along the bridge. You could come back from a ten o'clock movie at the mall, midnight on a school night, and see Frankie pedaling that bicycle, face set in an expression of grim determination. Frankie's parents never seemed to know where he was, and as long as he didn't get into legal trouble, they hardly seemed to care. In his endless wanderings he had made an astonishing range of acquaintances, but Patrick doubted if he would call any of them friends.

"Who hurt Manny?" Destiny asked.

"Haven't heard. Bet we could find out, though."

"Yeah, maybe," Patrick said. He glanced at Destiny. "We're not supposed to go over to the Edge, though . . ."

Frankie cut him dead. "Like *that* would stop you." Nailed. Frankie wheedled his way toward the kill. "Come on . . ."

"Well, if it's business."

Frankie held up two fingers. "Just business. Scout's honor."

"You were never a scout."

"Was too. Got kicked out for eatin' Brownies."

Destiny gave a disgusted laugh, and the kids weaved down the street, enjoying the day. For a half hour they passed out leaflets up and down Pacific Coast, then turned south along Main Street, past the Sizzler restaurant and the Rialto theater ("Recently remodeled!") and papered a parking lot next to a USBank. They went another block or so down, and were about to back off when Patrick saw Frankie staring at a blacked-out window below a sign reading *The Saddle Shop*. A lariat was painted around the edges of the sign. *Jesus Loves You* bumper stickers were pasted across the bottom of the window.

Frankie arched an eyebrow at them. "Shall we?"

Patrick felt disgust, amusement, fear, excitement . . . an odd mix of emotions that should have been competing, but weren't. "No . . ."

"Come on. Scared?"

Yes. "N-no."

But he didn't speak soon enough to keep Frankie from rocketing his bicycle across to the building. As they got closer, he heard the thump of iron on iron coming from behind the blacked-out glass. Metal sounds, and grunts of effort from men almost as hard.

Frankie pulled his bike up and grabbed a few printed sheets from beneath the book clip. Destiny stared in disbelief, and Patrick was almost speechless with awe at Frankie's daring. *This* was why he was willing to put up with the kid.

Christ. Nobody, but *nobody,* went through that door.

"Dare me?" Frankie said. At this point, no dare was necessary. Things had already progressed *way* beyond that.

"They'll eat your liver," Patrick said.

Frankie made a face at him, and turned to Destiny. "With fava beans and a nice kee-yanti? Dez. Dare me?"

Her eyes blazed, but she tried to act noncommittal. "Go ahead, idiot, but don't blame me."

Patrick motioned to Destiny to park her bike. He had only caught glimpses before this moment, and he was dying to see what the hell happened next. Maybe this would be the final chapter in the Crazy Frankie saga. If so, a witness was needed. He rolled his bike against the building, leaned it there and turned to Destiny. "Are you coming?"

"Hell, no. And you won't go if you've got the brains God gave a gerbil."

Frankie made a chipmunk face, pouching his cheeks and exposing his front teeth. "Then just wait here," he said. "If you hear a scream, run for help."

"I'll stroll," Destiny replied.

Patrick was right behind Frankie as he pushed the door of the *Saddle Shop* open. There was no tinkle or beep, as might have been expected if the door was the entrance to a shop or bar.

The room was dark and dank as a cave, just three overhead bulbs with circular shades casting fog-edged pools of yellow light on the floor. There was a bar to the left, but it was deserted at the moment. Later that evening, perhaps, it would be swamped. There were two billiard tables two-thirds of the way back, swallowed by shadows. A single bulky man with a shaven head practiced shots with almost mechanical precision. Chalked the cue, stroked, measured, chalked again.

In the very back of the room, however, was its oddest feature. Three heavy-duty weight benches, handmade monsters of chrome, padded leather and dark heavy wood, were arrayed as much for display as utility. Weight benches that might have been hewn from redwoods by Paul Bunyan for his *very* special friend, the Jolly Green Giant.

The six titans clustered at the benches fit the picture. Not one of them massed less than 220 pounds, with the largest nearing 300. Solid muscles, thick tendons, writhing snakelike ridges of flesh crisscrossing swollen chests. The air was a dense, tepid soup of testosterone and sweat.

Their bodies were laced with tattoos that melded lightning bolt images with steel guitars. In cartooned configuration, men with impossibly proportioned and vascular physiques flexed and posed. One of the athletes was etched with a bodybuilder Christ on the cross. This Lamb looked strong enough to flatten Golgotha, stalk down from his perch and slaughter a regiment of Roman wolves. The wall posters continued the same disorienting themes: gleaming muscle men rather obviously posing for the pleasure of other muscle men.

There was one man on each of the benches: two flat bench-press rigs and a leg-press device Torquemada would have swooned for. Apparently the victim was supposed to lie on his back and set his feet flat against seven or eight tons of iron plate loaded on the sled above. It looked like a surefire hernia generator.

Each had a spotter watching carefully, encouraging efforts with voices that were disorienting melds of Marine drill sergeant and seductive coo.

One was a red-haired crew-cut type, with a neck wider than his jaw line. Shoulders like the deck of an aircraft carrier were bursting out of his cutoff tank top. His legs were short in proportion to his torso, but of simian breadth. All of this was in contrast with his face, which was surprisingly mild. The small black eyes above his Roman nose were bright and intelligent.

Crew-cut leaned over the man on the weight bench, who was currently doing a pretty fair impression of a hydraulic jack. The bar was *bending* under its load, and the man on the bench vibrated with the effort to get it up one more time. Veins leapt out on his chest, popped out at his temples. His eyes nearly started from their sockets.

"Burning up there, baby?" Crew-cut said sweetly. "Come on, just two more—"

The other man, a suntanned long-jawed Gargantua tattooed from toe to eyebrow, managed one more, then hissed, "Jesus, Brando, I can't—"

Brando leaned close. "Make it worth your while, Cotter. Remember last Saturday? Give it to me. One more, sugar. Give it to me—"

Cotter screamed, set his sweaty hands and hoisted that heavy iron again. His arms locked straight, biceps and triceps ballooning grotesquely. His chest heaved as if an earthquake were erupting beneath his ribcage. He screamed either victory or agony—it was hard to tell which. That eruption of strength peaked and waned, and the bar trembled. In the instant before he would certainly have collapsed and crushed his chest into salsa, Brando snatched it from him with little apparent effort, and guided it back onto the safety bar with a clang. Cotter's gleaming, tattooed chest heaved like a beached blowfish. Cotter levered himself back to a sitting position, mouth gaping as he sucked wind. With obvious relish, Brando leaned over and gave him a sloppy kiss.

Patrick couldn't stop himself from gasping, "Gross!"

Only then did the men seem to see the kids standing at the door. They finished their last reps, and set the iron clanging back on the safety bars, mopping their faces with towels.

Brando seemed bemused. "Private club, kids. Get on out."

"Excuse me." For once, the unflappable Frankie seemed thoroughly flapped.

Cotter had finally stopped billowing. "This isn't for you, sonny boy. Come back in ten years." The other monsters erupted into good-natured laughter. Frankie took a step back, his jug ears red, his calm stamped flat.

Patrick took the flyers flopping from Frankie's hands and fumbled with them, evening up the edges. Startled at his own bravado, he held a couple of them out to the muscle men. "Seen you guys passing out pamphlets over at Twin Rivers," he said.

"Doing the Lord's work," Brando said without a trace of irony.

"Just thought you'd like one of ours." He held it out further, his arm shaking. Brando stepped forward, surprisingly graceful for a man of his intimidating mass, a gentle and utterly unthreatening expression on his face.

Brando looked at the flyer. And smiled. "Your mom?"

Patrick nodded.

"She has the little shop over across from the steak house?" Another nod. "Well, thanks, little brother. You guys take care. There are some real assholes out these days."

Frankie finally managed to get his throat open. "You hear about the stomping?"

"Yeah," Brando said. "Shit like that gets around. Someone likes to play with people who can't play back. Well." He rubbed his hands over his swollen arms. "Coolin' off. Gotta get back to work." He reached out and ruffled Patrick's hair, while Frankie looked on goggle-eyed. Then the big man turned his weight-thickened back to them, and headed back to the bench. "One more set!" he barked.

Cotter groaned. Brando turned the music back up, slid under the weight bar, set his palms firmly against the underside and hoisted it up.

Patrick watched for an awestruck second, and then backed out of the room.

"Goddamn," Frankie whooped. "He touched you man, he *touched* you!"

"What happened?" Destiny asked.

"Nothin'," Patrick replied. "Not like being a homo is catching or something."

Frankie leered. "You act like you *like* it. I think you *do* like it. I think that you should just go back in there right now and sign up. 'Oh, please, Mr. Homo, can I lick the sweat off your butt for you?"

"Jesus," Destiny said. "There is a lady here. Please?"

"Where? Where?" Frankie asked, looking both ways with faux concern. "Did I hit her? Is she all right?" They rolled their bikes out into the bike lane along Ocean Way.

"Oh, go spit," Patrick said.

Frankie made it up to them, actually paying their way into the matinee showing of the latest Jerry Bruckheimer action opus. Despite its R rating, the girl at the box office looked the other way, as did the teen-aged assistant manager. They bought popcorn and bonbons, and sat in the front row, riffing on the cornier lines of dialogue, cheering at the special effects and exaggerated violence.

Afterwards, they prowled the Twin City Mall. They bought yogurt at the food court while Destiny and Frankie talked about the fun they were going to have at summer camp in July. Patrick tried to suppress his raging jealousy, but managed only to conceal it.

"Too bad about Tanesha," Frankie said seriously.

"What about her?" Patrick asked, sliding his spoon up the little twisty mountain of frozen dessert. "Have you heard from her?" He stopped, smiling at the thought.

Frankie stared at him. "You didn't know?"

"Know what?"

"Jeez. I'm sorry. Her cousin Jeffrey told me that she got herself killed nearly two months ago, Pat. Oh, man." For a moment, all of Frankie's cavalier attitude dissolved.

Destiny set her yogurt down, blinking. "Is this one of your lousy jokes? If it is . . ."

Frankie shook his head vigorously. "Honest to God. She got hit by a car, man. Didn't even make it to the hospital."

"Oh . . ." Patrick tried to think of something to say, and couldn't. "Oh, man, I was just thinking about her this morning. Oh, man." He turned his face away from them, afraid for a moment that he might cry. The moment passed, and he turned back. "Why didn't someone tell us?"

"God, man," Frankie said. "I guess everyone thought someone else had told you."

"When did it happen, Frankie?" Destiny asked.

"On a Saturday, maybe seven weeks ago. I'm sorry, guys. You know, we haven't talked all that much lately. I just heard about it couple days ago."

Destiny was somewhere else. "Seven weeks ago? Wow. That's really weird," she said.

"Why?" Patrick had his voice back under control now.

"Just a dream. Maybe seven weeks ago. Dreamed that we were all back at Claremont, napping. Only Tanesha was flying. I remember that. She was above us, flying."

Tears sparkled in Destiny's eyes, and began to spill down her cheeks. Patrick put his arm across her shoulder, and she leaned into him, her face pressed against his chest, making little hitching sounds.

Frankie seemed completely at a loss, finishing his cup of yogurt with no apparent joy. By the time his spoon struck bottom, Destiny was done, but her eyes were still luminous.

"We have to do something. At least a card for her mom."

The boys nodded. Then Destiny sighed, and turned her attention back to her half-melted dessert cup. Patrick hugged her again, and then went back to his, but after a moment he looked up at Frankie, who seemed miserable. "Are you guys all right?" he asked.

Patrick nodded, but was silent until he finished his cup.

Then the three of them rose, bussed their trays, and left the mall without another word.

The sun was low in the sky by the time they unlocked their bikes and set out to distribute the rest of the flyers. They were down to the last few of them by the time they were back on Ocean Way and reached the Inside Edge coffee shop.

Patrick and Destiny looked at each other as if wondering what they were going to do. Then they jumped off their bikes and rolled them up to the front of the shop. They didn't bother to lock them. This time Destiny came inside, sandwiched between Patrick and an uncharacteristically sober Frankie.

Inside Edge was a deliberate anachronism, a paean to the tie-dyed, black-lit, psychedelic sixties complete with posters of Janis and Jimi and The Who. *Love the One You're With* bleated from waist-high tower speakers that resembled aged orange crates, but produced superbly clear digital sound.

Inside Edge was a favorite hangout for a certain element of Claremont: the radio station and bookstore crowd, the lunchtime chess and poetry bunch, the handmade pottery and flea market 15-minute portrait artists. In short, the town potheads.

Everybody knew that this was where the town dopers made their connections. The cops never exactly busted it, but Inside Edge had been tossed a couple of times. Nothing greenish-brown and illegal ever turned up: the proprietors were too smart for that. Legend had it that out in the hills north of town there was one hell of a fine little marijuana patch. It was said that carefully concealed fields produced a yearly crop of Cowlitz Coma, probably Washington's premier Two-Hit Shit. Further (so the legend had it) steady Inside Edge customers could make the connections necessary to buy discreet little baggies of bud.

Patrick already knew kids at school who smoked pot, and not one of them claimed to have acquired their supply from the Edge. If Rowan and her husband did in fact sell weed, they didn't sell to kids.

Rowan Rose was a flaming redhead in her late fifties, rather skinny upstairs, heavy down bottom, with a smile bright enough to light a billboard. Today, that smile looked a bit worried, as if she had been up half the night with a sick friend. Or perhaps a wounded child. "Hey, Frankie, Pat," she said, as brightly as she could. "How are ya? If you're looking for work—"

Patrick felt warmed and welcomed by her smile, faded though it might be. "Fine, Rowan. Just wanted to come by, say 'Hi.' " Her expression said she wasn't wholly convinced.

"Is that all?"

Destiny closed the door behind them. "Well . . . maybe we wanted to know about Manny."

Rowan's face darkened, and a shadow of suspicion crossed her face. A hugely fat, longhaired man in a checkerboard smock emerged from the swinging doors behind her. "What's up?" he asked.

"They were just asking about Manny," she said.

He tightened his eyes at them, and then relaxed. "Aw, hell, he's all right. We'll deal with this shit."

Frankie grinned at him. "How's the farm, Pork?"

Rowan's husband Ralph had been fat so long he didn't remember skinny, and was good-natured enough not to care. He had gotten the nickname "Pork" in Vietnam—originally a reference to his love of the Other White Meat, but in time a not-terribly veiled reference to his waistline. He narrowed his little eyes. "Ain't got no farm," he said.

Frankie wasn't taking "no" for an answer. "Why don't you roll me a fat one?" he said, innocently.

Rowan rolled her eyes as if she had no idea what he was talking about. "I tell you what," she said. "How about I set three hot chocolates at that table right over there?"

The spring afternoon was just beginning to cool, and that sounded like a stellar idea, one good enough to motivate even Frankie to shut up and let something nice happen for a change.

"Do we have a deal?" she asked.

"Deal," Patrick and Destiny said.

She leaned in until she was nose to nose with Frankie. "Then you can that kind of talk."

"Oops," he said, and sat.

Destiny sat kitty-corner to him, and couldn't help glaring at him with a particularly evil eye. "Frankie . . ." she began, and then trailed off.

Frankie shrugged. "Well, everybody knows they've got the stuff, they grow the stuff, and they deal the stuff—"

He cut off his dissertation as Rowan brought the hot chocolate to the table.

Rowan's face was both young and old, and she looked as if she had been an active and delicious part of the sixties scene in San Francisco, as if she had spent most of the last thirty years piling her worldly possessions into her VW van and truckin' on down the road after the Grateful Dead. When Jerry Garcia died, Rowan had worn black for a month. How exactly she had ended up in a town the likes of Claremont was a source of much quizzical speculation.

"Thanks, Rowan," Destiny said. She sipped carefully, swirling the cocoa against her tongue, and pronounced it Good.

Rowan hovered, not quite done with them. "Now," she said. "On the other subject. If it was true—and it's not, by the way—I certainly wouldn't give any to little weasels like you."

"And if we were big weasels?" Frankie asked.

"Come back and ask that question in ten years, and we'll talk again."

"Will the answer be different?" Patrick said.

"No, but we'll have fun talking." She winked at him. Rowan Rose was old enough to be his mother . . . hell, his grandmother, but there was something about her that gave Patrick that odd light-headed feeling. And made something deep down inside him feel . . . angry? No, that wasn't it. Confused. Jigsawed inside, sort of loose and electric. It felt a little like waiting to hit the opposing line in a good, rough game of football, all sizzling adrenaline. But why did he feel that about Rowan? Some part of him wanted to *hurt* something. But who? And why?

That he didn't know, and not knowing frightened him far more than had any of the make-believe violence in the afternoon's movie.

She leaned in close, as if she saw something in him that was of infinite interest. "And how about you, Pat?" she asked. "How are you?"

He felt dizzy, a little disoriented as he smelled her perfume.
Odd.

"Fine," he said. He felt a sudden, powerful urge to change the subject. "But I heard about Manny. What happened?"

Now her face fell. "He had an accident," she said.

"Yeah," Patrick said. "I bet Trask will help spread that accident around."

"That's not funny," she said. "Trask could have one, too."

They looked at each other, and Destiny laughed. "Trask? Nothing can hurt Trask!" There were four trophies set on shelves behind the counter and over the speakers. Each portrayed little golden men performing a variety of punches and kicks. Those were Trask's trophies. Manny's big brother's trophies. Whatever had happened to Manny, surely Trask would sort it out.

Rowan's faint smile remained, but the light had faded from it. "It's not that simple, kids. It's not something I'm prepared to talk about. I know you mean well, but . . . it's not that simple."

Patrick's mind was buzzing. What was this all about, really? Trask looked like a hippie, but he was also the aerobic kickboxing instructor at the local kung-fu academy. He was tall and lanky and lean, and looked like he'd just stepped out of a *Baywatch* episode. He'd even won tournaments down in Portland. Trask taught the Kickin' Kids class where Herman Sevujian took his lumps, and was really pretty much a big teddy bear.

Patrick's gaze wandered to a silver-framed black-and-white behind the counter, a picture of Trask standing next to Chuck Norris himself. With all of that martial arts training, what in the world did Rowan have to be worried about?

"And he wouldn't be alone, either," Frankie offered. "He has friends over at the academy, if anything happened . . ."

Rowan's eyes were sad, as if she didn't want to be the one to introduce these children to the ways of the real world. "Trask is a very good fighter," she said proudly. "Manny's . . . accident was just that. An accident." Her face hardened, as if her words proclaimed that the ultimate, irreversible end of discussion.

Strange. Patrick had been at the Inside Edge only a few weeks ago, but something was different now. He saw her fatigue more deeply, could smell the fear radiating from her, a mixture of sour milk and talcum powder. He had always thought the Edge to be absolutely the hippest hangout, but if he looked closer he saw the electrical tape mending the chairs, the dog-eared books on the racks, the paint flaked away from the wooden chessmen on the game tables. Why hadn't he noticed before?

Perceive those things that cannot be seen.

Pay attention even to little things.

Those were Musashi's words, words he had learned so long ago they seemed as natural a part of him as his fingernails. They bubbled up in his mind as they often did when there was trouble. Suddenly it felt as if the entire situation were a game, one of those multi-level Star Trek chessboards, with the different people and facts balancing each other, separate but connected and interacting. And what was it that his instincts were trying to tell him?

Before he could finish formulating a thought, Destiny broke the silence. "Rowan," she said, "if it wasn't just an accident. And if—"

"It was an accident," she said. Rowan pushed herself away from the table. "The world is bigger than you think it is." She turned her face away from them, but not before Patrick saw a glimmer of moisture welling in her eyes. Rowan blinked rapidly. "You're smart, all of you. But you don't *know.*" Her eyes were bright and tight, as if she were only a twitch away from panic.

"All right," Destiny said, reasonably. Then as Destiny had a tendency to do, she surprised Patrick and took an entirely different tactic. "I wrote a story once, though, about some nice people who were being hurt. I mean, their youngest son was hurt, and the mother was afraid to let her older son settle it. In my story, they went to the police, and the police were able to handle things. Do you think that was a good story?"

Jeez, that's transparent, Patrick thought.

To his surprise, Rowan pulled up a chair and sat down with them. "I think your story sounds good," she said carefully. "Too simple, maybe."

Love the One You're With had ended, and now Jefferson Airplane's *White Rabbit* began its opening drumbeat.

"How?" Destiny asked.

Rowan paused, looking at them. Patrick's eyes were calm, his peripheral vision floating out, expanding enough to see that Frankie and Destiny were sharing the same peaceful oasis. There was no urging from either of them. Any of them. Just that restfulness.

Rowan's reticence sought eagerness on their part. Childish challenge, pity, nosiness, anything that it could push against, and found nothing.

Her shoulders slumped, a great sigh whistling out of her. "I don't know why I'm telling you this," she said.

Again, the kids said nothing, as if sensing that a single word might break the spell. Rowan examined each of their faces separately, and then quietly began to speak.

"Sometimes, the police want excuses to look into someone's business. And if you give them an excuse, they start coming around even when you don't invite them. Sometimes, it can lead to more trouble than the original problem."

"More problem than broken ribs?"

Rowan's lips opened in the slightest of weary smiles. "You didn't say that that was part of your story. But yes, some things are worse than broken ribs."

That was as much as Rowan was going to say. She stood. Pork was right behind her. "We'll handle this," Ralph said. "I've handled things before."

"That was twenty years ago," Rowan said gently. "Closer to thirty."

"I still know how to protect my own," he said. Her thin arm slipped around his waist. Patrick had studied the Vietnam era in school, and found himself wondering how an ex-hippie and a 'Nam vet had ended up together. They'd created two sons, wrestler and karate-fighter, but both known to be pussycats. How had this odd family settled in a nowhere town like Claremont, brewing espresso, selling books and running a discreet pot farm somewhere up in the hills? You never knew.

Maybe Ralph read his mind, or something close to it. The big man turned, stared studiedly out of the front window in a rather absurd attempt at nonchalance. "You live over in the trailer park, don't you, Pat? Over near Cappy's bunch?"

Rowan gave her husband a dirty look. He shrugged. "Just a fucking question." He winced. "I'm sorry. I shouldn't have said that. Listen: forget about it."

White Rabbit wailed its conclusion. No new song filled the void, and the silence stretched on.

Images and labels danced in Patrick's mind: Cappy and his vile crew. The youngest member of a family of fighting hippies. A coffee shop with a reputation for pot.

And what was Cappy's reputation? Hadn't there been whispers there, too? Hadn't he seen one of Cappy's crew, one of the motorcycle creeps, riding up behind the football field at the high school, seen some of the high school stoners going back to meet him?

Know the Ways of all professions.

Rowan and Ralph wouldn't be partners with Cappy.

What if they were competitors?

"They know you won't go to the cops?" Patrick ventured.

Rowan's eyes opened wide, and Ralph coughed, covering his mouth with one thick hand. She lit a cigarette with her nicotine-stained fingers. Patrick saw that her hands were shaking.

At the absolute corner of his vision, Frankie inclined his head a fraction of an inch, nodding approval.

He wasn't sure what might have been said or done in the next moment, but suddenly Manny entered through the back of the shop. Manny looked like a big, healthy Kansas farm boy, his crimson hair a gift from his mother. Right now he had a painful limp, and favored his right side. He grinned ruefully. "Hey, Mom, Dad." He noted Patrick and his friends staring at him. "Hey, little dudes. It looks worse than it is, you know."

His brother and a couple of his friends crowded in behind him. One of them was well over six feet, lantern-jawed, with knobby hands and veined arms. The other was small, with very quick, precise movements and long black hair. He had a crooked, thin-lipped, reckless grin. These three pretty much ran the Claremont Kung Fu Academy. Patrick felt a violent itchiness in the air, as if the three of them were waiting for some crazy, half-starved, taloned raptor to roost.

Rowan and Ralph left the kids, and clustered around their sons and their friends, talking in low voices, occasional sharp bursts of forced jollity resulting in shallow laughter.

Once, Ralph turned and looked back at them, expression quizzical. Then he took his sons back behind the counter into the kitchen.

War talk, Patrick thought. *Oh, shit.* He thought about Cappy's bunch, and contrasted them with Rowan's family. He wanted to throw up.

They sipped their cooling cocoa. Rowan put another CD on the player. Procol Harum began to sing about skipping the light fandango, whatever the hell *that* meant. Another minute passed, in which Rowan busied herself rearranging cinnamon rolls and finishing her cigarette.

Then she stubbed the butt out, and went back into the kitchen. A minute later, Ralph came out, and waddled to the table. He stood looking down at them, his expression so odd he seemed almost to be a different man. He appeared distant, scared, defiant and completely walled in. He might have been standing atop a fortified hill, in fatigues and battle array, hands on an air-cooled .50 mm machine gun, gazing down on a horde of advancing Cong.

"You kids," he said softly. "You're pretty darned smart. Don't be too smart." That was all he said, but all of that odd, compressed energy lay behind those ten words, and it made Patrick feel like he had brushed against a beehive.

Crazy Frankie broke the silence. "What about rolling me a fat one? Whattaya think?"

Ralph snorted. "Chocolate's on the house."

Frankie made a face at Ralph's back as he disappeared behind the kitchen's double doors. Rowan reappeared a moment later, and busied herself at the cash register. She looked as if someone had drained three or four pints of her blood in the minutes since her sons had arrived.

The message was clear: *Drink your drinks and leave. This is family business.*

Destiny took another sip and stood. "Thanks, Rowan." Rowan nodded without speaking, still not meeting their eyes. Frankie finished his next. He tried to smile, but Rowan wouldn't meet his eyes. Finally they just backed out of the door and eased it closed gently, so that the bell didn't even tinkle. Something terrible, and terribly sad, was happening back in that kitchen. They didn't belong here.

The sad thing was, neither did Rowan and her family, and Patrick would have bet his left eye that they understood that better than anyone.

7

V ivian was closing up the shop, securing the door's double locks, and drawing the iron gate across the window. Business-wise, the day had been average, but there were . . . *extras* that quickened her step deliciously.

She carried a double armful of fabric rolls out to the parking lot and fumbled a little, searching for her keys. As she popped up the trunk she paused, listening to the drifting sounds of merriment from the Beefhouse across the street. It was still early in the evening. Things would get raucous around 10 o'clock, when the restaurant would shut down, the bar customers romping and stomping to the Nashville beat.

Even if she rarely indulged in that particular brand of merriment, she could still envy them.

Or would have envied them, under ordinary circumstances, on other days. Today, her heart was lighter than it had been in weeks.

Her battered black station wagon was twenty years old but still mobile. Sliding past the door, she grimaced as the rough, torn seat cloth scraped the backs of her thighs. The blanket seat-cover had ridden up a bit, exposing threads worn almost down to the springs. A tug at her stockings reminded her how very close to the edge she played.

It took three twists of the key before the engine turned over. Then she switched on the lights, illuminating more of the parking lot than she really wanted to see. During the day, the area looked downright respectable. Customers from the other shops filled the lot, and their noise and traffic helped to sustain the illusion of a bustling enterprise. At night, light from the street lamps seemed to flatten everything out, leached the vitality out of the buildings, made the entire area seem more than ever just another slum in desperate need of gentrification.

She pulled out of the lot and down a darkened street behind a new shopping center. Vivian had held her breath as the megaplex went up: There was always the chance that someone would open a costume shop there, and in fact she had considered bidding on a space herself, merely to reduce the probability of another costume shop moving into her territory. For a while a party-goods store had opened, but the clientele was so different that she was able to relax: no competition there, nothing that might pare a few vital dollars from her income, funds she could ill afford to lose. Fortunately the megaplex was mostly outlet stores, and pulled most of its customer base from traffic on the I-5.

The Claremont trailer park was a ten-minute drive from the shop, mostly twisty turns on narrow streets, finally crossing a bridge across the Cowlitz River, along River View, and finally to the place she called home. She checked the mailbox as she turned in the drive, pulled out a handful of bills and glossy ads for magazines she would never read, envelopes from banks begging her to take their credit cards. Nothing personal, nothing particularly interesting. She navigated the narrow streets, past the U where two trailers sat almost kissing, a familiar clutch of Harley-Davidson and Suzuki motorcycles parked out in front. Those trailers: one yellow with an emerald roof, the other an eyesore in primer gray, seemed to host an eternal party. A rotating clutch of rowdy men and shrill, gaudy women drank and laughed until three in the morning most weekends. Complaining brought out the cops—eventually. But it usually brought out the same cop, a beefy, sandy-haired borderline thug named Krup who was brother to Cappy's girl-friend. If Krup came out things usually quieted down, but on two occasions the complainants had met with mysterious accidents. Slipping on black ice. Falling down stairs. People stopped calling the police.

Past that trailer and a small forest of laundry trees was the southern fence. Through the fence, Vivian could see the worn and empty husk of Claremont Daycare. Its boarded-up windows still accused her. She hunched at the wheel and focused forward. The pain and guilt were no longer so overpowering, but she didn't like seeing the place. She wished someone would raze it to the ground, or at the very least rent and redecorate it. Failing that, she might have to move one day, just so that she wouldn't have to look at it every damned day of her life.

She might have moved already, but there was no other park north of Claremont, and moving to the south end of town, down by the mill, would be almost like moving over to Allantown. It would also mean separating Patrick from his friends, and she couldn't do that, not merely to salve her own conscience.

Vivian pulled up in front of her double-wide Monticello, approving of the way the little white Christmas lights shone through the trellised ivy. They twinkled slowly enough that one rarely noticed that the patterns rotated a hundred and eighty degrees every thirty seconds, lending a celestial effect to the walkway. It was just one of a hundred different ways that she strove to create a touch of magic in her life.

Vivian slid open the glass door, and sighed at the sight of the divine mess spread around the floor. The sigh wasn't one of regret or irritation, it was pure pleasure. Where other eyes might see a mere scrap heap of old clothes and tatters, hers saw nothing but possibilities, a thousand different ways that *this* and *that* scrap might couple, incubate, and birth a costume. This was *home*.

"Patrick?" she called.

From the back came a muffled "Here, Mom."

She went down the narrow hallway to the converted bedroom that served as a den. Patrick, Destiny and Frankie Darling were sprawled in front of the television, meditating on the Disney channel. It was all perfectly innocent, but Vivian felt a bit uneasy that Destiny's mother seemed so unconcerned that her thirteen-year-old daughter hung out, unsupervised, with boys. Or that Frankie's father, the Reverend Doctor himself, rarely seemed to know or care where his son was.

Frankie was the first of them to turn around. "Hi, Mrs. Emory," he said, with something in his voice that reminded her of that character in old *Leave It to Beaver* reruns, Eddie Haskell. *Good morning, Mrs. Cleaver, how lovely you look today . . .*

Patrick waved at her without taking his eyes from the adventures of Aladdin.

"Patrick—did you take the chicken out of the freezer?"

He nodded without turning around. "Yes, Mom."

Hmmm. She wasn't entirely sure why she even bothered asking. "Destiny, Frankie: you're both welcome to stay for dinner if you would like."

Vivian went out into the living room, so crowded with cloth and thread and equipment that it had become an unabashed sewing center. Her home computer, a Dell Dimension, sat watchfully on a cloth-draped dresser table. A tap of its scroll bar and the screen flashed to life.

She snuggled back into a plush-backed chair, and took another look through her mail. Nothing imperative or important magically appeared.

She turned on the computer, and signed onto AOL. The familiar "You've got mail" voice greeted her, and she clicked on incoming mail to find the name RSAND.

Allowing herself the tiniest of smiles, she clicked on the message again. "Dear Mrs. Emory—"

She read it twice over, then stared at the screen for a full two minutes before tapping out her reply:

"Of course I remember you. You were kind to me during that terrible trial, and you kept your word in ways that some of the other reporters didn't. We all appreciate . . ."

She backed up and reconsidered. All of them? What "all," exactly?

"I appreciate that. The next time you are through town, why not drop by the shop and say hello? Patrick and I would enjoy seeing you."

She stopped, fingers floating above the keyboard, debating whether to say more, and then added:

"This has been a stressful time due to a recent separation, with the seeming inevitability of a divorce."

Blushing at her own boldness she continued: *"A friendly face would seem nice right now."*

That was almost too much. She had never said anything that brash in her entire life. But she *did* remember him, and more important, remembered her own reaction to him. What would he think? Would he find her desperate? Lonely? Or just honest?

Her finger hovered over the "delete" key, then she clicked "send."

There was a short beeping interlude as electrons reshuffled, sending her message irretrievably out across the internet. The blush she had felt since first opening his e-mail that afternoon was beginning to spread, becoming a more generalized tingle. And that tingle became almost disturbingly localized, a sensation that she hadn't allowed herself to feel in months. Maybe longer.

"Girl," she whispered happily, "you aren't dead yet."

8

THURSDAY, MAY 10

Eighty miles northwest of Phoenix, Arizona, is the town of Prescott, bordered by cattle land to the south and east. Further to the northeast rise densely wooded hills, the Prescott National Forest, some of the most beautiful country in the entire state. Rising up above the high desert, this land is watered by the not-infrequent rains, and densely wooded with spruce, firs and ponderosa pines.

There are hundreds of campgrounds, public and private, including many set aside specifically for large group activities. Children come from around the country to camps run by the YMCA, Girl Scouts, Boy Scouts, and any other group that decides it would be a good idea to get a gaggle of kids or adults out of the city and a little closer to God and nature for a few days.

One of those camps is located in a box canyon, with steeply wooded hills on either side. There is one winding road in, down off the 89A between Mingus Mountain and the Potato Patch, through a branching warren of increasingly rough trails that would test the suspension of a tank, not to mention the Ford Bronco currently bumping along its knotted passages.

The driver was almost invisible behind the tinted windshield, and drove at a steady, almost prissily slow pace, like an elderly woman trying to navigate a road full of cats. The trail widened after a narrowing phase, and the driver pulled past a sign marked CHARISMA LAKE CAMPING GROUND, into a turn-out, and parked.

He eased himself out of the car with a rare fluidity of motion. The driver was a black man in his early fifties. His hair was almost shockingly white, but his face was relatively unlined, very rectangular. His arms were quite long, his hands a carpenter's or laborer's hands, strong with square-tipped fingers and scarred knuckles.

The driver was met almost immediately by a wide-faced, hearty man in his sixties in a red and black checkered shirt and blue jeans. His waist spread a bit, but his shoulders were so wide one barely noticed. He introduced himself as Del Withers. The driver said he was Mr. Park, and they shook hands. Park and Withers talked, and walked, roaming around the camp area.

There were twelve weathered log cabins, divided into clusters of four: one near the activity center, one near the dining hall, one near the baseball diamond and soccer field. Withers showed the younger man everything.

Park seemed intensely interested, asking many questions, listening patiently to the answers.

After another hour, they climbed the northern rise up to the lake itself. It was clear that the water level was unusually low, the rings of dried muddy residue suggesting that this year had been particularly dry. The same impression would be gained from studying the bushes and trees, the brown needles, the too-crisp leaves.

"We have a hundred and fifty acres here, Mr. Park. Our own wells, too . . . although we've had a very low rainfall this year."

Park nodded. "I noticed."

"Hope that won't cause a problem," Withers said, and then continued too quickly for his own taste. "Kids still love to get in the water, even if it's a little thick." He paused. "This is the only spot where a cell phone will work, by the way."

"Oh?"

"Well, also on top of those ridges east and west, and down south a mile or so."

"I guess I'd heard that."

There was a long pause. The younger man hadn't said anything, was just gazing ruminatively at the blue-green, placid surface of the lake. Then he turned and looked back south. From here, the entire camp and athletic field looked more than ever like a model set in the hollow of a saddle, the hills to either side rising up like short horns. The grade dropped away steadily for over a mile. Field, cabins, activity buildings, mess hall—all were spaced out along the shallow decline. The entire camp was framed by the brown, dry brush to the east and west. South, below the camp, the grass looked a bit brittle and brown, as if it hadn't seen a good rain in months. Still, there was a sense of peace, a natural beauty to the layout, as if its original architects had struggled to preserve the natural aesthetics.

Withers shaded his eyes against the sunlight, wondering if Park was visualizing happy children playing in the water or hiking up in the hills. Some instinct told him that those weren't Park's thoughts, but he couldn't figure out what *was* going on in the man's mind.

Park slapped a meaty hand against the side of his neck. "How are the bugs?"

"Those little black flies, and more mosquitoes than last year—but survivable. We lay in some Off, make the kids slap it on. They'll be fine."

The year had been bad for Camp Charisma. Several of their usual customers had gone as far west as California and as far north as Utah, concerned about the fire hazard. Withers *needed* this rental.

"Well, Mr. Park?" the older man said. "Do you think that's a problem?

Park, for all of his delicate motion, was very fit, hawk-lean, thick-fingered. He turned slowly, again. Absurdly, this time he reminded Withers of another bird, this time an owl. It seemed that Park's head moved first, followed by his body. "No," he said.

"I mean, they'll be able to swim. If these are city kids, they'll probably just love it. It's beautiful up here. Have you been to Prescott before?" He hoped that desperation wouldn't make his voice shrill.

"Yes."

Withers watched him carefully. There was something wrong, but he couldn't put his finger on it. Probably just his own discomfort at his situation. He knew that he should just press the sale, but decided that he had to ask another question. "Mr. Park—could I ask you why you decided on Charisma Lake?"

Park smiled at him. A perfect smile, one that might have been practiced in a mirror. At that moment, Park seemed the most plausible and engaging man Withers had met in years. "I'd heard good things, and the price was right."

Withers nodded. "Well, I can understand that—we had to lower a bit. What with the fire hazard, some of our usual groups were reluctant to book."

There was another subject that had to be broached, but Withers was reluctant to bring it up. "Your people understand about fireworks? I mean, we have zero tolerance. Fires are allowed only in the designated areas, and all counselors have to be drilled on procedure."

"No worries," Park said. "They'll be here a day early."

Withers felt his nagging sense of discomfort dissolving. Everything was going to be fine. "How many children are you expecting?" he asked.

"Five percent," Parks said, almost absently.

"Excuse me?"

Parks smiled like a man who had dropped a crouton from his plate, apologetic and ingratiating. "I meant fifty."

Fifty is three percent of what? About 1500?

"All coming from one school?"

"No," Park said. "From around the country." He didn't seem to want to volunteer more information, and Withers was about to ask when Park spoke up again. "We're a charitable organization. We identify children at risk who have managed to excel academically and in other ways, and we reward them with a week in the country and a thousand dollar savings bond. We're businessmen, but we hire experienced staff with YMCA and Girl Scout training."

Another level of Withers's emotions relaxed. That was something else that had nagged at him. Park just didn't seem like the kind of man to get down and dusty with a bunch of kids. More a headmaster type. Maybe military, or law enforcement. That was definitely an oddity. But if Park understood his limitations, and had the sense to hire some college kids to wrestle around with the campers . . . well, then, Park's square-cut business suit might have lovely deep pockets.

Again, Parks seemed to have read his mind. "I assume that a cashier's check is sufficient for the deposit?"

"Of course," Withers said.

Parks pulled an envelope from his pocket, and handed it over.

"Then everything is satisfactory. And I will see you again on June twenty-fourth."

They walked back down the hill to the parking lot. Park began gazing around the camp again, almost forgetting that Withers stood in front of him. He seemed to be memorizing the buildings and layout. Finally he nodded, satisfied with something that he had seen, or his own private thoughts. Without another word he returned to his Bronco, started the engine, backed it up, circled it, and began his way up the narrow trail. He hadn't reached the first set of marker stones before halting and backing up.

"Mr. Withers?" he called.

"Yes?"

"You live here on the grounds, don't you?"

"Yes. Me and Diane, the wife. We're always here when we have campers." Withers half-expected Parks to have some kind of objection to that, that he wanted to have the kids alone to himself. Right at that moment Withers decided that he didn't like the man. If Park said anything, anything at all that gave the slightest sense that he wanted fifty kids up in the mountains without proper supervision, Withers was going to turn the contract down. To hell with the fact that he needed it, that Diane would probably stamp her foot and get quiet and pensive for an hour or two. They could just scrape a little deeper into their equity credit line at Arizona S&L, and—

But Parks said, "Good." His smile sparkled. "Love for you to both be here. Help us celebrate the Fourth."

Withers scratched his head. "Sure thing. But no fireworks, remember."

"Zero tolerance." Park smiled warmly.

Park trundled the Bronco down the trail and away. The dust hadn't settled before Withers's wife Diane, a dumpling of a woman with deeply grooved smile lines at mouth and eyes, emerged to watch it leave.

"So," she said, and linked her arm with her husband's. "What do you make of that one?"

"Money's good, and we need it."

"But?"

"What makes you think there's a but?"

She poked her tongue at him. "That's your 'But' face. After thirty years, I should know."

The Bronco was making the first turn down the mountainside along the narrow, twisting trail. In a few moments, it would be gone.

"Well?" she pried, refusing to let it go. Her manner was teasing, but insistent.

He chucked her under the chin. "Let's pray for rain next year, all right?"

9

*E*yeful's offices were on the thirteenth and fourteenth floors of the Marcus Tower in Century City. The Tower was the most impressive building on the central L.A. skyline, made famous in the movie *Die Hard* as the doomed Nakatomi Plaza.

Sand had his own parking space, and an office cubicle with a door that actually closed: it should have been heaven. Fax and computer hookups, a three-line phone and a secretary only shared with five other reporters.

Marcus International, the conglomerate which owned Marcus Communications and *Eyeful,* also published *American Journal,* America's second-largest daily national, with numbers that made *USA Today* nervous about four months out of the year. It had better sports and financial coverage, and their Washington Bureau scooped *USA Today*'s about six times out of ten.

Once upon a time that one building, just off Avenue of the Stars, had held Sand's entire future. The plan was to start out on the middle floor, at *Journal.* With care and patience, he had worked his way up to the more prestigious magazines, maneuvering to snag that single killer assignment that might offer entrée to the biggest league of all. Not that Marcus Communications wasn't big. There were none bigger.

It was just that Marcus Communications had been founded by Alexander Marcus himself, one of Sand's few remaining heroes.

And even if the entire thing was run by the book, it was inevitable that a shadow as large as Marcus's would overwhelm any quality of journalistic work, and give the inevitable impression of a vanity publication.

That impression was bolstered during command performances like the current birthday party. Party, hell: it felt more like a postmortem. Marcus Communications employees milled about the conference room holding flowered paper cups half-filled with wine coolers or punch. The front of the room was dominated by younger reporters, corporate suits, and a few folks worried enough about job stability that they needed to practice their butt-smooching. The older, more cynical hands clustered in the back, sipping their watered Zinfandel and making tasteless jokes about zombies and vampires.

The publisher was Dorothy Spivey, an iron-spined, graying blonde Harvard MBA in her fifties. Spivey gave a formal speech clotted with fawning superlatives before escorting the grande dame herself, Katrina Marcus, to the stage.

Sand was in the back of the room, practicing his invisibility, sipping at a plastic cup of watered wine. A little cube of ice floated against his lip, and he sucked at it, and then chewed it out of existence.

Muriel Tong sidled up, her flat smile resigned but not resentful. "Once more into the breech, dear friends . . ."

He tried not to move his lips. "Every year they trot the old girl out." Disrespect was the expected response to the yearly ritual, but the truth was, he wasn't as cynical as the words implied. Marcus hadn't been an ordinary man. And if his mother seemed like just another old biddy who should have been playing Hearts and complaining about the oatmeal at some retirement home, once upon a time she must have been extraordinary.

Muriel stood close enough that her whisper warmed his ear. And points south. "Maybe Kitty's holding the strings, Renny. She's got over fifty percent of the stock, and loved her baby boy."

Forty years ago Katrina had been a great beauty, with jet-black skin and lustrous hair. But time had riven her painfully, the thick hair gone white and thin enough to need a glaringly obvious wig. Her left eye seemed partially occluded. She looked as if a cool breeze might send her spiraling into pneumonia. But as she took the microphone, some hidden well of strength possessed her, and she spoke with great presence.

"Thank you all for coming—"

"As if we had a choice," a well-marbled reporter said snidely, earning a dirty look from a junior exec and a thumbs-up from Muriel.

"—As time passes, my son's accomplishments seem all the more vital and important." She pronounced each word with painful precision. "It is the worst thing in the world to live beyond your children, but at least I know that the things Alexander Marcus created will live far beyond me. Thank you again. . . ."

There was polite applause, and Dorothy Spivey gave Mrs. Marcus her arm, and escorted her to a chair.

"And for my next trick," Sand whispered. As if on cue the room lights went down. A screen dropped from the front of the room.

"Ooh. Magic," Muriel said, resting her long, cool fingers on his arm. She was forty-three, gorgeous in a willowy way, and his boss's boss.

A professional-quality video was projected on the screen, recapping what everyone in the room knew about the storied, celebrated and entirely deceased Alexander Marcus. The unseen narrator was Laurence Fishburne. Sand remembered when he was Larry. "Born in 1930, in the fifty-eight years before he died in the crash of his Lear jet, Colonel Alexander Marcus lived enough for a dozen men. Korean War hero, media giant and Olympic silver medalist, he was also the hidden force behind some of the most important civil rights actions of the sixties . . ."

He'd only met Marcus once, at a reception about a year before his plane and body were fished out of the Pacific near Queen Charlotte Island up in British Columbia. With perverse precision, it was that very year's video on display tonight. He remembered the occasion clearly: a Christmas party in December of '87. Muriel had let herself be wrangled out of an invitation. She was just a junior editor then, a jade-eyed goddess with black hair falling straight to the small of her back, and a Masters in journalism from Columbia.

With one small warm hand on his arm, she introduced Sand to Marcus as "one of the bright young talents at the Times. I'm trying to coax him onto the winning team."

Then a leonine fifty-seven, Marcus was smaller than Sand would have expected, but then, from the stories and rumors, his accomplishments and the sheer driving force of his personality, one might have expected him to be seven and a half feet tall.

He was only a little over six, solid, with the gravity of a small black hole. People fought to keep from simply being sucked across his event horizon.

It's said that a few major movie stars, politicians and rock gods have a quality that projects beyond their physical selves. If they walk into an office, and you're in the next room, you can *feel* them through the wall. That's the story, anyway, but Sand had never experienced that effect until he shook hands with Alexander Marcus.

He was very dark-skinned, darker than most American black men. He should have had tribal scars on his cheeks. Shaka Zulu must have looked a lot like Alexander Marcus.

It was easy for Renny to understand why Marcus had remained so far in the background in the 1960s, allowing men like King and Jackson and Abernathy to take the lead during the civil rights struggles. Rumors abounded: His mother had never married his father. His eternally single status indicated satyriasis (probable) or homosexuality (not a chance.) The original source of Marcus Enterprise's seed money was a mystery, and the great man didn't want an investigative journalist to dredge up financial dirt.

When the Movement began he was still in the military, which took a dim view of its officers involving themselves in radical domestic politics. When he retired after his first tour as an "advisor" in Vietnam he was already a millionaire through canny stock and real estate investments. Legend had it that he had wanted his fledgling media empire to avoid possible censure in the South.

There were other public explanations why this wealthy and powerful man, known to have bankrolled several of the Movement's most sensitive legal fights, rumored to be a major deal-maker and power broker, had never led a march, never allowed himself to be interviewed during that entire decade.

But as soon as Sand met him, a deeper truth leaped out at him, hitting so hard, and so intensely, that it was startling no one had ever mentioned it before: Alexander Marcus was conservative white America's worst nightmare. He was a wealthy, ambitious, unapologetically masculine, fiercely intelligent, competitive, politically powerful black man. There was no question about it. He had succeeded in white America without changing one single essential iota of who the hell he was.

On the video, the reception line moved slowly past Emperor Marcus, who stood flanked by his bodyguard/assistants, the 'Nam vets usually referred to as the Praetorians. There was a smaller, white female figure in the group as well, a leathery little bit of a redhead with the brightest, most golden eyes he'd ever seen. They were like pools crushed with gold leaf, eyes that seemed to be watching everyone and no one. She was rumored to be a loan-out from the Secret Service.

It was strange to watch himself mouse through the reception line to greet his once and future boss. Marcus grinned at him, and clasped his hand firmly. Sand was shocked by the raw power held in careful reserve: Marcus could have crushed a raw potato with those rough hands. He had lost little strength since brushing the shot-put world record at the 1956 Olympiad.

The unmistakable, indelible impression was that he knew Sand's work, and was delighted at the prospect of having him on the team.

Furthermore, without saying a word, he managed to imply that he had personally requested that Muriel chat Renny up and bring him along. Damned if for a disorienting moment Sand didn't sense that Marcus knew his destiny better than the reporter did himself, and that the two of them shared a great and wonderful secret.

Then Marcus turned to the next person in the reception line. That massive focus slipped over Renny like a searchlight sliding over a rock. The absence left him feeling empty, a bit limp. For the first time in his life, he'd been touched by that quality some men call *greatness.* Throughout all history, men have followed the Marcuses of the world into the valley of the shadow. They've risked fortune and soul for the honor of serving such men faithfully. Sitting at their feet. Sand felt shaken, slack, hungry. For all his posturing and protestations of independence, Sand knew instinctively that he would accept Alexander Marcus's orders, and feel blessed to be fortunate enough to do so.

The realization had shaken him to the spine.

Laurence Fishburne was still talking, his voice containing strong echoes of his *Othello,* as if overwhelmed by the majesty of his subject. Or maybe just overcompensating for the mediocrity of his dialogue. "—A man of the people, Marcus never lost touch with the thousands of employees who daily strove to bring, in his words, 'an honest day's news for an honest dollar' into approximately one-fifth of all American homes. . . ."

Renny watched Marcus on that video, nodding his massive head regally as the crowd moved past him one handshake at a time, and a chill swept him. Quite simply, he'd been awed by the man. He suspected that many of the others, now clustered at the back of the room in the shadows and making jokes, had been awed as well. That Marcus had shaken and inspired them in a way that was now almost embarrassing to admit, that it had become fashionable among the painfully hip reporting staff to mock the yearly ritual remembrance.

Like most people, he'd always assumed men like Marcus led through domination, that they somehow inspired a doglike devotion through projecting some untouchable, unapproachable quality. But the actual aura of the man spoke a different truth. *I am you,* he said without speaking. *The best and strongest part of yourself. Do not follow me. Follow my path, and I will take you with me. There is not a one of you who could not achieve what I have done, were you to travel deep within yourself, and follow your most basic nature. It is our nature to succeed. Whoever told you different, sold you short on yourself, has lied. I am here to awaken you from the dream.*

It was almost overwhelmingly strange to watch the video image. What a different man Renny Sand had been then. A younger, better man. Sometimes, fourteen years was an entire lifetime.

Muriel peered at him over the rim of her glass. "Impressive, wasn't he?"

"Mmm-hmm. I wanted to have his baby."

She laughed throatily, and linked her slender arm through his. "Kitty might still have some sperm samples. You could check."

"His mom?"

"They were very close. Some say he never married because of her."

"Or the Goon Squad."

She laughed again, the long and slender line of her neck catching his eye for the first time that night, reminding him of . . .

He caught his breath. "Yeah." Renny fought to fasten his attention elsewhere. "Where are they now?"

Muriel pursed her lips and touched a slender finger to them with slightly forced elegance. "Rumor says D'Angelo's playing sheriff somewhere in the southwest. The rest of the Praetorians just scattered." She took another sip.

"And the woman?"

She chuckled. "Oh, that was Kelly Kerrigan. She was secret service, assigned to him in '87, while he was still running for president. They called her 'Gramma' even then."

"Wonder if there isn't a story in her."

She smiled approvingly. "Not a bad idea. Maybe I'll have someone look her up." She paused. "The Praetorians served with Marcus in Vietnam, back when we were just 'advisors.' Story is that he simply saved their butts, and they came back, black and white, swearing that he was the best officer in the war, and committed to him. When he went into business, he offered some of them positions, and they came. Those who weren't really suited to lead, he made his private guard. They are more than just loyal. I think that their greatest regret is that he dropped out of the race in '87."

Sand nodded. "I can understand that. I was disappointed myself. The polls put him pretty high. Got the skinny on why he flaked?"

"Oh, I know where a great number of bodies are buried," she said. Someone pressed her from the other side, and suddenly Sand became aware of the warmth and weight of her firm and shapely hip against his. "But you don't get it out of me that easily."

"Oh? Why not?"

"Because then I wouldn't have any leverage over you."

"You need more leverage than being my boss?"

"You exaggerate."

"Yeah, right. Well, you could probably get my boss fired, anyway."

"Ah," she said. "But I wouldn't." Her eyes narrowed until they resembled a cat's. "Couldn't you tell? I'm the kind of girl who likes to be in charge, but not *too* much." Her laugh was musical, and very very young. "What would you say," she said carefully, "if I suggested that we get out of here, go back over to my place . . ."

Renny had the urge, that was certain. He and Muriel were probably two of a type, even if there was a power differential between them, and had been for three long years. Once upon a time, they'd been on track to a live-in relationship. These days it was a now-and-then thing. When Muriel said *now, then* it happened. The whole thing felt a little cheap, but the visceral memory of her strong, slender, welcoming body was just too tempting.

"Sure," he said. "I'll meet you there."

10

DIABLO, ARIZONA

Bobby Ray Kerrigan kept a companionable silence as his wife Kelly drove their beat-up Chevy truck down the rutted dirt road. They were heading back to town, traveling through scrub land a little east of Diablo, the western-themed tourist town a hundred and forty miles southeast of Phoenix.

At almost seventy-five, even devoid of the jet-black hair she had loved, Bobby Ray was lean and handsome, at least in Kelly's eyes. Kelly herself was nearing seventy, but still had all of her red hair and most of the 30-20 vision in her gold eyes. Gravity had taken a bit of a toll, but she was still fit and trim, and walked as lightly as a forty-something aerobics instructor.

If there was a shadow in their lives, it was Kelly's unequivocal knowledge that she would outlive Bobby Ray. Not a misty *someday,* either, but soon, according to the sad eyes of Phoenix General's geriatric oncologist. The tumor was growing again and they had run out of effective medications. Radiation had worn Bob to a nub, and the malignancy was currently too large for an operation. If they could shrink it again . . .

But that would require an experimental protocol, and although Bob was on the short list, the clock was ticking, and time running out.

Perhaps not this month, or the next, but his body was no longer the reliable engine it had been when they were married back in '58. They had had four good decades together. It wasn't enough, but it was all they were going to get.

The distant *crack-pop* of gunfire grew steadily louder and more urgent as they trundled down the dirt road toward main street. Kelly's smile broadened and thinned as she heard it. She gripped at the wheel with her leather gloves, bowing her buckskin-clad arms with controlled excitement.

"Sounds like they're at it."

"Yep." Bob's pale blue eyes, clear and sharp, narrowed as they scanned the approaching parking lot. "Lotsa folks. Been a hot day."

"But a good day."

He chuckled. "Ain't they all?" That was her Bobby Ray. God, she was going to miss him.

They laughed at the small joke as Kelly pulled into a dirt parking lot packed fender to fender with dusty cars and trucks. Not many tourists: these were mostly townies. A few people were still unloading guns and equipment. Many wore spurs, chaps, or cross-draw holsters. Others were decked out as trail hands, gamblers, bankers, or school marms.

About seventy percent of them were men: leathery ranchers, townsmen, retirees, shopkeepers—the salt of the town. They were parking, unpacking, checking their weapons with professional care and placing them in little shooting carts with the loving delicacy of mothers depositing babies in bassinets.

As they passed Kelly, they tipped their hats politely.

"Evenin', Miss Kate," one of them said. He was Diablo's longtime barber, and knew full well that her given name was Kelly.

"Evenin', Buffalo," she yelled back.

Bobby Ray levered himself out of the truck and walked back to the tailgate, favoring his left hip. "Well, Miss Kate, think you can take it?"

"One shot at a time, Pecos," she said philosophically, easing her voice into a far more pronounced western twang. "One at a time."

She very carefully and soberly removed her weapons and checked them. They were prized possessions: a Third-Generation Colt in .45 Long Colt (Very Good condition, worth about $1,100), plain blue with hard rubber grips. Her shotguns were Overland 12-gauge doubles, with .28-inch barrels and exposed hammers, and double triggers. Circa 1985 vintage (the Rossi factory stopped manufacturing them in 1988), they were plain blue with walnut stocks.

The rifle was also a Rossi, a Model 92 copy of the infamous Winchester 92, a lever-action with a 24-inch half-octagon barrel and a brass blade front sight.

The dust in the parking lot was high, even though the day was beginning to cool. As she checked the action and housing, none of the men and women, or even the children walking past, paid much mind except to say "howdy." Not a single shooter allowed his rifle or handgun or shotgun barrel to point toward himself, another human being, or the town.

Up at the sky, down into the ground, out toward the desert.

That was the rule, and there were no exceptions. Violating this rule was an instant DQ: no argument, no exception, no second chance. Among these people, weapon safety was as automatic and important as breathing.

She sight-checked that all cylinders were empty before placing her weapons in her little rolling wooden shooting cart. Ammunition was carried in a separate compartment.

Bobby Ray had watched soberly as she completed her check. He nodded, and they started out across the parking lot. To the west, the sun had sunk to an orange glow along the horizon. The artificial lighting winked on.

Picnic tables dotted the tough brown grass between the parking lot and the row of low, caramel-colored buildings sheltering Helldorado, Diablo's largest tourist trap, and home of the biggest and most popular shooting range within two hundred miles. Children scampered and scrambled around the tables, finishing their picnic suppers, playing games, awaiting the next round when Daddy or Mommy would shoot again.

The tourist stage was closed today. Helldorado was hosting its annual all-day event featuring both day and night shooting. Whole families had been there since noon, and the entire affair resembled nothing so much as a church social wreathed with gun smoke.

They said words of greeting to familiar faces. Almost everyone was familiar, either a townie or from nearby Fairbank, or Tombstone. A few familiar faces were from as far away as Tucson or Littletown.

As they approached the range the crowd thickened, and Kelly nudged her way through to get a better look.

A man in his fifties dressed in a bowler hat and spats—somewhat like Butch Cassidy—stood behind a waist-high wooden barricade, facing three five-inch porcelain plates suspended at eye level on white poles. A light to his immediate right flashed green. His right hand blurred to his hip, clearing leather. The shots that followed were so rapid they sounded like a short string of firecrackers. The targets exploded into powder and splinters, side by side by side.

The crowd applauded politely, and another man stepped up to the platform, toting a double-barreled shotgun. The announcer introduced him as El Condor.

El Condor was as long and wiry as a pipe cleaner. His teeth were so discolored and misshapen it was rumored he considered chewing tobacco one of the four basic food groups. He was dressed with shoulder-crossing bandoliers and a serape. He wore an obviously fake, droopy mustache, and had doffed an oversized Mexican sombrero.

Bob nudged her. "Still in the specialty shooting."

The bandito's weapon was open and unloaded while men were downrange, setting up four porcelain targets. As soon as they were done he loaded up, then stood relaxed, eyes closed. After a few seconds, he nodded.

About twenty seconds later, the green light flashed on. El Condor fired from the hip, both barrels roaring. The targets simply disintegrated. He shucked shells and reloaded with incredible speed, then fired again, and two more targets exploded into splinters.

Kelly applauded with the rest of the audience. There was a short lull as the crowd drifted about twenty-five yards to the left, to another set of targets and shooting stages. She stiffened slightly as the next man walked up.

He was in his fifties, rangy, his golden hair receding but still beautiful. He was muscular, very erect, relaxed and confident. His sleeves were rolled up. His forearms were covered in a sheen of golden hairs that glinted in the light.

"And now Angel Eyes takes his position," the announcer said. Kelly smiled thinly. The new man's name was Tristan D'Angelo. Kelly Kerrigan had known him for fifteen years.

He had two pistols holstered at his waist, ivory-handled Colt Peacemakers, Model 1878 Single-Action Antiques in custom rigs. For any other man, the weapons would have been much, much too valuable to fire. But D'Angelo was easily Diablo's wealthiest citizen, owning half the town including the Helldorado stage, and he reveled in his reputation as a man who would trash a $40,000 investment by pulling a trigger.

He stood totally relaxed, yet with a curious electricity about him, as if he were less a creature of sinew and muscle than bundled wires and greased cogs.

This stage was very different, set up like a Hollywood back lot stage, with a row of storefronts to either side, funneling toward a point a hundred yards ahead, much like parallel tracks meeting in infinity.

D'Angelo stepped out, his hands hovering over his pistol butts, and he nodded.

This time there was no green light. Instead, in the window of one of the buildings, a silhouette revolved, revealing the image of a masked man with a gun. D'Angelo drew smoothly, fired two, three times before another window to his left opened—revealing a mother holding a baby. D'Angelo's hand twitched, but he didn't squeeze. A man-shaped target dropped from a bordello balcony. D'Angelo missed his first shot, and got two others off and into the black so quickly that the crowd never had a chance to react.

With a deliberately nerve-wracking rattling sound, a little track between two buildings began to move, carrying a silhouette of a man holding a young girl, a gun at her head. D'Angelo's left hand blurred, and the Peacemaker sent two slugs into the kidnapper's head before most of the observers had fully registered the scenario. And so it went with the next two, each villainous target drawing two shells, one innocent target almost drawing a shot before D'Angelo's hyper-adrenalized senses could stop him.

He called "I'm out!" and slid the revolver back into its holster as the crowd applauded.

There was a pause while the targets were checked, and about ninety seconds later the announcer's voice rang out again. "Seventeen seconds—with one miss. That brings Angel Eyes right up even with Pecos Kate in the shoot off. Where is Miss Kate? Anyone seen her?"

"Right here," Kelly yelled. "Bobby Ray had to deliver a rifle up to Phoenix. Told ya I'd be back."

As the crowd laughed, D'Angelo sauntered over in their direction.

"Hello, Miss Kate," he said, calling her by her competition name. He nodded in Bob's direction. "Pecos. How are the hotcakes?"

She ignored the implied jibe. "Drop by sometimes, try a stack," she said.

"Been here long?"

"Just got in."

"Too bad. See me shoot?"

She nodded, her face remaining studiedly neutral. "Seen it before, Angel."

Now his face lit up, with a very different, warmer, entirely more personable smile. This smile was wholly genuine, and almost neighborly. "That's right," he said. "You have, haven't you?"

Smile still warm as toast, D'Angelo walked away, calling back over his shoulder: "See you at the stage."

Bob spit into the dust at his feet. "I don't like that man," he said.

"Aw," Kelly said. "He ain't so bad—if you like reptiles."

"I do like snakes and such." He paused, and made another spitting sound, although this time his mouth was dry. "And I *still* don't like that man."

She nudged him affectionately. "Probably mutual, you'll be glad to know. Come on—let's get set up. Want to get warm."

Kelly moved to her practice area, and ran though her mental checklist, inspecting her equipment carefully. When she was satisfied, she took a box of shells from her cart's ammo dump, and loaded carefully.

After she had inspected her handiwork and was satisfied, she flicked on the little microphone at the side of the stage. "Mr. Earp?"

The answering voice came from a little box speaker by her head, not the big P.A. honkers. "Yes, Miss Kate?"

She deliberately accentuated her twang. "I'd surely appreciate two targets."

"On their way," he answered.

Keeping the Rossi 12-gauge's barrel pointed high, she walked out onto the range, and waited. Two targets, one at two o'clock and one at ten, popped up from a low stage. When Earp spoke again, he used the P.A.

"How do you want it, Miss Kate?"

"On your mark," she said tightly, just loud enough for her words to reach one of the range masters, and be relayed to the unseen Earp.

Kelly Kerrigan seemed to pull inside herself, and her grandmotherly aspect simply disappeared. Suddenly, she seemed not exactly younger, but somehow more *vital*. Ageless perhaps. She was so calm and inside herself that she seemed not an ordinary part of the time stream.

The light blinked, and Kelly fired twice, a *da-dum* beat taking just over half a second.

She shucked her shells and reloaded without taking her eyes from the targets. The world outside the shooting stage had temporarily vanished for Kelly. She fired twice more, and the last two targets exploded.

Behind her, the crowd applauded wildly.

Only then did she emerge from her near-somnambulant state. For once, the announcer's flattened mechanical voice sounded impressed. "That's some shootin', Kate. Good thing it was just practice, or old Cody would be disappointed."

"Ain't gunning for Cody," she said flatly, shucking her shells. The unvoiced question: *Then who* are *you gunning for, Kate?*

"Well, you get ready. We got the finals coming up."

She nodded and walked thoughtfully back to the ready line. Several of the spectators congratulated her, offering encouragement for the match to come.

She acknowledged most of them politely, but didn't relax her thoughtful expression until she was back at Bob's side. He took the shotgun from her, checked it, and slid it into their cart. "Good shooting, hon."

"Want to take a try?"

His smile was warm, but brittle. Bob Ray Kerrigan might have been only six years older than Kelly, but it had been a hard six years, filled with hospital beds and needles and specialists with cool, sympathetic eyes. "I had my time," he said. "Get yours."

She bussed his cheek warmly, and then rested her head against his for a moment. "I'll bring it home for you, Bob," she said.

"Just have fun, dumplin'."

Kelly spent the next half hour getting loose, practicing with the Colts, the Rossi Overlands, and the Model 92. She didn't try for maximum speed; accuracy was marginally more important, that illusive sense of connection between eye and hand and weapon. But her accuracy never flagged. She wasn't showing off: the next round, the final round, would tell the story.

The sun's orange rim had long since vanished from the mountain ridges to the west, and the desert's chill descended with a vengeance.

Jackets and serapes had emerged from baskets and car trunks. Folks kept moving just to generate body heat.

Kelly and D'Angelo stood in the midst of a saloon mock-up, surrounded by metal cutouts of gamblers, bartenders, dancing girls and inebriates of all stripes.

A rickety wooden stairway led to a second level. Recorded laughter flowed from behind closed doors. In the upper corners of the saloon were two video cameras, nestled behind heavy glass.

Outside the set, a crowd of almost a hundred and fifty spectators watched the action on television monitors, a safe distance from any potential ricochets.

"Marshall Earp"'s voice cut through the crowd sounds. "This is it, ladies and gentlemen. By mutual agreement, the finals will take place on the action stage. Ladies first!"

One of the observers at the back of the crowd yelled: "Sic 'em, Kate," and Kelly waved to them.

Without a visible trace of nerves, she stepped forward. She wore an 1890s riding skirt and a fringed bolero vest, gloves with embroidered gauntlets, and a kerchief with a silver buffalo neckerchief slide. She was the very picture of a frontier woman as she sashayed into the bar.

This time her Colts hung comfortably at her waist. Her shoulders were relaxed, but her fingers tingled as the warning buzzer sounded.

The plywood barman revolved 180 degrees. One second, he was simply polishing a shot glass. The next, he had a shotgun snug against his shoulder, leveled at her face. Kelly responded in a heartbeat, taking him between the eyes.

That was only the beginning of the challenge. Almost simultaneously, a number of the other targets flipped as well, some of them remaining harmless, some suddenly brandishing handguns, rifles, shotguns, knives. The air was filled with a rolling, roaring thunder and the stench of gun smoke. Ten shots total: five in each weapon, with an empty chamber under the hammer for safety. Kelly not only had to determine which were friendly and which hostile, she had to do it in an environment where the loudspeakers blared their own gunfire, and a shrill buzzer sounded, the overhead lights flashing like a strobe.

Once she hid behind a table, shucking shells and reloading, controlling her breathing to keep her hands steady. She popped back up to shoot again.

When she had emptied both six-guns, she slid them back into her holster, raised her hands and cried: "Out!"

The crowd applauded, and met her with handclasps and congratulations as she exited the stage. Range attendants scurried in to count the bullet holes, and emerged about two minutes later, making thumb's-up signs. They conferred with Earp, a broad, big-bellied man with bushy black eyebrows. He did some quick doodling on paper before coming to his conclusions. He flipped on his microphone. "That was some serious shootin', folks! Let's give the lady a hand, for an overall score of eighty-eight."

Bobby Ray hugged her briefly, their embrace interrupted as D'Angelo strode up to her. "Good going, Kelly. I knew *you* wouldn't have lost anything."

His face was perfectly pleasant, but Kelly knew that tonal inflection had been aimed at Bobby Ray. She squeezed her husband's hand and said: "Show us how it's done, Angel Eyes."

He nodded, tipped his hat and strode up to the line. Swathed in black, D'Angelo looked every bit the classic villain from *The Good, the Bad, and the Ugly.* He strode into the bar and stood, his guns snug in their cross-holsters.

Kelly watched on the television monitors, noting that he chose a position slightly angular to the bar, slanting his left shoulder a bit. The barman would be at his left peripheral, the gambling tables more central, and the shadowy second story just above his line of sight. She knew that he was de-focusing, waiting for movement, balanced and hyper-ready.

When the silhouettes flipped and the claxons sounded, D'Angelo was a machine: he drew and fired, drew and fired in perfect, almost ghastly smoothness and deadly accuracy. Headshot, headshot, headshot, reloading with nerveless efficiency that shaved clear seconds off Kelly's time. Finally he holstered his weapons, raised his hands and shouted: "Out!"

The audience applauded. Even without checking her watch, Kelly knew D'Angelo had beaten her time handily.

"Earp's" voice came back over the intercom. "We're doing a weighted count right now, folks, and—D'Angelo is at 89!"

Kelly sighed, and extended her hand. "Good shooting, Angel," she said.

"Maybe next year," D'Angelo said, genuinely gracious now that victory was assured.

Then the speaker crackled again. "Not that easy, folks. New rules instituted this year, say that if the final scores are within two points we get a draw-off. A draw-off, folks!"

At that, the crowd murmured and then applauded its approval. This was something new, using new equipment installed within the previous six months.

Bob smiled wanly at her. "Feeling game?" he asked.

The truth was that her wrists and hands were aching a bit. Bob knew it, but she was damned if she was going to let a little arthritis get in the way of her victory. "Never better," she said. "Bring it on."

"That's my girl."

The quick-draw stage was set up rather oddly, with two side-by-side platforms. Highly reflective Mylar sheets were positioned in front of each. Kelly's sheet was canted a few degrees, so that D'Angelo appeared dead center. D'Angelo's mirror showed Kelly. The sheets were about two feet apart, and in between them a signal light glowed red. In a few seconds, it would switch to green.

Behind the Mylar sheets, at chest and head levels, were broad sensor strips. The setup, known as a "Diablo," was of D'Angelo's own design, and if he hadn't owned the range, wasn't sheriff and didn't own a third of the property in town, it would never have been allowed. Most other clubs considered it just too damned close to shooting at a live human being.

Which was, for Tristan D'Angelo, the entire point.

Kelly watched her opponent's image. His smile, distorted by the Mylar, seemed almost inhumanly cold. Despite her best efforts to remain calm, Kelly shivered. *Just the cold,* she lied to herself.

It was hard for her to meet D'Angelo's eyes, and both of them knew why.

One part of her mind thought of nothing but the signal light, even now preparing to turn green. Another part of her floated away, remembering another time and place. . . .

It is Salt Lake City. July 23, 1987. She could no more forget that day than she could the day of her marriage. Less. Alexander Marcus is addressing a crowd at Salt Lake's Utah state fair park, out on North Temple Drive. Perhaps 11,000 people have gathered to hear Marcus speak of foreign policy, and national defense.

The crowd is rapt. He is, after all, almost legendary, a figure re-

membered not only from Vietnam, the Olympics and the post-civil rights era dialogues on race relations in America, but as a Presidential advisor and media giant. Most of the crowd is white, much of it Mormon and only recently of the official opinion that African-Americans were indeed fully human. Yet they respect him as a warrior who fought for his country, and then fought his country itself, in the service of the freedoms promised in the very documents that created her greatness.

Kelly is on duty that day, on loan from the Secret Service, in respect of Marcus's years of service, and in response to the abnormally high number of death threats he has received. Marcus does not feel the need for such official protection—he has his own men—but he likes Kelly, and enjoys having her around.

D'Angelo flanks Marcus, and on the other side, a black man named Wisher. Both were with Marcus in Vietnam, and both are superb soldiers.

In the midst of an especially impassioned segment of his speech a white man stands up from the audience, waving a gun.

People dive for cover. Kelly and Wisher dive for Marcus, pulling him under protective cover. The man in the audience fires, and it is obvious that his intent is lethal: the bullet misses Marcus's head by a fraction.

The action thus far has taken a mere instant. The would-be assassin fired through the crowd, winging one older man, muzzle-flash blazing in the face of a black woman just in front of him.

Kelly peered out around the podium, and what she saw next would haunt her the rest of her life. In a single smooth movement former Master Sergeant D'Angelo drew and fired. She would never have chanced such a shot: there were too many people still milling in confusion, diving for cover, too much noise. But the single bullet passed between two panicking women and took the would-be assassin directly between the eyes, snapping his head back. He knocked over the folding chairs behind him, spraying blood and bone and tissue across the row, sprawling limply, limbs still trembling.

She remembered looking at D'Angelo, wanting to congratulate him on the incredible shot, then saw the expression on his face. He wore the very slightest of smiles, a grin of satisfaction, but more than that, of pure pleasure. An expression swiftly veiled. But she saw it, yes she did. . . .

*   *   *

Kelly saw that same smirk now, on the face of Angel Eyes. A killer's smile, mistaken by everyone in the crowd as nothing but play-acting. Not playacting at all. She knew, beyond any question, that D'Angelo wished that this was for real.

He winked at her.

The light flashed green. Kelly reached for her gun with reflexes honed by countless thousands of repetitions, no conscious thought once the prearranged signal had been received—

But before she could bring her gun level, D'Angelo had fired, striking dead between her eyes. There was utter silence among the observers, and then Marshall Earp murmured: "Good goddamn."

Kelly dropped her gun back down, not even bothering to fire, and closed her eyes. The last thing she saw before she closed them was the cold ivory arc of D'Angelo's lips.

11

Muriel and Renny drove separate cars, and on the way to her house he stopped at the liquor store and bought a thirty-dollar bottle of White Star champagne: decent but not great.

Ms. Tong lived in a split level duplex off Sunset Boulevard, just behind a billboard advertising HBO's *Sex in the City* comedy show, with a gargantuan image of Sarah Jessica Parker's insinuating smile. Her house was a French-vanilla three-story condo, with six small windows facing south over Sunset. The roof sported a blue-tinted skylight that ran from wall to wall. In fact, if Los Angeles had much of a night sky, Muriel's view would have been spectacular. But between smog and a horizon clouded with artificial light, the few stars that shone down from above were dim and almost sad. The moon was a pale orb low on the horizon, surrounded by a misty ring.

Muriel thanked him for the gift, and fetched a pair of glasses. She filled both and handed one to Renny, and they climbed to the roof.

Framed against the glittering city, she was a glory to behold. Her jaw line was still strong as a girl's, with a swimmer's body and a swan's neck.

(Like whose neck, Renny?)

Her laugh contained some elusive element of self-mockery, and she was inviting him to share in the joke.

A pair of shiny black all-weather chairs were perched at the roof's edge. She eased herself into one, watching the traffic down on Sunset. The bleat of horns and purr of engines intertwined and drifted up as music, an organic urban impressionism. So many people in a hurry to go so many places. Los Angeles was his town by birth, but that bitch-goddess Career had taken him so many places: D.C., Miami, Chicago, Seattle. Returning to the Big Orange wasn't quite like a homecoming, because this part of Los Angeles wasn't his. His city had been the Baldwin Hills area, the district called "the Jungle" by cops and residents alike.

It felt very strange to return here after all these years, to sit with the beautiful boss in her two-thousand-dollar-a-month apartment, looking out over a city that sometimes seemed as alien and unknowable as the surface of Mars. Or for that matter, his own future.

He eased himself down into the chair next to her. For a few moments they just sipped in an easy silence. A low current of sexual attraction sizzled, something quite familiar, slowly ramping its way toward spontaneous combustion.

"So," he said, more to interrupt that silence than anything else. "Why don't you tell me about Colonel Marcus's campaign?"

"Well," she said, and took a sip. She rolled her head back, exposing that lovely fine length of neck. "In some ways he was a very private man, so it was surprising that he thought about running in the first place. He had always been the man *behind* the curtain. With King, with Malcolm, and others: funds, influence, guidance. But somebody got to him, and convinced him that he was the man for the job. Could he really die without taking a shot at it?"

"Hmmm. So you don't think it was a personal quest?"

"It was." She sipped at her drink. "Very personal. Marcus'd done the humanitarian work of a dozen men, but you had better believe that there was an ego in there. Maybe the healthiest I ever met. Under it all, I do believe Alexander Marcus was convinced that he could do anything, anything at all, and succeed." She paused, took another sip. "And maybe if you went deeper, what you had was a mischievous little kid who just wanted to play with the biggest train set in the world. Do you remember how it was?"

Hard to forget. Marcus orchestrated his non-campaign beautifully, hiding his political affiliations but making it clear to anyone with a teaspoon of brains that he was available for public office. Watching both Democrats and Republicans scrambling around was funnier than hell. Marcus was a cross between those two wild cards of late Twentieth century politics, Jesse Jackson and Ross Perot. Like Perot, Marcus could fund his own campaign, go third party if it amused him. But like Jackson in the Eighties, he was untouchable. His war record, as well as his civil-rights background, made it very difficult for people to criticize him without opening themselves to charges of racism.

What a roller coaster that six months had been! Both sides knew that, were Marcus to run as Vice President, he could coast their candidate to the White House. If he were to run independent, he could pull veterans, women, minorities, Democratic moderates and liberals of both parties, sufficient to make the '88 election the alley-fight of the century.

Renny had always thought politicians required a kind of plastic shell around their hearts, something slick enough to let them walk through sewers without picking up a fecal glaze. That probably explained why he'd never involved himself in politics. Deep down he probably feared that he was more Velcro than Teflon.

"So what happened?" he asked.

"The bigger the likelihood that he would actually run, the more hate mail he got."

Her eyes were like cool green stars, sparkling just over the edge of the glass. She was challenging him to hear what hadn't been said, to piece it together. And then, she waited to see how he would react.

"Because he was black?"

"It would appear so."

"Death threats?"

"The nastiest you've ever seen. 'Nigger, your sorry ass won't live past inauguration day.' Stuff like that. I dated a secret service guy for a while, and he'd never seen mail so venomous."

"And this despite his approval rating?"

The edges of her mouth curved downwards a bit, her eyes hooded. She was disappointed. Muriel had expected him to be more acute.

Sexual attraction is a strange thing. At the same time that it narrows your focus, it can also, temporarily at least, seem to increase intelligence. Maybe the part of you engaged in the mating dance knows that this is for all the marbles, and squirts a little extra IQ juice in there. His brain cells jittered to a sizzling mariachi beat.

"No," he finally said, slapping his forehead. "I'm wrong. *Duh.* They didn't send it *despite* the approval ratings. They sent that mail *because* of the approval ratings."

"Bravo," she said.

"Because there was actually a chance that he might get elected."
And he did understand. There were times he could almost feel sorry
for straight, Christian white American males. Blacks, Hispanics,
women, gays . . . if they fail, they know who to blame. It is so easy to
fall back on "they stopped me," whichever "they" happens to be most
fashionable.

But what if you're white, and male, making that fabled run up the
pyramid of success? There's only room for one at the top, and by the
time he gets there, he's old and tired. The rest of them have to blame
someone. So it's the minorities, the Jews, the damned liberal media
conspiracy, or *something.* Anything. Anything except looking into
themselves and seeing that the entire system, even for the winners, is
set up like a big dog race. Yeah, the dogs got fed at the end of the
day. And yeah, all of that running's good exercise. But the mechanical
rabbit is always out in front of you. You were never meant to catch it,
just to run for the cheering crowd.

Worse still, from time to time they make a mistake at the track, and
a dog catches the metal bunny. From that day on, that dog will never
run again.

And therein lies a clue to why the Elvises, John Belushis and Michael Jacksons of the world self-destruct: They tasted the rabbit.

"So he was afraid of getting killed?" That didn't seem to fit what
he knew about Colonel Marcus.

She shook her head, although this time there was no disapproval.
"No, I don't think he would have cared. But Kitty raised him by herself, and he was devoted. She'd worried about him through Korea, and
Vietnam, and the civil-rights times. I believe Alexander thought she'd
die if anything happened to him. I do believe that stolid, sexy golem
of a man backed out of the race because of her."

Sand could see it all: the private debates, the pleas, the call to duty,
and finally the admission that America, or Freedom, or the Cause, or
Business had claimed enough of him. One could almost hear Kitty's
demand that her sonny boy not place himself in harm's way yet again.
They said Ted Kennedy had done much the same for Rose.

"So there we were," he said. "Working for one of the twenty-five
richest men in America, decorated war hero, silver winner in Mel-
bourne, the only black man who could have been president in this
century, and knowing that he was completely and utterly a mama's
boy."

"I wouldn't suggest that you ever phrase it like that. Ten years dead, he'll still probably kick your butt."

She chuckled, and leaned back into her chair.

His mind spun away into the silence. He tried to keep his mind locked on the silky, golden length of the woman next to him, but instead, his thoughts went back to the family he'd met in Claremont, six years before. He'd often thought of them, and the strange thing was that the chance for an invigorating tumble with Muriel Tong just brought them more vividly to mind.

Sand kept thinking about the kid Patrick, and his mother Vivian, seeing something in their eyes that spooked him.

They didn't have money. They weren't the kind of people to have success in any of the traditional west-coast ways. But they had something that he'd never really possessed. Something that he probably feared he'd never have. Family. One thing was certain: whatever the future held for that boy, Patrick Emory was going to have his family behind him, all the way.

And that triggered something new inside Sand, a kind of longing that went far beyond mere sexual hunger. Beyond it, but inclusive of it: a sweet-sour ache that made his groin feel tender and tight. He turned and looked at Muriel. She was very close, short straight black hair lustrous, lips soft and moist, eyes luminous.

It would have been ungentlemanly not to kiss her. So he did. The old Renny Sand would have gone for that and the whole enchilada and damn the consequences, damn the fact that on some very deep and basic level he knew that the relationship was the *Titanic*. He didn't want to ride a boat that was going nowhere but down. *Been there, done that.*

The kiss ended.

She rolled back to her chair, her eyes gently inquisitive. Measuring, unsure, surprised that her offer had been acknowledged and refused. Women like Muriel weren't used to things like that.

"Something wrong?"

Yes. I drove past a town I hadn't seen in years, and now I can't get a woman I've never touched out of my mind.

"It's not you," he said honestly. *It's not who you are. It's who you aren't.* "It's just not the right time. I'm sorry, Muriel."

Her eyes flashed fire, so briefly it was like a spark in the night. Then she lowered her lids, and looked away.

Renny felt a sudden burst of pity for Muriel Tong. En route to her career, she had sacrificed whatever hopes of home and hearth that might ever have graced her youthful dreams. Children? Husband? Perhaps the comfort of growing old with someone who, whatever physical changes time and tide wrought, would always see the beautiful young girl she had once been.

Now, as the Big Four-Oh came and went, she was doubtlessly seeing one set of doors opening, another closing tight. Regardless of the trash-heap he'd made of his life, she and Renny were kindred spirits. Because they were, she used to be able to count on him for an hour or two of moist, fevered, meaningless amusement. Could trust him to make the moves, say the words, leave in the morning—or that night— without leaving any essential part of himself behind. No psychic follicles in the hairbrush of her heart. So to speak.

But that boy in the courtroom . . .

During the past week, he'd thought so much about Patrick, his mother, and her smile.

Her answering e-mail message: *If you find yourself in this area again . . .*

Mere politeness? But if it was mere politeness, why mention that her marriage was troubled? Was she so isolated and alone?

He longed for a place to pause. A place to put his heart. And in the face of that realization, he just couldn't pretend any more.

But he could pretend to pretend.

"It's the fact that I'm your boss?" Her voice brought him back. Muriel took a sip, but hadn't busied her hands quite fast enough to conceal the tremble.

He accepted the olive branch. "Yeah. But I tell you what: What if I quit and go to work for *Newsweek,* and we fly off for a dirty weekend in Puerto Vallarta?" As if *Newsweek* would have him.

"Sure," she answered, watching him carefully. "It's a date." She smiled. When she smiled, her eyes crinkled. When her face relaxed, the wrinkles didn't.

12

There wasn't a whole lot more to say, but they spent an hour saying it, pretending that the intent of the evening's invitation had been conversation and camaraderie, rather than a solid, practiced roll in the office hay.

He made his excuses and headed home, driving down Sunset to Westwood to the Woodley Towers. The Towers were reasonably upscale, appealing to UCLA students with wealthy parents, or low-rent cosmetic surgeons working out of little cubbyholes on Santa Monica boulevard.

He checked his computer for messages, and in the midst of all the ads for triple-X rated delights, he found a bunch from friends and contacts, and one that instantly caught his eye from Costumes, Period. Vivian had put him on her mailing list, which apparently went out to over two thousand friends, customers, and suppliers across the country. Most of it was general talk, a mention of new offerings, and notices about something called a Renaissance Pleasure Faire to be conducted in Northern California. Apparently, several of her costumes were on display there.

At the bottom of the flyer she had tacked a more personal note: *"No, not looking for any promotional help, and I bet costumes bore you. Just saying 'hello,' Mr. Big-Town Reporter. Vivian."*

He leaned back, one knot of tension in his chest dissolving, another one tightening. He could feel the door opening between them. She was throwing out the fragile, tentative line. A chance for Sand to tell her who he was, *really* was.

And for some reason, the knowledge of her interest was almost paralyzing. Some small, wounded voice asked what any decent woman would want with *him.*

He walked out to the balcony and looked out over the jeweled strands of the city lights, and felt his heart breaking. He could barely afford the Towers on his current salary. It made him feel like a fraud. But some inviolable part of him still dreamed of bonuses and book contracts. Maybe he operated on the theory that if he lived the lifestyle he wanted to reclaim, some tiny spark inside him might rise to the challenge. He believed that was called "fake it until you make it."

Of course, they also call that "self-delusion."

Not his fault that he thought this way. His mom, bless her heart, got him started in the psycho-cybernetics loop back when he was a kid, and it could be as addictive as cocaine.

He'd known too many people who wanted something, and went after it, and just didn't have what it took. They broke their heads and hearts and spirits on the rocks of insufficient talent or luck. He sometimes thought that what *might* work, in terms of self-improvement efforts, would be a national talent test, followed by a barrage of psychologists to help people cope with the cold reality that they just didn't have what it took.

Reporting was sort of an accidental profession. Through all high school he was certain that there was a novelist lurking under the surface, burrowing steadily upward, eager to emerge to acclaim and applause. Sympathetic counselors had advised him to join the school newspaper. He was given the example of all kinds of great novelists who had started out or moonlighted as journalists: Twain, Steinbeck and others. They said an ambitious young man could learn discipline, and make contacts, and learn research and clarity, and all manner of other crucial bits by going this route.

In college, he took the plunge and chose Journalism over LACC's creative writing department, which seemed full of blue-haired little old ladies who wrote astrological poetry, and professors who spent years drafting, rewriting and polishing a single short story.

He waited tables at Denny's morning shift, went to school in the afternoon and wrote at night.

Some say that everyone has a novel in them. By the late nineties, Sand figured that if there was one in him, it had to be the ugliest, most misbegotten breech birth in history.

Get far enough along that rocky road and you forget why you ever wanted to be a writer in the first place. Instead of passion, all you get is a dull ache, like a rotten tooth, if you don't pick up one of the old projects every month or two.

"Out of the cradle endlessly rocking," the poem goes. Sand's high school English teacher explained Whitman's words as an observation that the experiences of childhood are with us for a lifetime. Hard to argue with that.

Sand was an only child, mostly raised by a divorced mother. His mother and father split the sheets when he was eight, probably because Dad spent too much time chasing his own dream, singing. At least the old man had made it *part* of the way there. Never to the top, but close enough to covet the view. He sang with some of the best: Nat King Cole, Ray Charles, Johnny Mathis. But his voice wasn't strong enough, or original enough, to sustain a solo career, so he never quite made it. Working the night shift at the downtown post office was a poor substitute.

Renny had a nasty suspicion that Mom married Dad assuming that she'd hitched her wagon to a star. When Daddy's career went bust, when talent and ambition carried him no further than a two-bedroom house in South Central L.A., the marriage started to curdle. But this was just supposition. Truth to tell, he didn't really know: it was murder to pry information out of either of them.

Mom was always scared that baby Renny was going to follow in Dad's footsteps, and do something just as rash. God knows he never meant to hurt her, or hurt anyone, but maybe that's exactly what he did.

Along the way he had the hideous misfortune to learn that a steady paycheck is the most addictive drug in the world. If he'd never gotten that first job at the San Diego Examiner, interning that summer of '80, who knew what might have happened.

Not that he stopped writing fiction. Not at all. But his first novel, *Timestream,* made the rounds of twenty-two publishers, and then sat in the big green filing cabinet in the corner of his living room. Three years later, his second, *After the Fall,* made it to eighteen houses. It took four years to finish the next one, *The Equation.* All three were science fiction, all of them metaphorical journeys along an inner road.

He remembered working on *The Equation* furtively, at night, with a bottle of beer on the side of the desk. By this time, the suds were a necessity: he needed a little help getting going.

The first two books were written while working at the *Examiner,* and then later in San Jose at the *Chronicle.* The third was written in Minnesota, at the *Twin City,* a weekly liberal rag with a readership of about half a million.

The first two books he wrote in the morning, bounding out of bed, showering to heat his body up and spending a half hour on the treadmill, then another shower, then eating yogurt out of a cup as he sat at the computer and pounded out five hundred words or so, every damn day.

Going to work after that regimen felt downright righteous, no matter what lame story they threw at him. He could always tell himself, "I'm not here for the duration. Just passing through." However silly that might seem in retrospect, that perspective actually put some extra bounce in his step. By the third book, he'd started to view the computer with suspicion.

An old *Peanuts* comic strip was one of Sand's favorite memories. In it, Charlie Brown's beagle wrote prospective editors a note reading: *"Dear Sirs. I recently sent you a manuscript. You were supposed to publish it, and make me rich and famous. If you were not aware of this, I hereby give you thirty days to correct an intolerable situation. Sincerely, Snoopy."*

Every day, Sand felt more like Charlie Brown's hallucinating pooch.

Discipline and creativity began to break down. It got to a point where only three hundred words a day made it out of his computer. After a year, he had an unpublishable chunk of garbage, twice rescued from the trash can. And the computer keyboard became a thing to fear.

Maybe he should have gotten damned mad instead of frightened. Fought back by launching into another book. But the fear grew too large, loomed like some kind of grinning jackal over his crippled ego. No idea escaped unscathed. No word made it onto the page without merciless critique, and in time, he lost what remained of his confidence. There was just some little place inside him that didn't have the ability to climb that mountain again, to put his chin up again, and take the chance of another knockout. It happens to boxers all the time. Good boxers. Promising fighters. They never make it back.

He kept promising himself that he'd get back to that next book, that he'd finish it, polish it, send it out.

And he didn't.

The work that was certain: the newspaper work, the magazine work, called to him. He wasn't risking himself, because his heart wasn't in it. He could make money, and hide behind cleverness, and no one would ever know that he wasn't giving them anything of himself.

No one knew, no one cared. Least of all Renny Sand.

And that was how, ten years and three relationships later, he had found himself working in Los Angeles, flirting with a Pulitzer, courted and groomed for duty at Marcus Communications.

That was also how he had, with the very best of intentions, made the very worst mistake of his life. A little mistake named Benny Alvarez.

And how he ended up in a pissant town called Claremont, covering a little trial for Marcus Communication's lowest rung, *Eyeful,* and meeting a woman who touched him in ways he didn't think he could be touched anymore. How he ended up years later driving back through that town, and reawakening memories and dreams that he had never allowed to emerge into the full light of day.

And how, ultimately, he ended up declining an interlude with the firm, warm body of a woman who knew too much about him, knew that once upon a time he'd been on the way up, that now he was holding on for dear life.

And lastly, how he happened to be sitting on the terrace of his Westwood apartment, looking out over the rail at a city that didn't know his name, drinking his third canned daiquiri, breath hitching in his chest as the pain slid away into a bubbling black haze.

Packed away somewhere in a box was his third novel, the stunted literary albatross that he might as well hang around his neck as tangible evidence of failure. He'd carried that cold dead thing with him from job to job, swearing that one day, somehow, he'd pick it back up again, begin to write again, and dig himself out of this hole.

But even if he couldn't do that, he could do something else, and this he pledged:

He would make this city know who he was. He would make them talk about Renny Sand. Make them eager to open their papers and magazines to see if his byline was on an article, a news item, a column today. He'd win their love.

He'd find a story bigger and better than the one that had gone so terribly, fatally wrong. They'd know Renny Sand, by God.

And if he could do that, maybe he would be able to return to that lethal manuscript, and resurrect from it the spirit of his aborted dream.

I'm a writer, damn it.

13

THURSDAY, MAY 17

O tis Emory worked the gears on his Peterbilt, sliding the fork under a 500-pound bale of particle board. The front springs sagged as he levered the load up. Gravel crunched beneath the wheels as the tractor found its balance, and then shifted into reverse. He backed up until he had a clear run down the aisle.

He was a man of power and strength, a man intended for hunting, or fighting, or crashing through an opposing line to sack the hapless quarterback. Otis was too damned many years past eighteen now, but on good days he still felt the springy power in his legs and back, still felt that crazy electric juice in his blood that said One More Game. Just one more good game. *Once more, let me hear the crowd roar, and watch the cheerleaders twirl, and feel my body doing what it was meant to do. What I was born to do.*

That was on the good days.

On bad days he thought about shuttling endless flats of pre-cut board onto boxcars or ships that would take them to Albuquerque or Salt Lake or up the Columbia River to primo markets in Japan. Eight, ten, sometimes twelve-hour days that stuck a hot, dull knife in his lower back no matter what salves or crèmes or pills he tried. Or he thought about what had happened to his family, and tried to wrap his mind around the possibility that it was actually over with Vivian.

That was hard to take. He still remembered when Vivian was sixteen, the sweetest thing he had ever seen. She still was, but back then, the admiration was mutual, and passionate, and if they had been naïve and frightened on that first night up in Riverview cemetery, there had been something special about that cool, dark grass, their sleeping bags linked together as tightly as their bodies. She had trembled, her small hands laced around his neck, but her eyes were clear and focused on his, and they said *yes, yes, I want this, Otis—*

"Big load there, Oat," Ellie Krup said.

Otis yanked himself out of his reverie, and focused his eyes on a buxom blonde with a sharp nose and wide, generous lips. She smiled at him in a lazy, predatory fashion. He had known Ellie Krup almost as long as he had known Vivian, back when Ellie was a sexy cheerleader, too strapping to be called "cute," with a taste for running backs. Black, white, color didn't matter at all, as long as they wore the green and gold.

"You handle it nice and easy, Oat." He smiled a bit, not too much. Ellie was more than a flirt. She was trouble, and it would be very, very foolish to ever forget that.

"Always do, Ellie," he said.

Ellie Krup ran her portable scanner over the UPC bar code on the side of the bundled lumber, checked the display, nodded at what her clipboard computer told her.

"Seen that. You got a nice, light touch. Gets the job done, don't it?" The way she smiled at him gave him an odd, crawly sensation.

"Always has," he said neutrally.

"I'll just bet."

She was about to say something else, about to define the playing field more precisely, when Cappy emerged from around the corner.

Cappy Swenson was an out of towner, had only arrived in Claremont three years ago, but had found a way to fit in pretty quick. The first year or so the big, bearded man had ingratiated himself, or created pressure, to land random jobs around town. He had finally ended up here at the lumber mill, working around the shipping department. Not long after that he'd actually moved into their trailer park. Ugh.

Cappy processed packages from all over the country, and sent out the same. And Otis suspected that Cappy used Claremont Lumber's shipping as a cover. That he had contacts across the country, and that something (the rumor said drugs), went out, mixed in with invoices, samples, orders and returns. He couldn't prove anything, but Cappy drove both a new Ford SUV and a Harley, lived in Riverview trailer park but wore enough gold chains to put down on a decent house.

He purely stank of trouble. Otis knew the type as far back as high school: Cappy was one of those hard, dangerous bastards who would whisper things about your mother across the line, go out of their way to hurt you, to land on top of you or step on you, spear you across the knees sideways, taking strange and savage satisfaction from the music of snapping bones. Otis was wary of Cappy. Cappy was big, used to the whole world backing down from him. Otis didn't back down, and that aroused some little primal knot of cells in the back of Cappy's skull, something from the dark, cold days when cavemen fought to the death for the honor of screwing the shaman's daughter.

Cappy was dangerous, Cappy was with Ellie, and Ellie liked to push the edge. This was one pure-D rotating bastard of a situation: no matter which direction you viewed it from, it stank.

Otis got his little tractor in gear, and trundled it up the row, hoping that he wouldn't have to deal with Cap then. Or later, for that matter.

For a long time, now, he'd had an itch that he and Cappy might come to conclusions one day. If that was so, it was so, but he sure as hell wasn't going to help it along.

"What was that about?" Cap said.

"Just talking," Ellie said, too innocently. Her voice was studiedly little-girl, *daddy why are you looking at me that way* innocent. She sashayed away, deliberately exaggerating the roll of her hips as if trying to provoke him. Then she looked back over her shoulder to be sure he was watching, and threw Cappy a kiss.

His thick lips curled into a heavy smile, but as soon as she was gone around the corner, Cappy's face went flat and thoughtful, his bushy brows pushed together into a solid line.

Otis drove his rig up past the roll-up door into the dock, set the bale down with the delicacy of a mother laying her first born into the crib, and backed away.

He parked the tractor in one of two parking slots marked out with parallel yellow lines, hopped out and began to fill out his clipboard. He liked the job, but sometimes had to be extra careful with the math. If he was a little better with the numbers, maybe he could think about going for an office job. It would be nice to get in out of the weather. He used to like the outdoor work, but lately, just the last couple of years, the pain in his back had become more than an occasional groaner. Now he had to be careful how he rolled out of bed, how he picked things up, or it would feel like someone was playing a blow-torch across his lower spine.

This was one problem, he thought, that won't improve with age.

Maybe he could take some night school classes. Pat was always encouraging him, and telling him he could do it. That boy! Always filled with ideas, always figuring out ways to beat the world. Too young to know that you can't. Otis *knew* this for a fact, but had to admit that when the boy said those things, Otis could almost believe it *was* possible to win. Just maybe it was.

He was totaling up the last column when he heard Cappy and some of his friends approaching from the direction of the roll-up.

Two of them. Not the bikers that hung around the trailer park. None of *those* assholes worked around here, although sometimes he saw them out at the shipping bay, after the supervisors were gone. He hunched that they were bagging more than sawdust.

"Can I help you?" Otis asked casually. Cappy came closer. The man was big, big enough to give Otis just a little sour taste in the back of his throat. But Otis was a big man, too, and damned if he was going to give Cappy the satisfaction of seeing his fear.

"I was thinking maybe I could help you," Cappy said.

Otis looked around. It was four in the afternoon, and the loading dock was quieter than usual. He had a feeling that just maybe nobody wanted to be around right now. There was a big old torsion wrench in the back of the Peterbilt, just behind the seat. He could see its handle from the corner of his eye, and that was a very comforting sight in-deed.

"And how is that?"

"Just wanted you to know that any time you want to talk to Ellie, you find me and talk to me first."

"I'll keep that in mind."

Cap's rage was palpable, like jagged fingernails drawn lightly across the back of Otis's neck.

"Let me do you another favor."

"Wasn't sure you'd done the first one."

The edges of Cap's mouth turned up in something that might have been intended as a smile. "Just a way of talking, bro. I'd suggest you listen. What say you and your boy stay out of my business. Healthier all around like that, don't ya think?"

"My boy?" Suddenly the lights seemed to dim, all of the sights and sounds on the loading dock focusing to a point. "What the hell does this have to do with Pat. You threatening my son?"

What in the hell was this all about? He'd thought it was about Ellie, just typical hillbilly bullshit. But this was something else, originating from some other concern altogether. Cappy's "business," perhaps?

Before it could go any further, one of the managers, a tall thin long-timer named Weatherby, climbed stiffly down off the dock. He may not have had any real clue what was going on, but he had to have the general idea.

Cap sprouted a wide, watermelon-eating grin, and used a gravelly Rochester voice. "Never threatened your boy, there, Otis. I's juss an avvocate of higher *edjumacation.* You remember what I said, now, Otis." He gestured at the expanse of carefully stacked planks. "Hey! Real good job there. Mill's proud of you, boy!"

Weatherby watched the three of them stroll off, and then turned to regard Otis. Otis's shoulders slumped, the tension draining from them as the danger retreated. "Everything all right here?"

"Just fine," Otis said, picking up his clipboard again. He hardly realized it, but his hand had found its way behind the seat, and was grasping the wrench as if he wanted to crush fingerprints into the handle.

"You watch out for Cappy," Weatherby said. "He's a nasty customer. We know he's not straight. One day we'll catch him and be able to get him out of here."

"Until then, I've just got to watch my own ass."

"That's about right."

Weatherby paused as if there was something more that he had to say, but then just shrugged, smiled faintly, and left.

Otis sighed. It was hard to admit how scared he had been. Even more troubling was the fact that Otis knew himself too well to believe he could leave things at this. He was going to do something about his fear of Cappy. He had always done something about fear. Sometimes, too often, it was something he regretted later.

This wasn't over, not by a long shot.

14

JOURNAL ENTRY #2:

Although genetic components of intelligence probably cannot be increased, there are biological aspects (nutritional, neuro-transmitters, other ergogenics), and certainly conceptual aspects which can. Practice with a given family of tasks certainly decreases "fuzz," and practice in so-called lateral thinking increases creativity. We are determined to increase functional efficiency, not to mire ourselves in a tired debate about whether intelligence, and/or the ability to measure it, exists at all. The ability to think "outside the box," while avoiding a full breech of social walls, is another quality which can be taught environmentally. In order to implant such patterns, Aristotle must employ activities in all major sensory modes, not merely the visual/digital featured in 90%+ of standard IQ tests. . . .

SATURDAY, MAY 19

Traffic was still light along Ocean Way. Most of the traffic flowed west, and as more late sleepers rolled out of bed it would thicken as weekenders headed to the beaches forty miles distant for an overdose of sand and sun. Spring was warming now, and when it didn't rain, when the sun drove the clouds away, the days whispered promise of cookouts, vacations, toasty sand and endless body surfing.

The morning was foggy, but that low mist would burn off soon, birthing an afternoon of miraculous clarity and warmth, one of those Northwest days that makes the long rainy season seem a fair price.

Frankie, Patrick, Destiny and Shermie were kamakazing down Angel Avenue onto Ocean Way, touching their brakes as little as possible. No one wanted to be King Wuss.

The light ahead turned red. They applied friction to wheels just in time to turn the dive-bombing descent into a controlled stop. Patrick gloried in the wind screaming past his hair, filling his world with the sense of being temporarily *out* of control, followed by a jolt of will and skill as he wrenched himself back *into* control. It was the sweetest and most exhilarating experience he knew.

When they screeched to a halt, they were laughing. No one else took Claremont Hill at a dead roll in the fog. No one else dared.

"Now *that*," Frankie said, "was way twisted."

"Wanna pump back up, try it again?" Destiny's eyes sparkled.

"Almost, but not quite." Shermie was shaking, the adrenaline dump nearly overpowering him. He regarded Patrick with shrewd eyes. "You know, I was watching Charlene last night, and I'm telling you that she wanted to slow dance with you."

"God," Patrick said. "You are so full of crap."

"You were just scared," Shermie insisted.

Destiny was curious now. "Scared of what?"

Frankie barked laughter. "Scared he'd get a boner half a meter long."

Destiny grimaced. "God," she said. "Barf much? You are disgusting, Frankie."

"Thankyaverramuch," Frankie said, his lip in an Elvis twist.

They slid down the street. Morning mist still hung low to the pavement. They had an odd sense of owning the world, of moving through a landscape that was theirs alone.

They talked comfortably, and with little speculation on the possibilities of the coming day. Perhaps there would be adventure of some kind. Perhaps a game, or a movie, or maybe they would just spend the time together relaxing, enjoying the companionable silence. Without verbal discussion, they had somehow come to an agreement that they would spend the day in each other's company. For all of their complaining about Frankie, he was one of *Us*, not one of *the Others*, the rest of the world. The ones who didn't, couldn't understand.

They rolled their bikes east along Ocean Way for a couple of blocks, pedaling their bikes as slowly as possible, enjoying the fog and the company, when Patrick suddenly pulled up short. "Wait a minute," he said. "What the hell happened here?"

They had just rolled past the Atomic Burrito stand, and were looking back at the Inside Edge coffee shop.

Destiny let her breath out in a long steam-kettle sigh. The front of the shop was smashed. It couldn't be easily seen from the street: you had to be rolling or walking down the sidewalk, and until now, there had been too much fog and too few pedestrians.

But *they* could see it, and they understood the implications just fine. One at a time, they hopped off their bikes, walked down the driveway to the window, and peered inside.

"Jeez," Frankie said. "Who did that?"

Patrick put his kickstand down. "What happened here?"

Hermie Shermie was shaking again, as if the previous adrenaline hadn't worn off. "We don't want to be here, guys. We don't want to be anywhere around here."

"Man," Frankie said. Patrick couldn't help but notice the excitement in his voice. "Somebody really trashed the place."

They stepped through the door carefully—the coffee shop's glass door was broken. Ignoring the voice of reason, let alone the accumulated wisdom of countless *Nick At Night* reruns of *Dragnet* and *Adam-12,* Patrick reached through the front door's broken glass and opened the door from the inside.

Destiny was not happy at all. "Oh, man—guys—you shouldn't be in there. Somebody is going to see . . ."

Frankie was openly scornful. "Nobody saw all night, did they?"

Patrick seemed almost in a trance. He walked in, looking at the broken chairs, the paint-splashed walls, the defaced counters, the torn books, but gave them only a cursory glance. His eyes were immediately drawn to something that seemed out of place in the middle of the trash-strewn floor.

It was a plain red house brick, weathered, cracked. It might have been pulled out of someone's garden wall. A sheet of white paper was folded around it, fastened with a rubber band.

"Look, man," he said, and picked it up. He popped the rubber band off and slid the note free.

Frankie snatched it from his hand, and began reading aloud. His forehead crinkled. " 'You assholes want to settle this? Meet us under the bridge at midnight.' "

"Is that corny, or what?" he said, but handed the note to Hermie. One at a time, they all read it, and then stared at each other.

Patrick was the first to speak. "This can't be happening," he said.

Frankie looked disgusted with him. "Oh, it's happening, all right."

Destiny nudged a piece of broken glass with her toe. "Will Rowan call the cops?"

"I don't know," Patrick said. "If they do, bet you that whoever did this—"

"You know who did this," Frankie said. "It's Happy Cappy and the Fuckwads."

"You're just guessing," Shermie said.

"Hell I am. Those assholes will know if Rowan calls the cops, all right."

"How can you be sure?" Shermie said again.

"Haven't you ever watched television?" Destiny asked. "If these guys are selling serious drugs, you think they don't have a connection in the local cops, someone to tell them when a bust is going down? They obviously knew how to shut the burglar alarm off. They don't want an audience. This is *personal*." No one argued. They had all watched too many cop and detective shows to disagree.

Potheads Rowan and Pork might be, but Patrick had too many memories, good memories, of afternoons in the shop, hot cocoa, of gentle ribbing with some harmless folks whose business just happened to overlap with the most vicious bastards in town.

"Probably won't call the cops anyway," he said slowly. "I think this thing has been heading to a showdown for months. This is it. Pork doesn't want the cops in his business."

Hermie made a sound like someone sucking at a joint. And Destiny gave him the nastiest look imaginable.

"Somebody's going to get killed," she said.

Frankie seemed lost deep in thought, so deep that they seemed a bit surprised when he roused himself and said: "I hope so."

They looked at him, holding the brick in his hand. The beginning of a cold, cruel smile curled his lip. Patrick was the first to reconstruct Frankie's thought process, and the light burst behind his eyes like an exploding star.

15

JOURNAL ENTRY #4:

Determining the goal is one step. Proposing a means to achieve it is another. But there is also the necessity to correlate results, and publish for replication. Due to the proposed double-blind nature of the initial experiment, it was initially feared that it would be problematic to gather the data without raising suspicion. But since all preschool computer systems were enabled for automatic downloading of updates, it was also possible to upload results, keyed to the individual child. Dosages of ergogenics could be computed by standardizing the percentage or weight of

mixture per snack, and tracking the amounts of each snack consumed. Simple evaluations disguised as general achievement or progress tests gave further insight. All in all, Aristotle proceeded more rapidly than we had hoped, and more positively than we could have dreamed.

Then, of course, there was the unfortunate event in Washington State. Although an isolated instance, safety suggested that Aristotle be suspended until a full evaluation could be completed. . . .

PALO ALTO, CALIFORNIA

The two men had landed at San Jose International Airport an hour earlier. One of them was white, the other black with very white hair. Aside from that, they might have been brothers. Both were in their fifties, both very fit; neither betrayed much emotion. The black man presented a credit card issued in a name that was not his own, and rented a Camaro. They took the 880 north to the 580 East, cutting across Hayward and Castro Valley, through rolling green hills.

They took the Vasco Road off-ramp north up to May School Road, passing a Texaco and Mobil gas station, a Denny's, a few private homes, and then finally reaching a smaller, privately maintained road.

A sign to the right read: ADVANCED SYSTEMS. A key card in the slot of an electronic reader opened the gate. They drove a few hundred yards along a twisting gravel path to a pleasant green building with broad windows looking out onto a featureless expanse of hills.

The white man pressed a button on the main door, and announced himself, saying: "Martin Schott." The black man said: "Mr. Wisher." These were their real names. In addition to their other, more specialized skills, both men held college degrees: Wisher a Masters in Psychology, Schott a B.S. in Political Science. Familiarity with organizational structures and the specialized jargon of an establishment like Advanced Systems had made them ideal for this assignment.

The door opened, and they were welcomed into a foyer without a receptionist's desk. A broad, smiling, pale man with a deeply receding hairline greeted them. "Mr. Schott! Mr. Wisher! How good to meet you at last."

"Dr. Dronet," Wisher said, and extended his hand. His face was smiling, but behind his sunglasses, his eyes were flat.

Dronet led them through narrow halls back to a conference room looking out through one of the broadest picture windows, onto the valley and the freeway running through it. There were five people in the conference room at the moment: three men, two women. All of them were dressed for comfort, except one man who stood, his bald pate glistening in the overhead light. He wore a cheap, shiny J.C. Penney suit, although everyone in the room knew that he could have afforded much better. That was just Jorgenson's way, and he was brilliant enough for his eccentricities to offend no one.

Dronet presented their guests, who were seated, brought drinks (a cranberry spritzer for Mr. Wisher, a diet Coke for Schott), and there was a friendly, congratulatory buzz of light conversation as everyone waited for the meeting to come to order.

"Well?" Jorgenson said to Schott and Wisher. "We've all looked at the data. I see no reason not to announce Aristotle's success."

Wisher opened a briefcase, extracted a slim sheaf of papers. "Very impressive, yes." He paused, as if he needed to scan the columns of figures again. In reality, every number had been checked and rechecked, every conclusion reconsidered and extrapolated by minds far colder than any Advanced Systems personnel could have imagined. "The average grade point is 3.7, up from 2.7 in the control group. IQ points average about seven points higher—"

"Which means," Jorgenson said, "that while the process doesn't *increase* intelligence, it *does* enhance focus. A student given Aristotle can be relied upon to score at the upper levels of his potential. We're not changing genetics here."

Wisher nodded, and stood, walking around the room slowly. "When you first contacted us with your situation, it seemed . . . well, incredible. You can imagine why we want to be as certain as possible that there are no mistakes, no repercussions. After all, there was the problem in Washington. . . ."

Jorgenson waved his hands, seeming to pooh-pooh the idea. "Claremont? That was years ago. We have monitored the children since that time, and they are doing quite well." He shuffled a stack of papers, searching for something. "See here."

Schott smiled. "Oh, no. We don't have any problem with your figures. The concern is more one of public image. There are corporate concerns, family concerns . . ." He smiled broadly, and gestured expansively. In the moment that Schott gestured, and all eyes were on him, Wisher slipped a thumbnail-sized adhesive pad onto the back of a television monitor. Anchored to the pad was a tiny black metal rectangle.

Jorgenson nodded understandingly. "We understand. You knew the man himself. He was friend to you, and mentor, leader. Of course you would have these thoughts. But this is such an exciting development."

One of the other men, a black man who looked like a barrel with arms, cleared his throat. "This is about the children, and *only* the children. We have the preliminary data. We are tracking them now, and things look excellent. We need to disseminate the information."

"Which is," Park/Wisher said, "impossible to do without revealing names and procedures, some of which will raise eyebrows."

"What are you asking us to do?"

Schott laid his hands flat on the table. "Let's not wait months. A few weeks. Say—until the middle of July. Give us time to prepare the family, to confer with the editors and board members. If this needs to be spun, we spin it. But we agree. It's about the children."

The others harrumphed and shifted uncomfortably in their seats. One of them, a small blond man wearing a checkered shirt, said: "Listen. I agree with you that we have a winner. Grades, behavior, general health, all indicators are up, but these are external indicators. We need better testing, and that will be difficult to get, unless we go public. In order to go public, we have to be very, very certain that we aren't liable for lawsuits . . ."

"That's absurd," one of the women complained. "We've done nothing wrong."

"That's not the point. We agree that the Washington incident was merely an illusion, a coincidence having nothing to do with our project. Several of the children were being abused at home: the physical traces were discovered, and the prosecutors lumped all of the evidence together and tried to make a case. Nightmares, ugly dream drawings, bruises, genital trauma . . . that poor school caught hell. The point is that, merit or no, a lawsuit will prevent us from going national. Who is going to back us if someone is screaming sexual abuse?"

Wisher finished his circuit of the room, and sat down again. "Believe me, whatever concerns we have right here in this room, the media will blow them up a hundred times larger, regardless of our motives, and regardless of the ultimate worth of our efforts. Give us a little time."

"I think we all want the same thing," Schott said soothingly. "We're so close now. Just a little longer."

There was a bit more discussion, followed by agreement. Wisher and Schott made their goodbyes, and left the boardroom, and then the building.

In the car, Schott pushed an AC adapter into the cigarette lighter, and clipped it to a device as large as a transistor radio. He attached an earphone to the box, and slipped its button-sized speaker into his left ear.

"Reception?" Wisher asked tightly. He seemed almost mechanical now.

"Very good," Schott said blandly. "A thousand yards, easy."

"That's all we need." He paused. Then: "What are they talking about?"

Schott touched the ear button, nesting it more carefully. He squinted his eyes, and listened: "*. . . wonder about that one reduction series Wisher asked us to run, identifying the fifty children at greatest risk. Unstable families, arson convictions, reports of animal torture or bed-wetting. Strange stuff. What do you make of that . . . ?*"

"Just stat stuff," Schott said, closing his eyes. "Crime statistics. Unemployment rates." Almost a full minute passed as he listened. "Risk factors on the kids. Everything our tame shrink identified as critical points. The boss was right about these researchers. They're sharp. Give them enough time, they'd put it all together."

"Jesus," Wisher said. His voice was tired and worn. Almost as if overcome with the wonderment of it, he asked: "And we have to kill them all, don't we." It wasn't really a question.

"Can you think of any other way? You've looked at it. You tell me another way. Fifty kids now, or maybe a thousand innocent victims down the road."

They had made it back to the main road now. They paused at the stop sign, and Wisher leaned his head against the steering wheel. When he looked back up his face was calm, and flat again, impassive, but for just a moment there had been a crack in his calm, and underneath it had been something as bright and hot as a flow of lava. Fear? Pain? Anger?

"No," he said. "It just seems like there's no end to it."

"Then buck up, soldier. Keep your focus. I don't like this any better than you do."

Wisher took the main road down, and then returned to the freeway. "I'll do this," he said quietly. "I'll do what I have to do, but then . . ." His voice wandered off.

"Then what?" Schott said.

"I don't know," Wisher said. "I don't know what comes after. I'll do what I have to do, but then . . ."

Schott watched his friend for a few seconds, and then turned and looked out the front window at the traffic. "After it's over, Chuck," he said. "Until then, keep focused."

Wisher nodded, and drove on.

16

A rainy night in Claremont.

Most of the town seemed to revel in its rurality, but the main strip was raucous with card casinos, C&W-themed bars and even what passed local muster for a nightclub. Baja Bug VWs, trucks and SUVs were parked up and down Main Street. Their owners might have been going to gamble, or heading to the town's largest movie theater, the Rialto, (newly refurbished!), or to one of the local party spots. Traveling further down the streets, there were darkened windows of the banks and pawn shops and payday loan services that had made such inroads in this section of town. Traveling another block or so brought you to a section where most of the businesses were closed for the night. It was darker here, less inviting. On this block, you would find a bar with rain-streaked, blacked-out windows. The sign above the door read: THE SADDLE SHOP. MEMBERS ONLY.

A few pickup trucks and cars were pulled up tight outside the Saddle Shop. It was well off the nighttime's beaten track, but from time to time a man entered or exited the building, his coat pulled tightly around him.

They were usually between nineteen and forty years of age. Almost all were phenomenally muscular. If you were to follow one in after a car pulled up, you might notice that his swagger increased as he reached the Saddle Shop's front door, even before he could hear the music blaring from within.

The music was loud, insistent, driving, vital. Its beat cut right through any notions of romance, to a core of animal sexuality that practically washed the room in male hormones.

The room was packed belly to butt with men. Most were dressed similarly to men who might have entered any other doorway along the street: as farmers, truckers, cowboys, construction workers. They had the bodies to match. No beer bellies here, no scrawny legs, no desk-bound bad backs. These men put as much careful care into their appearance as the women in the Logger Lounge three blocks north.

There were no women in the room, but the men danced. In corner tables there was low, intense conversation. In the shadows at the back of the bar, and sometimes at the bar itself as the night wore on, there was considerable hot, sweaty physical contact, although there was no actual sex. Sex, however, was mere minutes away, in a drive up any of the unlighted roads leading to the hills, or down around the rivers, or in the apartments or sprawling ranch houses all over town. No need to risk undue legal attention.

Creased black leather molded around sculpted chests and arms and backs. The air swam with sweat and an unmistakable, undeniable stink of *maleness.*

The men drank, and danced. A song extolling the virtues of raw animal copulation blared from the loudspeakers. The men arm-wrestled, and talked low or loud, and watched each other with slitted eyes as they figured the evening's moves.

Then the front window exploded, glass shards spinning into the dance floor as if a bomb had exploded in the street. A brick spun through the room, bounced off a table and rebounded onto the head of one of the construction workers. It slid to a stop against the wall under a poster of a bare-chested Brad Pitt.

The music died, and the room went deadly silent.

Brando, owner and bartender, walked around from behind the bar and crossed the room. No one else moved.

He hefted the brick. It was covered with plastic. Slipping off the rubber band, he unpeeled the wrapping.

The front door slammed open and a tree-trunk of a man named Hogie ran out. A few seconds later he reentered, shrugging his massive shoulders. "Nobody out there, Brando. Gutless assholes ran."

Brando's face was red with rage, but he was terribly silent. He hefted the brick again, and then with a careful hand, unwrapped a note nestled beneath the plastic. His eyes moved over the paper, reading it twice, and then passed it to one of the others.

"I'll kill 'em," he said quietly. "They'll wish their mamas had chosen the coat hanger."

17

The Allan Street bridge spanned the Cowlitz River, separating the old town of Allantown from the newer burg of Claremont. Over the years, Allantown and Claremont had grown larger, merging to the point that there was no dividing line save the river that ran under the Allan Street bridge.

Allan Street had become increasingly run-down over the years. The Chamber of Commerce office of Allantown was only staffed half the time. The old Deluxe theater tried to reinvent itself as a theater pub, then ran free broadcasts of sports and WWF wrestling spectaculars in an attempt to lure people into its pizza-and-beer bar, finally succumbing to the fall of the entire neighborhood.

Some said that it was all to the good, that the decreased values of the property made it easier to buy up the buildings with an eye to constructing a second bridge, one that would be four lanes wide instead of two, facilitating faster travel between the fusing halves of town.

But for now, the nights here were dark and quiet, most of the traffic passing a quarter mile to the north along the Prosper Street bridge. Here, shadows engulfed a once busy district even as early as eight in the evening. By midnight, no one passed this way at all.

There was a pedestrian lane along the bridge, sheltered from the motorized portion by a low wall. The pedestrian lane was a grille rather than solid concrete, and the rain ran through it to the darkened currents of the Cowlitz below.

This dreary night, there were two small forms crouched behind the low wall, boys who were supposed to be home in bed.

Patrick stole a glance at his watch. He was shivering, and not entirely due to the evening cold and wet. A truck rumbled up on the bridge, vibrating it to its foundations, its headlights sweeping across the cobblestone, brighter and colder than the eyes of God.

He crouched tighter, lower, and then jumped again at another sound behind him.

"Jeez," Frankie said sourly. "If you got any froggier, you'd turn green."

"I just don't like this," Patrick said. "If my mom takes a good look in my bedroom, I am like so screwed."

"This'll be good," Frankie said. "This'll be *really* good. Hey, Pat . . ."

break out the snacks." Beneath a plastic drop cloth he held his father's
Sony video camera, complete with infrared night vision. "Let's get
ready to rumble," he said. "I am ready for fight night."

"*Jesus,*" Patrick said. His voice complained, but his eyes were excited. "You are so sick." Patrick wanted to be here, and he didn't. His
stomach was tied in a knot, had been ever since he'd thrown the brick
through the painted-out window of the Saddle Shop, whipping around
the corner on his bike at mach speed.

"If you think it's so sick, why are you here?"

"To keep you out of trouble," he said.

"Shhh," Frankie said. "Someone's coming." The roar of approaching motorcycles built and then died away. Kickstand sounds, and then
some low, confident laughter.

The boys shut up, and peered down through the grill. A cluster of
shadowy shapes, perhaps eight of them, moved down to the bottom.
They were big, solid, and Patrick instantly recognized them from the
trailer park. He had seen them outside Cappy's trailer for months,
laughing and joking, and going about their terrible business. He didn't
know them by name, except for one who he had heard called Flanagan,
a mountain of tattoos and earrings and long greasy hair, and the one
called "Torque."

Flanagan was the only one who spoke. The rest were quiet but
almost seemed to vibrate with a kind of crazy energy. "Think they'll
show, Torque?" His voice was just audible through the traffic. The rain
had decreased to a mist.

"Torque" Marcello worked at the Li'l Car garage out on River View
road. He was skinny, and looked something like a forties-era Sinatra
after sandblasting, his features too vague and uncoordinated to have
any impact. Marcello had a kind of crazed, jittery energy. His voice
was a gravelly baritone, and he was never seen without something at
the corner of his mouth: a cigarette, a toothpick, a segment of plastic
straw. He had a younger brother named Toby who had flunked two
grades, and was the oldest kid in their school, an aggressive little thug
who strutted the halls like Godzilla.

These two easily dominated the other six. "Who the fuck can say?
Karate assholes might think they can kick their way out of this, but
it's gonna be a nasty surprise."

Torque spit, pulled a slender stick out of his pocket, inserted it in
his mouth, and twirled it.

Flanagan shrugged the shoulders of his windbreaker, and held a palm up, satisfied that the rain seemed to have decreased. "Fire that up," he said. There was a brief, bright flare of flame, extinguished by a gust of wind. Then a second flare, and the sweet stink of smoke rising up through the air, detectable even twenty feet away.

Laughter. "Assholes got good weed, though."

More nasty chuckles followed that.

Patrick rolled over to his left. Frankie had the Sony trained down through the grill. "Are you getting this?" Patrick said in a dead whisper.

"Every word," Frankie said. "Do you think we might be able to enter this in some kind of contest? *America's Sickest Home Videos*?"

Patrick silently mouthed the words *shut up,* then said in a voice softer than a whisper, "Do you want them to hear you?"

As if in answer to them, down below, Torque inhaled deeply, and then looked around. "Did you hear that?"

"What?" Flanagan said.

"I thought I heard a voice. . . ."

Up on the bridge the kids froze, terrified, and ready to flee. Suddenly, there were voices. A dozen voices.

Flanagan flexed his shoulders. "This is it," he said confidently. "Finally forced those pansies out."

Almost on cue, the rain picked up again, harder and colder now.

One of the others nodded his head enthusiastically. "Gonna stomp the shit out of . . ." He focused his eyes on the figures emerging from the shadows, heading down the side of the embankment from Allan Street. "Those hippies," he said, and there was something almost like reverence in his voice as he finished the words, something that was in terrible contrast to the expression on his face, which suddenly seemed very like a little boy's.

Emerging from the rain, a dozen strong, came the men of the Saddle Shop. The smallest of them dwarfed Flanagan and his crew, made them look frail and utterly vulnerable.

There was a long moment in which the two groups stared at each other, and no words were spoken. Then Flanagan said what all of them had to be thinking. His voice was high and wavering, and filled with terror and loathing. "Shit, man. It ain't the hippies—it's the faggots!"

Even atop the bridge, Patrick imagined he could hear Torque swallow. "Now, hey," he said lamely. "We ain't got no beef with you—"

Brando smiled like a butcher eyeing his favorite turkey on Thanksgiving eve. "We got one with you. Which one of you uncle fuckers threw this?"

He heaved the brick at them. If Torque hadn't slipped to the side it would have smashed his nose through the back of his head. It winged past his shoulder, landing in the mud just behind him.

Torque's expression was almost farcically alarmed, the face of a comic drunkard who has stumbled into his own open grave. "Man, listen, we didn't . . . this ain't got nothing to do with—"

He didn't have time to say anything else, and no other speech was needed. Brando slid in a long step, and a great gristly knot of a fist slammed into Torque's face. It made a sound like a mallet striking a side of beef.

Torque went down hard, and the fight, such as it was, was on.

There was swearing, and thrashing, and the shadows melded there in the wet beneath the bridge. Flanagan's men formed a square, stood shoulder to shoulder and back to back as the Saddle Shop boys descended on them. The battle, if one-sided, was not without its small heroisms.

None of that made any difference in the end.

Atop the bridge, Patrick watched, his eyes wide. Frankie taped. There was little sound but the distant traffic, and the grunts and sounds of exertion below. Chains flashed, and once, a switchblade knife gleamed. A crack as the knife-wielder's arm was broken with a length of aluminum pipe. Someone went down, and mud splashed.

But there were no gunshots, and for a very long time, no cries for mercy.

No one ran. To their credit, the bikers stood like brothers during the entire debacle.

It was entertaining at first, and Patrick found himself cheering silently, having the time of his life. Happy that Frankie was taping this. It was the caper to end all capers. . . .

And then the horror began.

18

Patrick managed to get all the way back to the trailer park without being seen. He had stopped three times along the way. The muscles of his diaphragm still ached with the violence of his retching.

He was very, very careful to go in the back way. On this night, more than any other in his young life, he didn't want to be seen by Cappy or any of his people. Hell, no. *Please, God, no.*

He walked his bike the last hundred yards to the dark, wet, quiet place that was his home, a greater and colder darkness alive and gnawing inside him. He had to stop twice and steady himself, but didn't dare to close his eyes. Every time he closed them, the same images spooled out behind them. He couldn't tolerate that. Even if he had to prop his eyes open with toothpicks, he couldn't see even one of those images, ever again.

Luckily the goat in the next yard didn't make a sound as he pulled in. His bedroom's side window was unhooked. He scrabbled over the sill and into his room without making a sound. He dumped his wet clothes in a corner and crawled into bed.

Patrick stared into the ceiling. In the back bedroom he heard his mother's breathing. What he wanted more than anything in the world was to just go in there, climb in bed with her, tell her the things that he had seen and heard, and beg her to make it all better for him.

Without really realizing that he had done it, Patrick curled into a knot, his thumb slipping into his mouth. He stared into the wall, into the darkness, and when he did, the images from the bridge came back to him. . . .

The night went colder after the sounds of fighting died down. With hands that trembled, Patrick reached out for Frankie's camera, and used the zoom to focus on the shadows below.

Distantly, a steam whistle blew. Everything seemed as far off as a cloud in a fever dream, including the few cars crossing the bridge, belching fumes across the pedestrian wall.

The bikers were done, finished. Surely now the men from the Saddle Shop would walk away, laughing. Surely.

The wind quieted so that they could actually hear what was happening below. It had stopped being funny some time ago.

A whisper of a voice. "Tough assholes when you're beating the hell out of some harmless hippies, or some femmie little high school kids."

"What kids? I don't know anything about—"

"Lying motherfucker. Thought you'd move up the food chain?"

"Sorry," Torque wheezed. "I'm so damned sorry." He held himself as if his ribs were broken. Patrick had seen the kicks and blows, and didn't doubt it for a minute.

"Damn right." Brando chuckled. And the man next to him wiped blood and rain from his face, and shared the dark humor. They scanned the empty office buildings to either side, as if checking to see that they were utterly alone.

"Please," Flanagan coughed wetly. "Just leave us alone."

Brando said the next sentence as the wind picked up again, drowning him out. But they heard the first ten words as he began to unbuckle his belt. "I'm afraid this is going to be a long night."

Patrick lay in his bed, afraid to close his eyes. Too tired to leave them open. Somewhere out in the night, by the bridge, he had lost something terribly important.

And for the first time in years, he prayed, prayed that God would forgive him for his part in the evening's events. But even as he prayed, there was another part of him, a part that was deeper than his conscious sense of self that said:

You did it.

And was glad.

19

LOS ANGELES,
SUNDAY, MAY 20

Renny Sand entered his apartment in an unusually buoyant mood. He just about danced into the bedroom to change into sweatpants and jogging shoes.

In the corner of his bedroom was a ProForm treadmill, a recent acquisition and the current savior of his soul.

He jumped on it, set it for a medium level thirty-minute program, and began to run, letting it take him through a series of fast-slows and changes of incline. He imagined himself running along a country road, say, in Washington. . . .

Now he was beginning to sweat, and once he started, he wasn't the kind to do things halfway. Sand shadowboxed, bouncing on the whirring belt, pretending that he was going twelve rounds with Sugar Ray Leonard.

Then the phone rang. He got off the treadmill and answered it, the sweat beading and dripping down his face.

Blowing hard, he said: "Yeah?"

"Renny? It's me."

Muriel's voice was instantly recognizable. He grinned, wiping his face. "Muriel! Great! I was waiting to hear from you. Listen, I've had more thoughts about that article."

"Renny . . ."

"Listen," he went on, not really hearing her. "I'd like to tie it in to a nationwide angst thing, a search for answers in the continuing debate about health care, and child care in particular. You know, that the mothers were projecting their own guilt at not being with their children during the day. I bet we could get a quote from Dr. Laura!"

"Renny, listen to me," she said firmly. "The article isn't going to happen."

There was a long, painful beat, a moment in which he was uncertain if his ears were working right.

"What?"

"We're not going with it, Renny." He heard her this time. There was no mistaking it at all. His mind spun. "But I've got . . . I can do this . . ."

Muriel was unmoved. "We need you on the other piece, Renny."

He sat down hard on the bed, holding his head in his hands. He felt as if someone had clawed out his stomach. It was only at this moment that he really *got* how many of his hopes had lain squarely in this one chance, this one idea. Such a slender thread it seemed now. . . .

"God, Muriel . . ."

"It's a good story, Renny." She said it with a kind of bland, medicinal kindness.

Despite that, he saw her saying it while filing her nails, with a smirk, as if she knew, and knew that *he* knew, that she was hammering the nail in his career's coffin. "She's a hooker," he said numbly. "She's writing a tell-all. That's not news. It's . . ." he searched desperately for a word. "It's Novocain."

She was unmoved. "It's business, Renny."

He held his head in his hands, cradling the phone between ear and shoulder. "What is this really about, Muriel?"

There was no pause at all on her side, nowhere for him to insert an imagined guilty conscience. "You know the answer to that, Renny. We need you on something where we don't have to worry about sources."

Her voice was very steady, surgical. "You do understand my reason for concern."

That headache, the one hammering away at him behind his right ear, became a roaring, angry thing now. Yeah, he understood, but pretended not to. "Is this about us?"

For the first time there was a pause. With a small, dirty satisfaction he wondered if he had hurt her.

When she came back on, the flat strength of her voice told him that he was dead wrong, and that he had said almost precisely the wrong thing. Her words were clipped, professional. "Don't flatter yourself. And don't blow this, Renny. It's a good story. Bring it in."

Then she hung up. He stared at the phone as if it were a snake, and set it back on the cradle gingerly. He squeezed his eyes shut, the sweat drizzling down his face and puddling on the carpet.

Then he screamed, and virtually hurled himself back onto the treadmill, cranking its incline up to ten degrees and its speed up to six miles per hour, running and running until his legs burned and his chest felt as if someone had poured molten lead down his throat. He slipped, almost tripped, and in falling yanked the little red safety key out of its slot. The treadmill sighed, slowed, and then stopped. He staggered off, legs wobbling. The room reeled around him as it always did when he pushed too hard. It was a familiar sensation: running hard and going nowhere.

He wiped his cheeks, uncertain whether the moisture on his hands was tears, or just more goddamned useless sweat.

20

Claremont, Washington,
Monday, May 21

A crush of students streamed through the front doors of the Claremont Middle School. It was a spacious red brick building, which shared a parking lot with the high school only a few hundred yards west. They also shared a stadium, whose bleachers rose intimidatingly high above the field.

Patrick rode his bike up to the front, and parked it. He fastened the lock, and got his books from the basket.

Frankie approached him from the blind side. "Boo!"

Patrick started, and looked like he wanted to punch the boy, who brayed laughter. Despite Frankie's attempt to seem merry, there was something almost glacial behind his eyes. "Jesus. Don't do that, man. What are you so freaking happy about?"

Frankie was bubbling. "We did it, man . . . we did it! You should see the tape. . . ."

Patrick grabbed Frankie and spun him around, slamming him against the wall. Their faces were so close they were almost kissing. "That was the biggest, stupidest mistake anyone ever made. You need to get the hell rid of that damned tape."

Frankie sneered at him. "Who are you kidding? I'm sendin' it to *Hard Copy.*"

They stopped, temporarily ending their conversation as Toby Marcello, Torque's younger brother, walked past. The kid wasn't strutting today. His black hair was an uncombed mop, and his dark blue eyes were bloodshot. His body, usually a solid, threatening monolith, now just seemed heavy. The kid looked as if he hadn't slept or changed his clothes in a month. He pushed brusquely past Frankie and Patrick.

Toby was glancing around, his eyes slightly defocused. He seemed frightened, disoriented. Disheveled.

Frankie had the good sense to wait until Toby had passed to continue his crowing. "Can't you feel it? Everyone knows something happened. No one is talking. I hear that three of the assholes left town last night. Never coming back, man."

Patrick's head pounded. "Will you keep your voice down? This is a nightmare." He pushed Frankie away so hard that the boy stumbled a step. "Leave me alone."

Frankie crowed laughter after him as he ran up the steps.

Patrick tried very hard to study in history class, and to hear what his teacher was saying.

The lecture was on the Civil War period, and on the display table at the front of the class were models and pictures of the relative positions of the different armies during the battle of Gettysburg. The teacher was Mr. Schmeer, a well-intentioned but bland man with a voice that would induce sleep even if he were announcing winning lottery numbers.

"Although the shots at Fort Sumter officially began the bloodiest struggle of American history, in reality the pressure had been building up since before 1776, when both sides realized that a compromise, struck to create a country strong enough to stand against Britain, could not long endure half slave and half free. . . ."

Patrick was listening to the lecture, and noticed as always that every time a teacher said "slave" some of his fellow students looked at him. But neither lecture nor irritation could spare him the terrible images that flashed to mind.

Behind a curtain of black rain, two groups of men fought. Blows were struck, and vengeance reaped.

With a terrible force of will he wrenched himself out of the fantasy and again followed Mr. Schmeer:

"In one battle alone, more Americans died than in all of World War Two. A terrible, terrible reparation for the institution of slavery, a foreshadowing of the terrible price in human freedom and dignity that continues to be fought to this very day."

Patrick heard Schmeer, but saw Torque bent over a trash barrel in the rain beneath the bridge, pleading not for his life, but for his dignity. Perhaps his soul. Patrick clapped his hands to his ears.

God. The screams. The screams.

"Mr. Emory?" Pause. "Mr. Emory, is my lecture that offensive to you?"

Patrick tumbled back into awareness, and saw that the entire class was staring at him. His hands fell away from the sides of his head. "Sorry," he said lamely. "I have a headache. I'll be all right."

Schmeer continued on, but kept a careful eye on Patrick for the rest of the class.

Somehow, the boy managed to drag himself through the rest of fifth period, and dashed out into the hall before Schmeer or any of the students could try to console him.

Destiny Valdez caught up with him in the hallway. "Patrick?" she said. "Patrick? Patrick!" She said his name three times before he heard her.

Desperately, he wrenched himself out of the daydream, and looked at Destiny with haunted eyes.

She looked at him with genuine concern. "Patrick?" The other kids flowed around the two of them, like water parting around a rock. "Patrick?" she said again, and this time Patrick attempted to formulate an answer.

"Mr. Emory?" That voice came from behind him. "Is there something that we should be aware of?" It was Mr. Schmeer, looking not at all regal behind his horn rims.

"No," Patrick said, struggling to snap out of it. "Nothing at all."

But Destiny was watching him, and she looked worried.

At lunchtime the kids sat together, except for Frankie. Frankie sat with the leadership class, which as usual he held in effortless sway with a seemingly endless stream of conversation. They were the beautiful people, with moneyed parents and hefty allowances. They had perfect bodies and faces, the kind whose photos looked great on banners and posters, who could win election to the kind of high-profile offices that meant nothing to anyone but college application evaluation committees.

Frankie could talk circles around any of them, sometimes wrote jokes for their assembly-hall speeches, kept them cracking up at noon. But they knew that a specimen like Frankie could never get elected, and laughed at him behind his back. Frankie, on the other hand, knew that their brief and meaningless tenure as Class President or Treasurer was likely to be the high point of their entire lives, and laughed at them just as hard.

Shermie Sevujian shook his head. "How can he stand it over there? They're just so gay."

Patrick was quiet, watching his friend. If Shermie had been on that bridge Saturday night he would never have used that term again. Never.

Shermie took another couple of bites out of his peanut butter sandwich before he realized Patrick was staring. He stopped chewing. "What? Whatisay?" he said, confused.

Destiny sat right behind Patrick, and probably hadn't taken her eyes off him for two minutes.

"What happened, Patrick?" she said finally. "I know something happened Saturday night. I can feel it, all over the school, but nobody seems to have any idea what it is."

He ate very slowly, as if afraid of choking. His mouth half-filled with food, Patrick said, "You don't want to know."

She stared at him. "What did you do?"

Across the school yard, Frankie turned and looked at them, almost as if he had overheard the conversation. Then slowly as a drowsing basilisk, he turned back to the kids in the leadership class, and continued to hold court.

And with the voice of someone much younger than his years, but eyes as old as God, he told them. Patrick hadn't wanted to or planned to, perhaps, but was helpless to keep his secret inside him. When he was done, they were quiet for almost two full minutes.

"Jesus," Shermie said in frightened and respectful awe. "And you *saw* that?"

"Can't get it out of my head. I don't think I'll ever get it out of my head."

He looked over across the school yard at Frankie, who was laughing up a storm with his friends.

He sighed deeply. "I guess some people can just . . . do things. That need to be done."

Destiny laid a hand on his shoulder. "They hurt people, Patrick. You were trying to set things right."

He tried to find comfort in her words, but instead seemed to be fighting a chill, as if a bit of winter wind had come impossibly early, or late. "I think someone is going to die over this. I just don't know who."

"I wish you were coming to camp with us," Destiny said fervently.

Shermie fidgeted uncomfortably, and wouldn't meet their eyes. He looked around the yard until he saw a clutch of boys heading over to the athletic field. He looked at Patrick without quite meeting his eyes. "Looks like they're getting a soccer game going. I'm in."

The others nodded understanding, and Shermie moved off, leaving Patrick and Destiny alone on the bench.

Patrick looked at the two-story school building, the heap of brick and stone surrounding him, and for a minute, it felt more like a prison yard. "Only a few more weeks," he said wistfully. "And then summer."

"That will be good," Destiny said.

"Will it?" Patrick said. He pushed at a twig with the tip of his toe. "You're going away."

She shrugged. "Two weeks at camp."

"Then a month at your grandmother's, in Utah."

She laid her hand softly over his. It was soft and warm. "It's not so bad."

He turned away from her, and said so softly that the words barely reached: "I'm going to miss you."

Destiny smiled. "I think that's the first time you've ever said that to me."

"I was thinking it," he said. "You feel it, don't you? I'm just all confused. The things I saw under the bridge just made it . . . sharper. I hardly recognize myself right now. And I want to."

Destiny smiled at him more gently. "What would Musashi say?"

He laughed. "Not much help. He wasn't into relationships much. But Marcus used to say that the most important thing in his life was his relationship with his mom. He said she kept him sane."

She nodded. "Is there any chance you could talk to your mother?"

His expression was horrified. "I'm sorry. Stupid question."

For a time they sat, just feeling the air move around them. Then finally he spoke. "Summer dance is coming up. Would you maybe—?"

She shrugged regretfully. "Billy's already asked me, Patrick. You know that."

He turned away from her again, his heart thundering. His face felt like it was on fire. "You gonna go with him forever?"

She looked straight ahead, and for a moment he wondered if she had heard the question, whether in fact he had made a terrible mistake in saying that. Then, almost without moving her lips she said: "Maybe not even all summer."

He turned, and looked at her with hope in his eyes. "Really?"

Destiny stood up. "I've got to go now."

She stole a glance, making sure that Billy wasn't looking, and leaned over to peck Patrick on the cheek. Then she left him there on the bench, by himself.

He saw Frankie with the leadership class, Shermie with his soccer game, Destiny with her tall, lean, pale boyfriend. Patrick sat there alone, the darkest, somberest face on the entire school ground.

21

TUESDAY, MAY 22

Renny Sand parked his Toyota in an underground lot, and took a token from a little attendant, a pale, withered old guy who made Renny wonder if the last three generations of his family had all been raised underground.

The hotel desk called Penelope Costanza's room for him, and if they felt any discomfort with their guest's notoriety, they didn't reveal it. It was just business as usual at the Beverly Palm. He doubted if they really cared whether their guests were radio talk-show hosts, expatriate dictators, or former madams. As long as the bill was paid and no one set fire to the rooms, that was all that concerned them.

Ms. Costanza wasn't actually paying the bills, of course: the deep pockets belonged to her publishers. Her expense account must have been a doozy. The cheapest room in the place, off-season, had to be about three hundred a night, and Tiffany wasn't traveling third-class. Her room was on the fourteenth floor, and as Sand walked across the gold-and-marble-trimmed foyer, he had the distinct impression of being watched, measured, and found wanting.

He approached room 1412, and knocked.

The door was opened by a sloe-eyed creature in a brocaded satin dress slitted almost to her waist. She was Chinese, gorgeous, her eyes as hard as diamonds behind the deferential manner. "Mr. Sand?"

"Yes. And you are?"

"Shan," she said.

"Shan. Is Ms. Costanza in?"

"She is waiting for you." Shan gave the distinct impression of being disappointed that he wasn't late, or rude, or hadn't presented her with some other excuse for a disapproving stare.

The hotel room was late-nineteenth-century simulated to a turn. The outer room was designed as a study. A gold-inlaid Empire clock rested on the mantel, beneath a painting labeled *The Outing,* green trees shading to gold against a foam of clouds, by a painter he didn't recognize named Johann M. Culverhouse. Picnicking and horseback-riding in a pastoral setting, superbly rendered. The walls were covered with gold-mounted paintings, and he suspected that many of them weren't reproductions at all. Chairs, tables, chandelier—all were Neoclassical, still generations removed from Arts Nouveau or Deco, suggesting an elegant echo of an older country with deeper roots.

Through the wall-wide window, Los Angeles was simply breathtaking.

"Walk this way, please," Shan said, perhaps noticing his reluctance to leave the study.

"If I could walk that way, I'd be in the wrong business." She frowned at the old, lame joke, and led him into the master bedroom. She opened the door, entered with him, and closed the door.

The bedroom was just as ornate. The four-poster bed was all hand-carved wood and handmade quilts framing a mattress thick enough to sink the *Titanic*. All of the artificial light was oblique, seeming to seep in from the corners and edges. The rug was a tufted blue-gray rife with garlands of stars and golden feathers. He took a long moment's breath, letting it sink in.

"Mr. Sand?" a husky voice behind him inquired.

He whipped around to face a tiny woman who, Sand swore, hadn't been there when he first entered. Her eyes caught his attention first. They were pure feline, half-lidded, harmless as undetonated land mines. Penelope Costanza was barely five feet tall, molded like a young Elizabeth Taylor, and carried herself as if she were playing Cleopatra. She took tiny gliding steps, almost as if her feet had been bound in her youth. She offered her hand, which was small and pleasantly warm. It took close inspection to verify that this woman was, indeed, in her fifties. She wore a brocaded emerald and silver Chinese robe, and it fit her like a glove.

"Ms. Costanza?" he asked.

"Please. Penelope." Her manner was calculatedly self-deprecatory.

"Penelope, then."

"We haven't much time," she said, and seated herself carefully on the bed. "I hope that you don't mind this venue. It's been a long book tour, and I enjoy transacting my business . . ." she paused, and lowered her lids.

"In the bedroom?" Bizarrely, he found myself himself responding to her, felt his lips growing heavy and clumsy. His face felt hot.

"In my bare feet," she said, delighted with his discomfort. "It reminds me of my childhood."

Right. This was a game, and she had, in some odd way, taken first blood.

She motioned him to sit on a bench at the side of her bed. Shan sat in a straight-backed chair near the door.

"Not much about your childhood in your book, Penelope."

"Right to business are we?" She twinkled at him. "I suppose it's as well. You work for *American Journal,* don't you?"

"No. *Eyeful.*"

"But still Marcus Communications?"

There was something just a little odd about the way she asked that question. Insinuating, but not quite insulting. He wondered at that, but didn't bristle. Yet.

"Do you mind if I set up my tape recorder?"

"I would prefer it. Memory is so . . . flexible."

That task occupied his hands, but his mind was buzzing, wondering if he had merely imagined the odd inflection.

"So. You came to Hollywood in . . . 1957?"

"Yes," she said. "Seeking fame and fortune."

"And made a few small films."

"Yes. *Caltiki the Immortal Monster*—down in Mexico. And a couple of Beach Party films. But I soon discovered I had . . . other talents."

"You seem to have a unique perspective on that." He pulled out his notebook, and quoted from a Xeroxed clipping. "In your book you said: 'I discovered that there was a supply-and-demand vacuum. Intelligent, beautiful, adventurous women without a touch of slutty nature, who could be relied upon to make a good impression in any environment . . .' "

"Yes. I had more knack for making friends than acquiring cinema roles. While disappointing, one makes adjustments in life. Merely by introducing my male and female friends to each other, I generated a very reliable income stream."

"You . . . pimped your friends?"

"No, of course not. I arranged encounters. Adventures. What two adults do behind closed doors . . . on a deserted beach . . . on boats or in cabins . . . that is, of course, up to them."

Right. He skimmed his notes. "Now, for several years you were the . . . *friend* . . ."

"Mistress. I prefer that word." She seemed to be talking to herself. "Master and Mistress. Both are roles of power. Neither role is shameful or tawdry, except for small, shame-filled, tawdry minds."

Somehow, she had caught him off guard again, and he didn't like that feeling at all. "Yes. Of Louis Fillipo, one of the most powerful men in Las Vegas. A mid-level singer—"

"He opened for Sinatra," she sniffed. "That is hardly mid-level."

"Sorry. Who graduated to guest services and then casino management. Sometimes known as 'Louis the Fixer.' "

She laughed delightedly. "Mob Chic, my dear. He just loved to have people wondering how deep his connections went. . . ."

And so it went through the afternoon. Shan fetched fizzy water for Sand as he asked questions, and Penelope laughed her way around him, flirting with salacious revelations, then coquettishly avoiding any names that hadn't already turned up on the police blotter. Anyone who watched *A&E Biography* or read the *Enquirer* could probably guess half of them: the bodybuilder turned box-office giant who was addicted to prostitutes. The faded star of a comedy-suspense television show who turned discreet tricks for five figures a night. The child star turned infomercial queen who was caught in the locker room of a major southern California university's football stadium, giving her all for the team.

He'd pretty much given up getting anything that would be really usable. The entire interview was becoming exactly what he had feared: a puff piece for a whore with a golden contract.

Throughout it all, she teased him, and there was something about the teasing that was not entirely friendly. A couple of additional times she mentioned *American Journal* instead of *Eyeful,* perhaps a jolly reminder of how far he had fallen in life. She also made it clear (indirectly) that there was something about the entire company that was worthy of scorn. That simmering contempt, just beneath the surface of her apparent bonhomie, took him to the brink of distraction. Sand wanted to grab her and shake her.

He was frustrated with the afternoon, with the fact that he was conducting the damned interview in the first place. This wasn't news. This wasn't anything remotely resembling news. And every atom in his body resented the fact that, in all likelihood, this was all he was good for any more.

So when he began to put up his briefcase, and she laid back on the bed and looked at him through those slitted copper eyes, there was a challenge of some kind there that he couldn't afford to think about.

"Well," he said. "I guess that about covers it."

Penelope was lounging on the bed now, watching him very carefully. "Are you sure that there's nothing else you want?"

"This is strictly professional," he said, trying not to let his voice crack.

"Oh, I am. But you're cute, in a kind of severe way. I remember the article you wrote on the Gary Hart scandal."

That startled him. He hoped she wouldn't notice. "You remember that?"

She looked at him like a cat who has recently cleansed her paw of cream. "Charming boy—sex is my business."

For the first time, she seemed to be looking at him directly, and now he realized what had put him off before. She had considered him a useful tool. And she had, for a flickering moment, seemed to be making a veiled sexual offer. Or had she? And if not, then what? And why?

For the first time, he had the sense that he was looking at the real Penelope, and there was something hard, and cruel, and ruthlessly intelligent in there. Something inside him took a deep breath.

"I also remember the article on the cocaine," she said.

It took everything he had not to react. Yes. The cocaine. The mistake of a lifetime. The kind you don't come back from. The kind apparently remembered even by eight-bit hookers in thousand-dollar-a-night hotel suites.

"I'd rather not talk about that."

"That's why you're here, isn't it?" She studied her aqua-blue fingernails. He couldn't believe what he was hearing. What in the hell did she want?

"Excuse me?"

"A writer of your quality. That's why you're interviewing a sixty-year-old madam instead of covering Washington, or Wall Street. Isn't it?"

He stood. "Thank you for your interview. I wish you luck with the book." *Bitch.* He slammed the briefcase lid down, and stood up.

But she had a hold of something. There was something so insinuating in her voice that he couldn't just let it go.

"Have I offended you? I didn't mean to."

Yeah, right.

"I read your piece on Marcus, Reynard Sand," she said.

"You do your homework."

"As it happens, yes. You've written about him several times. You even helped kill a story about him once."

He paused. "And how would you know that?"

"It's my business. It concerned one of three subjects I found of greatest interest."

"Sex, of course. Vegas. And . . . ?"

She drew a little silver box out of the dresser next to the bed. When she flipped it open, he could see the little plastic bag. She looked at him as if hoping he would be shocked. He merely felt tired. "Cocaine, dear boy. Would you like a line?"

"No, thank you. And Marcus?"

She nodded, her eyes holding steady on his. "Yes," she said. "I suppose Marcus is the fourth."

"I guess he fascinated the whole country."

"Brilliant young Harlemite, raised by a single mother, who rises to power, wealth and acclaim? Of course he fascinated us." She spooned out a little pile of white powder. "Do you like what you do?" she asked. Something in the words told him that they were a little closer to the truth, closer to some revelation of what this was all about. "I was frank with you, Renny Sand."

"You are selling a book. This is my life. It's not for public discussion."

"I understand people, Renny Sand," she said. "Especially men. I collected them—the powerful and the poseurs. You are something odd—a lion pretending to be a lamb."

There seemed a shimmering about her, something quiet and deadly. "What is this about?" He knew, could sense, that she cared not a jot for him, or his career, and yet it somehow served them both to act out a charade. Leaving him to ask again, more stridently, if silently: *What the hell is this about?*

"I have something for you. Something that could help you get back on top."

His antennae were up, and he sensed that he had heard the truth, and also a terrible lie. "Why would you want to help me?"

"First, I want the truth about something," she said. "I want to know what happened to you."

Another pause. His mind was reeling. "It's not an accident that I'm here today, is it?"

"No," she said.

"Why me?"

"Tell me," she said again. "What happened to you?"

"Why should I tell you?"

"Because I have something for you, Renny Sand. Pulitzer-nominated investigative reporter who reveres Alexander Marcus, who now spends his days flacking for elderly whores." With a gold-plated razor blade she chopped a dime-sized pile of coke into a fluffy row, and snorted half of it through a silver straw. Then the other half.

"Jesus," he said. "I'm out of here." He headed toward the door. Sand wanted to hit something. He wished that Shan were a man, and that she would try to stop him.

"There are stories I left out of the book, Reynard Sand."

"Don't call me that," he said. But her voice stopped him. His emotions were devolving to total confusion. "That's hard to believe," he said without turning around. "People like you will say anything to get what they want."

"People like *us,* Reynard." Another thin sniffing sound. Then: "Would you say that I am honest, Mr. Sand?"

He wanted to lie, but couldn't. "When it suits you."

"I can help you."

"Why? Why me?"

"Because I want to know the truth. And because I want the truth to be known. And you can give me both. But it must be today, Reynard. It must be now."

He could hear his own heartbeat, and the traffic far below on Sunset Boulevard, but nothing else. "It's that big a story? Isn't it dead by now?"

"Stories like this never die, Mr. Sand."

Hating himself, he turned and came back to his chair.

He gestured toward Shan. "Have her leave."

Penelope Costanza motioned, and the girl disappeared.

He sighed heavily. "I don't know why I'm doing this, but I guess I'm going to do it. I hope you don't mind if I say I don't like you."

She placed one delicate hand over her breast. "You wound me."

"Oh, please. But I can trust you for ten minutes. Quid pro quo?"

She nodded.

Sand crossed and then uncrossed his legs, trying to delay the inevitable. Then he leaned back in the chair, and spoke words that he hadn't breathed to a soul in years. "Let's say there's a reporter for the *L.A. Times,*" he said. "Young guy, during the Reagan administration. He hears Nancy ranting 'Just Say No' until it's coming out of his ears. Then one day he hears that during Vice President Bush's tenure as chief of the CIA, huge amounts of cocaine were smuggled into the United States, and sold to finance covert operations."

"A slush fund."

"Gigantic. Hundreds of millions. He was able to trace the connections down from the top—following the money. And up from the bottom, dealers in Texas and California who had made connection with Contras and black ops men running the whole thing."

"The kind of story that can make a career."

"Or get you killed. So. This young reporter was putting it all together, when his editor, who had given him ten months, came to him saying that *Newsweek* was getting ready to run their own story."

"Time pressure."

"The reporter had two weeks. Two weeks to get it sewn up. To find the missing link that would cement the entire string top to bottom. Because every step had to be validated at least two ways. He didn't have it, but knew of a guy named 'Benny.' "

"Benny."

"Benny Alvarez was a go-between. The reporter knew everything about him, except that he hadn't been able to meet him. And Benny died."

She closed her eyes. "You wrote about that. A drug-related shooting?"

"Yes. So . . . I 'found' an interview with Benny, and printed it. It was my missing link. And the *Times* printed it. Pulitzer nomination. Job offer with Marcus Communications."

"What happened?"

"Funny thing. Benny wasn't actually dead. The worm was actually in witness protection. He read the article, stewed over it for a couple of years, and then threatened to break cover unless I paid him off. Even getting the threat out was enough for his people to find him. And kill him."

"But the damage was done."

"Yes. It couldn't be proven, but everyone knew I'd lied. And everything came unraveled."

"Your career . . . ?"

Renny didn't hear those words the first time she spoke them. Didn't hear them, but *felt* them. His career. Watching everything he'd worked for since college going down in flames, feeling homicidally angry, then suicidally depressed when he realized that he had only himself to blame. He could count on the fingers of one hand the pains that had remained with him throughout his life. His first dog's death. His first heartbreak. The day his father walked out of his life. The day his cancer-ravaged mother stopped recognizing him.

And the week his career crashed and burned.

"Nothing could be proven," he said, his voice a hoarse whisper. "Everyone knew. I was already at Marcus, riding high, and suddenly I was poison. It was a long fall." He paused, feeling the weight of the truth. "So I'm here."

"Interviewing me, instead of the President."

"Yes."

"You stopped talking about that young reporter."

"I guess I did." His hands were shaking. He pulled a cigarette out of his briefcase, and lit it without asking permission. They were just two addicts, having a friendly little chat.

"You don't like me," she said, "but you trust me, don't you?"

"I guess you're right." He exhaled a slender plume. "Anything else?"

"No," she said. "How do you feel now?"

He searched inside himself for the answer, and was surprised when he found it. "Strange. Better."

"As I felt when I had written my little book."

"So." He inhaled again. Strangely, exhaling, he felt more of the weight lift. What he had done was inexcusable, but not beyond comprehension. He'd let anger and fear and competitiveness eat at his judgment, until he ran out of reasons to Just Say No. "So," he said. "It's too much to hope, but what's the story you're dangling in front of me?"

She sipped her tea. "The recorder is off?"

"Yes."

She slid the little box of cocaine out of sight. "You did not hear this from me," she said.

He considered her carefully. This didn't seem like the same woman at all; if he wasn't entirely mistaken, she seemed just a bit fearful. "All right," he said.

"Perhaps thirteen years ago this happened. Things were at their peak. I was supplying girls to Hollywood, and some to Washington, through trusted connections. The girls were run as an escort agency. An up-front fee was paid, the girls would negotiate additional services, and I received a portion of their earnings."

"Pretty much what you described in the book."

"Yes. Remember when I mentioned a girl who became greedy, who used me to make connections and then made dates directly, to deny me my percentage?"

"Yes. You said she left your employ."

"Indeed. I called her Majel. Her real name was Courtney Piper. And the customer was Alexander Marcus."

"Marcus?" Renny had heard rumors about his fondness for prostitutes, so that wasn't surprising. He had the distinct feeling that she hadn't finished yet.

"Yes. December of '88, in San Francisco. I had supplied ladies to Mr. Marcus before. Consistently, they had reported that he was rough, and generous and incredibly virile . . . considering that he had only a single testicle."

"What?"

She grinned at him. "Didn't you know? No, I don't suppose you would. They said he had had reconstructive surgery. He was scarred, as if he had been in some horrible accident."

Jesus.

"I had had problems with Courtney before, knew that she had a pattern of sneaking to see her previous clients, and making money without sharing it."

He felt his mouth pulling into a frown. "So . . . what happened that night?"

"She called in sick—as she had done before. I have a contact who saw her entering a restaurant, a block from the Plaza Hotel, where Marcus was staying. I was ready to fire her the following day."

"And?"

"And she never came in."

"Never?"

"No."

The single syllable hung in the air like a bad smell. He wanted to shuffle papers, or light another cigarette or something. "Did you ever see her again?"

Penelope reached into her drawer, pulled out the little box and prepared another serving of cocaine, chopping and fluffing it before answering. She looked up at him. "Are you sure?" she asked. For a moment he wondered if she meant *are you sure* about that question, but then realized she was asking him if he wanted a snort.

"No, thank you. Did you ever see her again?"

She sniffed deeply, and then wiped tears away from her eyes.

"Yes. Once more. At the morgue, a week later."

"A week."

She daubed again. "She was found in the mountains above Santa Cruz. Her hands were torn with what the coroner called defensive wounds. The police officer said that she was naked, and bruised. Her feet were abraded, as if she had run barefoot across rough terrain. The police thought she had been hunted. I barely recognized her: her face had been *chewed.*"

The bottom fell out of his stomach, and he fought against a sour, ugly taste in the back of his throat. "Chewed?"

She lit a cigarette, and sat, studying him.

"Bitten," she said. "Disfigured."

"By an animal?"

She smiled at him. For the first time he noticed that her teeth were small, perfectly formed, improbably, artificially white. "Human teeth, they said."

His mind was buzzing, but the thoughts were still fluid, had yet to solidify into any conclusions. "What else?"

She snorted the other half of her line. "That is all," she said.

"Did you tell the police?"

"No," she said. "It was months later that I heard the story of the restaurant. And who would believe it?"

Who, indeed. "That's it?"

She said nothing.

"What exactly are you saying?" His voice had a quaver in it that he didn't like at all.

"For forty years, I made my living reading people, as I read you. I met this man once, shook his hand, watched his eyes as they roamed my body, heard his voice without electronic filtering." She leaned forward. "I *felt* him, Renny Sand. And I tell you that what he loved most in the world was not sex. Not money. Not anything but power—and there is no greater power than that of life and death. Of knowing that there are no rules." Her words were simple, and unadorned, and spoken with absolute conviction. Sand found himself drawn in by them, to them, and had to remind himself that conviction didn't mean accuracy.

"That's crazy."

"Yes," she replied. "Isn't it? But I give it to you. It is now yours."

"This is nothing," he said. To his disgust, Renny realized that even as he said it, he was busy figuring angles.

She watched him shrewdly, and he realized that in a game of poker, this woman would have already won his underwear and pink slip. She had known a hundred of him. Sand didn't have the slightest idea who she really was.

"You don't believe that," she said. "You are not sure what it is, but you do not believe that."

He stood. If nothing else, he had to get away from her damned self-confident smirk, the obscene implication of her words. "If that's all you have to say, I'm out of here."

"Mr. Sand?"

He wanted to hit her, and wasn't entirely certain where the anger came from. "What now, damn it?"

"You believe I tell the truth?"

"I believe that you think you're telling the truth."

"That is enough, for now. You will look into it." Annoyingly, it wasn't a question.

He slammed the briefcase closed again, and without a backward glance, left the room. On the way out, Shan opened the door to the hall.

"How much of that shit does she put up her nose every day?" He wanted to hear a brain-killing answer.

Like her mistress, Shan was way ahead of him. "Not enough to cloud her mind," she said.

22

CLAREMONT,
THURSDAY, MAY 24

Cappy Swenson and "Toad" Wilcox hadn't slept in three days. For Cappy, the world was beginning to fill with sticky strands of pink spider silk. He could barely see them, but could feel them when he waved his hands, or stalked in increasing frenzy from room to room. They brushed against his face and hands, were easier to see in darkness than in light. When he lumbered into the kitchen to run his face under the tap, he walked through walls of the stuff. When he stumbled back out into the living room to snort another short, thin fluffy line of crystal meth, the spiderwebs got into his eyes, his mouth. Another line, and the world went white for a moment: no trouble, no spiderwebs, nothing but pure adrenaline as his synapses fried.

Ellie Krup had been up for thirty-six hours. It had been a party at first, but now she was yapping at him, screwing up his ability to think, and he needed to think. He paced, and ranted, and slammed his fist sideways against the trailer's paneling, shaking the entire house. He had pushed her twice, and slapped her once, and she just kept yapping. He was going to settle her down harder pretty damned soon, if she didn't get out of his face.

He made another line disappear up his nose, whipped his head back as the first sour tingles hit, and heard her say: "You've got to slow down on that shit, Cap. . . ."

Like the bitch wasn't first in line for his leavings. He glared at her, a red haze boiling at the corners of his vision. He itched, dammit. His joints felt swollen and loose at the same time. Ellie looked like shit. Her eyes were squiggled red as a plate of marinara. She shrank back, and he turned back to his favorite topic. "I bet the fucking Canadians set this shit up. Canucks control the border, think they can flood us with their cheap shit. What do you think?"

Ellie grimaced. "Cap, I dunno. I really don't."

Howie "Toad" Wilcox leaned in and snorted one of the remaining lines. Wilcox looked just like his nickname: short, thick body, long legs, squat hairless face. Toad had been Cappy's closest friend for ten years. They'd celled together down in California, at Tehachapi State, then ridden cross-country for years before falling into this gig in Hicksville, Washington. "I say we kill those fucking bastards."

Cappy glared at him. "The faggots?"

"Hell, yes!" Toad said. "Who else?"

Cappy stopped still, gaze defocused as if searching deep inside himself for the answers. There was wisdom in there, a regular fucking font of it. "Give it time," he growled. "All things in time. First, we find out what the fuck is going *on* in this town. We've got enemies."

"Fuckin' A," Toad said.

Cappy sat on one corner of the living room couch. It groaned and sagged beneath his bulk. The pieces were coming together in his head now. Yeah. He could feel it. "And they're getting together, moving against us. They want a fucking war, that's what they'll have."

"Cap, honey . . ." Ellie said.

That was the last straw. As she moved toward him he backhanded her savagely. Her head whipped back, and she stumble-flew back against the wall, stunning herself, and slid down, too dazed to move. Blood trickled from her nose.

Cappy looked at her dully, appreciating the precision of the blow, then spooned another line out, and sniffed, trying to clear his head.

"This shit is just too fucking good," Toad said.

"Cap," Ellie pleaded.

Cappy looked at her incuriously. She seemed kind of funny, crouched there with the blood oozing over her lips. "You want a fresh one?"

She shook her head frantically and cowered back. She said nothing for the next two hours, just watched as Cappy and Toad snorted, and planned, and the night stretched cold dark fingers toward morning.

23

SATURDAY, MAY 26

Lee was the last one to join their circle, and Patrick had the feeling that he had barely convinced himself to come at all. The boy was pushing his bicycle up the path to the meeting spot long after Destiny had already called them to order.

They spoke of business, of the health of the web page, and the lawn-mowing venture. For almost a half hour, Lee looked at them, as if he was about to explode, and then said: "All right. All right. What happened? I know you guys are holding back on me. You've got to tell me what happened." His eyes were wild. Without knowing, he already knew too much, and it was nearly killing him.

Hermie, Destiny and Patrick looked at each other. There had been an agreement not to let the secret out any further. This was the kind of secret that got people killed, and for Lee to be burdened with it as well . . .

But it was the thing that everyone knew and no one discussed, and it was killing their friendship. So Patrick told the story again, as simply and directly as he could. The air seemed to grow chill as he did, and Lee just stared at them, his mouth working without words emerging. Then when Patrick finished he just said: "Good Christ. Oh shit. Oh, man, guys—this is bad. This is the worst thing I've ever heard in my life." He stood up, and wouldn't look at them, pacing back and forth, seething with nervous energy.

Then he looked at them, and shook his head. "I can't be a part of this, man. This is just too much." And he got back on his bike. "I'll call you guys in a few days. I need to chill out. Oh, man." And he bumped his bike down the wooded path, and away.

Patrick looked at Destiny and Shermie. "You guys?"

"He's right," Shermie said. "It's the worst thing I've ever heard." He paused, looking at the ground, shaking his head. "But I'm with you, bro."

Destiny nodded.

Patrick stood up. "Well, I guess there isn't a whole lot more to talk about right now. Let's call it. We'll . . . we can talk in school next week, all right?"

Shermie waved his hand. "You guys go ahead. I need to kick it a bit. Just chill and think."

Destiny pulled Patrick away, kept him from hovering over his brooding friend. They steered their bikes down the path, sharing discipline and focus in a cocoon of silence. He let her get a little ahead of him, and watched her. The sun and shadow played on her, filtering down from the trees like green netting.

They turned right onto River View Road, rolling into the bike lane. She slowed so that he could catch up—

And then the world went crazy.

From two different side roads, first four, then six motorcycles appeared. To Patrick on his little bike, the choppers seemed impossibly gigantic, the gargoyles squatting upon them mythically imposing in black leathers.

With a single glance, Patrick was absolutely certain that one of them was Cappy. The bikes thundered down from the hillside, appearing almost out of nowhere, and went into idle, coasting, almost walking along as the riders examined Patrick and Destiny.

They were hemmed in by the wall of flesh and steel. Five men, one woman. The woman was Ellie Krup, and she was larger than half the men. Her wind-whipped hair was a dull blond, her square jaw almost hidden by her collar. She wore no leathers, and her upper arms were massive, her knuckles creased with ground-in dirt.

They glanced at the kids, and one of the bikes swerved over a bit as it popped out of idle, so close that Destiny gasped.

Destiny's face was strained and ashen.

"Let's just stop." Patrick was praying to himself: *Please God, don't let them know. Please, Jesus—*

Before they could begin to slow, one of the choppers swooped up behind them, bumping their rear tires with its massive chrome fender.

Trembling now, Patrick looked up at the face beneath one of the helmets, the bearded face, the surprisingly clean and white teeth clenching a thin black cigar. The fleshy lips turned up in a jolly Santa smile.

In that instant Patrick saw the metal guard rail just around the curve. As clearly as an image on the Imax screen where he'd seen *Fantasia,* he saw himself and Destiny crowded closer and closer to the barrier, saw the "accidental" twitch of one of the choppers, saw their fragile little ten-speeds careening sideways and smashing into the barrier. Broken limbs at the best. The worst, they could bounce back out into traffic, and the next truck around the curve would plough them like a tractor.

He reached an arm out for Destiny. "Stop," he said, his voice suddenly fierce.

Destiny's eyes were wild. "But they'll hurt us."

"If they do, they do. But don't let them make it look like an accident."

Cappy's chopper brushed them, almost jolting them off their bikes, bouncing them forward. Patrick wanted to jump off his bike and run, but knew that to vault the waist-high barrier and run up into the woods would be even more perilous. Whatever Cappy intended, they couldn't eliminate the threat just by walking or running away from it.

For a seeming eternity the tableau was unchanged, and then they heard another sound, rumbling up the highway behind them.

It was a flatbed logging truck, stacked with immense, freshly-felled logs, chained in a pyramid. It roared up behind them heading for the Allan Street turnoff for the I-5 freeway, heading down to Portland and the docks. Its horn sounded like Gabriel's trumpet. Cappy looked around, and then back at Patrick and Destiny, and he made a gun of his thumb and forefinger, and slowly, deliberately dropped the hammer.

Cappy made another, broader motion of his massive arm, and the cycles gunned their engines. With a cloud of smoke, they swerved around the kids, and headed south down the road.

Patrick was breathing in shallow little bursts. Destiny's eyes were wide, her cheeks streaked with tears. She looked at Patrick, blinked once, hard, and said in a small voice, "God, Patrick. What have you done?"

24

S on of a bitch!" Otis Emory whispered, voice so deadly quiet that Patrick wanted to hide. His father's face was so distorted by rage and an almost palpably murderous intent that he seemed like a raving madman viewed through a funhouse mirror.

He knew that he had made a terrible mistake in giving his mother even the slightest hint of the incident on River View Road. He should have lied about his shaking hands, the wildness in his eyes, the nightmare of chrome and rubber that had ejected him shrieking from his sleep.

He understood Cappy's madness. At least, he thought he did. The bridge. That horrible night under the bridge was taking Cappy's organization apart, and the man was going crazy. Or was there something more? Something that connected Cappy's enterprise with Patrick and Destiny?

Like for instance the location of the club . . . ?

Vivian stood in their trailer's doorway, blocking it with her slender body. Otis tried to force his way outside, but so far she had refused to yield. His huge fists were knotted, forearms swollen until they threatened to burst his sleeves. "Goddamn it, Vivian," he said quietly. "Get out of my way."

Patrick tried to think, but couldn't. It was as if a huge smoky cloud of blood and ink was blotting out the words in his head. He clung to his father's massive right leg. "Daddy, no. Don't do this—"

Vivian's face was pale with fear and concern. "Otis, I don't want you going over there, starting something."

"That bastard tried to kill my boy!"

"We don't know that," she said. "We could call the police."

"Fuck the police. They *own* the police. There's something that I can sure as goddamn hell do. I can march over there and drag his hairy fucking ass out of that trailer . . ."

Desperately, Vivian said the obvious: "You're drunk!"

"Daddy—that's why I didn't tell you." Patrick babbled the words out, in a complete lather now. "I was wrong. I was probably wrong. I was just scared, you know? Just scared, and upset and mad." He was watching himself talk, watching himself fall apart, couldn't stop or slow the descent from logic into pure raving emotion. "Daddy, don't do this." His voice was a six-year-old's.

Otis wasn't listening. The anger and pain built up inside him, a yammering cacophony of voices that finally drowned out restraint, clouded his vision with violent need. No longer seeing or hearing Vivian, he placed one massive hand on her waist, and pried her out of the doorway. Not daring to meet her eyes, he squeezed past and onto the porch.

From across the way, he could just barely see Cappy's trailer. There was no roaring party over there tonight. In fact, there had been no parties for more than a week. *Something* had happened, something that was whispered about and hinted at, but that no one had dared speak aloud. He knew that some of the bums that usually hung around Cappy's place were no longer there. Fewer bikes. At work, Cappy had been barely contained, his eyes reddened, as if he was sampling too much of his own supply—or as if he was murderously angry about something. Something.

Cappy examined every passing face compulsively, searching for something. Guilt? Knowledge? He didn't know, but he knew that the thug had braced at least half a dozen men, had lumped three of them up. No one was talking, or no one knew why at least three regulars had just left town. Just picked up and vamoosed. He knew that. There was no explanation, but there were, once again, rumors. Something about the Allan Street bridge. But he didn't know, or care.

He only knew that something had almost happened to his boy, his only child, and that was more than he could tolerate.

Otis started down the steps.

Patrick screamed it: "Daddy, no!"

Otis felt like his ears were filled with cotton. He seemed to be viewing the world in slow motion, and through a red filter. His lips felt numb and clumsy as he said, "Watch an' see how it's done, boy." He descended another step.

Patrick still held his leg in a death grip. Otis hadn't even noticed. The big man pried his son away gently, careful not to hurt his fingers, and set him on the porch. Desperate now, Patrick pulled at his mother's arm. "Mom," he said. "Stop him."

For a moment, Patrick's voice shook off that childish cant; it was dead calm now. That change seemed to snap Vivian out of her trance. He managed to catch her eyes, and hold them. "You're the only one who can, and you know it."

There was something in Patrick's eyes that was older and calmer than God. She shook her head sharply, then ran down and around to confront her estranged husband.

"Otis!" She slapped him stingingly across the face. He whipped his head toward her, raising his clenched fist as if about to strike back.

"Otis Cawthone Emory," she said. "I swear to God if you go over there, and start anything, anything at all, I will never let you in my home again."

He looked past her, toward the trailer, and a thin sound escaped his lips, something that was almost a whine, a desperate, animal yearning, to vent his rage and frustration physically.

His eyes refused to focus on her, but they flickered a bit, as if some deep part of him, a part too small to halt or deflect the emotional avalanche, had heard.

She went on, her voice dropping to a hoarse, fierce whisper. "Never, Otis. You will never lie in my bed again. I promise you."

Now he looked at her, his desperation even more starkly vulnerable. "You not takin' anything away from me, Vivian. I already lost everything I love. Pret' near. I lost you. But I still got my boy. Can't let 'em hurt my boy."

She came closer to him. Placed her hands on either side of his face.

"We're still your family, Otis." Her face was tense, but her voice was calm and strong. "You haven't lost us yet."

"I haven't?"

Her eyes flickered away from him to Patrick, who stood on the porch. He seemed so small and weak. Frightened. Her eyes locked with Otis's.

"No. Not yet." She pressed her lips against his, very gently.

From deep within his chest came a mewling sound, something he didn't recognize.

"Come back inside with me," Vivian whispered.

"Inside?"

She kissed him again. He backed away from her, almost disbelieving. Her fingers circled his fisted hands, smoothed them open, guided one of his broad hands to the warm swell of her hips. His expression was that of a little boy offered a sweet he knows he does not deserve: suspicion, hope, longing.

She nodded gently, and took his hand, and led him like a trained bear back into the trailer. Past Patrick, who watched her with shining, worshipful eyes.

25

Patrick rolled off his mattress silently. Without the aid of external lights, he felt his way through a maze of books, magazines and model cartons, to his swivel-bottomed computer chair. He touched the space bar to get a live screen, and logged onto AOL.

A few keystrokes took him to the kids' chat room. There he scanned a list of subjects: Baseball, Music, Education, Dating and Miscellaneous. Cruised miscellaneous and scanned down a list until he came to an odd one: Musashi.

He relaxed a little, more than he had in the previous three hours, hearkening to the moment when he wondered if his father was going to die. Four years ago he had received an Instant Message on AOL inviting him to check out the Musashi room. Out of curiosity, he checked it out, and was instantly addicted. The nine principles of Japan's greatest warrior were its bylaws. He no longer remembered where he had first heard the Nine, but they now seemed to be engraved upon his heart.

Do not think dishonestly.
The Way is in Training.
Become acquainted with every art.
Know the Ways of all professions.
Distinguish between gain and loss in worldly matters.
Develop intuitive judgment and understanding for everything.
Perceive those things that cannot be seen.
Pay attention even to little things.
Do nothing that is of no use.

He loved those rules. Tried to live by them. Read every version of the *Book of Five Rings* he could find, from Clavell to Kaufman. One day, he would study sword, would really understand what those words meant, and where they might lead you. Some of Japan's greatest businessmen and warriors had, as had many Americans, including his personal hero, Alexander Marcus. Marcus had started with nothing, with less than Patrick had, and built himself an empire.

Ever since the day a fourth grade social studies teacher had read Marcus's life story to her class, he had known this man would be his role model. Had searched out and read everything he could on this great man.

Musashi Miyamoto. Alexander Marcus. Great men. Great examples.

In the Musashi Chat he had found kindred spirits. Claremont, Washington might well be the very definition of lame, but there was a big world out there, filled with brothers and sisters, a family he had never met.

There were three people signed on to Musashi at the moment: Ronin3, Hamlet007 and Virgo. Patrick's name was Marcus9.

Patrick spoke aloud as he typed. "Hi, guys. What's up?"

A chatter named Blckbelt signed in and answered. *I'm up for testing next Saturday.*

"Still into the gay kwon do?"

Manners . . . Ronin3 typed.

Yeah, Blckbelt said. *Or I'll kick your butt right through the screen.*

Virgo got into the discussion. *How r you, Marcus?*

He paused. What did he want to say? In some ways, it was as easy to talk to these guys as it was to Shermie and Destiny and Frankie. Virgo was in Mississippi. Ronin3 was in South Dakota. Patrick had family he'd never met. "Things are kind of weird here."

What kind of weird? Virgo asked.

"My mom and dad are back together, but not really. It's confusing."

Ronin3 typed, *Perceive those things that cannot be seen.*

Hamlet007 had been lurking, but now jumped in. *Pay attention even to little things.*

Patrick brightened a bit. That name was familiar. Only one person he knew would label himself after a brooding, half-crazed Danish prince and a British agent. "Hey, Frankie."

Don't call me that. Hamlet's the name.

"I'm the one who's screwed up today," Patrick typed. Little knots of tension floated away, just by tapping the keys.

How so? Ronin3 asked.

"I don't know what I want. It's good to have Dad back, but I don't think it's good for Mom. I know what I want, and I think it's not good for her. This sucks."

A lurker named Barnum675 jumped in. *Keep busy, tiger. What's up with the projects?*

"Everyone here is on-line—we mostly spend spare time distributing flyers and marketing for the local businesses." Thinking about business helped to take his mind from his personal problems.

Good deal, Ronin3 said. *I like to try to get other kids working for me, so I can sit on my butt more often.*

Tom Sawyer, Blckbelt said.

Yeah, answered Ronin3. *But I've never been able to figure out how to get people to pay ME to do my work.*

And at that Patrick managed to laugh. It was forced at first, and then, although quiet, grew deeper and more healing. He hunched over the keyboard, and lost himself in the community of friends he had never met.

But somehow, he sensed, he *would.*

26

Shadows filled Vivian's room. Otis was heavily asleep in the bed next to her. For two minutes she listened to him snore and then slid out of bed, and into her nightgown. She slipped into the bathroom, and closed the door behind her. She looked into the mirror at her smudged, puffy face, staring as if trying to see the girl that she used to be. Then she began to cry.

She dried her tears and listened carefully to a tap-tap sound, put her ear against the wall, and smiled faintly. She left her bedroom and walked down the short hall to Patrick's room. She could hear him giggle.

And in spite of the pain she felt, she managed to smile.

Patrick was bent over the keyboard, tapping away. His bedroom door opened, and he was too lost in cyberspace to pay any notice.

He was talking with someone named Kipper6.

I found this jammin' book on co-op ventures. Finding people who have a customer list that matches yours, but is in a kinda different area?

"How so?"

Like if you do car detailing, and there's a car wash that keeps a list of their regular customers. That kind of thing.

"Cool! 'Know the ways of all professions.' I—"

He looked around, and saw his mother in the door.

"What exactly are you doing?" Vivian asked.

Patrick hit a button on his machine, and it shut down.

He turned to her. "Just having a little trouble sleeping," he said.

Vivian nodded. "Me, too. Your chat room friends?"

"Yeah."

"Some of them are east coast? It must be three o'clock!"

He smiled sheepishly. "Some of 'em are in Europe, I think."

She shook her head in disbelief. "Well, you've still got a few inches left to grow. You need your sleep."

He flexed his right arm, making a muscle. Or trying to. "Nope, doing fine."

"Sleep, young man. Hop into bed, and we'll just forget that this happened for now."

Relieved not to be punished, Patrick made no protest, just followed her orders. Vivian kissed his forehead, and then turned out the lights and left the room.

Patrick lay in the dark and looked at the computer, its screen giving off a soft green phosphorescence in the darkness. He longed to sneak back up and rejoin the chat room for just a few minutes, but instead murmured to himself, like a catechism: *"Do not think dishonestly."*

Then he yawned deeply, suddenly feeling the fatigue, and slid more deeply beneath the covers, closing his eyes.

27

Vivian sat in the living room, staring at her computer screen. She had a separate e-mail folder set up for her correspondences with Renny Sand. Her finger touched the button on her mouse, and she dragged the entire folder over to the trash bin, and dropped it.

Then she lowered her head, and began to cry. Who was she kidding? She was trapped, trapped by a life that had once seemed so full and promising.

An hour ago she had made love a lie in her soft, wide bed. She might never sleep there again without remembering what she had done.

But Patrick's eyes . . .

What was true? What was the lie? She didn't feel dirty, or used. She just felt lost.

In the last weeks she had received several notes from Renny Sand, mostly just updates on his career. The longest had been three hundred words of pure disappointment when an anticipated assignment fell through. She remembered feeling sorry for the disappointment, but glad that he had chosen to share his feelings with her.

Then, just days ago, an odd mixture of excitement and anger blossomed in his careful, polite notes. Something that had happened during his most recent interview that made him reach out to her as a friend.

. . . and when this woman mentioned Marcus, and told me things she thought would shock me, she was right. I was surprised how deep it went. Sure, there'd been hints in the media about his predilection for prostitutes, but I just didn't need to go there. I

**have few enough heroes any more. It got worse than that, but it
wouldn't be right to go into it right now. . . .**

Alexander Marcus. Most of the world knew that name—Patrick had
done a project on Marcus for his American History class, and had a
picture of him on his wall. He had quoted the man, but then so had
news commentators. Marcus was black, wealthy, and had been raised
in poverty by a single mother. Easy to see why Patrick would look up
to him.

But Renny's mention of Marcus seemed strange. Another hero-
worship thing? It seemed an odd way to reach out, but even so, she
took a bit of comfort from it. She wondered what the "worse" might
be, and figured that if it was really important, it would end up on *60
Minutes* one night. Whatever it was, she just prayed it wouldn't hurt
Patrick.

But that was all foreground. In the background, flowing smoothly
as a river, was communication. She and Renny had begun to share
thoughts. She spoke of her shop, he of his job. Small hopes and
dreams. Likes and dislikes.

She never opened one of his notes without a tingling sensation
bouncing between her heart and her tailbone, and she instinctively
knew that the same was true for Renny.

Like it or not, distant or not, strange or not—they had a relationship.
Something was budding.

A bubble of hysteria broke the artificial surface of her calm. *What
would Musashi say?*

Where had *that* come from? Oh, God, Patrick and his *Book of Five
Rings.* He said that he'd learned about it in one of Marcus's biographies, which listed it as the great man's favorite book. When Patrick
finally bought a copy at Barnes and Noble, he had read the entire book
in one sitting, and then looked at her mystified, as if it contained the
hidden secrets of the universe. He had turned to her and asked: *Did
you ever read this book to me? Maybe when I was a baby?*

A book on killing people with four-foot razor blades? Hardly.

He scratched his head. *Weird, Mom, it's like I already know this
stuff.*

She had read it, and found it mostly impenetrable, but when she
began to apply it to sewing, some of it made sense. *Know the Ways
of all arts. Know the Ways of all professions.*

Studying other art forms—pottery and painting, macramé and

sculpture, did give her ideas for her own work. Costuming was three-dimensional art. Wearable art. Studying drama, and the art of the stage, told her even more. And magic—the art of illusion. So Musashi, the ancient sword-killer, had touched a basic principle that held true even about something apparently as far removed as sewing.

Somehow, it was calming to her to think about this. *Do nothing that is of no use.*

She was chewing her guts out because she had slept with her husband to save his life. Because she was being "unfaithful," in some inexplicable way, to a man whom she had only met once, seven years ago, for three minutes. It was absurd, and seen through that lens, she found it within herself to laugh, quietly.

Damn, life was so strange.

Thank you, Musashi. And Alexander Marcus, for bringing him into my son's life.

She clicked the mouse again, opened the trash can icon, and dragged the letter file back out. What the hell. Even if the entire relationship was nothing but a fantasy, she was in the business of fantasy, wasn't she?

Everyone needs a little fantasy from time to time. She just needed a little more of it now, that was all. *The whole damned town is going sour,* she thought, *especially for the children.* She wasn't the only one who felt that way, but most people traced the problem back to the preschool trial. She knew better, and so did Patrick's friends, and their parents.

The problem started earlier, had begun with sun and sand, and ended with tragedy. . . .

28

I *t was a day in early October of 1994.* For the older kids, school had already begun, and the weather had begun to break, gray skies crowding out the sunshine in the way it always did. Summer had been beautiful, so lovely that between late May and September, it had been possible to forget the bleakness of winter.

The gorgeous summers were one of the factors keeping her in the Northwest, even after discovering that her skills with needle and thread might be sold more dearly in Los Angeles or at least San Francisco.

She and Otis had actually spent a month in southern California, staying with cousins while Otis interviewed for work. As wonderful as she thought the city was (the nightlife along Sunset and Santa Monica and the Crenshaw district!), when no work materialized and they returned to the Northwest, she had been relieved, even when the first serious and unmistakably frosty nip hit the air.

This was *home*. This was *right*. This was what she knew and understood. Cold, wet winters with the promise of snow. Springs like the kiss of an awakening goddess, and summers bright and hot and alive enough to make you forget the lip-cracking winter cold or the endless spring rains. A verdurous cascade of leaves and grass and needles that looked and felt and smelled as if it would go on and on forever.

And when it began to shift, when the first breath of cold signaled the end of summer, and the beginning of a long, long fall, a tumble into the maw of winter, it triggered something within her. It signaled that time changes, the year turns. *Another year gone, Vivian. Another year closer to that final cold.* There was work to be done, cloth to stitch, long, slow love to be made in the depths of the marriage bed, and children to bring squalling and yawping into the world.

She could, year by year, feel her body changing in a way she knew would never have happened, had things worked out differently. Had Otis's job not fallen through, had she joined the tribes of the endless spring, in sunny, sunny California.

And now was one of those times. The mornings had begun to bare their teeth. She was awakened by the feathery whistle of wind from the Columbia River, an arctic whisper under her nightgown, tripping along the spine. Oh, sure, by noon the sun would be out, and the sky would try to convince you that it had all been a joke, that the cold wasn't real, that the summer wasn't over.

But nightfall came much earlier now.

So before the weather broke, she decided to take the last good weekend and drive out to the beach, to take a last look at the sun-swallowing waves before they turned cold and gray. The beach wouldn't be crowded: by now the vacationers from Spokane and Eugene would have retreated from the shores, packed up their summer vacations and returned to their lives.

But from Claremont, the drive was no more than forty minutes, straight out the Coast Highway, then south a bit, through the industrial maze and past the little mom-and-pop restaurants selling their fresh seafood specials and hot pastries. On the way back from the beach, Otis would probably pull in at one of them, and celebrate the day with a warm meal.

But now they sought one of the little wooded coves in the stretch of Oregon State Park along the coast, one of the areas that shifted so abruptly from woods to beach, soil becoming sand in the stretch of a few feet, leading down to cliff or cove, and hard, flat waves.

The families caravanned out: The Wallaces, Sevujians, Darlings, Valdezes and Emorys.

The kids were all about six then. Lee and Herman would be in kindergarten in a week, the others would stay behind in Claremont Preschool. The quintet would be broken, and in the way that things went in the world, it was possible that they would never be the same again.

Otis pulled their battered station wagon with its BACK OFF, I'M A GODDESS bumper sticker into the county parking lot at eleven in the morning. It was deserted. There were traces of a hell of a party the night before, and motorcycle tracks spooling out along the sand. Most of the beer cans and bottles had been scooped up in a big net and deposited near if not *in* a trashcan, but a few stray sun shirts and cutoff jeans were still sopping and bereft of owners. Otis picked up a halter top with one huge finger and dangled it sardonically.

"Must have been a hell of a party."

Their dog Willie was running back and forth along the beach, barking at the waves and the birds, reveling in the thundering avalanche of new smells. Willie was a medium-sized mutt, maybe thirty-five pounds, a cross between a Labrador retriever and a Doberman pincher. Patrick adored him, and had raised him from a puppy. The dog's mother had been a Lab, a class project at Claremont Preschool, all of the children pitching in with effort and money to raise her from a pup. She managed to run away for a couple of days one spring, and returned looking oddly abashed. Sixty-odd days later she bore a fine spanking confusion of puppies, and their teacher held a litter lottery.

Frankie, Patrick, Destiny, Lee and Shermie had pooled their tickets, vowing that if any one of them won a puppy, *all* of them would have a puppy. Patrick won the mutt, and had made as good as he could on the deal. Willie made the rounds of the other kids' houses, as much as their parents tolerated. But when it was time for him to come home, when the last of the parents dropped him off at their trailer park, Vivian thought that she saw a special perk to the mutt's ears, a little extra spring to his step.

Willie loved them all, but he belonged to Patrick.

The kids were fanning out across the beach, running and screaming, throwing rocks at the surf. "Don't go too far!" Otis called.

"And stay together," Mrs. Sevujian added. "Stay away from the rocks." She pointed at a finger-shaped rock pile that speared out a hundred yards into the surf. Waves hissed and coiled and broke at its base. The kids loved to play on it, but one mistake could cause a tragedy.

Another group partied about a hundred yards further down the beach. Black smoke rose in wisps from their oil can, was caught and spun by the wind, and dissolved into the salty air. It was too distant to see their faces, but easy to imagine that they were happy, laughing, sharing love and companionship and grill-striped hot dogs on the last good weekend of the year.

Vivian and the other parents busied themselves setting up beach chairs and collecting wood. Afterwards they peeled down and smeared on sunblock in token acknowledgment of the waning sunlight. It was warm that day, but not hot by any measure. The sky wasn't overcast— it was merely cool, as if they were viewing it through a pane of refrigerated glass. The wind carried a clear message, reinforced by the gray clouds: Winter is coming. Enjoy the day.

And so they did. Within an hour, the fire pit was going, and the cars, unpacked, yielded drinks and salad and various meats to be roasted at the pit.

Some of the older kids were plunging into the water, and the younger ones had gained permission to join them on a buddy system: each of the younger children was joined to an older, who had the responsibility.

Vivian wasn't completely comfortable with this: she saw some of the glances between the teenagers, and suspected that the energy between Delta and Robbie, for instance, fourteen and fifteen respectively, was beginning to build. Delta was ripening quickly, and she was ready for some adventure.

At fifteen, Frankie's older brother Robbie already drew the attention of older girls (and women, if one paid attention to salon gossip). He was tall, athletic, intelligent. His parents were the Reverend and Mrs. Darling, the only ones of the group who hadn't needed financial assistance to get their child into Claremont. Considering Claremont's sliding scale, that meant that they were paying a pretty penny—but Frankie's father was the associate minister at Lord's Grace Baptist church, his mother the dental hygienist who had snagged him. They had been eager for her to get back to work, and considered Claremont Preschool their best bet. She was a willowy brunette gone a touch soft around the middle. The Reverend Darling looked as if he might have stepped out of a funeral home ad in GQ.

At any rate, what was abundantly clear was that Robbie, good at football and baseball, a terror on the dance floor, and a fair little scholar, was headed for great things.

The Darlings had had Robbie when the Reverend was forty-one, and his bride thirty-five. Rumor had it that five or six years later Mrs. Darling had suspended her birth-control pills due to her husband's seriously diminished sex drive. As it happened, there was still one shot left in the clip, and in 1988 Frankie was born.

Frankie was a stubby six-year-old, sweet-natured and intense. His parents treated him with a sterile kind of affection, but brother Robbie just flat loved the kid.

And the love was reciprocal—Frankie followed Robbie everywhere, in a manner that most older brothers found downright embarrassing. Not Robbie. The fastest way in the world to start a fight was to say something negative about Frankie, imply that he was a little slow mentally, or simply too sickly to survive.

Frankie wasn't slow, Robbie insisted, although Frankie's speech could be a little hard to understand. You just needed to listen carefully to him. "And you should see him with video games. He's a whiz."

And Frankie never looked at Robbie with anything less than adoration. No one cheered harder than Frankie when Robbie charged past the goal line for a touchdown.

No one, except perhaps Delta.

Delta Valdez was Destiny's older sister, sloe-eyed and dark skinned, perhaps mature beyond her years, but still not fully ripened by half. She carried with her the hint of a phenomenal maturity, a certain promise of the flesh. Everyone knew, but no one said anything about it, certainly not to her father, who was prone to jealousy. Perhaps too damned jealous.

The beach outing progressed, a slow crescendo of sun and sand and warming then cooling surf, games of tag and tubs of ice and beer, volleyball and treasure hunting, naps on grainy blankets and the sounds of children begging their parents to run with them, play with them, applaud as they risked life and limb.

And the parents got into it as well. Once upon a time three of the five fathers had played football. Stiff joints and bad backs were actually forgotten as reluctance grew into acceptance, which evolved to enjoyment, and then eagerness and finally competitiveness.

Now, this was just the parents. Robbie wasn't a part of the game, and the teenagers found themselves in the water watching the younger kids—whichever of the younger sprouts weren't watching the parents make fools of themselves.

And that was the way it evolved. The three groups:

Parents and adult friends, those who played and those who cheered or watched and made sarcastic commentary. Teenagers, who were charged with the care of the younger kids. And the children, who were herded back and forth like calves, shrieking with pleasure from one makeshift game to the next.

In the main it was a wonderful day. A twisted ankle here, a mild sunburn there, and Mrs. Valdez, who was working on a miniature castle of beer cans.

And a little flirting. Well, that was to be expected. After all, why in the world would the former front line of Claremont High bare their chests and shoulders and huff and puff in the sun if not to win the admiration of the former cheerleaders?

And at this remove, everyone remembered having run the long ball, having sacked that quarterback who went on to play a minor position for the Chargers or the Dolphins. And due to the inevitable damage wrought by gravity, friction and time, the Reverend Darling, who never indulged in anything more strenuous than recreational tennis, found that he could compete quite well with yesteryear's beefy gridiron giants.

The beach had been staked out, the fifty yard line demarcated by a wire trash basket and the tumbled pier of rocks pointing out toward the horizon. Teams were drawn up, five to a side, former football players and former cheerleaders, a teacher, a couple of accountants . . .

All of the parents and step-parents were out on the playing field. The battle was surprisingly evenhanded, with Otis facing the beefy Joseph Sevujian, who was a year younger and therefore had never faced him in varsity ball. Both had wondered what this moment would feel like, and they grinned and grimaced at each other as only aging jocks can.

At first, Vivian watched from the sidelines. She lounged in a folding chair, her eyes sheltered by a pink, floppy sombrero. But as the game got more competitive, one adult after another was pulled onto the field, until every parent was co-opted, and the sun and beer-drenched hilarity had engaged them all.

The time seemed to float by. Vivian went out for passes, got knocked rump-over-teakettle in the sand and came up laughing. She was supposed to just grab the flags trailing from the runners' trunks, but with the agreement of all concerned touch slowly turned to tackle. Although tackles were hard, they were fair, and no one was hurt. The afternoon went on like this, and perhaps, had things not gone so terribly wrong, Vivian would have remembered it as one of those wonderful, perfect late-summer days, the kind of day about which people say: "Remember that game? That great game? I'd like to have another game like that."

But days like that, *times* like those, can never really be recaptured, because there is a magic that happens when your attention is in one place, and something slowly, gradually builds at the periphery of your awareness, and when it does, it has a life all its own.

In this case, all of their initial attention had been on the children, on making sure that the kids had a hell of a day. And with their attention there, something else had a chance to grow, something good and strong, and that would remind them of the lost days of their youth with every deliriously wrenched joint, every deliciously pulled muscle. And the new thing, that subconscious thing, slowly pulled their attention away, creating a perceptual hole.

It was only later, at the hospital, trying desperately to understand how the day had gone so badly wrong, that they had pieced together the truth and determined what had actually happened.

While the grown-ups had reveled in their creaking joints, almost all of the kids had headed into the surf. Under the watchful eyes of the older teenagers the kids had enjoyed these last hours of summer, and the hard, white sand upon which the waves pounded their steady, eternal rhythm.

There were enough of the older children to watch—just barely enough. Hermie's older sister could watch the two-year-old Sevujian twins, and thirteen-year-old Brett Wallace supervised the others. But like it or not, Robbie and Delta were the backup. They needed to watch Destiny and Patrick, but most especially, they needed to watch Frankie.

Because if there was any wild card in the entire situation, it would be adoring, helpless Frankie. He stayed on the beach most of the time, making sand castles, drawing his name at the tide line, and watched Robbie playing in the sun and the surf.

And, of course, at Robbie's side was Delta, so long of limb, with ready smile and full, beautiful lips. Delta of the long, straight hair that streamed behind her in the water like a dark halo.

Almost inevitably, Robbie had noticed that all of the adults, distant on the beach, were occupied with their game. . . .

He spit out a mouthful of the salty water and turned his eye to Delta, who swam close to him, then pushed away, laughing like a seal. It was only natural that he would look for Frankie, and see him quietly occupied on the beach, far from the sparkling line where the tide darkened the sand. Frankie was never adventurous. Frankie never really took chances. And Frankie was something very close to a perfect alibi.

So, with everyone occupied watching someone else, or the sand, or the ball, or the waves, Robbie and Delta worked their way over behind a boulder on the long rocky spur, and found themselves completely alone.

He was fifteen, but despite being a young man of extraordinary physical presence, had had very little experience with girls. Being a Baptist preacher's son was both a curse and a blessing. Girls were fascinated with him, but kept him at a slight distance, simultaneously idolized and isolated.

So despite the (allegedly) rampant deflowerings accomplished by his contemporaries, Robbie had found himself, thus far, suspended between heaven and hell, between the good girls, who often wanted to but wouldn't, and the bad girls reputed to doff their drawers at the drop of a hint. And despite the aforementioned perfect qualifications, Robbie was a little too intimidated to "go" with a girl who really knew her way around.

But Delta . . .

Well, Delta was Delta. They had been friends for years, and if their relationship had never gone beyond the pecking stage, it was solely because Mrs. Darling had kept an eagle eye on him, completely aware that he was, quite simply, a catch by any standards.

But on this day, when she pushed herself up out of the water, the droplets shimmering on her skin like diamonds, and peered at him challengingly, it was too easy for him to finally abandon the shyness and inhibitions, and flow into her arms. And he found, in that hot wet embrace, a kind of blistering pleasure that no pass interception had ever afforded.

He lost time, and he lost awareness, as for the first time in his life, he pushed himself up against the body of a willing woman who was wet and more than half naked, and realized that she hadn't shied away from the rigidity in his trunks. She had in fact, pressed herself against it, and Robbie knew absolute and total bliss at the same time that his subconscious whispered to him *you ain't seen nothing yet. . . .*

Frankie saw his brother disappear, saw the last few strokes as their heads disappeared around the corner, and he sighed.

It wasn't as if he wanted to get his brother in trouble. He loved Robbie. It was just that everyone watched him so closely, thinking that he couldn't do anything, that no one trusted him to take care of himself, and that was just wrong, because he *could* take care of himself.

He wasn't weak, his *body* was weak, and there was a difference. He didn't understand quite *how* there was a difference, he just knew that there was. And that one day he would show people.

The condescending eyes were on him *all the time,* to the point where it was hard for him to play his favorite games, the private games, during which he came closest to being who and what he really was. He knew that someone might catch him, and even at the age of six, understood that no one must catch him, no one must find out.

And he knew ways to keep them from finding out, too. He didn't know quite *how* he knew, but there were voices in his head that told him the things that he needed.

Do nothing that is of no use.

Pay attention even to little things.

He could hear the voices, and struggled to understand what they meant, or why he heard them so clearly, and as yet, did not know.

But one day, he would.

As far as today was concerned, what Frankie wanted to do, more than anything in the world, was slip out into the water, to feel its warmth against his skin. He had always had a strange and healing affinity for water, and resented the fact that everyone always watched him when he went into it.

But no one was watching him now.

Very carefully, Frankie stepped out onto the wet sand.

Behind him, the sounds of the football game drifted across the beach, and overhead, the gulls called to him in their skawing, mournful refrains. The summer was going away, like everything went away. Like Frankie would go away, one day.

Frankie's toes rolled onto the sand and he shivered with delight. The water felt warmer than it looked. He already knew how it would feel to have the water roll up over his feet, and ankles, and calves. How it would feel lapping at his thighs, and then that place between his legs, and then his tummy. The water was almost a living thing, like a friend.

Frankie moved out into the water until it lapped at his chin, then took a breath, and went under.

Vivian saw what happened, but only after it began. The football game was rough when it should have been rough, and fun when it should have been fun, one of those delirious exercises in excess that results in bruises and sprains to be savored for weeks to come.

But in the daze of sun and sand, it was her head that came up first, her ears that first heard the thin, reedy call above the sound of wind and surf, the high "help me . . . !" that twisted through the wind, and turned to look out at the water, toward the sun, low enough in the western sky to force her to shield her eyes, and saw the tiny head bobbing in the water, and felt the breath catch in her throat.

"Oh my God," Evelyn Darling said, beside her. "It's Frankie."

Robbie had just finished the longest, sweetest, wettest, and saltiest kiss of his life when he heard the sound. It wasn't exactly a complete word. He and Frankie had this *connection*. Everybody knew it, and it wasn't something that he could exactly explain. Most of the time, he just *knew* if there was something going on, knew if Frankie needed him, or wanted him, and he was happy to help out.

When on the football field, somehow he just knew when Frankie was watching. When baby bro was there, Robbie ran a little faster, hit a little harder, jumped a little higher. He knew that those hits and jumps had to carry his brother along with them, that that was as close to glory as Frankie was ever going to get.

He knew that he needed to keep an eye on Frankie, that there was more at stake than just his brother's physical health. The attachment was something fierce, and savage.

Despite that knowledge, he had taken a few moments to himself, enjoying the first strong steps along a pathway that promised to be long and sweet and warming throughout the days of his life.

But despite the pleasant, almost opiate haze that enraptured him further with every successive kiss, Robbie was yanked into complete alertness by the sight of his brother's head a hundred yards from shore, his small arms thrashing weakly. And without another thought, without even the memory of that last, sweetest kiss, he put that young, strong body into the greatest action of his life, and cleaved out toward his brother.

Frankie was afraid. He had, at first, been enraptured by the sensation of the tide tugging at him, lifting his toes above the sand, a sensation of flying. For an instant he knew what his brother felt when he was floating up and up above the heads of the tacklers, diving for that ball, nothing but daylight between his feet and the ground.

Then suddenly he was tumbling, the waves tossing him from above, the rip pulling from beneath. He didn't know which way his head should go, he was thrashing and didn't know which way was *up,* and he was breathing water, and suddenly all of the thrill, all of the exultation, everything was forgotten in the sudden, drastic revocation of his God-given right to breathe.

Frankie flailed his thin arms, thrashing toward the eye-stinging sunlight, hardly believing it when his head broke the surface again, when he gasped for air and found it. He blinked the water from his eyes, and tried to focus. In every direction he saw nothing but ocean, nothing but horizon, and knew he was going to die.

"Frankie!"

The sound was distant, and weak. But as he was lifted on a swell he was able to thrash around in a circle and see the beach, and the frantically gesturing people on the distant beach. Those sparkling sands seemed so impossibly far away that his tiny store of hope was utterly extinguished.

In that moment, all the regret within him burned through all the self-justification, all the heroic image, and all that remained was a terrible urge to live, combined with a terrible fear of death.

I'm not ready. . . .

And distantly, he heard a cheer, but couldn't grasp it.

I'm sorry. I never meant to hurt—

The wave slapped him, pulled him under again. He swallowed another mouthful of water, and this time it went down. The pain in his chest was awful, was a sucking black hole in his heart, pulling him down and down in a swirling funnel, tiny bits of images, and they were frightening, and he suddenly knew that he was a *bad boy,* who had done *bad things.* God had been watching after all, and now Frankie was going to pay. God had seen the kitten. Frankie hadn't meant to hurt it. He just wanted to make it do what he wanted it to do, and it wouldn't, and he got mad. And oh, God, he was sorry—

But then Frankie felt his brother's arms around him, knew that strength, heard Robbie saying "I've got you, Frankie." His heart soared, because, apparently, God hadn't been watching at all.

With perverse precision, another wave struck them, and this one jolted them sideways. But Robbie had him, had *them,* those tireless arms and legs striking out, the breath not even ragged, marvel of marvels. Frankie could spare a little attention, could catch a glimpse of the shore, and saw his father diving into the water, and his heart lifted again—

As another wave, stronger this time, slammed into them, driving them further sideways, and this time he heard just a ragged edge to Robbie's breathing. Despite a jolt of fear he knew, just *knew* that his brother would make it, had the strength and the courage—

And then remembered, in some small room in the back of his mind, that the waves came in threes, in rising, steady rhythm, that the third was almost twice as large as the first two, and twisted himself around against the pressure of his brother's arm. He saw the third wave, standing against the sky, dwarfing the sun, drowning the world, and had time to say: *I'm sorry*—before the watery cliff collapsed on him, and then there was nothing but a vast sideways motion, an avalanche, and then a great smashing jolt, and then blackness.

From the beach, the unfolding tragedy had a solemn, balletic grace, a kind of clockwork inevitability which, in retrospect, made it all so terribly worse.

For a moment, the adults barely reacted to the cry, and then as heads turned and the realization truly settled in, the Reverend Darling shook off his shoes and plunged into the water, hitting the edge of the shallows just in time to catch a wave coming in, which pushed him back toward the shore. When the swell died down and they were able to see what was happening, both heads were above water, and Robbie was making his way toward shore, his meaty arm cleaving the water.

Robbie's father struggled with the waves, getting caught by swell after swell as he fought his way out.

The children were gathered at the tide line, watching the drama silently. They weren't really afraid, because if there had ever been a hero among them, it was Robbie. But watching him on the gridiron, or swinging for the fences was one thing. Those were games, and this was real life. Still, reality or not, in an odd way this was just another episode of the *Robbie!* show. This was just another chance for that perfect heart and perfect mind in that perfect body to display its prowess, and they didn't know whether to pitch in, or just applaud as he sidestroked manfully toward the shore.

Then the first wave hit him, and they held their breath, watched the two small heads go under and then bob to the surface, watched the obvious moment of disorientation, and then Robbie swept toward the shore again—

And the second wave hit, taking them toward the spur of rocks—

And somewhere deep inside Vivian, she sensed disaster, sensed a trill of impending doom, but it was still filtered through the sense that Robbie was larger than life, and it was, after all, not much different than watching Magnum P.I. hanging from a helicopter, legs flailing, as the commercial break came and told you some wonderful news about low-fat dog food.

So if this was another episode of the *Robbie!* show, then this was the moment when the music would rise up and up, and this was the moment when the announcer would tell them that *Robbie!* would be right back after this important announcement.

Only another voice in her head kept shrieking: *They're just children. . . .*

The third wave hit, carrying both of them against the rocks, and without exactly hearing the impact, they could *hear* it. Oh, yes. It was the sound not of bones breaking, but of dreams fading, or hope dissolving, spring gone to winter in a single freakish May snowstorm.

Where Robbie's head had smacked against the rock it was smeared with blood. An instant later another wave swished, washing the stain away. Both heads disappeared.

Now, when it was too late, everyone dived into the water. Robbie's father reached the rocks a few moments later, but there was nothing and no one to be seen.

Perversely, now that the surf had done its damage, it seemed to quiet, almost as if it appreciated the value of a diminuendo. Another three sets of strong arms were there within fifty seconds, and a minute after that, of diving and bobbing and frantic searching, Robbie and Frankie had both been located, and were being hauled toward shore.

Neither was conscious.

Someone ran for the parking lot, for the telephone booth in the parking lot, to make an emergency call. The people from down the beach were running over, one of them offering a cell phone.

Vivian didn't move, just gathered Patrick under her arm, feeling the perverse gratitude that it was not *her* child who was in such terrible trouble, and recoiling from the inevitable guilt that she would even feel such a natural, human emotion.

She began to pray: "Dear God, please help those children, please let them live, let them breathe."

Mr. Sevujian was a volunteer fireman, and grimly performed CPR compressions on the younger boy. The Reverend Darling worked on the elder, but every chest compression brought another trickle of blood from Robbie's terrible scalp wound. Mrs. Darling was sobbing and shrieking, the sunny, perfect last summer afternoon suddenly transformed into the worst day of their lives, the worst day in the history of the world. Long before the sound of sirens announced the arrival of the ambulances, everyone knew that Robbie was dead.

She remembered the moment when Frankie woke up, when he vomited water and rolled onto his side in a fetal position. It took a few moments for his eyes to focus. He sat up, and Otis helped him to stay erect. "Momma . . . ?" he said, and looked around.

Vivian remembered that moment, because she remembered her stomach lurching sideways.

Frankie's father, the Reverend Darling, ceased his labors and regarded his living son.

The Reverend glanced from Frankie to his perfect, dead son, Robbie who had perished in the rescue of his brother. Something like a dark, electric cloud passed behind the Reverend's eyes, something so huge and swollen that for just an instant it seemed that his head itself would become distended. He did not move, merely stared.

Frankie's mother stared as well, and then began screaming. The screaming didn't stop until the paramedics, who had been summoned to resuscitate a dead boy, found it in their hearts to give her mercy in the form of a needle, a needle long enough to guide her into the healing arms of sleep.

29

LAS CRUCES, NEW MEXICO,
MONDAY, MAY 28

Wings tipped in scarlet, a single hawk soared high on the shimmering thermals. Miguel Sanchez's open eyes reflected its image without seeing it, or anything else.

The boy was small for his age. He sprawled, broken on the sidewalk, arms and legs twisted into a posture attainable only by the injured and the dead. Blood matted his limp, dark hair.

There was a crowd gathered around him, and some of them spoke in frantically fast, pain-filled Spanish.

"Dios mio, Miguel, Miguel—" one heavy woman cried, and then, against the advice of others in the crowd, dropped to her knees and cradled his head.

Several members of the crowd knew the Sanchez family, knew enough to know what a horrible coincidence this was. After so much pain in her life, Stella Sanchez had won the lottery, made plans to travel all the way to Spain in just a few weeks, taking her family and many cousins with her, only now to face the awful loss of her only remaining child.

In Spanish, some of the crowd asked if anyone had seen what happened, wondered how the boy had fallen out of the apartment window. Others scrambled to call for the ambulance. A few murmured softly to each other that there was no use in it, that the boy was obviously dead.

And it was such a shame. Miguel was such a good boy, never a bother, always a help. And considering his no-good *maleton* of a father, an abusive, *asqueroso* son of a bitch who should *come mierda* in New Mexico State prison for the next hundred years for strangling his own daughter, it was a miracle that the boy was turning out as well as he did. But he was. Always polite, and courteous, ready to help, industrious, and just as bright as a star. He had so much light in him, that boy. He was going to *be* something someday, they had all known.

And now Miguel Sanchez was dead. Another tragedy, like so many others in the *barrio.*

It was just a shame.

A block away, a black car sat parked next to the curb, two men in the front seat, watching the crowd.

One black. One white.

The car pulled away slowly, too slowly to be of any notice to the grieving crowd, and then picked up speed, finally turning onto El Paseo Street to merge with the traffic.

Wisher drove, his expression rarely changing as he cruised the streets. No matter what the heat, he rarely seemed to sweat. "Nice town," he said, lips tight. "Just a perfect fucking town."

When Schott replied his voice was flat, as if he were speaking under duress. "Gotta wonder about the nightlife."

Wisher shrugged. "Got beer and titty bars. What else do you want?" His hands gripped the steering wheel hard.

"A movie theater," Schott said. "I'd like to see a movie." His voice was rather small for a man of his size. Disorientingly soft for a man of his violent experience. "Movies help me relax." He loved them, especially old movies he had watched as a child. Schott had a library of over five hundred video and DVD movies. Since this whole thing with the kids had started, he had become almost addicted to the television and movie screens, absorbing everything from *Jason and the Argonauts* to Disney's *Robin Hood* to the Tyrone Power *Mark of Zorro,* as often as time permitted.

"We don't have time for that," Wisher said. "Room's got HBO. After we finish linking up, watch whatever the fuck you want."

"Let's do it," Schott said.

Wisher nodded without making a verbal reply. Five minutes later, they reached the place where El Paseo turned into Union Street, crossing the 10 Freeway.

Wisher turned into the parking lot of a Motel Six, just another of those anonymous economy mega-chains stretching from sea to shining sea.

Wisher let them into their room. The beds hadn't been slept in, the luggage hadn't been unpacked. The two moved with a numb familiarity born of years . . . no, *decades* of interaction. Synchronized, but not quite alive and spontaneous.

Wisher opened a flat briefcase, and extracted a Dell Inspiron laptop computer. He connected its modem to the side of the room phone. Booting up, he opened a program called Conferex Secure.

As he did, Schott turned on the room's air conditioning. He bent down, holding his face to the flow of cool air, enjoying the faintly metallic tang. Then he straightened, feeling the mild pain in his lower back. That was a nagging, constant companion now. Once upon a time, his body had been invulnerable, immortal, bulletproof. That was thirty years and two wars ago.

Once upon a time, also, the world had seemed much more black and white, cut and dried. He hadn't found it to be the moral equivalent of Dr. Dolittle's mythical pushme-pullyu. Everybody's right, everybody's wrong. No up, no down, everything goes sideways.

Even that slightest touch of whimsy triggered a savage longing for simpler answers. He forced himself away from such speculation and set up a compact video camera, hooking it into a port on the rear of the computer.

After about forty seconds, a box appeared on the computer screen, accompanied by a blinking cursor.

"Ready," Wisher said blandly. Schott opened a little black book and began to read:

"Zebra, zebra, copy one seven eight."

Wisher typed the characters in, and the computer began to beep, dialing.

Nothing.

For the first time, Wisher displayed an emotional crack underneath the reserve. "Fuckin' piece of shit—"

Schott looked at him curiously. "Did you dial 'nine' for an outside line?"

Wisher stared at the computer, and then his anger evaporated into that curiously flat affect. "Oh. Right."

He called up a command screen, and clicked the "dial 9" option. He pushed the dial box again, and this time the call went through. There was a *hiss* as the computer connected, a sibilance Schott had always considered disturbingly like the warning call of an angry rattlesnake.

The connection went through, and information was exchanged.

News of death delivered exchanged with word of progress in other allied matters. Just information. It was impossible to treat the faces and names as belonging to real children, real human beings.

Schott knew Wisher actually *had* children, although he hadn't seen them in over a year. Schott had none. Disturbingly, one of the small, smiling images across the line looked much like a blend of Schott and his first wife. What he called the Good Wife, the one he had really loved.

What was this kid's name? *Jessica Range*. Cute name. Blond hair, brilliant green eyes, chubby cheeks. Twelve years old. Schott could see himself sitting across from little Jessica, eating Sugar Frosted Flakes and talking Pokémon strategy.

Please God. Keep her off the list. Keep this one off my list. I don't know how much more—

Then Wisher ended the call. He copied a bit of information off the screen, then closed the case. "Amarillo, day after tomorrow," he said.

Then Wisher stripped off his clothes and went in the bathroom for a shower. If he went according to pattern, he might be in there for a half hour.

Schott rolled onto one of the beds, picked up the remote and switched on the room's television, flicking channels until he found Comedy Central, which was running a marathon of British sketch comedy. Five minutes of *Benny Hill* convinced Schott that it wasn't his kind of thing, and he kept flipping until he found the Cartoon Network. Then he sighed, and watched, and laughed until his sides hurt, and never once thought about little Jessica Range, who lived in Minnesota with her alcoholic father, who, according to plan, had a little more than a month to live.

That was all right. Just not this week. And not at Schott's personal hand.

A small mercy, that was. But sometimes, in life, that was all you got.

30

TUESDAY, MAY 29

Renny Sand wound his way through the warren of cubbyholes to his desk, angry almost to the point of exploding, but not quite certain why.

Lisa Cortez, the features reporter across the aisle, studied Renny as he fumbled through his morning calls. Finally, Lisa stood and leaned her elbows on the cubicle partitions and asked: "Hey, Renny—I never asked you how the interview went."

He didn't need to ask which interview. "Just great," Sand said, and glared at her.

Sand pivoted to his desktop monitor, pulled out the keyboard and booted up. The computer screen asked for his authorization code, which he punched in above the little green glowing cursor. After a minute a menu appeared, asking his pleasure. He typed in the words "Alexander Marcus," and a moment later was rewarded with an immense list of articles.

Sorted for date, the most prominent cluster was composed of articles about Alexander Marcus's death.

What a week that had been. In March of 1988, en route from Alaska to California, Marcus's Lear jet simply exploded. Some of the wreckage had been recovered, and enough of his body to be positively identified. Examination of the wreckage had revealed no explosive residue, and there wasn't enough of the engine recovered to make a full evaluation possible. "Fuel-line malfunction."

Even the memory of it disturbed him. At the time, he'd been just another shell-shocked face in a room full of dumbfounded reporters too whiplashed to stop their sobbing. Very unprofessional, a display like he'd never seen in a room full of journalists, as if it were 1963 and they were in Dallas, hearing the news from JFK's cavalcade.

He closed that article window, and went on. Sand typed a second word: "Chicago."

The list shrank, but still filled the screen.

He paused, a man about to step over some kind of invisible line, and typed: "vice raid."

An article appeared detailing the raid of a high-level whorehouse in Chicago in 1989. He remembered that article because he had contributed to it. It was a scandal, because several political figures were implicated—none of them named in the article.

Renny drummed his fingers on his desk, and then picked up the phone, punched four keys, and waited.

A woman's voice answered. Uncertainly at first, then with growing confidence, he said: "Hello, Madeline? How are things down in archives?"

"Renny Sand?" she asked, her voice rather cynically suspicious.

"Why, I'm just simply super. Everything down here is super. And how are you?"

He ignored the wariness. "Just great. Listen, I need you to access some information for me. Ready?" He read off a list of dates and reference numbers.

She hawed as she scribbled. "Got it. Couple of years, you'll be able to access all of this stuff right from your desk."

"Then I couldn't come down and flirt with you, now could I?"

She laughed at him, and hung up.

Renny threw his coat over his shoulder and hurried out, drawing the bemused expressions of his cubbyhole mates.

They had watched him for a week since the infamous interview, and it was obviously clear that *something* was bothering him. They were just waiting to see how long that *something* would fester before he exploded.

And now, just maybe, it had happened.

The research and storage facility was in the second basement of the Tower, and reminded him of nothing so much as a medieval catacomb with fluorescent lighting. One of Marcus's innovations in the news industry was a central repository for a reporter's research materials. In most news bureaus, individual reporters jammed their desks (and sometimes homes) with stacks of index cards, sheafs of paper, four-inch by eight-inch reporter's notebooks, and shoeboxes filled with cassette tapes. The basement at Marcus Communications housed all of this material, moderately well cross-referenced. The practice had been one part legal hedge against lawsuits and subpoenas, and another, equal measure anal retentiveness on the part of Marcus Communications.

There was an ancillary warehouse in Santa Monica, and others in London, Paris and Moscow serving the foreign branches. A million-dollar digitizing program was putting it all on-line, but until that cyber-day dawned, there was Madeline.

Madeline Lindrows was a plump woman somewhere in her forties, with wire-rimmed glasses and a healthy sensuality that fairly baked off her. She kept that aspect of her personality down to a dull roar at work, however, where she was hyper-competent and almost regal.

She led him back through the stacks, occasionally glancing at him back over her shoulder. "What article is this, Renny boy? You know, I don't believe half the things I heard about you."

"Thank goodness."

"The half I *do* believe bothers the hell out of me."

He couldn't quite bring himself to meet her eyes. They were too direct, too challenging, saw too much.

"I shouldn't believe the other half, should I, Renny?"

Sand finally managed to face her squarely. Although he had five inches on her, he felt almost as if he were looking up, as though she stole the moral high ground just by waking up in the morning.

"Just believe I'm coming back," he said.

She sighed, as if she had hoped for another answer.

"Well," she said, "try this desk." She indicated a little wooden model complete with a computer terminal. She pulled a metal tray with a bulging file folder out of a shelf, and plopped it on the desk. "You say 'hi' on your way out, Renny."

"Thanks, Mad."

"Keep your facts straight, Renny Sands."

He winced, but kept his painful thoughts to himself and began to leaf through decade-old notes, refamiliarizing himself with the sordid details. About five minutes of fishing about and he found what he was looking for.

The note was marked "kill file." It read:

Unofficial reports consider the entire situation sensitive. The arrest took place during the 1986 Congress for Racial Harmony in Chicago, and was considered to represent police harassment of several leading civil-rights figures. Names were withheld, but it was believed that among those present at the party was Alexander Marcus—

He scanned further, finally finding an address for the party: 1608 Fountain, Chicago.

That was the crucial bit of information. Renny fired up the desktop machine, and typed it in. After a moment, a second story appeared.

Prostitution ring busted. Mr. Marano Smith, charged with operating a telephone call-girl ring that stretched over the entire Great Lakes area . . .

A little buzzer went off in the back of his mind. "What is it? What is it . . . ?" he murmured.

He continued to scan, then sat back with a dissatisfied look on his face. Then he cleared the screen and typed in: "bite marks."

A huge list of stories scrolled past. He added "Chicago" to the search. It still filled two screens. "Prostitute" was his last filter, and then at last he had a list comprising no more than five or ten entries.

The first to catch his eye was a "Mary Anne Dowling," killed in 1989. The story listed her as having died in a wilderness area on Lake Michigan. Bite marks on her face. She was mentioned in connection with a Mr. Marano Smith's call-girl operation.

This was ugly, and getting worse. Renny wrote "Marcus" on a sheet of paper, and drew a line linking it with "Marano Smith." Then he drew another line linking Smith to the girl, Mary Anne Dowling.

And followed it with a large question mark. What was this? He had two girls connected with Marcus, who had died in similar circumstances. *If* there was a connection, what was it? Marcus had had some very rough characters around him—the bunch sometimes called the Praetorians. Ex-military, riding his coattails. To hell with what Penelope "Happy Hooker" Costanza had implied. It would be one staggering story even if Marcus had "merely" engineered a cover-up for the benefit of one of his thugs.

"Thin," Renny said quietly. "Very thin."

Two hours later, he stood smiling before Madeline's desk. She doffed her wire-rims and smiled up at him tolerantly.

"Maddy?"

"Yessss?"

"Listen—who would you say had the most complete biography of Alexander Marcus? I mean a complete itinerary—speeches, appearances, vacations . . ."

She frowned quizzically. "Going back how far?"

"What have you got?"

"Well, there is a compiled itinerary going back as far as his early military service, then into civilian life—so many biographies and articles have been done on the man. What's up?"

He had already considered his answer. "I don't know. A story proposal. Embryo stage right now. Can you get that for me?"

Madeline gave him a very strange look indeed. "Sure, I guess so," she said finally. "Take me a few minutes—you're on terminal twelve?"

"Thirteen."

Renny bought himself a cup of coffee. By the time he returned to the terminal the biography was shimmering on the green-tinted screen, a timeline of Marcus's military and civilian service, with tons of meetings, speeches and vacations.

He read, and noted the reporter's name, and went back to Maddy again and again for notes. He sorted through bundles, reading, scanning, correlating . . .

Two yellow legal pads later, he looked up at the clock and found that six hours had passed. His head ached and his eyes burned. Without realizing it, he had entered into one of those zones of concentration so total that the building could have burned down around him, and he wouldn't have even heard the fire trucks.

Sand hated computer screens, and had made a printout of the bio. Working through the FBI links to local law enforcement, he'd also created a list of crimes that seemed to match the two prostitutes. Then what he had to do was cross-reference the crimes with the Praetorians. That was where the notes came in.

This was going to be a staggering job. The Praetorian core group consisted of perhaps six men who surrounded Marcus regularly, as bodyguards, executives, and assistants. If one of them was involved in something like this, Sand was going to have to cull him carefully, rule out the men who couldn't be involved, and zero in on a pair of likelies.

First he had to see whether there was any pattern at all. After all, two cases meant nothing. What was the old saying? *Once is happenstance. Twice is coincidence. The third time, it's enemy action.*

So he began to check down the list, starting from scratch as if he had never heard anything about either of the girls.

There were fifty-eight profile-matching murders over the last decade of Alexander Marcus's life. Sand selected the first one, a poor thing named Crystal Philips from Boise. He checked Marcus's itinerary, and found that he had been in London at the time, with his coterie in full attendance. Good.

The next was Nadine Fumitomo, in Honolulu. Sand tensed a bit, but Marcus had spent that week in the Soviet Union.

The next two were a bit bothersome, because there was no listing at all for Marcus's whereabouts, which probably meant that he was just taking care of minor business in the United States. If Sand continued to pursue this, though, he'd have to hunt that information down.

The fifth stopped him cold. Her name was Heather Albany Cross, and she had died a cold and lonely death on a road north of Salt Lake City, on July 24 of 1987.

Marcus had given a speech in Salt Lake the day before.

Happenstance.

He went down another six names before the next match appeared. Name: Fidela Braga, a known prostitute in the Hispanic section of El Dorado, Arkansas. The day following her death, Alexander Marcus had dedicated a library in Little Rock.

Coincidence. Oh, God.

He was sweating now. Four names later, that sweat went cold. Joyce Kitteridge, a runaway from Boston. The seventeen-year-old had died north of Miami. Her body was found in a drainage ditch, face chewed until she was almost unrecognizable. Two days later, Alexander Marcus was in South Beach, addressing a minority-themed small business convention.

Renny's stomach felt as if it were full of bleach. Marcus was there. The Praetorians were there. Who had done these terrible things? And was it even logical to protest that Marcus couldn't have known?

In fact, a low and terrible voice whispered to him, *isn't it most likely that—*

"Hey, Renny," Madeline said, a darkly curious tone to her voice. "What in the world are you up to?"

Oh, nothing—just the complete and utter destruction of the last of my heroes. Nothing much at all.

"—We're closing up here."

His watch said another two hours had passed. God in heaven—he'd been here almost ten hours, and hadn't even noticed. The entire desk was covered with printouts and scraps of paper, boxes of notes and index cards. He tried to put on his most innocent expression, knowing just how little muster it would pass. "Can you just let me close up? I'm good for it."

She chewed on the end of a pencil. "Must be something interesting. I haven't seen you like this in a long time."

He curled his lips up at the corners, hoping that it was a disarming smile, but afraid that the effect was lame and shallow. "I'm hoping."

She nodded. "Okay. Don't get me in trouble, now."

"Scout's honor."

She ran a warm finger along the back of his neck. "Don't forget your friends," she said, and took a step away, then paused. She turned.

"Renny," she said, "this article is in-house? I mean, it's for a Marcus Communications company?"

"Absolutely," he lied without hesitation.

She sighed. "Then there's something you should probably have." Another pause, as if uncertain whether she should speak. "About fifteen years ago, Marcus blocked publication of an unauthorized biography. The writer had a choice of half a million dollars, or five years in prison on a burglary charge."

"A setup?" Renny was aghast.

"Sort of. Receiving stolen property—something about some files from Marcus's house. At any rate, I know there's a copy of it buried in his personal effects. Interested?"

"I'm salivating already."

"Then I'll see what I can do," she said, smiled again, and left.

He sighed a deep sigh of relief when she vanished, and turned back to the computer.

The computer's lime-green cursor blinked at Sand patiently, his wish its command.

The breath seemed to catch in his throat. He wasn't aware of where he was, or even *what* he was. It was as if a stone had been lifted from his head, or heart. The pain he felt was a childish pain, a disillusionment pain, the agony of having your favorite fairy tales ripped brutally out of your heart. The dirty, molten, eager joy was an *adult* joy. Despite whatever pain he felt, the joy, germinating within him, stronger with every passing moment, was greater still.

For the first time in almost six years, he was a reporter again.

"Holy shit," he said. And meant it.

31

PHOENIX, ARIZONA,
WEDNESDAY, MAY 30

*E*very city has a jungle. During the day, many of them are commercial strips near residential districts, often near airports or other high traffic areas. They are usually in moderate-to-low-income areas. Industrious and bustling during the day, twilight signals a tawdry metamorphosis.*

Shuttered windows, barred doors, emptied parking lots . . . these create an entirely new habitat whose denizens are both predator and prey.

Although pharmaceuticals are often available nearby, few of the

*animals in this jungle are, in the strictest sense, drug dealers or ad-
dicts. The drug they sell is fantasy, or physical release. The drug they
seek is money, or a sense of control. They are female in body and male
in personality. They dress for display of, and swift access to, the wares
they offer.*

*Their customers rarely approach on foot. Depending on the time of
the month, the time of the night, and the need for a fix, it is either a
buyer's or seller's market.*

*One car is cruising the jungle, like a lion stalking the Serengeti. In
the car is a buyer. He is a white man, taller and heavier than average.
He is in his late fifties, but the extra weight is muscle. His motions are
very precise as he steers the wheel, searching for what he needs.*

*He doesn't know exactly how to find what he's looking for. He does
know that for years now, ever since that wonderful, terrible revelatory
time in Southeast Asia, he has been able to find it. He watches, con-
siders, and discards several possibilities before finding the one he
wants.*

*This one, the one in the iridescent green hot pants, is not tall, not
short. Her face, scrubbed clean of makeup and graced with an honestly
joyful expression, would be pretty. It is not pretty now. It is too . . .
specific. She is selling a product and whoever she is, whoever she woke
up as this morning, is irrelevant. Whatever small beauties she might
have had to offer, she is not beautiful now, no more than a can of
Comet or a Craftmaster hammer is beautiful, except in its utility. It is
not dark yet, not even twilight, but she is already on the prowl.*

Both predator and prey.

*When he pulls his car up next to her she turns to him and begins
the conversational dance. Both want to know how much, what, where,
how. Each has reason to be cautious. Different reasons. Early in the
conversation he says the magic words, "I'm not a cop." Prices and
services are negotiated. He tells her that he wants her to meet an
important man. She says that's fine, but even if it's only him it's all
right, because he looks nice. She would like to get to know him better.
He opens the car door and she climbs in. The last thing she says before
the car begins to move down the boulevard is "My name is Talisa."
She holds out her small, soft hand as if to shake.*

*"Hi," he says, both of his hands steady on the wheel. "My name is
Tristan. Tristan D'Angelo."*

32

Journal Entry #6: Imprintation Methodology

Our goal is simple: to provide disadvantaged children with the core psychological and emotional tools requisite for success. Of course, this involves identification of desirable traits, formulation of such traits into a coherent template, and transference of that template to the experimental group.

Even before the primary determiners are extracted from the Model, the subject of imprintation methodology must be addressed. The ultimate decision was that the combination of several differing approaches would achieve optimal effect. In summary, those approaches are:

1) Nutritional optimization. This is multiphasic. Children must be supplied with all basic nutrients essential to physical and mental growth. Experiments in the Third World suggest that this can be accomplished for a few cents a day per child. In addition to ideal levels of proteins, carbohydrates and healthy fats, it is possible to go even further to provide a perfect physiological environment. Neuroenhancers—acetylcholine and norepinephrine precursors are considered to be the safest of the effective ergogenic psychotropics. These will be selected from only those compounds most thoroughly tested, erring on the side of inefficiency rather than placing any child at risk. We believe that a suitable "cocktail" can be derived from 100% safe, organic compounds.

2) Window of imprintation. All evidence, especially research following in Piaget's footsteps, suggests that the ages from 2 to 5 years are most conducive to the kind of imprintation we propose. The acquisition of a test group suitable for double-blind testing, a minimum of 2,000 children within this age range, is a major logistical challenge.

3) Mechanical methodologies. Several are suggested. Psycho-physiological "patterning" requires an actual adjustment of physical movement patterns. Although there is no parallel to this in Western education, esoteric Eastern disciplines such as Sufism, martial arts and yoga have long theorized a body-

mind feedback loop, where an improvement or true modification of body performance affects the mind, and vice versa. By studying and extracting unconscious micro (i.e.: subliminal reflex habits and skin conductivity patterns) and macro (breathing patterns, body language, coordination, etc.) physical responses, then embedding as many of these as possible at the pre-conscious level, it is probable that deeper levels of correspondence to the Model are achievable. Physical games, dances, specialized "jungle gym" apparatus and other tools can all be used to mold the subjects into the Model's idealized patterns. Subliminals, implanted in both auditory and visual modes, have proven effective in laboratory settings, but they must be of "burst" duration (less than .1 second), ultra-high frequency, low-volume, reverse-masked and "blended" with the auditory track. The information is therefore "everywhere" and "nowhere." Similar multiphase techniques can be applied visually.

4) The acquisition of a suitable Model's belief systems, physiology, thought habits, philosophies, value structures, problem-solving modes, and emotional anchors mapped in a multidimensional grid gives us a personality matrix so complete that computer games can be formulated to literally mold a Target's subconscious while never conveying a single overt instruction. In combination with the above factors, we feel that there is an excellent potential for transferal of the deepest and most powerful programming from one ideal mind to thousands of young subjects. And once the window of imprintation is closed, external factors will have less influence than the implanted programs, which, like the most potent seeds imaginable, will continue to germinate. . . .

CLAREMONT

The preschool's shell was boarded and cold now, a dead spot on the local map. Patrick still felt drawn to it, like a rat continuing to search a maze long since bereft of cheese.

They snuck back inside about once a month. Lee Wallace, the most agile of them, had discovered the way in. He'd climbed up a rainspout, then edged his way around the roof, finding a trap door where workmen gained access to the evaporator cooling system. From there, Lee worked his way to the attic, and from there to a trap door in the back bathroom, the one where old Mrs. Coffee used to squat and stink the place to kingdom come. From there, he could easily open the office door, and then the side door. Then they were in.

There were no lights in the building, but daylight still glimmered outside. Summer was almost here, and in the Pacific Northwest the sun shone from six in the morning until almost eight at night. The louvers were tilted to catch and slot the late afternoon light.

Patrick felt like a pilgrim returning to the land of his birth, a supplicant entering a temple. Perhaps an archeologist excavating the tomb of a lost pharaoh.

The dust lay thinly on the floor, undisturbed for weeks. All of the fancier equipment was gone, but chairs were stacked against the wall, as if awaiting the return of the students who had once filled them.

Patrick closed the door quietly behind him, and the five stood gazing, feeling something very much like awe.

"It looks so small," Destiny said.

"That's just because your butt's gotten bigger," Frankie said, and there was slightly nervous laughter all around.

It was true—the room *did* look smaller than it once had. More than that, it seemed unutterably sadder.

Patrick remembered the first day he was ever brought in. How scared he was. How his mother had introduced him to the nice lady in the pink and blue floral-patterned dress, and had said: "Patrick, this is my friend Mrs. Coffee. She's going to take care of you today. Won't that be fun?"

He realized now that it had been a kind of ritual, something to help him feel more at ease, that Mrs. Coffee, the woman decked in wildflowers, hadn't been his mother's friend at all. That day, he had been shown around the schoolhouse and the yard with all of the jungle gyms and the moving, spinning, balancing things. At first he had been frightened by all of the noise and color and motion, then raw pleasure took over. He recognized some of the kids who were in his own trailer park, and others he had seen at the Fred Meyer store, or the Twin Rivers Mall. He was only four, but he was a Big Boy. With that facility only children possess, Patrick made instant best friends, and before twenty minutes had passed was playing and running, and jumping and singing and laughing as if they were all his long-lost cousins.

Patrick glanced over at Destiny, remembering the first time he had seen her at the preschool. She'd been playing a video game, something that looked a lot like one of those shooting games—*Doom,* or *Duke Nuke 'em* or something like that. The kind of game with puzzles and monsters and a terrific selection of lethal weapons. There were differences: there was no blood in this game. The "monsters" were more like triangles and rectangles and other things. From time to time they would flash, and then change to another shape. You had to be fast to shoot them and stop them from shifting.

After watching her for a minute, he realized that there was a pattern to the game, a relationship between the colors and the shapes. Every time you shot them in one way, one thing happened. When you shot them in another way, another set of things happened. He was delighted, and tried to take the gun away from her, but she held on for dear life.

He stopped yanking because he didn't want to be a Bad Boy, and maybe not be able to come back to this place, because he was already beginning to love it. He didn't want to miss out on something that might just turn into more fun than he had ever had before.

So he sat and watched her. Finally he realized that she was *really* good at this, and laughed, and clapped delightedly, almost as if he himself had been the one playing the game.

After a while, she stopped playing and turned it over to him. Mrs. Coffee came over to him, and said, "Hi, Patrick. This is what you should do. Do you know how to spell your name?"

"Yes," he said.

"Good." She gave him a plastic gun with a little lightbulb at the end of the barrel. She fiddled with the television set, and the alphabet appeared. "Go ahead," she said.

At first he was confused, but when he pointed the gun at the screen a tiny dot of light appeared. Moving the gun moved the light, and every time it touched a letter, the letter began to sparkle. He pulled the trigger when the "P" gleamed. There was a snappy *pow* sound, and the P appeared on a line at the bottom of the screen.

He understood! One letter at a time, he shot his name off the screen. After he was done, and the letters PARTRICK EMORY glittered on the television, Mrs. Coffee touched the set again, and the triangles reappeared.

The two triangles floated around. When he shot and hit them they began to line up, and when they were on top of each other the gun in his hand tingled, and made happy sounds.

He gurgled with joy, temporarily unable even to express himself in words. This was fun! This was good. He spent the next hour making the triangles and squares and circles line up. There were certain patterns that earned him a little tingle, others where music played, and a few where the plastic gun buzzed, and a little metal band around the handle shocked him just enough to make him frown.

And every day after that, if he played there were different tingles. Some of them felt good and warm. Some of them hurt just a tiny little bit, and when that happened, boy, he didn't want to do *that* again, but by that time he liked the cartoons and the tingles and the sounds of the music, and everything was just great.

Patrick could hardly wait to come to the center every day. There were always different games, and new songs, and cartoons. He never saw these cartoons on his TV set at home, although sometimes they actually featured familiar characters. They didn't look quite as good as on television, a little simpler maybe, but there were Fred Flintstone, and Space Angel, and the Gummi Bears. The voices didn't sound quite the same, either, but it was still a load of fun.

And so were the games. Where did they get all the games? Had the ladies who ran the center created them? Some were games of hiding, and coloring inside or outside lines, depending on the sounds and colors from the television box. And video games. But there were other things too.

There was a man who came in and led them through exercises that were kind of like Jackie Chan kung-fu stuff, where arms and legs were moving in weird ways, and it was impossible not to say *Hyahh!* and *Hah!*, and everybody laughed.

But when he did it right, he felt good somehow, as if the movements he made in the air were shapes, like the triangles and rectangles in the games. He felt *good* when he did it right, and somehow bad when he did it *wrong*.

After a while he was just enjoying the movements. He wasn't learning kung-fu stuff, because when he got into a little fight with one of the other kids in the trailer park, he couldn't use it at all, and ended up with a black eye.

But when he played softball, or soccer, somehow he and the other Claremont Daycare kids were just a little quicker than the others. He liked that, so sometimes he would practice the exercises at home, make a little dance out of them. If two of the daycare kids got together at the same party, and there was music, they would dance together using the moves. They called it the Claremont Groove, and the other kids thought they were goofy, but cool.

Mrs. Coffee found out about the dancing, and asked them to do it for her. When the dance was performed, Mrs. Coffee got excited and made a phone call. Two weeks later, when they put a video into the television, it featured a man and a woman and a bunch of kids, and they were doing the Claremont Groove to music, and having fun. Patrick really giggled at that, because he knew where it came from.

And all the games! And all the songs, and poems! The snacks weren't all that good-tasting, but he always had energy to play all day long, and his dreams were brighter and louder than they had ever been.

Dreaming began to change. Some of the books at the preschool were about kids who could wake up inside their dreams, who could make their slumber worlds into anything they wanted. Those kids would walk around all waking day saying "Am I dreaming now?" and stuff like that, and then they started saying it in their dreams, and they would wake up inside their dreams, and take control.

And darned if it didn't actually work! In fact it worked so well that maybe half of his dreams were "awake," where he could turn monsters into sheep, mountains into clouds, or fly faster than a jet, on command.

And every day, the daycare ladies asked him to draw pictures from his dreams. He did, and no matter what he drew they loved it, as if they didn't care how well he drew, as long as he did. Every morning he drew one of those pictures, from the dream he remembered best.

Even when his dreams started to become nightmares.

Patrick, Destiny, Frankie, Shermie and Lee sat in a circle on the floor, holding hands. This was a game that they had learned in the school a long time ago. There was no one to play it with now, except each other.

They had to laugh, at first, because this part of the ritual was so silly. But they managed to quiet themselves, then started breathing with slow and steady control. As usual, their exhalations were interrupted by giggles. Destiny said "Shush!" and they started quieting down a little.

And then it began. The trick was, without any kind of plan, to all begin to breathe in the same way, in the same pattern. Inhales and exhales together. This wasn't something that they had been taught. It was something that had started happening spontaneously.

They remained in that state for almost twenty minutes, just breathing, descending into a well of peace and contentment so deep that when Destiny's watch beeped them back to awareness they felt a sense of resentment.

Lee was the first to find words again. "One of the times that my mind drifted, I thought about Mrs. Coffee. Remember her?"

Patrick did remember her, and her memory triggered an oppressive sense of loss and confusion. Patrick thought of the last time he had seen the woman who had nurtured them. She hadn't looked huge and powerful and all-knowing that last time. She seemed shrunken and somehow lost, peering out at the courtroom as if somewhere, in one of those faces, she could find the answers.

"Why do you think that Darnell lied like that?"

"We don't know that he lied," Destiny said reasonably. "We weren't watching all the time. We don't know everything that happened."

Patrick wasn't convinced. "I don't think that it was Mrs. Kellogg or Mrs. Coffee at all. I think that . . . well . . ."

The others stared at him, and he found it difficult to speak. They waited. There was no hurry, no sense of anything other than that here, with each other, they had all the time in the world.

"I don't know what happened," he said. "But it's all a buncha crap. We all had nightmares. Sure. But so what?"

"So what," Lee agreed, as if that dismissed the subject.

They shared the booty bought from web pages, bottle deposits and mowed lawns: cartons of orange juice, low-fat Triscuits, Power Bars and fresh apples. None of them liked candy much, another thing that made the other kids mock them.

Once, achingly long ago, they spent all their days here, had been closer to each other than to their own families. But now they could already feel the world tugging at them, pulling them further and further apart, and the feeling was frightening.

Meal completed, they carefully wrapped their trash up in the little brown paper bags. Destiny collected the bags, and stuffed them all in one larger sack, then rolled the top down tight. When she finished, she exhaled a long, thin stream. "Can we nap?" Destiny asked somberly. Despite her youth, at that moment, she seemed like a little old woman, already riven with fear and regret. And they looked at each other, knowing that there was something real and true here, something healing, and nodded.

The cupboards were no longer stacked with blue blankets. The sound system had been gutted long ago, and the television sets and computers were gone. But the room, its dusty floors, the light streaming obliquely through the windows, still brought a strange and soothing kind of comfort, and that was no small thing in their lives.

They all had thin blankets or sheets in their backpacks, and rolled them out on the floor. Destiny placed hers neatly, pivoting around on her knees with the kind of quick, clever movement that Patrick loved to watch. She stopped, and bit her lip, and said, "Promise. Promise that we'll always be friends."

Patrick felt a swelling within him, one part the primal, youthful ache that wants to say, *yes, yes, always and forever, we'll be together, we'll be friends. . . .*

But he knew that it wouldn't really be that way. He *paid attention to little things*

(where had he first learned to do that?)

Lee's father was already talking about moving on, opening a print shop in Moscow, Idaho. Wanted to be closer to his aging parents. And Shermie's dad was talking about Tahoe for the summer, out on a houseboat owned by a half-brother. And Destiny would be at camp, and then her grandmother's. So there wouldn't even be one last summer to cushion them. Even as Destiny said her piece, they knew that what she had asked was impossible.

This was all there was. Maybe all there would ever be again. No matter how much they wanted to hold their friendship together, they weren't the ones who made decisions. They were just the ones who lived by them.

But there was no use in bitching about that, none at all.

Do nothing that is of no use.

And Patrick wouldn't be the first one to say that the dream was a lie. He couldn't, didn't, have the heart for it. So he said, "Sure. We'll always be friends." And they held hands and hugged each other, and spread the blankets, lying down like the petals of a daisy, all five heads toward the middle.

They settled in. Once, some of them had slept on sides and some on their stomachs. But that was at the beginning, and now they all slept the same way, flat on their backs. The instant they started, Patrick felt the rhythm start to pull him, felt the call of their shared pattern, breathing funneling like a river slowly picking up speed, slowly accelerating toward a roaring falls.

It was so strange, and there was nothing that he could have done to stop it. Too many hundreds of times he had floated in these currents, and closed his eyes, listening to the sounds around him, each and every sound only taking him deeper and deeper into the dream.

Strange, but comforting in a way even his own room at home never was. This was home. These were his brothers and his sister.

Rapidly, rapidly, they fell toward sleep, even if it was only for a few minutes, even if only for a fragment of shared dream.

In that dream, Patrick was grown. He moved through a world of buildings that sometimes transmogrified into trees, if he took his eyes from them for more than a moment at a time.

When he moved through the concrete canyons, he turned to catch a glimpse of himself in a window, and was impressed by himself. How strong he had grown.

("Just wait till you're all grown up, boy," his grandmother had said, and he had heard that, and thought that it would take an impossible time, would take until forever, and yet here it was already.)

He was tall and strong, and handsome, wearing a three-piece suit of some kind, and his eyes were piercing. And from somewhere, something in the very back of his mind said:

"Are you dreaming now?"

And he knew that he was. How he knew, he wasn't sure. It was something about looking at his reflection. Something about seeing himself, and giggling to know that the world of dreams was different from the world above

(below)

where he was limited to those things and experiences that the flesh could comprehend.

But the concrete towers melted away. Suddenly he was in a forest, and the forest was dark and deep, and he had promises to keep, and miles to go . . .

He stopped that thought, because there was a wind winding through the forest behind him, one that plucked at his clothes and his hair, and suddenly he had no other urge but to *go, go, go,* to run, and he was running, and not even certain why. The air around him was swirling as if in a whirlwind, and the leaves were bursting into flame, and he was picked up and whirled around and around in a world of—

Patrick sat up suddenly, completely out of the dream that had abruptly turned into a nightmare.

The others were sitting up, too. He came very close to asking them if they had dreamed, or *what* they had dreamed, but at the last instant something warned him not to.

Destiny looked a little flushed, but Lee and Shermie just looked groggy, and then a bit closed-down, as if they were thinking something that they didn't want to say.

Broach it? Not? Before, there was always a deeper sense of connection after their naps. Now, there were barriers, and he didn't know why.

Again, he started to say something, and then changed his mind.

No. Let it go. So what that they had changed? Everything changes. Everything dies.

33

LOS ANGELES

R enny walked through the offices feeling more confidence than he had in years. The overhead fluorescents seemed brighter, warmer. Paper-clotted desks looked busy and productive, not desperate. Cubbyhole cloistered coworkers seemed somehow more lively and attractive; even the general background buzz of ringing phones and clipped conversation was more attractive and welcoming. Renny may have been emotionally conflicted, but he was also cooking. Yes indeed, the man was on *fire*.

Muriel was lost in a maze of papers and Post-it notes in her glass-walled office, but her eyes were drawn to him, as if threads or wires connected them. He felt *hooked in.*

"Renny?" she asked.

He stopped, not irritated, not excited. He was expectant, contained, safely within the circle of his own power. "Yes?"

"Would you step in here for a minute?"

"Sure." He was almost laughing to himself. There was a touch of hysteria in that humor. *I'm juggling a bomb here.* "What's up?"

She let Renny into the office, thought for a moment, and then closed the door behind him. "Have a seat."

He sat "Whuzzup?" There was something in his voice that he didn't entirely like. The pressure of keeping the secret was starting to wear him down. Here he was, in Marcus's building, on Marcus's payroll, slaving to uphold his honor, sitting on a secret that could bring the whole empire crashing down.

Muriel sat on the edge of her desk, and shifted one tanned and muscular leg over the other. She smoothed her dress down. "Well . . . I have to admit that I sort of thought you'd fall on your face on the hooker piece."

His smile felt nailed into place. "Now why in the world did you think that?"

"Well—you'd intimated that you thought it was beneath you. And your recent work hasn't had . . . that spark."

"And?"

"Well, I read your piece, and I was blown away. This is really good work."

"Thank you."

"In fact, I'm thinking of kicking this up to *Quanta.* Barry and I had lunch today, and he thinks he can use it. Frankly, it's too good for *Eyeful.*"

"Always good to hear." Sand wondered if he should put a bit more enthusiasm in his voice. Surely she knew that a month ago, he would have crawled across a mile of broken glass to hear those words. Now she was playing with Renny. Testing him. Watching him. Damned if she didn't seem just a little nervous about him.

Muriel drummed her fingers on the desk. He didn't speak.

"Why," she said, "do I have a feeling that you've got a secret?"

"Everyone has secrets."

She nodded without agreeing. "How do I put this . . . ?"

"Simply and honestly?"

She laughed. It wasn't the deep, throaty, healthy laugh that he remembered. It was something else. It was worried. "All right. You seem a lot more like the man I met seven years ago. More . . . alive. Or something."

She probably thought he had a girlfriend. And maybe he did: hardly a morning passed without a note from a very special lady in Washington. And almost every night he sat and wrote her of his days, visualizing her smile as she read the little inconsequentials. Three days ago they'd Instant Messaged each other for an hour. Life was good, but that wasn't what Muriel was sensing, oh, no. Not at all.

His smile remained right where it was. "I just love my job," he said.

"Renny, Renny, Renny," she said, unconvinced but not knowing quite what to say. "Well, congratulations, I suppose. Oh, and by the way, there's a package on your desk."

"Thanks." He got up to leave.

"Renny?" she said.

"Yes?"

She sighed. "Never mind," she said, and then turned on a glimmer of her old, girlish charm. "Liar."

He grinned at her and left.

34

Renny drove home along Santa Monica Boulevard, hitting every red light, his mind buzzing, spinning. When he turned off Westwood into the parking lot, he was on autopilot, and couldn't really remember how he had found his way home. He tucked his package, a thick manila envelope, under his arm and ran up the stairs, checking left and right, up and down furtively, as if afraid of surveillance. The key fumbled its way into the lock with damn little help from him.

Every sound seemed unnaturally loud, every shadow in the hallway was a snoop and a spy. He wedged his back against the door as he closed it. The bolt slid in thickly, and the lock clicked into place. Then he finally turned on the lights.

He threw the envelope onto his couch and forced himself to head to the kitchen and make himself a cup of coffee. The familiar ritual: measuring out the dark granules, replacing the filter, pouring the filtered water, even waiting for the first sigh of steam, all had a calming effect on his restless mind. He lit a cigarette as he waited, watching the glowing coal consume paper and tobacco as he drew. He barely tasted it, but the nicotine rush was divine.

Finally he had a cup of steaming java, half of his second cigarette, and the nerve to venture back into the living room. He sat at his desk, sipped, turned, and stared at the wall.

The living room's floral green wallpaper was covered with faxed and Xeroxed photographs of murdered women. These were taped to copies of headlines, articles, interviews, speeches, webzine profiles. To gain a sense of Marcus before he retired from the armed forces, he had researched Marcus's unit, and tracked troop movements with declassified military memos.

All of this work in order to document Alexander Marcus's motions over the last thirty years. The further back he went, of course, the sketchier the information became. Despite that handicap, Sand had found thirty-eight cases (thirty-eight!) of women, generally prostitutes or runaways, murdered with facial wounds attributed to human bites. All were within fifty miles of a Marcus appearance.

Thirty-eight. There might have been two, or three, or five times that number. God in heaven.

Every time he looked at the chart, his stomach dropped again. Holding a secret of this magnitude was absolutely killing him. Sand was shaking as he turned on his desktop computer. As it booted, he opened a book from a stack of books and magazines that he'd collected.

Well, this was it, the story he had searched for his entire life. All he had to do was be certain. *Really* certain. Of two things:

First, of Marcus's guilt. It looked inarguable now. It wasn't one of his bodyguards. It wasn't a coincidence. It was Marcus himself, and if anything, the Praetorians had helped him cover it up.

Second, he had to be certain that he, Renny Sand, could actually break the story. He was killing a part of himself by doing this, and could hear it screaming in the very back of his heart.

Finally, Renny picked up the manila envelope and opened it. About three hundred pages of manuscript bound into a blue folder slid out. *Alexander Marcus—A Life in Shadow.*

He read into the night. It was pulp stuff, digging into Marcus's childhood in ways no other biographer ever had. The reporter, a former *Washington Post* columnist who wrote a single best-selling exposé before spiraling into alcohol-fueled depression, had apparently unearthed sources no one else had ever discovered. Fascinating, sleazy, and slightly embarrassing. Revelatory, but certainly far less damning than the information currently displayed on Renny's wall.

He hated every word he read, but couldn't stop himself.

What happens when you kill your heroes? When the last of your illusions is dead?

Maybe, just maybe that's when you finally become an adult.

Or maybe he was just lying to himself. Again. He had become so very good at that, over the years.

But he had a thread now. Amidst all the lies and tacky self-justification a slender thread connecting him to something honest. A thread that stretched from Los Angeles north to a place called Claremont.

Renny continued to read.

35

Talisa Kramer couldn't breathe. The air was so tight, so hot, that every attempt to salve her lungs brought more pain than relief. Without much success she fought to place the events leading to her imprisonment in some kind of order, some kind of logical sequence.

The main thing was to avoid panic. Panic was a killer, however reasonable a response panic might seem.

A mad bubble of laughter gurgled in her throat. She didn't dare to let that bubble rise. Laughter was the last thing she could afford. Laughter would be the beginning of the end, the admission that her sanity had broken, and that regardless of her captor's intent, her mind was already lost. That the body of Talisa Kramer might live on, but her spirit was dead, or transformed into something unrecognizable.

She lay on her side in an utterly dark, confined space that she could only believe was the trunk of a car. A car. Now she remembered. She remembered traveling to the motel in a car. She remembered that the room had been far away from the road. More cars. There seemed to be a tiny island of memory, surrounded by an ocean of dread. Her mind was only giving her a few pieces at a time, just enough to allow her to understand what had happened, but nothing more than that.

She remembered what had happened in the room. Strange. The thin man had promised her a secret, promised that someone famous would be waiting for her, that it would be a special treat.

This would be good. She had had famous men before. A rap singer who had done a gig in town. Another time, she serviced the host of an MTV game show. They were the same as any other men. When she first began this long, lonely road, some part of her had expected that famous people might be different. Nicer, perhaps. Sexier. Perhaps she expected them to be bigger down there, or somehow golden. . . .

But she found that they were just like other men, except that they had more money, and expected others to see their importance, to be cowed by it.

But the promised "important man" hadn't been in the motel room. And although disappointed, she had already been paid, and went through the motions as she had so many times before.

The night began reasonably enough, with Talisa maintaining the kind of control that she liked. When in control, Talisa never sold herself, only rented. She determined the time and the place, and the ways, and the price.

She had control when she walked the street near the airport. She liked the sounds, and the smells. She liked the old walk-up flophouses, and the ancient women peering down from the second-story windows. She liked knowing that if she made a single misstep, she would join them one day. There was something frightening about that, but exciting, too. It tested her control. It was like walking a tightrope across a pool of sharks. Every additional twenty-four hours of survival reinforced her essential uniqueness. Not everyone could walk that line without falling off. She had something special. She was a star, only no one had realized it yet.

A girlhood in Innes, Texas, had been made tolerable by dreams of Hollywood. She dreamed of the glitz, and the images from the glamour magazines, and the movies where golden people made golden love to the accompaniment of stereo-surround soundtracks. In her fantasies, sex wasn't this wet, grubby thing that she had learned in the backseats of cars, in dingy motel rooms, at the blunt, weathered hands of the man her mother wanted her to call Father.

So she left home, hitching, planning to hitch all the way along the 10 Freeway to Malibu. Talisa would wait tables, and eventually someone would discover her, because there was something inside her, something deep and hidden, that she knew was pure, and good.

She had heard stories that some people, when they hurt, when they were in a bad situation, psychologically abandoned their bodies. Talisa did not. Instead, she went deep within, and there she found peace.

That peaceful place inside her had sustained her through eight years of horror. No matter how bad things had gotten, she could contract to a mote small enough to slip into safety, and there she remained, within a tiny ray of light, feeling no slightest connection to the body around her.

And if things had gone wrong, if she had run out of money and needed to do things on the streets of Phoenix that she had never thought she would do, then it wasn't Talisa that was violated, it was merely the darkness surrounding her light. They could never have her light. Their hands and their tongues and their sex never reached deep enough to touch her light.

Whoring was, after all, just acting. It was pretending to be someone or something that they wanted. And she was good at it, as she'd known she would be. She had only to pull back into the light. Then the dark part, the irrelevant part, could be shaped into anything she wanted it to be.

She was only acting, merely portraying a character when she paraded her wares, turned her head saucily when a car horn beeped. She was only courting an Oscar or an Emmy or a Tony when she went to her back or her knees in a hotel room, and told them how great they were and how much she wanted them, and by the way, for an extra ten bucks they could have her ass as well.

It was all just an act.

But she wasn't acting now. She was more frightened than she had ever been in her entire life. Judging by the smell and the burning sensation between her legs, she had already soiled herself.

It had started with the pale man, the one who was tall and thin, and seemed to be covered with a sheen of thin, golden hairs so fine that they shone like oil under the streetlamps. He had pulled up next to her on Main Street, and she had approached the window as always, and been drawn into his eyes. For a moment, she had lost her place in her practiced spiel (*Wannadate, baby? Lookin' goodtonight, baby. Where's your woman, can I be, could I be, do you wammetobe ya baby tonight?*) and was lost in those eyes. Her stepfather had had eyes like that, on the occasions when he came home drunk, but not angry. Those nights, he would sit, watching television late and sipping beer. She would curl up next to him on the couch just to be near him. Sometimes, after her sow of a mother tottered off to bed he would look over at her with eyes like marbles frying in hot oil, and those blunt rough hands would close on her.

This man had eyes like that. He picked her up, told her what he wanted, and took her to the shadowed and secluded motel, where he said that the important man would be waiting.

At first she had been delighted, felt beautiful, desired, important.

And then came the swift, sudden pain around her throat, and she had awakened here.

Had she done something wrong? She could only think that getting in the car in the first place had been a terrible mistake. Had she failed to please? She couldn't see how. She had given more of herself than usual, even offered some of the light, just a touch of the light, something special for a special evening. She had given him real smiles, real laughter, even allowed him to kiss her wetly.

And perhaps, just perhaps, that had been a mistake. Perhaps in giving something of her true self, she had offended him. Perhaps her mother was right. Perhaps she was utterly, irredeemably corrupt, and all she had to offer the world was her darkness.

The car stopped. She heard clicks and vibrations, footsteps, muttering. Then the trunk opened. She tried to kick up, but was blinded by the sudden flood of light.

Then she was crouching by the side of the car, naked, shivering in the night cold, still blinded by the light. She heard him say: "Run, bitch."

"Why?" She was humiliated by the weakness in her voice. She tried to find a place within her that was strong, and confident, something to believe in about herself, a place to make a stand.

She tried to find the light, and couldn't.

The tip of a boot found her ribs. She gasped, sudden pain flooding her, making her cry out with shame and surprise. "Because it's time."

Talisa found her balance, managed to fight her way to her feet, and on numbed legs began to hobble toward the safety of the open desert. Safe. Perhaps she could hide. "You've got two minutes," he said, and then she heard the rustle of clothing.

She ran. Her feet were immediately savaged by rocks, and pine needles, and the shocking night chill. She heard her own voice praying, heard herself scream without sound.

Cramped and cold from her time in the trunk, her legs failed her, but adrenaline and a young, strong heart did not. Long ago she had read somewhere that an actress's body was her instrument, and she regularly went to the 24-Hour Fitness center in Paradise Valley, pumped on the stairmaster, sweated through the aerobics classes, and did everything she could to keep her instrument in proper condition.

Talisa swore that releasing her had been a mistake. She could run. She could hide. She could think. She would survive. In school, long ago, she had run track, and knew that if you could just find a rhythm within yourself, everything came more easily. If she could just find that, just manage to breathe with her legs, just stop the fear from strangling her, just find a little speed . . . somewhere up ahead of her, she heard car sounds, truck sounds. A road. Or was that an echo?

Her ankle turned on uneven ground, and she tumbled, caught herself, scraped her hand on a clump of cactus needles. She went down to the ground, and stayed there for a moment, trying not to make a sound. Perhaps if she was silent, if she was very, very quiet, she could remain hidden. But was silence any protection? Was shadow?

Moonlight glimmered through the sparse cloud cover, its cold light bathing her in silver dust. There were lights ahead, and highway sounds. She wasn't sure where she was. By the time she had regained consciousness in the car trunk, she had already been on a highway. North? East? She thought that they had headed north, away from the city.

That might be along the 17 freeway, although it was possible that the thin man had taken her east along the 10, back toward Texas.

Her eyes were adjusting. In some odd way, the depth of her fear was forcing her to a greater, deeper, hotter aliveness than she had ever known. It was forcing her to drop her acts. All of her acts. Not the salty hooker, seasoned and cynical. Not the blushing schoolgirl or the temporarily out-of-work actress, not the fantasy stepdaughter that she played so well.

None of those roles fit at all. And yet, it didn't stop there, either. The old Talisa, good girl, bad girl, wronged child . . . none of those roles had much to do with this. It was as if every successive step peeled her a little closer to the core. And what she discovered in her mad flight, listening to the hard-packed sand crackle behind her, knowing that death was oh, so very close, was the part of her that wanted desperately to live. A part of her craved life, loved air. In those moments she knew that the dreams of Hollywood and fame and fortune and even romance were irrelevant. That what mattered was this, was the exhilarating joy of merely being alive, alive to feel the pain in her feet as she slashed them on rocks, alive to feel the hot wind whistling in her lungs, even alive to feel the fear chewing at her.

Because fear wasn't so bad. There was one Talisa, running naked through the desert, and there was another Talisa, above the running Talisa, watching and aware and cheering her on. And it wasn't completely fragmented, because the watching Talisa joined her, and there was a pure moment, when all the women-children within her flowed together, and they were as one.

And she was alive, so alive, and the crest of the hill was so close, and if she reached it, she could stand there, headlights splashing over her like waves, and they would see her naked body, and stop, and then—

Something hit her from behind. The air *whuffed* out of her. A moment after that she felt herself slam breathlessly into the ground, her mouth and nose crushed into the sand.

A knee in her back. A fevered, muffled laugh.

Then the pain began. It wasn't so bad at first, because she had the trick, the terrible trick she had learned at the hands of her stepfather back in El Paso. She gave the thin man the darkness, and didn't even associate the gobbling cries for help or mercy or an ending with herself. It was too far away, too distant. It was just an actress, on a distant stage.

And finally all of the darkness was gone, and there was only the light, the real Talisa, no place to hide, no place at all. And the voice was her own, and the pain was her own.

And ultimately, the death was her own, and if it was hideously long in coming, it was, in the final analysis, as good as any death that had ever been given anyone, anywhere, at any time. And most importantly, unlike most things in Talisa Kramer's short and unhappy life, it was hers and hers alone.

36

CLAREMONT,
THURSDAY, MAY 31

Claremont's largest movie theater was a triplex set in the corner of the main mall, sandwiched between an Arby's roast beef and a Twilight Bowl with a sign advertising CHICKEN NIGHT TONIGHT!! in garish green letters.

Patrick generally liked the theater, except that they never seemed to have hot dogs: they were either just sold out, or the frankfurters were still frozen, or the dogs on the little rotisserie machine had been there since noon and were roughly as appetizing as week-old roadkill.

Patrick still wasn't sure what was happening with his mom and dad, but there seemed at least a glimmer of hope for their future. Otis had stayed over one more time since that night of drunken rage, and if Patrick hadn't heard his parents arguing through the wall, he would have felt that life was beginning to normalize.

Beside him in the darkened theater, his father chortled at the inane antics of two actors in a regrettably bad action-comedy. The actors were thrashing about to little effect, and in general seemed rather embarrassed. Theatrics like this popped Patrick right out of the illusion of a film, and reminded him that he was watching actors reciting lines in front of a camera. He *hated* when that happened, and it seemed to happen more often to him than it did to most kids. Even most adults.

His dad seemed completely into it all, rocking back and forth, laughing and pounding his hand on his knee, big booming laugh filling the theater. Usually Patrick was a little embarrassed by his dad's exuberance, but considering they were two of only four people in the entire room, it was difficult to get himself to care.

Despite the empty theater and the bad movie, it was a chance for him to kick back, share popcorn with his old man, and for the two of them to be, well, kids together.

By the time the last bridge had been blown up, the last lame joke tossed off, and the credits rolled, Patrick and his father were the only ones remaining in the theater.

"Damn good movie," Otis said, stretching. "Not many people here, though."

"At least we could find a seat," Patrick said brightly. He pitched his empty popcorn box into the trash as they passed. "Two points."

Although it was only a little before nine o'clock, the theater lobby was almost deserted, one clerk and the manager watching them leave with tired, bored expressions. Patrick made a little check mark in his head, cataloging yet another career that didn't interest him.

What did he want to do with his life? There were a ton of things that didn't interest him, but he wasn't at all sure what might. Doctor? Lawyer? Indian Chief? He felt a deep sense of confidence that he could have any career he was willing to commit to, but . . .

They were halfway across the parking lot now. The few cars parked here belonged to theatergoers attending other movies at the multiplex and bar patrons at the *Lucky Lady* next to the theater, so it took a minute to really register that his dad's truck was surrounded by motorcycles. Cappy and four of his boys were there, along with Ellie Krup, who sported a lovely black eye.

Patrick got a little closer to his father, whose fists were already knotted. "You're blocking my truck," Otis said.

Cappy spit on the ground and rolled his shoulders. "Little bird said you wanted to talk to me the other night."

Otis looked at Patrick. And then back at Cappy. "No. I didn't."

"Didn't have any problem talking to my woman," he said. Ellie flinched as he said the words. "Why don't you talk to me?"

Otis's arm wound tighter around Patrick. "Look," he said. "I don't want no trouble."

"I just bet you don't." He hopped down off the hood of Otis's truck. "Oops," Cap said, without looking down or behind him. "Looks like you got a scratch on your truck here."

"Where?"

Very deliberate, Cap pulled his hands out of his pockets. He was holding a half-dozen keys set on a brass ring. He ran the longest across the truck's hood, leaving a jagged scratch. "Here," he said.

Otis's shoulders tensed. Patrick felt a dizzying jolt of fear, as if he had never completely left the nightmare on the bridge. "Dad, no."

"You talk pretty big when you're backed up by four men," Otis said evenly.

Cap raised an eyebrow. He gestured toward the others almost as if he had forgotten they were present. "Oh. That? Ain't nothing. They don't get involved."

"Right," Otis said. He stood in front of Cap for a tense second, and then reached around him to open the door.

" 'Scuse me," he said with forced politeness.

He slipped Patrick into the truck, then walked around to the other side.

Cap clucked. *Buck-buck-buckaw.* "Fuckin' pussy," he said. "Nigger faggot."

Otis paused. He looked through the window of the truck. Patrick shook his head an urgent *no*.

Otis closed his eyes, as if this was the greatest test of faith of his life. Then opened the door—

Cappy punched him on the left side of the face.

"Dad! No!" Patrick yelled, while another part of him screamed *kick his ass.*

Otis wheeled, and punched with a straight left hand that struck Cappy squarely on the nose. No getting past it now: the fight was on. Cappy was taller, and bigger across the shoulders, and his face glowed with anger. Patrick should have been terrified, was ashamed that he wasn't frightened for his dad, but Otis had already hunched over, protecting his chin with his fists, turned a little sideways to protect his groin with his knee. He stepped back, shook himself, and slid back into range.

What Patrick knew, and Cappy didn't, was that his dad had done a little boxing way back, and still knew how to put it together. Cappy was a bully, a bruiser, a thug. Otis could take him. If it was a fair fight, he just knew Dad could do it. God, please.

Cappy tried a kick that would have been merely sloppy on a football field, but was downright foolish in a street fight. Otis caught Cappy's leg under his arm, and buried his fist almost to the wrist in Cappy's swollen gut. The bearded man exhaled a huge gust of sour air, and stumbled back, gagging.

As promised, the other bikers were just watching. So far. Patrick didn't just watch: he *felt* the action. His own hips and shoulders twitched as every punch was thrown. This was nothing like watching a fight on television or in a movie. It was sweat and fists flying, blood at the corners of mouths, muttered curses, grunts of effort, narrowed eyes and savage grimaces.

Cappy punched Otis in the face, then missed badly with a swing, stumbling to catch his balance. He pivoted to face him again. Otis took a big step in, and with skills unused since the glory days of high school, punted Cappy in the crotch.

Cappy sagged and doubled over, mouth pursed in an "o" of surprise. Patrick was sure that that was the end of it, would have to be the end of it, but incredibly the giant staggered forward and drove Otis into the side of the truck. He windmilled, smashing Otis in the ribs with brutal roundhouse punches. Now Patrick was afraid. This was a slow-motion nightmare: every punch took forever to land, every snap of his father's head lasted for an eternity. This was a syrupy world of pain and terror that seemed one with that terrible night on the bridge, like a river of molten violence that flowed just beneath the surface of his life, erupting to the surface at its unknowable whim.

"Dad!" Patrick screamed.

Cappy smashed the side of Otis's head into the driver's window. The glass cracked, leaving a smear of blood from a cut ear. Otis's eyes were glazed, his knees wobbly. Cappy wound up with a looping right—

The bikers cheered—

And at the very last moment Otis moved two inches to the left, slipping the punch. Cappy's fist smashed into the window, through the window, cracking glass and breaking knuckles. The giant roared with pain and backpedaled. Otis grabbed Cappy's arm, swung him in a circle, and smashed his head into the truck. Cappy bounced away, right into Otis's fist. Left, right, left, right—Otis chopped Cappy down with a determined, almost workmanlike rhythm.

Cappy fell to his knees, and looked up at Otis with an expression of hatred mixed with a vast and almost childlike confusion. Then he toppled over onto the side of his face.

There was a moment of silence. The other bikers looked at each other, and their fallen leader. It was an ugly moment.

A blinking red light slid over them. Patrick whipped his head around in time to see a police cruiser turning their way.

Cappy pushed himself to hands and knees, and then staggered up. He looked from his men to Otis and back again. He wobbled to his bike, and looked back at Otis bleakly. He opened his mouth as if about to say something, then perhaps thought better of it, and just got on his bike. The air around him seemed to shimmer. Patrick thought that he had never seen a more dangerous human being in his entire life. Now, more than ever, Cappy frightened him.

Cappy rode away, his men following.

Otis limped to the truck, and slid in beside Patrick. He wheezed, fighting for air. They looked at each other for a long moment, then Otis stared straight forward into the darkness.

He was still breathing hard. "Self-defense . . . ?" he croaked, expression pleading.

Patrick threw his arms around his father, and cried, and they held each other in the darkened parking lot.

37

DIABLO, ARIZONA,
SUNDAY, JUNE 3

The morning sky was crested with dense, white clouds, shielding the town from a piercing sun. Its citizens had no illusions: by noon the cloud cover would bake off, and southern Arizona would face the sun's full fury. For now, it was a welcome relief.

At the Diablo Grocery, the ice machine was working overtime. Its ancient compressor labored, unable to keep up with the demand as Kelly Kerrigan and her husband Bob loaded groceries into their truck.

"I was thinking blueberry," Kelly said. "Remember the tarts you made last President's Day?"

"Surely do. Watch your thumb, there." He slid in a twenty-pound sack of flour.

"Heck, Bob, we had three requests for the recipe, and in my book, that makes it . . . kind of . . ." She shoved against the bag, making room for a flat of strawberries. "*Oof* . . . obligatory . . ."

He mopped his forehead. "Ooh. Kinda early in the morning for them big words, ain't it . . . ?" Bob poked his head up as a police cruiser crunched across the gravel into the parking lot. Kelly watched it with a guarded smile on her face. There were two people in the car, one of whom Kelly didn't recognize. Sheriff D'Angelo got out from the passenger side. His clothes were theatrical, more nineteenth than twenty-first century, a cross between Wyatt Earp and Marshall Dillon, with ten-gallon hat, cowboy boots and tin star. The Colt .45 at his belt, however, was completely functional.

"Hey there, Angie," Kelly said with a broad, guarded smile.

"Kelly." D'Angelo grinned back at her. "How you doing today, Bob?"

"Every day above ground is a good day."

"Amen to that," D'Angelo said. "Saw the truck, thought I'd come over, find out if you folks needed a hand."

"No," Bob said carefully. "I think we can manage."

A cloud overhead had shifted, and a shaft of sunlight fell directly on the parking lot, seeming to increase the temperature by fifty degrees.

"Oh, I know you can, Bob. Just being neighborly."

Kelly wiped her hand across her forehead. "Sure appreciate that. Good shooting the other day, Angie."

"Just lucky. Better be, when the competition is as good as you. Sorry you weren't out there too, Bob—takes a little of the starch out of it, you know?"

He ignored the remark. "Who's the new kid?" Bob thumbed toward the man behind the cruiser's wheel.

"Oh—driving? This here's Riley Woodcock. You remember Riley?"

Kelly nodded her head. Another Praetorian. She hadn't seen him since . . . Utah. "It's turning into an old boy's club around here. How goes it, Riley?"

Woodcock tipped his hat. He was a raw-boned Okie, in his fifties but, like D'Angelo, lean and fit. He carried himself with the erect posture of the combat soldier he had once been.

"Charlie still on leave?"

D'Angelo nodded. "Leaves me short a deputy—Riley's filling in for a bit. Be talking to Charlie later, though. Should I say howdy?"

"You do that," Kelly said.

"Well, all right then. You two take it easy, and you get inside, Bob. Gonna be a scorcher."

"You bet," Bob said.

D'Angelo got back in the cruiser, and tooled off. Bob shoved the last bags and boxes into the back of the truck violently, bruising corners and probably cracking eggs. His breath caught, and he was suddenly pulling for air, face gone slightly red, but he held his hand up to silence Kelly when she tried to speak.

They got in the truck and began to drive. Bob was silent as they drove through the narrow streets of residential Diablo, just two blocks off the tourist strip.

They parked behind a carefully maintained nineteenth-century two-story clapboard house. The yard sported a rock garden and fountain, and was shaded with a cedar tree.

Kelly carried a bag of groceries in each arm, but Bob could only manage to carry one up the steps through the screened back porch and into the kitchen. She set the bags down on a sturdy table in the center of her kitchen, and snuck glances back at him as she stored eggs in the oversized refrigerator and bread in the pantry.

Bobby Ray slammed his groceries down on the kitchen table, then stalked out to the shed behind the house, unlocked it, and disappeared inside. Kelly held her temper, putting away the rest of the groceries herself. She brewed up a pot of tea, waited for it to whistle at her, and then chose two flowered mugs from the cupboard and filled them brimfull.

The shed was Bob's workshop, and by unspoken rule she never entered without knocking. Carrying two steaming mugs, the best she could manage was a foot-knock, but Bob answered promptly, and she eased in.

The room was dark except where the gooseneck lamps curled over vises and drill-presses and reloading equipment. Here in this room, Bob was still the man he used to be. The outside of the shed was weathered wood, but inside the walls were steel-reinforced. He probably had a half-million dollars' worth of rifles and handguns in that room: muzzle and breech-loader, antique harquebus to competition Feinwerkbau model 300S 4.5mm 10-meter rifle.

After Kelly, his only love in the world was his guns. He could spend days in his shop, modifying the rifles other shooters sent him from across the state, experimenting with cartridges, filling dozens of notebooks with sketches and designs for specialized weapons he would never have the time to create.

His great loves were the Western lever-actions: Spanish Tigre 44/40, Winchester 1892 eleven-shot with the 955mm barrel, the 336 CS Marlin with a tubular seven-shot magazine. They were toys, tools, pets, and he pampered them endlessly.

If one was his special love, it was the Sharps 1853 sporting rifle, the deadly "Buffalo" with a gray steel frame. He had two, one taking .45 paper cartridges, and the other modified for .44 long-barrel. He was deadly accurate with either, and could send a slug down its twenty-six-inch barrel into the bull's-eye at 250 yards.

Over the last three days Bob had partially disassembled the rifle, working on the double Stecher trigger, tightening the pull.

She set the teacup beside him, but he ignored it for a minute, working at a metal spur with a black piece of emory cloth. Then he picked the cup up without looking at it, and sipped.

She watched without speaking at first, but finally said, "Bob? Honey? What is it?"

He put the cup down, and hung his head without looking at her. He had doffed his cap, revealing a completely bald scalp, marred with dark red discoloration. "That man. He just . . . treats me like I'm already dead."

"Just being friendly. Friendly as he knows how. Don't you fret none, hon."

"I guess. Sometimes he is friendly. Hell, he helped us buy this place." Of course that was just business: Angel owned a piece of the local bank. "But, I don't know . . ." He took another sip. "Maybe its just me. Most of the time, I'm all right. All right. But now and then, I just think about all the work I'm leaving you with."

She understood. There was painting and planting to be done, the cactus garden was edging toward raggedy, and the family room branching off from the kitchen was unfinished. Its floor was half-stripped, the walls only partially painted. Once, they had dreamed of turning it into a den or hobby room, but Bob was just plain running out of energy, and she needed all of her focus to keep the B&B running.

"Bob, you just shut up. You're not leaving me just yet. Not for a long while. And we bought this together. This was *our* dream. My dream." A Texas Ranger, a Secret Service woman. A chance meeting in Fort Worth, and instant attraction. A long-distance courtship, followed by a marriage that had given both of them the combination of intimacy and space that two career-driven, high-octane achievers demanded. Then retirement together in a town whose roots rested in a simpler, less political time. Dreams of warm, quiet nights, laugh-filled days. "You helped make it happen."

He turned away from her and made a funny sound, something halfway between a laugh and a sob.

"Bob," Kelly said. "Bob, you listen to me. Just stop it now. We got a lot more living to do. Together. Just stop it." She wrapped her arms around him.

He pressed his face against her. "Just . . . hold me?" His voice was muffled.

She stroked his hair, gentling him as she scanned the walls of rifles. Bobby was selling off the least precious, those that hadn't too deep a place in his heart. The Dreyse 1857 Prussian cavalry carbine, but not the 9.5 Wm. Read Plains rifle with the beautiful woodwork. The Corsican light-infantry 17.5 mm, but not the 1819 Hall breech-loader flintlock. Tidying up. Saying good-bye to the world.

He sighed. "Let's get the rest of the groceries."

"Already got 'em, Bobby Ray."

He nodded ruefully. "Art of living, ain't it? Volunteer to help just after the job's done." He rubbed her nose with his. "How about this. Maybe I can do a mite more painting on the side room after dinner."

"Maybe later," she said softly. "When it gets cooler. You just work on your Sharps. She's a good old girl."

"The best," he said. "Just like you." He rested a hand on her still-slim waist, and another on the roundness below it, and nestled his chin on her shoulder. It had been two years since Bobby Ray's body had functioned fully, not long after the sad-eyed doctor had begun talking about anti-nausea drugs and chemotherapy. Two years of chronic fatigue and muscle wasting; but there were many ways an ingenious and giving man could share physical love, and thank God they had never allowed shyness or prudery stop them.

She felt the blood heating in her face, and knew that this would be one of those nights, the ones she would remember after he was gone.

She was careful to blink the tears out of her eyes before she let him see her face. "You just save your strength, you hear? And we'll see what's cooking for dessert."

38

D'Angelo pulled up in the tan sheriff's Jeep. It was air-conditioned, but he rarely turned it up high. He liked the heat, enjoyed the fact that if he relaxed just right, the temperature barely seemed to bother him. Other men would sweat and groan, and D'Angelo's thighs barely dampened beneath the leather pants.

He was in his fifties, and never worked out in a gym, but his body was still lean and aggressive, had yet to soften at jowl or gut. He moved like the lifelong predator he was: every step, every gesture compact, economical, and somehow *wary*.

The offices of the Sheriff's department weren't large, but adequate. The front receptionist was an older woman, Grace Marchini.

"Good morning, Gracie," he said casually. *And isn't it a shame I can't tell you exactly* why *it's so good.*

"Morning, Sheriff," she answered. "Good trip?"

"They were biting." *Oh, yes, indeed they were.* "Calls?"

"On your desk."

"Thanks," he said. *I like you, Gracie. I like you so much I wish I could show you the souvenir in the Jeep's trunk.* A stack of envelopes sat in the in-basket, and he browsed them. "Bring me back a cup of that good coffee, would you?"

"Sure thing." She dimpled at him.

D'Angelo went back into his office, and sorted through his mail. As he did, Gracie brought him a steaming mug of coffee. The sheriff sipped with satisfaction.

"Your husband's damned lucky I like the old bastard. Half a mind to just shoot him and keep you to myself." *And peel you with a can opener. Right in front of him, while he's watching his guts spill out. But that would be too close to home. Too close for comfort.*

She giggled, as he knew she would, and her cheeks colored. "You'd never keep up with me, Angel."

"Probably right." He grinned. "I'm going to walk the boards." She nodded and disappeared. Anything that came up while he was gone could wait a spell.

He turned right out of the front door and headed down to Silver Street, Diablo's main drag. A stagecoach rumbled past, crammed with tourists craning with Kodaks and Sonys to capture a bit of the Olde West. Diablo was a mining town, established in the 1860s. It had been just a supply store and a saloon, with a few hardscrabble farms around.

Over the decades, it grew. By the 1890s it was the second-largest town for a hundred miles, just behind Tombstone. Like Tombstone, Diablo had almost died in the first decades of the new century. Not until the tourist explosion of the 1960s resurrected Tombstone did anyone even pay attention to the single convenience store and gift shop that composed Diablo.

But somehow, Diablo grew. Old houses were declared state monuments, the opening of a new cave to the north brought spelunkers and tourists down from Phoenix, and a big Clint Eastwood western in 1980 rebuilt half the town. Investment money began pouring in. Somehow, it became a popular retirement spot for state and federal lawmen and ex-military living on pensions and enjoying new identities as Pat Garrett and Jesse James, putting on three shows a day for the tourists, and parading the authentic wooden sidewalks as mythic men of old.

Diablo came back to life; greater life, in fact, than it had enjoyed in its youth.

Tristan D'Angelo had retired from Marcus Communications a wealthy man still in his prime, and found Diablo to his liking. He bought property, worked for local law enforcement and then ran for sheriff, putting enough money and charm into the campaign to smoke the competition.

This was *his* town now, and he'd had more than enough juice to get the loan for Kelly Kerrigan when she retired. Yes, that had been a good thing. He walked the streets, past the barber shop and the soda stand; the little restaurants that had two menus, one for tourists, one for locals; the nickelodeon where silent westerns and a slide show of Diablo's history played from nine in the morning until ten at night. He passed saloons with the double doors, four curio shops with carved topaz and hardwood in the shapes of noble Indians, an ice cream parlor advertising Italian ices.

The tourists gawked at him in his finery, and he tipped his hat politely to them, imagining that he was in another era, another time, with other responsibilities. . . .

And other pleasures. Yes, the pleasures.

"Afternoon, Sheriff," a little boy said to him, and he tipped his hat, making the boy's day.

Yes, the pleasures. He still remembered the girl's screams, muffled though they had been by a wad of her own clothing. And when someone finally found her body, in a year or ten, would that last scream still be in her throat?

The shopkeepers greeted him, the other cowboys (no real ammunition in their belts) stepped out of his way, and in every way, this was a fine, fine day.

Alexander would have liked this day, he thought. D'Angelo owned half the town. Bought it with Marcus's money. He was the sheriff, thanks in part to Marcus's media clout. There was damned good hunting within three hours' drive. And an hour's easy flight landed him in Los Angeles, home of the best hunting in the world.

Alexander would have appreciated all of it, especially the irony.

Too bad you couldn't be here, he said to himself.

Too bad you got sloppy, Alexander.

Too bad I had to kill you.

39

CLAREMONT,
FRIDAY, JUNE 8

The Claremont Lumber yard stretched over three hundred acres of land, nestled between the I-5 freeway and the Cowlitz River. Day and night, trucks, trains and boats carried an endless stream of logs in, and hewn planks or raw lumber products out.

Driving his little forklift, Otis Emory negotiated a vast interconnected warren of mills, offices, shops, storage sheds, ship docks and truck parking, meeting halls and cafeterias. Claremont Lumber directly or indirectly employed almost a third of the town's entire population, down from almost ninety percent at the turn of the century.

The payroll offices were next to the Claremont Lumber Credit Union building, the town's largest financial institution. On the first and third Thursday of every month, the employees lined up for their checks at noon, or waited until five for the checks to be brought around to their various posts.

Otis parked his tractor in a COMPANY VEHICLES ONLY space and entered the payroll office, waiting and chatting in line with the men before and behind him, pretty much enjoying the day, and looking forward to having his money in his hands instead of behind a sheet of one-inch bullet-proof plastic.

The woman behind the counter was too old to flirt as she did, but she never seemed to let that stop her. "Another fat one, Otis," she said.

"*Could* spend it all right here," he said, and leered at her.

She blushed prettily, the reddening visible through the thick make-up, and handed him his envelope. "You get along to that pretty wife, now, you hear?"

" 'Nother time, maybe," he said.

He went out to his car in the parking lot. Otis paused for a moment, alert, scanning the lot. Cappy had been avoiding him. Otis had caught only two brief glimpses of the man since their altercation. Was that good? Would it be better if Cappy threatened him? Promised revenge? Offered apology? He knew only that his gut felt as if it were full of frogs.

There was nothing threatening, no sign of anything to concern him even in these nervous days. Just some knots of people scattered here and about talking. He shrugged, got in his car, and drove out of the lot.

Brogan's was one of the oldest bars in town, a mill bar run by a family that had once cut board for old man Claremont. One fine day in '37 someone swept up two of Billy Brogan's fingers from the sawdust-speckled floor, and packed them in ice. The nearest hospital, down in Vancouver, had reattached them, but in a couple of weeks they turned black and greasy and had to be taken back off again, and Billy Brogan won permanent disability. He had used the settlement cash to open the bar.

One of Brogan's sons worked the mill, the other worked the bar. And a generation after that, the bar was the family business, and the only sawdust any of them breathed was sprinkled on the floor to soak up the beer.

The eternal party had already commenced. Reba McIntyre was asking *"Why Not Tonight"* in the background, and a few of the patrons were swaying their shoulders to the beat. Otis sat at the bar.

Cory Brogan was a beer-barrel of a man, just a bit over six feet tall, but carried it like seven. "Otis," he said in greeting. "Haven't seen you in a while. Usual?"

"Just a beer. Taking the kid shopping tonight."

"Got it," Cory said, and drew a foaming glass of Miller. "What for?"

Otis sighed. "Gym stuff. Shoes, shirt, pants. I remember when tennis shoes cost five bucks. Now you got to take out a mortgage. Nikes, Adidas, New Balance. Wow."

"I'm in the wrong business." He slid the glass down in front of Otis. "Here you go."

Otis drank. Then too casually, he asked: "Seen Cappy around lately?"

"No. Not really. Not since you handed him a whuppin'."

Otis laughed. "Got around, huh?"

"Yeah," Brogan said, but didn't laugh along. "Chuckle now. But Cap's a mean one—I wouldn't turn my back on him."

"Don't intend to." Otis sat for a minute, just drinking and thinking. He was going to have to deal with Cappy again, he knew it. But with every sip of his drink, it got easier and easier to remember the victory, and forget the uncertainty and the fear. Hell, he had thumped the bastard once, he could do it again.

Except that next time Cappy wouldn't hold his boys back. Next time, it would be a mob scene, and that was going to be ugly.

When he looked up at the clock, forty minutes had passed.

"That gonna be it?" Brogan asked.

"Maybe a whiskey. Just one."

"Just one. Right you are. Hey, Otis, what time does the store close?"

"Store?"

"You know, the one you're taking your kid to?"

"Oh, yeah. Sure. How could I forget?"

Brogan looked at him carefully, shrugged, and went to service other customers. Otis sat alone, staring into the reflection in the mirror behind the bar. The guy staring back at him looked big, dark, confused. And not nearly drunk enough.

Patrick waited by the window. The headlights of a car slid by, followed by a long dark Chrysler.

That wasn't his dad. He shifted, looking over at Cap's trailer. It seemed quiet over there, darker. It had been, since the night on the bridge. Worse, since the parking lot. Something had changed over there, and he wasn't sure what. As if a great weight had descended upon them. The air felt compressed, as though at any moment it might explode.

"Where is he, Mom?"

He had murmured it to himself, but somewhat to his surprise, she appeared behind him, laying a comforting hand on his shoulder.

"He'll be here, hon. I'm sure he's just working a little late."

He glanced at the clock. It was six o'clock.

His mother tried to comfort him, but he just continued to stare, almost unblinking, into the darkness. Three times she had asked him if there was something wrong, as if she sensed some deeper significance in his distraction and nervousness in recent days.

She busied herself with small things, and the next time she came back to stand beside him, it was almost six-forty.

"Store closes in twenty minutes," Patrick said dully. There was something else burrowing around inside him, something far stronger than a lust for new shoes. It was genuine concern, fear that something might have happened to his father, an emotion so deep and selfless that Patrick might have been the adult, and Otis the child.

"I know," she said, "but . . ." she was interrupted by the sound of another car pulling up. This time, thank goodness, it was his father.

Vivian's hand tightened on his shoulder. "Wait here a minute, darling."

Patrick shrugged her hand away. "I'll get my coat."

Vivian wrapped a shawl around her shoulders, and stepped out on the porch. Otis appeared, just the slightest bit unsteady.

"You're late," she said.

"Just a li'l bit."

"You've been drinking."

There was a Band-Aid on the side of his face, and when she tried to get a closer look, he drew away. "Ain't nothing. Don't have to make no case out of it."

"I don't like you taking him when you've been drinking."

"I had one beer. A li'l whiskey. Ordered another one, but didn't drink it."

She watched him carefully. Lying had never been one of his faults. "Why not?"

Otis hawed a bit and finally shrugged, as if unable to devise a really good answer.

Something occurred to Vivian, and the realization saddened her. "Me?"

He shrugged again, seemingly more a big kid than a grown man.

She reached out and touched his cheek, just below the bandage. "What happened?" she asked.

Otis's only answer was a shrug. A little boy's shrug. An *I don't know what happened to the cookies* shrug. She saw it then, saw that the boy she had fallen in love with was still there. The only problem was that the girl he loved was gone.

"Otis," she said, as tenderly as she could. "This isn't going to work."

His face went slack, but before he could speak, Patrick appeared on the porch, bouncing out almost on cue. "Ready!" he called, and piled into the car.

Otis shuffled his feet as if working up his nerve to speak, but the clock was running. Instead of talking he just nodded and climbed behind the wheel, backing up without looking at her again. As if he were afraid of what he might say in response.

Patrick and his father sat quietly as the streets rolled past, some of his ebullience vanished now that they were alone.

"We're already too late to shop much."

"Oh, shit, Pat. I'm sorry. Listen, though—we can be quick. You know what you want, right?"

"I don't know." The boy was unconvinced.

"Oh, come on." They had pulled out of the trailer park, and were driving down River Front. The western hills cast deep shadows, mimicking a deeply orange dusk.

Otis shifted uncomfortably. "What then? You want to just go home?"

"Yes," Patrick said coldly. Then a moment later: "No." He shifted, uncomfortable in his seat. "I don't know."

Then in a very small voice, he said: "Maybe bowling?"

A huge grin creased his father's face. "Now you're talking! Tell you what: I'll get my ball, and we'll have a great time over at Starlight."

Now, at last, Patrick smiled.

Otis lived in a rather ratty apartment building behind the Fred Meyer department store at the east edge of town. It was a small, unattractive, decidedly bachelor building, a place Otis had never expected to stay in more than a month or two. They bumped up into the parking lot.

Something glimpsed in a shadow behind the building reminded Patrick of a motorcycle: glimpsed, not seen. Perhaps even imagined. He wanted to tell his father to back up and take another look, but realized that he was wrong. It hadn't been a motorcycle, just a set of box-springs leaning against the alley wall. Yesterday his fevered imagination had transformed an abandoned clothing rack into a Harley. This had to stop, before he made an idiot of himself.

Otis turned the engine off, but left it in the ACC position, so that the radio stayed on. "I'll just be a minute," he said.

"Okay. Dad?"

"What?"

"It's okay about the shoes. We can get 'em later."

"Was thinkin' that way myself."

And he got out. Some country western ditty was playing on the radio, someone howling about his wife running off with his dog, or vice versa. Something. He looked up at the apartment. He couldn't quite see his father's window, then leaned further sideways, and could make out a dark window. He blinked thoughtfully, and looked at his watch.

The song about the dog finished, and then another one came on, a guy singing that his girl was more laughs than a stack of comic books. Patrick liked that one.

Then he heard a motorcycle starting, perhaps as close as a block away. He looked up at the apartment again, and the window was still dark.

He exited the car, and walked toward the stairs. Distantly, someone laughed. The motorcycle sound dwindled.

One step at a time, he took those stairs, more confusion than fear on his face. He reached the landing. His father's door was closed. Patrick reached out and gripped the handle. It wouldn't turn. He knocked on the door. Nothing. He looked to either side, and the corridor was utterly empty.

He reached into his pocket, and found his key. He pushed it into the lock, twisted, and opened the door.

A slowly widening wedge of light pierced the room's darkness. Patrick felt numb, disconnected. Through the wall, he heard that song, that damned song, no longer funny, some stupid hillbilly ranting about how his girlfriend had her daddy's money and her momma's good looks, the beat a distant, driving pulse. He took a step forward, and his foot thumped into something. His breathing was so shallow it was hardly better than holding his breath.

Otis Emory looked as if he was curled onto his side, sleeping on the floor. Patrick touched his shoulder, got no response. He pushed with all his strength, rolling his father face-up. "Dad . . . ?" Nothing. No mark, no motion.

Patrick felt as if his insides had turned to ice. It wasn't his father lying on the floor, and it wasn't he, Patrick Emory, who rolled his father onto his stomach to inspect his back. It took only a minute to find the tiny hole at the base of Otis's skull. Feeling ever more disconnected from reality Patrick felt the wound, the sticky warmth of Otis's blood coating his fingers. It was a simple puncture, one that had severed skin and punched a pencil-thick, roughly triangular hole in the base of his father's skull.

Patrick stared at his soiled hands, distantly wondering what it would take to clean the blood from beneath his nails. Something in his mind simply shut down, as if a wall had fallen over his emotions. An image came to him, clearly, too clearly. So clearly. *Cap sitting on the porch of his mobile home, cleaning his fingernails with a triangular knife blade. Smiling.*

Without a word, or a sound, he laid his father's leaking head on the ground, stood, went to the telephone, and punched in the numbers 911.

After he said the things that he needed to say, he folded his legs and took his father's head into his lap, breathing through his mouth, staring out into the darkness with unblinking eyes. His ears were closed to any sound but the beating of his own heart, and the fragmented thoughts running in his mind like crazed rats in a barrel.

I did it.

He's dead because of me.

Daddy, I'm sorry.

Daddy . . .

And then finally, flatly, *I'll kill them all.*

40

SOUTH DAKOTA,
SATURDAY, JUNE 9

The rented Pontiac sat in a rest area turnout, near the outskirts of the town of Whitehorse. Through a combination of modem and digital phone, Schott and Wisher were hooked into the net.

Schott, the larger and older of the two men, had wandered off for aspirin and a couple of Cokes and brought back two frosty cans while Wisher worked the computer.

"Hot," Schott said, handing over a Tylenol blister pack and one of the colas.

In the back seat, Wisher nodded without speaking, tapping at the keyboard, maneuvering through cyberspace. He paused long enough to push two capsules out of their plastic cocoons and wash them down with Coke. Maybe they'd kick in before his head exploded. Maybe.

"What's the word?"

Listening to Schott's voice was like chewing on aluminum foil. " 'Proceed to staging, complete unless you receive contrary instructions.' "

"Oh, Jesus," Schott said.

Wisher's head pounded. He took another swig, contemplated another tablet, and changed his mind. Everything would be all right. Just give it a little time.

His switched his attention back to the computer. He clicked on a file folder, and the screen asked him for a code word. He typed in "Eltotsira."

A list of names emerged, some of them scored in red. Several had pictures beside them. They were all pictures of children. One was a beautiful young black girl labeled Tanesha Evans. One was a sweet-faced Hispanic boy with ancient eyes. Those eyes bored into Wisher, seemed to be asking *do you know what you're doing? Do you realize what you've done?*

No, I don't.

"What?" asked Schott. "Did you say something?"

"No," Wisher mumbled. "Nothing." He bit his lip hard, using the pain to push away the weakening thoughts.

A long-haul trucker pulled into the space just behind them, brakes squealing and hissing. Wisher looked back over his shoulder. The truck's gigantic grill grinned at him with metal teeth.

Wisher grimaced to himself, and returned his concentration to the screen.

Half of the children were white, with some indefinable hollowness about their eyes, a roughness of complexion that suggested their families were trailer trash, mining stock, federal cheese-eating hillbillies.

Wisher clicked off the Hispanic boy, whose name promptly went red. He massaged his temples. He had forgotten to take Miguel Sanchez off the list in New Mexico. He was losing focus. It was so easy, so damned easy to lose focus, and he couldn't afford the luxury.

The list was long, almost a thousand names, but fewer than two hundred had pictures beside them. Wisher studied the list carefully. "Acceptable risk," he said to himself.

"What?" Schott asked. He was sitting on the front passenger seat, door open and his feet hanging out.

"He said that we were now at a level of *acceptable risk*."

"Is that what that fucker called it? Shit." Schott spit Coke on the ground and tossed his can toward the nearest trash barrel. The can spun end over end, spraying brown fluid until it clanged home.

"Then the rest can wait for Independence Day." Wisher sank his head down into his hands, squeezing his eyes shut until red and white dots formed in the darkness behind his eyelids. "Acceptable risk," he said. When he closed his eyes, he saw the faces of the dead, and those who soon would be.

And prayed for their souls. *I'm sorry. Please forgive me. I don't know what else I can do. If there's another answer please show me, tell me.*

He waited, but the only reply was silence. Wisher opened his eyes again. The screen was still in front of him, and he felt a vague sense of disappointment, as though if he prayed hard enough, they might disappear.

Names were clustered together into states. One alphabetical subgrouping was headed "Washington." In Washington, there were two pictures. One of them was labeled *Frankie Darling,* a little freckled face with sad, deep eyes. The other one was a Hispanic girl named *Destiny Valdez.* Both read: *Confirmed.*

Wisher hit the SEND button. The computer uploaded. The program terminated. He closed his eyes, squeezing hard. "I think you'd better drive," he said.

"This is the last one?" Schott asked.

"Until the Fourth, yes."

Schott grunted and slid over behind the steering wheel, while Wisher climbed into the front seat. He sat, with the motor idling, his big hands on the wheel. "Do you believe in God?" he asked.

Wisher shrugged, and then nodded. "Fuck. I don't know. Maybe. Yeah, I guess I do."

Schott shook his head slowly. "We had better hope to hell you're wrong," he said, and then backed them out of the lot.

41

The wind blowing off the Cowlitz seemed to cut right through the sweaters and coats of the mourners at Riverview Cemetery. Patrick and his mother Vivian stood stock-still at Otis Emory's gravesite, listening to the obsequies through a shroud of grief and pain so thick it was difficult to draw breath, to think, even to feel.

Frankie's father, the Reverend Darling, performed the ceremony. The Reverend was a good but somber man who spoke in measured tones. "—And although life can seem painful, and even unfair, it is to be remembered that the days of a man are few, and that what matters, what has and will always matter, are the things that we leave behind, the people we love and the deeds we do—"

Vivian wept quietly, lost in her pain and regret. Lolly Schmeer and her husband Kiefer stood to her right. The others were neighbors, friends, a few relations. Otis's sister Melanie, a large, dark woman with damp rings beneath her eyes, had flown in from Los Angeles. His uncle, a slender, tidy man with salt-and-pepper hair, had closed up his Atlanta barbershop and come west for the interment. Otis hadn't seen Uncle Gerald for years. He would have been happy.

But Otis's eyes were closed now. He couldn't see the gray sky, or the mournful faces. He couldn't hear the sobs, or the Reverend's fluid words. The time for all of that was past.

Briefly, starkly, Vivian remembered another time here in the graveyard, a Saturday night, so long ago. Two sleeping bags joined at the zipper, two young lovers joined at the heart, dreaming of a life together, rejoicing in the Now. All gone, now. All hopes dashed and gone. She was barely coping. Barely.

She pulled her attention out of the past and onto her son Patrick, who stared straight ahead without a single trace of visible emotion on his face.

Each of us deals with grief in her own way, she thought. Still, she would have felt better if Patrick would let himself cry. Or scream. Or get angry. There was nothing.

And that frightened her.

*   *   *

Patrick turned, just enough to see Lee, and Shermie, and Destiny. Lee and Shermie's parents were there. Destiny's weren't: She had car-pooled to the funeral with Shermie's folks. Frankie stood next to his mother. As soon as Patrick's eyes found him, Frankie nodded. Destiny nodded. And Shermie.

Lee kept his eyes away, and Patrick accepted that.

A decision, once made, creates its own path. A great man said that. And the path Patrick intended to walk was not for everyone.

In fact, it was for no one except the damned.

"I'm so sorry, Vivian," Mrs. Hiroshi said. She was Patrick's school counselor, a short, brown, solid woman with a high, sweet voice. "And in some ways your separation makes it especially hard."

Vivian's eyes were clear, but not steady. "Wondering if it would have worked," she said, a tiny catch at the back of her throat, like a hiccough, tugging at every word. "The part of me that asked him to leave wants to crawl into a hole and die. I'm sure that in some ways Patrick blames me."

Mrs. Hiroshi shook her head. "He's a much better boy than that. Look at him. Little soldier."

They turned to look at Patrick, who stood in a silent circle of his friends. Destiny had folded her arms around him, her face nestled against his neck.

"I just don't know," Vivian said. "I've tried. But it seems like every decision I make is the wrong one."

"You're doing a wonderful job," Mrs. Hiroshi said. "Nobody blames you for what happened. Before, or now."

Vivian watched her son, and the woman's healing words seemed to wash over her without dampening the flame of recrimination. "I wake up in the middle of the night, and ask myself who I am. What kind of mother would leave her child with people who could even be ac-cused . . ."

Mrs. Hiroshi shook her head. "A human being," she said. "That's all any of us are. And we make mistakes."

Lee's mother, Ellie Wallace, had joined them. She was a thin woman, who had the slightly loose-skinned look of one who has lost weight too quickly. She placed her hand on Vivian's shoulder. "Stop it. If there was anything wrong with that place, those people—it would have cropped up by now. My Lee is a joy. He doesn't get into trouble. Fact is, he helped us get out of it. I don't know what I'd do without him."

She and Vivian had never been close, but right now Mrs. Wallace's eyes brimmed with empathy. "Have the police come up with anything?"

"There's a man who . . . might have had something to do with it, but at the time of the mur . . . of Otis's death he was getting a traffic ticket on the other side of town."

Ellie sighed. "If there's anything I can do, Vivian."

Vivian nodded. "I hear that you're moving to Idaho."

A small smile. "It looks that way."

"Well—don't let Lee lose touch with Patrick. Not for a while."

"Oh, I don't think that's a problem. There's the web page."

"You'll get through this," Mrs. Hiroshi said. "I promise you."

Vivian wanted to agree, but through a gap between two mourners she could see Patrick. The five kids were clustered . . . no, only four of them. Lee had already excused himself, and was heading back to the car, leaving Shermie, Frankie, Destiny and Patrick alone, together.

Patrick's face was still a mask, but when she looked with her heart instead of her eyes, he seemed to her a wounded, stricken animal.

Vivian and Patrick slid through the parking lot, passing Cappy's corner. The giant was on the front porch, leaning against the rail, watching them. Without a smile or any real expression at all, Cap took his cap off and held it over his heart. *Sorry, kid.*

Patrick saw him, said nothing. His face didn't twitch. Vivian could feel Patrick's energy, like a dark storm cloud looming on the horizon, lightning sizzling around the edges. Bright enough to burn the eye, too distant for her to hear the thunder.

He was watching Cappy. She knew it. He thought something. Suspected something. Or did he actually *know* something?

They parked the car, and she moistened her lips, searching for the right words. "Patrick," she said. "Is there anything you want to tell me?"

He turned and looked at her, the soul of emotional immobility. "No, Mom. Nothing."

She searched for the words. "Did anything happen between your father and . . . that man?"

He cut her off. "Mom—if something had happened, I would have told you. What reason could I have to keep a secret?"

Despite his words, there was a wildness in his eyes, and it terrified her. His eyes and mouth were set, utterly intractable.

Then he leapt from the car, and was gone. Vivian looked after him, afraid, but uncertain what she was afraid of.

Vivian entered her house alone, feeling small and cold. She sat heavily in front of her computer, and brooded for almost four minutes before turning it on. Maybe there was an e-mail. Something to lift her spirits, although God knew that on a day like today that might require one of Otis's forklifts.

That thought brought fresh tears to her eyes, and she almost turned the machine off. Then she clicked the AOL button, and watched while a series of sign-on screens paraded.

"You've got mail!"

Her heart raced as she clicked the little mailbox. Her embryonic smile died as she saw that it was all junk, and a pair of sympathy notes from friends in Michigan and New York. She was reading through the second one when a little sign popped on:

Will you accept an Internet Message from RSAND@Marcus1?

Shocked and delighted, she clicked YES.

Hi, she typed.

Hello back. How are you? I was doing some research, and your name popped up.

It's been a bad day. My ex-husband died, and the funeral was awful. Why had she typed that? She and Otis were separated, not divorced. She had pressed SEND before she noticed the mistake. It was too late now.

I'm so sorry. Is there anything I can do?

Now she paused. She wanted to say: *Would you fly up here and hold me?* But that, or anything close to it, was completely beyond her.

Can you tell me why there is so much pain in life? I think my son is almost out of his mind with it.

I don't know, he typed. *The trite answer is so that we'll recognize the good times.*

Are there going to be good times? I wonder. It's been so long since anything I would really call a "good time." She hesitated before sending that one, but finally gave in.

Yes, there will, he said. *You have people who care about you. At least one.*

She held her breath. *Can we be friends?*

If you'll let me be, he typed. *I wanted to get to know you. Maybe I was jealous of your husband, but I never wanted anything to happen to him. He seemed to be a very good man.*

He was.

Give it some time, he wrote. *And if you need to talk to someone, you know where to find me. And when it's right, when everything is right, I would like to take you to dinner.*

She was aware of breathing, of the sensation of her hands on the keys, of a strange and healing heat rolling through her body.

I'd like that too.

42

Claremont Junior High School was closed, empty, deserted in the darkness.

Frankie, Patrick, Destiny and Shermie sat on their bicycles, looking down from the rise above the school's parking lot and main buildings. They were all thinking the same thoughts. All pretense of squabbling between them was over.

"How did you find it?" Destiny said quietly.

"We'd heard the motorcycles for weeks," Patrick said quietly. "Every time we had our meeting, we heard them. We knew that Cappy had a piece of land up in the hills. It wasn't hard to find."

"I recognized the smell from biology class," Frankie said. "Didn't have to get too close. Stayed in the woods and waited for the wind to shift. It was ether." He locked eyes with them, as if waiting for the significance to sink in. "And more, man. San Jose porker Web site says to watch for a cat-piss smell."

"It's a litter box up there," Patrick said.

"Then we know what they're doing," Shermie said.

Frankie was the only one of them whose voice held any emotion. There was something of excitement there, as though the dark potential that always lurked beneath the surface had finally found a vent. "I found *Uncle Fester's Meth Lab book,* on-line."

"How did you do that?" Patrick asked.

"Went to Dogpile dotcom, did a search on "Ether" and "Meth." Whattaya think?"

A police car cruised past them, its cold white eye sweeping. A beefy cop leaned out of the window. "You kids all right?"

"Just fine," Destiny said.

The cop watched them for a moment, as though some instinct had alerted him that everything was *not* all right. Everything was, in fact, pretty fucking far from all right. In fact, it was all too possible that things would never be all right ever again.

But he cruised on, seeming to ride on a breeze that swept in off the sea, carrying with it a cold, wet scent of dead lost things.

"The rest of this is mine," Patrick said. "I don't want you guys involved."

"Too late," Shermie said.

Frankie passed over a thin sheaf of papers. Patrick read them carefully. "Can you get this stuff?"

Frankie nodded. "I found about fifty recipes, and kept looking until I found one that we can actually do."

Shermie looked at them, and his eyes seemed to become calculators. "This stuff is easy—you're talking any swimming pool supply store. What do they call it?"

"An oxidizer," Patrick said.

"And the other . . . let's see. Brake fluid? Hair oil?"

"We can do that," Patrick said. "We can do it, easy."

"What about the other choice? We want to have a fallback."

"Sulphuric acid is easy," Sherman said. "But the potassium chlorate . . . I'm not sure. Look." His finger traced the printout. "It says you can use potassium per . . . man . . ." He stumbled over the syllables, then suddenly sounded it out. "Permanganate. Potassium permanganate can be used the same way. What about that?"

"That I can do," Destiny said. "Mr. Mackie trusts me. The rest is just glass and aluminum foil."

For a time none of them spoke, perhaps seeing through the stillness of the night into the enormity of their proposed actions.

"Are you sure you want to do this? Some things you can't take back," she said soberly. "Not ever."

She looked at Patrick, normally the sanest of them, and saw that his face, in the cold overhead light, seemed strained and ashen. "And some things you can't ever *get* back," he said. "Like my dad."

No other answer was needed.

43

Mr. Mackie didn't look at all like the infamous balloon-headed counselor in the *South Park* cartoon show. He was a small, compact sort who doubled as the high school wrestling coach, and had a Master's in Chemistry. He was popular with the kids, at least partially for the speed and facility with which he broke up fights between the largest football players. In fact, half the fun of watching a fight develop was wondering just how fast Mr. Mackie would charge pitbull-fearless into the scene, and throw both offenders for a loop.

But at the moment, he was just teaching the Introductory Chemistry class. Mackie peered out from behind his wire-rimmed glasses as he walked the aisles, watching the kids complete their assignments.

Today's work was relatively simple, the production of some basic precipitates, and calculations designed to predict the color of a particular reaction.

He seemed generally satisfied with the results of the day's work, and finally clapped his hands. "All right, class," he said, "that's it for the day. We have a minute before lunch. Any questions?"

Destiny raised her hand.

"Yes, Destiny?"

"I'd like to get some extra credit—maybe clean up during lunch?"

The other kids groaned. One made a rude smooching sound against his closed fist.

Mackie seemed a bit put off, but then shrugged. He was unaccustomed to the frequency with which Destiny and a few of her friends volunteered for extra work, but it was a relief.

"Well, I suppose—" The bell rang, cutting him short. He looked up at the clock, as though surprised to see the time. "Remember your homework. . . ." he said, but the words were drowned in the general rush for the door.

Destiny placed her books in a neat pile, and then began to clean up her immediate area, moving on to sweeping the floor and wiping the counters clean. Mr. Mackie read for about ten minutes, then stretched and looked up. "Listen, Destiny?"

Destiny answered cheerfully. "Yes?"

He stood. "I'm going to the cafeteria for a few minutes. You finish up here, will you?"

She twinkled. "You bet."

Mr. Mackie puttered about and then left the room.

Destiny waited a minute, then locked the door behind him. She opened the window. Patrick and Sherman climbed in.

Without saying a word, they began rummaging in cupboards and cabinets and the main desk, ultimately yielding nothing.

"No key!" Patrick called.

Destiny jingled her finger. On the end of it was a key ring.

She grinned at them. "It's great to be a lab rat."

"Bring on the cheese."

Sherman held a flask of something that resembled water, but burned the nose unless held at arm's length. He poured the fluid carefully into a second bottle held by Patrick.

A single drop went awry, spattering against Patrick's wrist. He cursed, and his hand trembled, but he didn't drop the bottle. Only after it was set safely on the counter did he jerk his hand away. "Ow! Damn, damn! Damn!"

"Oh, shit, man, I'm sorry!" Shermie yelled it, scrambling to turn on the faucet. They ran water on his wrist for two minutes, then Destiny poured half a box of baking soda on the wound. Patrick looked at her, eyes bleak but watering.

"Patrick," she said softly.

His voice was thick in his throat. "Later."

"Got the permanganate?"

Destiny nodded. Patrick had his tears under control. The acid burn was a raw, discolored spot on his wrist. It could have been far worse. Patrick seemed to have dammed the pain up somewhere inside him. "Destiny," he said. "Thank you."

Impulsively, he kissed her cheek. Her eyes widened but there was no time for reaction as Patrick and Shermie scrambled back out the window.

The boys landed heavily on the far side, scanning for witnesses like the conspirators they were, then moved off into deeper shadow behind a row of azaleas. Patrick groaned as his wrist brushed against the side of the building. "How's that arm?" Shermie asked.

"All right," he said. "Just a drop. Just a drop." He looked his friend carefully in the eye. "Maybe this *should* hurt, Shermie. Maybe pain is the only thing that's really real."

"You scare me when you talk like that," Shermie said.

"You should be scared, Shermie. We should all be scared."

44

At four o'clock that afternoon the kids headed up to Rev. Dr. Darling's five-bedroom house off Old Mill Road up in the hills east of the I-5. Carrying their various packages, the kids took their bicycles up Mill Road through about two and a half miles of winding blacktop lined with small package stores, rural schools, and a single fire company.

When they reached the Reverend's green mailbox they walked their bicycles up the driveway to the top, past the Cadillac with the *Jesus is Love* bumper sticker. The Darlings had an acre of fenced yard. A black-dappled horse stood looking at them with what Patrick felt was a mournful expression, tail swishing slowly back and forth.

Frankie's mother was in the living room, performing some light housekeeping duties with an air of focused distraction, as if part of her was very far away. "Hi, Mom," Frankie said glumly. Her lips twitched up in greeting, whatever slight pleasure she might have taken in his arrival vanishing from her face when she saw Destiny. Mrs. Darling nodded without speaking, and continued to shuffle magazines.

The living room's wide picture window looked out on the valley below. It was graced with a fireplace large enough to roast a whole hog, and two couches in shades of brown and black. That earth-toned color scheme dominated through the room: drapes, rugs, chairs, even the abstract print hanging on the wall.

The only break in the monotony was the mantel above the fireplace. There were six pictures of Frankie's deceased older brother Robbie: Robbie running track, Robbie hitting the long ball, Robbie in a swim meet, his long, smoothly muscled limbs cleaving the water like a young Poseidon.

From where Patrick stood he could see down the hall toward the bedrooms, and glimpsed the corner of a tall redwood trophy case. It too was filled with Robbie relics: trophies, photos, scrapbooks.

Nowhere within easy sight was there any evidence that Frankie lived here at all.

At the back of the hall was Dr. Darling's study. A thin strip of light under the door suggested he was in there working, as did the Cadillac in the driveway.

Undeveloped woods stretched out behind the house. Once upon a time Reverend Darling had plans to build a guest house, and had already poured the concrete pad when his elder son died. The slab was stained by weather, wet leaves and random animal droppings. No one had been up there for months, but Patrick had always thought it could be converted into a gazebo. Instead it stood as a monument to lost love, and Frankie's failure to convince his parents that they had another son to raise.

Shermie, Destiny, Patrick, and Frankie spent the first few minutes setting up, getting ready, preparing compounds, hauling water up the hill. All the time Frankie's attention split between the task at hand and glances back downhill at the house. No one stirred, no one paid any attention. Patrick had a sense that in a wistful way, Frankie wished that he would get caught. Anything was better than believing his parents didn't give the slightest damn.

Shermie produced a tube of hair oil. Squeezing out a finger-length, he mixed it in an empty tuna can with fluid Destiny had obtained at the sporting goods store. Setting the tin cautiously in the middle of the concrete pad, they stepped back, watching Patrick's pocket watch, waiting. Ten minutes passed, and nothing happened.

Frankie slapped his forehead. "That's not working. Maybe the wrong oxidizer?" He picked up the tin cup and dunked it into a pail of water.

"Let's try this again," Patrick said. They were all much too nervous, and in a situation like that people make stupid mistakes, silly mistakes, the kinds of errors that get people killed. Next time they consulted the written instructions and mixed more carefully, poured it all into the metal cup and waited.

Ten minutes, and nothing. Birds mocked them from the trees.

"All right, let's try the next formula. And let's leave the old one there—maybe it just needs more time." For the next two hours they tried different mixtures, setting the cups in a widely spaced circle. They were working on the seventh when the sixth erupted into flame.

Hands shaking, Shermie made very careful notes on a pad of paper.

His expression was strictly clinical. Patrick had the sense that Shermie was lost in a world of abstraction and numbers, anything to shield himself from knowledge of what they were about to do.

They tested the mixture three more times. No question about it: it worked. According to their instructions, when mixed together the oxidizer and the fuel generated heat. The heat built up until it exceeded the container's ability to radiate it, at which point the little heap of chemicals smoked and burst into flame. The flame was blue-yellow, and flared three feet into the air accompanied by a sound like a low-yield rocket engine. When the fire burned down, it left a black bubbling tarry mass in the cup. A smoky, bleach-like stench filled the air.

Speaking for all of them, Frankie said, "Awesome."

They discussed containers, detonators, timing and other concerns. No one mentioned human lives. They tested the mixture twice more, in sunshine and in shade, noting the difference in combustion time with a change in ambient temperature.

After three hours the shadows were lengthening, and a mild rain began to fall. They tested the mixture again, and even with the watery mist, it smoked and sputtered and popped into ignition.

"Jackpot," Patrick said.

They came down from the hill. It was time to go, and they had all the information that they needed. None of them were in a talkative mood. What they were about to do was entirely too sobering, even for Frankie.

In the kitchen they prepared peanut butter and bologna sandwiches and ate them out on the porch, the silence slowly growing oppressive.

The Reverend and Mrs. Darling entered the kitchen together. His father glanced out through the window, giving Frankie a small, low-wattage smile, the kind of smile someone might give seeing a new puppy in the hands of a barely remembered acquaintance. Frankie returned it in kind. They drifted back inside. Patrick watched Frankie.

The brief light in Frankie's eyes had retreated somewhere deep inside him. At that moment, Patrick understood Frankie better than he ever had. Understood what Frankie saw and felt. He suspected that Destiny understood the same chasm. Without being told, he knew that Lee and Shermie knew the same darkness, and feared it with all their hearts.

45

Patrick was eating salad, baked chicken and fresh rolls with his mother. Over the sound of her radio they could hear a party, or perhaps a fight, going on over at Cap's trailer.

Vivian was trying to eat, struggling to maintain her calm, but her hands shook every time she brought the fork to her lips. A hoot of laughter arose from the other side of the park, followed by motorcycle sounds.

Patrick squeezed his mother's arm, and she looked up at him and tried to smile. She touched his wrist, a fond gesture, but he winced.

"What's wrong?" she asked.

"Skinned my arm playing soccer today," Patrick lied automatically, and pulled his arm back.

"Want me to look at it?"

He shook his head. Vivian studied him carefully.

"Is there anything you'd like to tell me? Anything I should know?"

"You've asked that before, Mom."

"I just feel . . . I don't know. Patrick, if I asked you a question, would you answer it? Honestly?"

Patrick hesitated.

"Honestly, Patrick. I need this." She was breathing in small sips.

"All right, Mom. I promise. What is it?"

She took a deeper breath. "Do you blame me for what happened? I mean, I asked your father to move out. And he was living in that terrible neighborhood. Maybe if . . ."

She put her head down, then looked back up again. "Because if you do, I just wanted you to know how sorry I am, how terribly sorry."

"Mom, no. I promise. I absolutely don't blame *you*."

He got up, and scraped his plate carefully into the sink. Every motion seemed almost preplanned, robotic. As if he was operated by strings from above.

"Patrick," Vivian said. "Are you all right? If there was anything wrong with you, if I lost you . . . I don't think I could bear it."

Patrick turned and looked at her with eyes that were as ancient as the Pacific. "Fine, Mom," he said. "Never better."

*   *   *

The clock read one o'clock.

Patrick's motions were almost preternaturally controlled. He carefully crept from bed, and to his mother's room. He nudged the door open wide enough to make out her shape beneath the covers. She was asleep. With every breath, her body shook beneath her blankets. Even asleep, she was crying.

He waited at the front window, watching Cappy's trailer. Patrick didn't yawn, wasn't bored, his thoughts didn't wander. He just watched, blinking as slowly and regularly as an iguana. At 2:30, the bearded giant emerged, pounded his palms against the swollen bulk of his belly, and jumped on his motorcycle. Before the roar died away, Patrick had slipped through the front door.

He unchained his bike and rolled it silently away from the mobile home before seating himself and pedaling out onto the dark, wet road. After four minutes he stopped popping gravel beneath his wheels, and was on the main road heading north. Another fifteen minutes and he came to the section of the woods just north of their old meeting place.

He rolled his bike up the dirt path, until he came to a fork in the road. He took the right path, past a sign saying PRIVATE PROPERTY, NO TRESPASSING.

There was another fork up farther, and he wasn't sure which to take. Then he sniffed. As the breeze shifted, he caught a smell like a fully loaded litter box. He hared to the left.

He paused again, eyes closed, letting himself acclimate to the darkness before he continued. Dirt and gravel crunched under his wheels and heels. One careful step after another, he went higher and deeper into the darkness between the trees. When his sensitized eyes caught the very first glimmer of light ahead, he took his bike off the road, and laid it carefully on its side.

Patrick paused again, listening. Nothing. No sounds at all with the exception of wind and soft animal noises. Crickets, night wings. And then human words. Arguing. "Keep it up . . ."

A fragment, not a complete sentence.

"Behind, motherfuck—"

He went down on his belly and wiggled in closer, commando-style. The wet grass dampened his shirt and slicked his face and palms. From the closer vantage point, he saw an oddly shaped house. It looked like something built of several different trailers patched together haphazardly to make a single dwelling. He counted four people through the windows. Two wore gauze masks. Closer now, he could hear more yelling. Patrick crawled, elbows scraped by rocks, face stung by low branches. Onward he came, clinging to the shadows.

"Shit!" Cappy's voice. Patrick could hear it clearly now. "I'm telling you that it's shit, and it isn't good enough to sell to a fucking retard!"

"Well, your fucking chemist went south on us. Small matter of someone corn-holing him, near as I can tell. Now I can Nazi this stuff, or bathtub it for you, but we gotta make smaller batches, and if you don't have his connections, it isn't going to be as pure—"

A flat smacking sound, and someone cried.

"Don't you *ever* talk to me that way—"

Patrick crawled around to the other side, and he could still hear the muffled sounds.

"Place stinks! One fucking match and the whole place—"

There was a sudden pause.

Cappy's voice. "Wait. Did you hear something out there?"

Patrick froze, willing himself to invisibility. If they caught him, they would kill him. He watched them balefully, a tiny fragment of his mind wondering why he wasn't afraid.

Cappy waddled out onto the porch, eyes sunken in the scarred puffiness of his face. His great meaty forearms rested on the wooden rails on the front deck. Cappy stared out into the darkness. He seemed gargantuan, but flabby. Hyper, but exhausted, a man burning his candle at both ends, then putting a blow torch to the middle.

He slid a thick tongue across his lips, then went back inside.

Patrick crawled more rapidly, taking a chance on sound. These last few yards, if someone looked in his direction, they would see him. There was no cover.

As he reached the edge of the house, the iron control that had sustained him seemed to dissolve. His throat closed so tightly that he couldn't breathe.

Things crawled under the house. It was damp in a way that suggested sewage and rotting garbage. Something dripped down from the floor panels, something that smelled like very strong cider vinegar mixed with ammonia. Every breath dizzied him.

Crawl. Breathe. Crawl. He found a vent almost a foot wide, and poked his head up through it.

Jackpot. He could see into the living room. A bunch of half-empty bottles sat just in front of the vent. He could read through the label from the rear, and it read: Danger-erlier.

The fumes were awful, and suddenly his stomach revolted. For a ghastly sixty seconds he choked on his own stomach fluids, suffering in a desperately imposed silence.

He dared not cough, just bore the awful convulsions and contractions until he gained sufficient control to choke his salad and chicken back down.

From his backpack, he extracted a metal can, the kind used to package brake fluid. He set it carefully on the dirt in front of him, using the rays of a tiny penlight to guide him.

The second item he pulled out was a condom packed full of powder, a special mixture of magnesium powder and a pair of common additives used by ordinary, everyday non-homicidal-psychopaths. It had been simple to acquire the chemicals—a hobby shop for the magnesium, Triangle Pool and Spa supply, and Kraagan Auto Parts. No one looked at him twice.

The enormity of his intentions hit him like a sledge. Patrick felt horrific claustrophobia. The darkness and wet, the smells and crawling sensations all closed in on him like a collapsing tomb. What was he doing? Just what the hell was he thinking . . . ? He started to snatch the can back up, when Cappy entered the room above him, booming: "You think I won't do it? You think I won't kill your yellow ass? Planted one asshole Wednesday, damn sure plant another one next week. All the same to me. Your call."

Patrick heard the other voice. Ellie's voice. Backing down. "All right, honey. Whatever you say."

Patrick's chest froze. Any small amount of humanity or regret he might have felt vanished utterly in that instant.

Dizzy from fumes and fear, he unscrewed the can and set it down again. With a penknife, he carefully poked a hole in the condom, and then lowered it into the can. He screwed the top on tightly, and set it under the leaking grill.

On knees and elbows, Patrick began to back out and away. Slowly at first, and then faster and faster. When he reached the edge of the house he paused. There were footsteps above his head. He had to wait. He couldn't wait. God, he was right under the *porch*.

More footsteps, then the sound of a zipper, and a stream of yellowish fluid arced out over his head into the dirt. Cappy grunted and sighed to himself. The stream stuttered, died. The sound of a zipper, then retreating footsteps.

Patrick's heart was almost bursting. Behind him, an irreversible chemical reaction was building up and up, and he was going to *die,* unless—

The front door closed.

Patrick edged out, crawling faster as he crossed the clearing's no-man's-land. When he reached the shadows he jumped up to a crouch and sprinted to his hidden bicycle, and rolled it down the hill and away.

46

Cappy stood on the porch again. For the fifth time in as many minutes he had returned there, staring, as if some atavistic cranny of his hindbrain intuited danger.

He lumbered back into the lab, the collection of bottles and beakers and tubs that turned raw materials like diet tablets into pure chemical gold. The resulting drugs his runners sold around Claremont, sending the surplus to Portland and up to Seattle.

When things were singing he had connections as far away as Vancouver, BC. If he could just get things running smooth they would dump this trailer setup and get with the smart way of doing things. To hell with making this shit on your own property. You rent a motel room or a beat-to-shit house in some nigger neighborhood. Make your score in a series of seventy-two-hour marathons, and when the place was so contaminated that the roaches couldn't live in the walls, you got the hell out and found a new place.

You did that over and over again, paying cash, using fake IDs, and in two years you could make a million dollars, cash. His whole future was right in front of him, if the clowns who worked for him could just keep their greasepaint on a little longer. That, and keep the competition under control. They'd beat the snot out of some coke dealers who had organized over in Allantown, and scared hell out of the hippies at the Inside Edge. A pothead could make discreet dope connections at the Inside Edge today, but you never knew what tomorrow might bring. Best to keep them mindful, a little nervous. Let them know who's boss. Hell, if they folded up shop there'd be less grass around town, and that might mean more customers for him.

True, he'd let his temper get the better of him. When he lost his chemist, when some asshole had set things up so that half his people got mugged and raped under the bridge, even Cappy could admit he'd gone a little nuts. Maybe big Otis had had something to do with it, maybe not, but Cappy had to admit that doing the bastard had certainly relieved his stress.

He felt much better now.

Cappy sniffed through his cotton mask. Even with the drops of Binaca on the strip covering his nose, the stench was barely tolerable. "Fucking stinks," he said, but there was something in the chemical smell that was new, something he recognized, and his drug-addled mind fought to categorize it.

One of the last things he saw was a curl of smoke rising from a grill behind a cluster of bottles. His eyes widened. There was a *pop* as a spiral of flame burst up.

The ether bottle broke.

Cappy's mouth opened to scream—

And suddenly the world was filled with flame.

Almost a mile away now, Patrick was pedaling like a demon. He heard the roar, turned and saw the orange and yellow fireball rolling up through the trees. It mushroomed in the night like a newly birthed sun, then died back down to a steady glow.

Patrick pedaled on, dimly aware that he was laughing and crying at the same time.

Vivian woke up in darkness, the fragments of a dimly remembered nightmare slipping away from her like skeletal fingers. Groaning, she rolled over and checked the clock. It was five in the morning. She was about to try to slip back into slumber when she heard a scratching sound, followed by a dull thump. Then, the rush of running water.

She sat up, stood unsteadily, wrapped her robe on and walked out to the bathroom. The light was off, and she flicked it on.

Hunched over the face basin, Patrick was washing his hands and face, scrubbing them raw. In the flat light his thin, dark body appeared almost emaciated. He flinched as the door opened, shivered as she approached, as if his every nerve was stretched to the breaking point.

She barely knew how to react, saying only: "Patrick . . . ?"

He looked up at her with red eyes and hollow cheeks. He reminded her of a concentration camp survivor. When she took him in her arms, he sobbed, pulling himself against her with all of his failing strength. His cries were those of an abandoned child, a shipwrecked mother who has watched her babies drown, an abandoned soul in hell's darkest dungeon.

Fear hammered at her. "Patrick? What is it?"

His thin fingers gripped at her robe, and he sagged so that she had to hold him erect.

Perhaps, she thought, perhaps he was finally grasping that Otis was dead. Perhaps he was finally allowing himself to feel the pain, the loss, the helplessness. In a way she was glad. He had been so stoic, so impenetrably distant, bottling his feelings so tightly that she feared for his mind.

This was better. Sometimes it was just best to acknowledge our terror of death, our feeling of utter helplessness in the face of such an overwhelming reality.

Then, distantly, she heard the sirens wailing in the night.

47

CLAREMONT *Courier,*
TUESDAY, JUNE 19

*P*olice report that the fire and explosion at Route 345 Riverfront Drive was not the result of a gas leak, as originally supposed, but rather the accidental explosion of a clandestine methamphetamine laboratory. Police discovered traces of "precursive" agents such as diet pills and Vicks inhalers, as well as lithium batteries, which imply that several different methods were being utilized to synthesize the illegal drug.

"This tragedy almost certainly has put the largest meth ring in the Pacific Northwest completely out of business," said Claremont Police Chief Darryl Haines. "There had been rumors of some kind of violence between them and a local group suspected of cocaine trafficking, and we may have to assume foul play until we have determined otherwise."

The explosion, at 3:30 A.M. on the 17th, originally seemed the result of spontaneous ether combustion, but recent discovery of what Vancouver arson investigators have referred to only as "a crude detonator" have suggested that the resulting blaze, which killed four and wounded one, may have been deliberately triggered. Killed in the blast were Reginald "Cappy" Swenson, 38, the suspected ringleader; Ellie

Krup, 32; Reginald Hernandez, 27; and William R. "Mocha" Coffey, 41. Wounded and in serious condition is Majel Burroughs, 20.

"Confidence is high that forensic investigation and Ms. Burroughs's testimony will bring this matter to a swift conclusion," Chief Haines said.

48

CHICAGO, ILLINOIS

I t was a scene played out too many times before. Two men. A hotel room. Seventeen miles northeast of them, a mother was crying.

But on returning to the room and hooking into their computer link, a flashing mailbox alerted Schott that one of their internet news-clipping services had struck paydirt.

Schott read several of the clippings, and made a disgusted sound. "Oh, Christ. We've got a problem."

Wisher read over his shoulder. "Claremont? Wasn't that where the school went bad?"

Schott nodded, and his fingers blurred over the keys. "We laid in some extra screening there. Looks like we caught something."

They talked for a minute or two, and then typed a swift query, and sent it out over the Internet.

They tried to play cards for the next hour, but couldn't maintain sufficient focus for a decent game. Too many miles, too many hotels, too many days, too many deaths. Regardless of discipline, or their understanding of necessity, the small faces were beginning to stare at them from darkened closets, dead television screens, closed eyelids. Restful sleep had become a fevered memory.

Within an hour, their phone rang.

"Yes?" Wisher said.

"I received the e-mail," a familiar voice said. "I would say that was very sharp observation on your part. You deserve commendation."

Wisher's voice didn't change. "Thank you, sir. But what now?"

"This man 'Cappy.' He's the same one suspected of killing the Emory boy's father?"

"Affirmative. Questioned and then released. According to a second article, there may be links between this man Swenson and a couple of Claremont P.D. officers."

"A town that size, it wouldn't take much to buy them. And the mechanism of the triggering device?"

"Don't know yet. But, hell, I could make a dozen timers shopping five minutes at any Seven-Eleven."

The man on the opposite end sighed. "Why didn't this boy come to our attention earlier?"

"His family situation seemed relatively stable. What do you want?"

"Send him an invitation."

"And if he doesn't come?"

There was no hesitation at all. "Arrange an incident."

49

WEDNESDAY, JUNE 20

Alexander Marcus's mother Kitty lived in a gated community in the northern end of the San Fernando Valley. If she hadn't had her son's millions, she would certainly have been in a nursing home, considering that she was far too frail to enjoy or appreciate the walk through the chaparral bordering her property. At ninety, Sand doubted if she could use the pool in her back yard. He hoped that she could walk, or wheel, or even drive to the top of her hill, from which she could enjoy a spectacular view of the San Fernando basin: Topanga, which was frankly spectacular. Chatsworth, Simi Valley, Agoura Hills . . . all the way to the Santa Monica Mountains.

Only the slightest of lies had gotten him an appointment: as one of Marcus's official biographers after the great man's death, he had interviewed one of Kitty's lawyers concerning Marcus's vast arts endowments. The estate was still huge, still managed by the same lawyers, and a call to the firm gained him access to the grand dame herself.

The guard at the gate was stocky, maybe Persian, the sort of guy you suspected might work a minimum-wage job during the day and study stock brokerage at night. He vanished back inside to check a clipboard or printout, and then opened the gate. "Have you been here before?" He was polite, professional and observant, his English heavily accented. The guard wasn't overtly suspicious, but Sand knew he was being thoroughly checked out.

"Nope."

"Then go up two streets, turn left and then right at Heartland. End of the street, there's a circular drive. Pull right in."

Sand thanked him, silently wished him luck with his Series Seven exam, and followed his instructions to the letter. Three minutes later he was in front of a two-story mansion with a white panel truck from St. Mary's ElderCare facility parked in the front. Two men were maneuvering a cabinet-sized piece of machinery out of the van as he pulled into the drive.

A broad-hipped pale woman in a crisp white uniform stood at the front door, watching them. Renny parked his car and walked up to her. She seemed of fairly typical nursing stock, with a stern but pleasant manner.

She switched her gaze from the panel truck to Sand as he approached. "Mr. Sand?" she said.

"Yes, that's me." She extended a hand larger, flatter, and stronger than his own. Pumping bedpans, he reckoned.

"I want you to understand that Kitty is very weak, and I don't want her excited. But it soothes her to talk about Alexander, so I approved fifteen minutes."

"I appreciate that." He paused as another thought occurred to him. "Did you know him?"

"Yes," she said. Her face was clear, but he could have sworn that something slid back behind her eyes, out of sight. If he hadn't been looking for it, he would never have seen it at all. "I've been with Kitty for twenty years. It almost killed her when her son died. Before they found . . . larger pieces, they actually searched the house for DNA samples, to verify the remains, did you know that?"

He grimaced. "That's pretty raw."

"Imagine that. I hope you're not a conspiracy-theorist. That would be upsetting to her."

"No, not at all. We just viewed one of his birthday tapes, and I thought that Kitty . . ." He corrected himself quickly. "Mrs. Marcus seemed so happy on that tape, and it occurred to me that it had been such a long time since anyone had spoken to her, and that is a real shame. She has so much to say."

That answer seemed to satisfy her, and she guided him through the house, passing vast expanses of glass and white pile rug, hardwood and stainless steel, swooping staircases leading off and away like the wings of great cranes.

Against the living room wall were trophy cases. Seven golden cups, and several plaques, all set with images of samurai swords. Above the cups were two gleaming *katana,* Japanese swords. Killing tools. So *those* were the implements that Marcus had spent so many thousands of hours wielding.

"Do you mind?" he asked the nurse. She smiled thinly, and led him to the case.

Beautiful, shining, thirty-six-inch steak knives. He could almost smell the sweat, feel the focus. It was easy to imagine Marcus on a white mat, dressed in one of those karate uniforms, slashing and striking at imaginary opponents. Thirty years he had spent practicing Japanese sword. Renny'd once read that the old swordsmiths would heat and fold the steel again and again, pound it flat, fold and heat and pound, until the sword was composed of thousands of tissue-thin layers.

Marcus had written an essay, published in the American Journal of Hoplology, a sort of esoteric kung-fu magazine. In it, he compared the process of purifying and shaping steel to that of refining human character, drawing on references as wide-ranging as Nietzsche, Musashi Miyamoto, and the unknown author of the *Rig-Vedas.* He spoke of his own journey, from fear and powerlessness to self-mastery, comparing it to such a process.

For any man less accomplished, less a warrior, less a staggering success, the article would have been considered puffery. But when Alexander Marcus spoke, people listened. He had even performed a sword dance of some kind on a documentary videotape. Renny had seen a snippet of it on his *A&E Biography.* Marcus was fast, fluid, extraordinarily precise . . . all of that was true. But Renny couldn't get past the feeling that the real secret of Marcus's success was his detailed visualization of actual opponents before him. When Marcus thrust, Renny swore he was cleaving flesh. When he whipped the blade at the end of his demonstration, returning it to the scabbard, Renny could almost see blood droplets spattering onto the mat.

He shook himself out of it, and let the nurse guide him up the staircase. The men from the truck outside were wheeling the motor through the front door. "What are they installing?"

"A special elevator rail system," she said. "Kitty will be able to move anywhere in the house, attached to her chair. From the bed to the elevator, up and down the stairs, out into the back yard . . . all automated."

"Nice."

"One of the things that money can buy. It can't buy her back her youth, or her health. Or her son." Again, that flickering darkness that Sand had a difficult time naming.

"So here we are," she said. "Fifteen minutes, Mr. Sand. Please don't make me regret this."

The bedroom smelled more like a flower shop than a sick room. Renny saw no scent-diffusers, but knew that they had to be there, just out of sight. Money.

The high-canopied bed was in the corner of the room, but Kitty Marcus wasn't in it. She was in her motorized chair, seated at a little writing desk.

"Hello, Mr. Sand," Kitty said. She was a large woman, impressive even in steep decline. Her bun of dark hair was almost certainly a wig, but an excellent one. She had a washerwoman's hands, broad and flat and weathered, and broad, hunched shoulders. Her face, once full with high cheeks and sensuous lips, was as dark and wrinkled as a raisin. She wore a blue flowered housecoat over a gauzy pink blouse. Kitty Marcus wore skillfully applied makeup: just a hint of color to mouth and cheeks, enough to soften but not deny the passage of time. Once, Renny thought, this woman had been extraordinary. "Please excuse me if I don't stand to greet you."

"Quite all right. It's enough that you agreed to see me on such short notice."

"Would you like a chair?"

"May I use one of these?"

He pushed a plushly cushioned wicker-backed chair over from the other side of the room. "Your house is very beautiful."

"And very empty, Mr. Sand," she said. Her voice was like an amplified whisper. "Since my son died, it's hard for me to fill my days."

"I can understand that." Careful words were the best route. "America's lost so many heroes. Sometimes I think we've lost our way completely."

Mrs. Marcus shook her ancient head as if it was made of spun glass. "I know exactly what you mean. My eyes aren't what they used to be, but I can still watch the TV a little. I swear that if I were a child I wouldn't know what to think. Who to listen to. Not even the President is required to have morals today." She seemed to go back inside her head, where she became lost in her own thoughts. Renny didn't really want to pull her back to the present, but didn't see his options.

He didn't want to lie to her. Lies had gotten him into so much trouble in his life. But this time, one more time, he was going to twist the truth.

"Marcus Communications is spinning off a new magazine for children. I thought of writing an article emphasizing that everyone, even the greatest people, started as children."

She nodded soberly. Her eyes went unfocused for a moment. Perhaps she was remembering little Alexander in short pants, running though the New York projects. "A very useful thing."

"So if you didn't mind, I'd like to ask you some questions about your son."

She didn't mind at all. So she spent the next ten minutes talking to him about Alexander Marcus's background. He was unusually small for his age, and the poorer sections of Harlem were somewhat traumatic for him. Although Sand didn't ask the indelicate question, he knew that Kitty had never married Marcus's father, and that lack of a man in the home hadn't helped things when intellectual Alexander had become the target of several area gangs.

"Was he beaten?"

"Oh, yes." Her voice was fierce. "But he learned to fight back."

"Did the other boys learn to accept him?"

Her voice dropped, as if concerned that she might be overheard. "They had to," she cackled delightedly. "He kicked their asses! But they weren't the worst. *They* fought one on one."

"Who were the worst?"

"The girls," she said. "Those girls. They were like packs of rats. Always after him, hurting him. They ruled our building." Her voice dropped. "They broke my leg once." She stopped speaking for a moment, and her old, tired eyes were distant. "He tried to fight. He tried to run. Nothing really worked. Eventually I found a way to move."

"To Chicago, when he was fifteen?"

She shifted uncomfortably, blinked several times, and then donned an uncomfortable smile. "Yes."

Renny inhaled deeply. That had been the first dangerous question. *Watch her carefully.*

He maneuvered his way back to safer territory. "Tell me about his first newspaper articles . . ."

She enjoyed recounting his days on the school paper, and his entrance into the ROTC. Her mood brightened considerably. Very carefully (he hoped) Sand selected a conversational lull to insert a few mild queries. "There are stories that your son did not run for President out of consideration for your wishes. What do you think about that?"

Mrs. Marcus chuckled. "Alexander always made up his own mind," she said. "If he didn't want to run for president he didn't run for his own reasons. He wouldn't do that to spare my feelings. He wouldn't have done it because of the threats."

"You know about the threats?"

"Oh yes, of course I know about the threats. Alexander and I talked about everything."

I'll bet you didn't.

"Then what do you think the real reason was?"

"I think he believed it would be an invasion of his privacy. The older he got, the less he cared about being a public figure." She smiled again. "You may discover, young man, as you grow older that fame and wealth are greatly overrated."

I'll just bet he wanted his privacy. "Your son was surrounded by many people. Some were business associates, others were with him in Vietnam."

"Oh yes," she said. "The Praetorians."

"Praetorians?" he asked innocently.

"Yes, that was his name for them. I don't think they minded very much. That was Caesar's imperial guard, you know. They were always around him. Bodyguards. Friends. I think that they reminded him where he'd come from. Thick as thieves they were."

"Did you like them?"

"Most of them. There were a few who didn't really fit."

"Who, for instance?"

"Oh, goodness, I don't remember their names." She stopped in thought. "But you know there was one I did like quite a bit. It was the lady. The woman."

That startled him a little. "The Secret Service woman? Kelly Kerrigan?"

"Yes. She was with him on that last trip to San Francisco. About four months before he died."

Renny paused and searched his notes. He had seen no reference to San Francisco in late 1987. San Francisco? "What was he doing in San Francisco? When was this?"

Her voice lowered to a hush. "Some sort of health tests. He was actually rather excited about them. He said he would talk to me about them later, but he never did."

"But the Secret Service woman was with him?"

She averred. *San Francisco.* Near Santa Cruz, where he had found reference to another dead woman with the same mutilations, the same bite marks. The same time frame. Since there hadn't been a stop in San Francisco on Marcus's itinerary he'd discounted it. Dear, dear God.

Renny made a few more minutes of mindless chitchat, hoping that the conversation would cover the genuine thrust of his inquiry. Whatever her son's sins, he was still her little boy, and she loved him and perhaps he had loved her even more than she ever knew.

But the reporter inside him couldn't resist asking, "In his biography, there are several mentions of hospital stays, when he was thirteen, fourteen . . . in that range. Were these associated with the gang incidents you mentioned?"

Her face grew tight, and he saw something behind her eyes that suddenly startled him. Behind the harmless old woman's mask, there was something predatory, hard. *There* it was, there was the will that could take a fatherless black child born in poverty and mold him into one of the most powerful men in the country. That something inside her was as merciless as an eagle's talons, and about as nurturing.

It was all he could do to meet her gaze.

"Yes," she said finally. "But then, as I said, young man, he learned to deal with it."

"And you moved to Chicago soon after his reconstructive surgery?"

The pink tip of her tongue flickered out, wet her lips, disappeared. "Alexander never wanted to talk about that," she said quietly.

"Before he died he gave a quite candid interview, ma'am. Apparently, he intended a complete biography. More complete than anything done previously."

She was listening! God! He fought to keep his hands from shaking. "I know that the man arrested—but not convicted—for the assault said he was protecting his wife's honor. Would you say that was true?"

She hissed, literally *hissed* as the memory was resurrected. That feral animal within her was rampant, overwhelming Kitty Marcus's studiedly genteel persona. "That bitch," she said. "She was his teacher. His *history* teacher. The slut. She'd screwed half the senior class, but Alexander was just a freshman. He was so large for his age. So bright." Her eyes were glazed with tears, the only soft things in a face strained with hate. Hate and . . . what other emotion? Guilt, perhaps?

"She couldn't keep her hands off him, and that stupid whore didn't know her husband was hiding in the house. Listening to them as she used him in her bed."

She swallowed and turned away. Her gnarled hands had drawn into knots. "He followed Alexander home. Pulled him into an alley. Pulled his pants down . . ."

She couldn't say any more. And didn't need to. *They said he had had reconstructive surgery. He was scarred, as if he had been in some horrible accident. . . .*

Renny tried to imagine the fifteen-year-old boy, big for his age, bright for any age, deflowered by his teacher, and then mutilated by her husband in some dark, wet alley. The pleas. The pain.

"When you arrived in Chicago, you moved to a . . . more affluent neighborhood. Alexander attended a private school." He took a deep breath. "Mrs. Marcus, the man who assaulted your son . . . was he well-to-do?"

She looked at him with no more expression than a cadaver. "He owned the largest furniture store in Harlem."

"And he never served time."

She exhaled a long, thin stream of air, and sagged back in her chair. "I'm afraid that is all, young man," she said. The nurse appeared in the doorway, doubtlessly summoned by the push of a hidden button.

"Mr. Sand," she said, "is leaving."

"You took the money, didn't you?" he said coldly. "While your son was still in the hospital, and the doctors were stitching his testicles together, you made a deal, and all of this . . ." he swept his arms at the walls, the lavish furnishings, the view beyond the windows. "All of this started with that deal you made, didn't it?"

"Get out." She refused to meet his eyes now.

The nurse clamped her hand on his arm. He looked down at the hand, and then at her straining face. "It's all right," he said. "I'm finished."

50

CLAREMONT

Destiny shared fifth period History with Patrick, and before they headed their separate ways for sixth (him to Geometry, her to Gym), they found time to meet at their lockers, to take a moment to talk before the next period swallowed them. All day Patrick had seemed drawn, haggard, somehow shrunken. There was a bright, almost feverish look in his eyes that frightened her. "Are you all right?" she whispered.

He gripped at her hand wordlessly, painfully hard. "I need . . ." he began. "I need . . . I can't sleep. . . ."

She had heard about the explosion, seen it on television and in the papers, but Patrick had refused to talk about it, and she was afraid to press. When he was ready, he would. They were family, and families knew how to keep secrets.

"Patrick!"

Destiny was jerked out of her reverie as Patrick's head came around. "Mrs. Hiroshi?"

The little woman strode toward them, waving an envelope excitedly. "Good news. Good news. You've won one of the Guardian awards, and have two weeks at summer camp, besides!"

Patrick stared at his counselor, searching her face disbelievingly. Then he sagged against the lockers, opened the envelope and read. He might have collapsed if there hadn't been a wall to hold him up.

"Well?" Mrs. Hiroshi asked. "What do you think?"

He looked from Destiny to the counselor and back again, then jumped up and kissed Mrs. Hiroshi's cheek. He hugged Destiny hard. "See you after school!" he called, and bounced up the stairs.

Mrs. Hiroshi watched him go, blinking. "I thought he deserved a little good news."

"That's an understatement," Destiny said. "Thanks, Mrs. Hiroshi." Then with more energy than she had felt in days, Destiny ran toward the athletic field.

Vivian was measuring Mrs. Fondelli, a fiftyish redhead who worked a cash register over at the Office Max. The manager was retiring, and the employees were throwing a costume party in celebration. Fondelli had chosen a black and vermilion Spiderwoman costume, and Vivian had also taken orders for a beaver, a fairy princess, and a matching Austin Powers/Dr. Evil set. Mrs. Fondelli held her breath and closed her eyes as Vivian measured, humming tunelessly, jotting the results in her black daybook. Mrs. Fondelli peeked at Vivian's scrawl, but was unedified: Vivian wrote in her own private shorthand, the numbers and symbols meaningful only to her.

Vivian's every movement was tight and controlled. Probably too controlled, and had been ever since the funeral, and most especially the fire. Cappy was dead. Even had she not believed him complicit in

Otis's death, she would not have grieved. Cappy was a thug and a bully. But her heart told her that Cappy *had* been involved. How then should she feel about his violent end? Relieved? But if the explosion was no accident, then what to make of the coincidence, of Cappy and Otis dying violently in the same week? Didn't that place her and Patrick within the circumference of a circle of violence and retribution?

And if Patrick knew more than he was telling, what did it mean that he was awake and cold even as the fire engines were racing to the site of the explosion? Nothing? Everything?

Distantly, she heard a police siren, and tensed.

Mrs. Fondelli opened her eyes. "Is there something wrong, dear?"

"No, not at all. Just pricked myself."

"You be careful, now."

The front door banged open, and Patrick entered. His bike was leaning against the front of the store.

"Mom! Mom, look at this! I won!"

"Just a second, dear. All right, Mrs. Fondelli, why don't you take that off now." The customer retreated to a changing room.

Vivian took the missive from Patrick's hands. "What's this?"

"Mom," he said breathlessly, "it's the camp. They said that they reconsidered me, and got a recommendation from one of my teachers—"

"Oh? Which one?"

"I don't know. That was anonymous. But I get the two weeks in Arizona, and a chance at the thousand-dollar college bond."

Vivian felt his excitement, and her heart hurt for him, but all she felt was fatigue. "Hon, I don't think this is going to work. I don't want you away from home for two weeks right now."

"Why not?"

Because I'm afraid you may have killed some people. "A lot has happened in the last few weeks. I'm still confused about some of it. I need you here, where I can be with you. And you can be with me. Patrick . . ."

"Mom," Patrick whined, "it's a *thousand dollars.*"

"And you're the only child I have. You're all I have, Patrick. I don't want something to go wrong. And there is something wrong, isn't there . . . ?"

She was very near tears, and reached out to take his hand. "Patrick. Sometimes we can't talk about the things that are really bothering us.

And we can't talk about the things we feel . . . or do. I've always tried to keep the channels open between us, but they've been closed recently."

He turned away from her, his fists clenched, his small dark face tilted at the floor.

"Patrick . . ."

"I need to get away from here."

"From me?"

His voice was terribly small. "From everything. Just for a while. Please, Mom."

She was silent for a few moments, and the void seemed overwhelming. "I'll be good," he said in a child's voice.

Vivian felt old. Of course he wanted to get away from here. Of course he wanted to be with his friends. But she couldn't. Just couldn't. "Maybe next year."

"There *is* no next year!" he screamed, face swollen with emotion. Patrick stormed out.

She looked after him, a flux of conflicting emotions. She read the note. It consisted of a few hundred words, a promise of different skies, different land, new friends. A few dollars. She crumpled the letter, then changed her mind, smoothed it out and stuck it behind the cash register. The wrinkled corner was still visible, staring at her accusingly. "Damn," she said.

In the half-empty parking lot of the Beefhouse restaurant across the street sat a sky-blue van with California plates, its hood and roof still powdered with dust from the drive up over the Cascades. Its windows were deeply tinted.

Inside the van, two men sat, listening to every word said in the costume shop. They heard Patrick's excited voice. They heard Vivian's emphatic "Damn."

Their names were Hennings and Fields, and they were the second team. Like Schott and Wisher, they were retired military, family men with homes and lives in other states. Like the others they also gathered information, but unlike them they had not yet been forced into direct action.

When the Emory boy's father was murdered, Patrick's chart went red. All news reports from Claremont were double-checked, and when a few days later an explosion killed several convicted felons who lived in Patrick's trailer park, that red light began flashing.

Careful inquiries suggested that the dead were part of a meth ring responsible for several unprosecuted acts of violence around Claremont, and their leader was rumored to have lost a fight with Patrick's father soon before Otis Emory was found dead.

Fifteen hours ago, the second team had bugged Vivian's home and store, and were monitoring all conversations, waiting to hear any discussion about the camp invitation. Judging by the last few words, the news was not good.

Hennings, a chunky dark balding man, was monitoring the radio. "Better call home," Hennings said. "It's a wash."

Fields's scalp was liver-spotted beneath thinning, pale red hair. At the moment, his mouth was twisted in self-loathing.

"He's a killer already, Chuck. If we ever needed proof that Wisher was right about the kids, this Patrick is it."

"Damn," Chuck Fields said.

Hennings ground his fists against his temples. "We're going green," he growled. "Maybe I'm going to hell, but I'm saving a few lives along the way. Get him on the phone."

51

SATURDAY, JUNE 23

Patrick straddled his bicycle at the top of Suicide Hill. He had pushed the ten-speed all the way up, too tired and unfocused to try pedaling. He pushed himself forward, rotating the pedals twice until the gears caught. He screamed all the way down, leaning into the curves, thrilled by the sensation of wind whipping through his hair.

When he skidded to a stop at the bottom he looked up at the top again, the blood pumping in his forearms and face, heart jumping in his chest. He felt about two hundred percent better. He turned the bike around and began to pump. At the top he paused, panting, but before his pulse slowed he turned the bike around and sped to the bottom again, his face a small dark mask of concentration.

He slewed around at the bottom of the hill, and then, without pausing, pumped his way back to the top again.

As soon as he was out of sight, the blue van pulled onto a side street intersecting Suicide Hill just before the last, ugliest curve. Hennings kept the van in Drive, and idled the engine with his foot on the brake.

"This is fucked up," Chuck said nervously. "What the hell are we doing. We're not supposed to kill kids. We're supposed to protect them."

Hennings spit out the window. "We are. From kids like this."

Patrick stood atop the hill, astride his bike, surveying his domain. From this elevated position, he could see the entire valley, all of the shops and streets, the river and the smokestacks of the bustling mill. His heart still pounded from the pumping climb up Suicide Hill, and the exertion was a cleansing thing, sweeping away the crippling guilt.

He had made mistakes, his father had made mistakes, everybody in this damned town had made mistakes, and just a few people had paid the whole bill. There was a dead place in his heart, a place numb and dark, and his mind tumbled toward it if he gave himself time to think and feel.

For just a moment another image flashed to mind: a blue van. On his way up the hill he had seen it parked in the Chevron lot. A blue van with out of state plates, and two men in the front. One white, one black. He had a vague sense of having seen them before. But where? Ah, well—it didn't matter. In a town this size you eventually saw everyone more than once.

Then he forgot about the van and started down the mountain. Faster and faster he rolled, entering a world of motion, all logical thought turned off. As he turned the last curve, he *felt* more than saw or heard the van coming for him.

He didn't have time to turn his head: that would have been suicide on Suicide Hill. But from the corner of his eye he saw the gleaming bumper, the gleaming eye of the headlight, the terrifying blue steel mass hurtling to crush him.

Time slowed, stopped. Patrick's concentration became so acute that he entered a kind of perceptual tunnel, all darkness with only the tiniest spot of light at the end. And in that very special place he seemed to have both all the time in the world, and no time at all.

To the left was the Van. Death. To the right, death if he went over the low rail and fell down the drop onto the reservoir's concrete lip. If he went straight ahead, the Van would catch him in maybe three seconds, smash him there or grind him into the rail. Death.

Without time for conscious thought Patrick hit his brakes, threw his bike sideways and jumped the instant his right foot touched the ground.

Forward momentum was transferred into a bouncing tumble, the bike cartwheeling an instant after they crashed down. Patrick screamed as his back hit the ground, then his shoulder hit the rail and the breath jolted out of him. He bounced up, over the rail, flinging his arm out and catching the edge of it with desperate fingers. He screamed again as his shoulder, elbow and fingers hyperextended as he gripped, trying to slow himself. He flung his other hand up, grabbed the rail with both hands now, and *slid* a dozen feet downhill, tearing the skin from his hands with the friction and uneven metal edges. Momentum ripped him free and he tumbled, fingers ripping at the ground as he twisted across three short feet of grass before he went over the edge.

His left foot went over the drop, and he knew he was dead, knew it, could already see his body fall down, hear his open, screaming mouth, see his head strike the concrete like a watermelon dropped off a bridge—

Then that dangling foot hit a water runoff pipe projecting from the sheer side, a few inches below the grass. The jolt went all the way up his leg, but it slowed him for a moment, and Patrick frantically hooked his right leg toward the same protrusion, floundered and then found it. And then he was hanging, butt dangling, both feet on the pipe, both hands clutching at the grass, straining to climb back up. The grass slipped beneath his fingers, then tore out in a series of furrows, and he slipped again, then found his grip and pulled himself back up. He lay there panting, face over the edge, staring down at the concrete floor thirty feet below.

Distantly, he heard a rumble as the van tore off down the hill. He had enough time to wonder: *which one of Cappy's friends did that?*

Something crazily like laughter escaped his lips, then he rolled over onto his back and passed out.

52

Angel of Mercy Hospital was located only seven blocks from Costumes, Period. Only eight minutes elapsed between the moment Vivian got the call about her son and her dash from the elevator on the fourth floor.

One Doctor Hubbard was waiting for her there, a man in his sixties with a sun-bronzed face and hair so full and black that it fairly screamed toupee.

"Mrs. Emory?" Dr. Hubbard asked.

"Yes. Is he—?"

He waved his hands at her. "Now, Mrs. Emory. Please be calm. That boy caught the luckiest break imaginable—if he'd gone off the edge, he'd be dead. Instead, just some bruises, and a strained shoulder."

Violence everywhere. Death and accident, injury and fear. Vivian's mind was so crowded with ugly thoughts she felt she was thinking in slow motion. "Can I see him?"

"He's resting just now, but . . ." He shrugged. "I think seeing you is better medicine than anything we could offer."

Clutching her purse in front of her like a shield, Vivian found her way to room 419, and eased the door open slowly, relieved beyond words when she saw the tiny sleeping form curled on its side beneath the thin blue blankets.

Patrick's face was bandaged along the left side, and his lips were split and swollen. His right shoulder was bandaged as well, and the elbow taped. His left eye looked as if someone had punched him.

She slipped into a chair beside his bed, leaning her head against the rail, slipping her hand around his. Even asleep, his fingers tightened on hers, and Vivian's heart sang.

"Pat?" she whispered.

Patrick opened his eyes groggily. The left lid would only open half-way. He seemed momentarily confused, as if not remembering what had happened or where he was. "Mom?"

"Oh, God," she said, leaning over to kiss his forehead. She was so relieved she almost lost the capacity for speech. "I was so worried. If I lost you . . ."

"You won't lose me," he said, trying to growl. "I'm too tough." He winced. Vivian flinched at the sight of her son in such pain.

"Mom," he whispered. "I have something I need to tell you."

"Shhh," she said, and stroked his brow. "We'll talk about it later." She glanced over her shoulder. A nurse had entered the room, and checked something on a clipboard at the foot of his bed.

"All right," Patrick said. "I'm sorry about running the hill. Suicide Hill. You were right. It wasn't very smart."

"Shhh," Vivian said, and blinked back tears. "Just rest right now."

When Vivian emerged from the room, her face was puffy with tears. She needed time to think, time to stop shaking, to try to think through the last few horrible days and make some kind of sense of them. The stress was crushing her. Every breath felt like inhaling water. More than anything in the world, what she wanted to do was curl up in her own bed and cry.

Before she could take a single step a nurse in a starched white cap collared her. "Chief Haines would like a word with you," he said.

She turned, and saw Haines approaching. She had seen him at town meetings, but they'd never spoken. He seemed a kindly man. He wore steel-rimmed glasses, had a shiny bald spot precisely at the crown of his head, and was as hard and round as an Idaho spud. The chief's eyes seemed tired, but the compassion in his voice was unmistakable. "Mrs. Emory? I want to ask you something which might be a little uncomfortable, but it involves your boy's safety."

"Yes?"

"To your knowledge, was your husband involved in any illegal activity?"

Her mouth went dry. "No. Why?"

He scratched his bald spot. "Well . . . recently, there's . . . a lot of violence for a town this size. Beatings, a gang war of some kind. Rumors about a fight between your husband and Cappy Swenson."

Was that Patrick's secret? "When?"

"You didn't know, then?" Haines was polite, but watchful. "It was only a week before his death. We questioned Cappy, but he had an alibi, provided by one of my own officers." The chief's face was tight. There was something that he wasn't saying. "We were hoping to break that alibi."

Vivian had the feeling that one of his officers was in for a long, hard week.

"Then we finally found the meth lab we suspected Cappy was running, and you know how and why we found it."

She clearly remembered that night. Patrick scrubbing his face and arms, his desperate sobs against her breast. Sirens in the night. "When it blew up," she whispered.

"Another death, more injuries. And now, the attack on your son—"

"Attack?" That word jarred her. "It was just a hit and run. Wasn't it?"

"Not exactly. The attendant at the Chevron station said that that van had been kind of lurking, almost waiting for your boy, or for somebody. We have a description but no license plate numbers. We might get lucky."

Almost waiting for your boy. "And you think that it might have had something to do with that explosion?"

"Ma'am . . . we don't know what is going on here, but these people . . . drug people can be paranoid and vengeful. It's just possible that some kind of war has broken out between two different factions, and that your ex-husband was involved. He was killed, and then in retaliation, the lab was blown up. Cap's people tried to retaliate by killing your boy."

Her legs felt unsteady. "Dear God."

"We don't know what to believe right now, but you and your boy might be at risk. You may not want to be in town for a few weeks— while we sort this out. Is there some place you can go?"

The nurse told Vivian to dial "9" for an outside line. She called Costumes, Period and spoke briefly with Charlotte Antony, her assistant, and got her to look at the slip of wrinkled paper tucked behind the phone.

She wrote the 800 number down, and then took a last moment to ask herself if this was really the best course. Vivian saw nothing else she could do, and punched the digits in.

A buzz, a click, as electrons flowed along the line. Then a male voice answered.

"Hello?" The voice on the far end seemed abnormally clear, as if they were very close, although the 800 exchange could have been anywhere in the country.

"Hi," Vivian said nervously. "My name is Vivian Emory, and you sent my son an application for the summer camp?" She hadn't intended for the last sentence to have a rising intonation, but couldn't control it.

She heard a brief pause, and then a cheery answer. "Yes. That would be Patrick. You declined the invitation. Or do I have the wrong information?"

"No, no, I did. Is it too late to change my mind?"

"Ah . . ." funny sound there, odd tone of voice. "I don't *think* so. He can make it after all?"

"Yes, but there is one condition. His father just passed away, and I . . . I'd have a very hard time letting him out of my sight for two weeks. Could you possibly use a volunteer? A chaperon or a cook? Would that be possible? I wouldn't want any money. I'll even pay my own board. I can help cook, and are you doing plays or skits? I can make costumes. Just please."

Another pause. "That might be a bit difficult, but perhaps . . ."

53

At one thirty in the morning, Vivian was still packing, arranging, trying to allow for any problems Charlotte might encounter at the shop, hoping that the girl would finally grow into the job. Finally, half-exhausted, she sat at her computer, called up the word processing program and jotted a note.

"Dear Renny," she wrote. *"Your friendship has been a life-saver during this period. I won't be able to talk to you for perhaps ten days. Things have been terrible here. Patrick and I are going to a summer camp in Prescott, Arizona, at some place called Weinstein's Folly. But when we come back . . ."*

She paused, her fingers hovering over the keys, and then typed again. *"Perhaps you'll be coming back through the Northwest again. Truth be told, I wish you would."*

She hesitated, wanting so badly to watch his face when he read it, hoping that she wasn't making yet another in a long line of mistakes. *"I have to trust the sense of connection I have to you. It isn't just in what's said, it's in the fact that we keep saying it, keep talking to each other, both wondering if there is anything there."* Her hands were shaking. *"I want to find out. No, strike that. I* need *to find out. If you feel the same way, please answer this. Leave a message on my machine. Something, anything to let me know that I'm not making myself into the biggest fool in the world. Maybe a big city guy like you doesn't have anything in common with a country mouse like me. But give me a chance to* prove *you wrong. I think I could."* She paused, her fingers hovering over the keys. *"I think I want to."*

Sometimes, you just had to step out on faith. She pushed the button, sending her message irretrievably out across the Internet.

54

A battered dust-gray Honda van struggled along the narrow dirt road up to Weinstein's Folly, a white Dodge SUV on threadbare tires bouncing along just behind. The van stopped, and a short, slim blond ball of energy clambered out. If Marty Feldman had sired a daughter with Goldie Hawn, their offspring might have resembled Janie Stein. With short blond hair, Armenian nose and boyish hips even as she neared forty, Janie combined the optimism of an eternal child with the discipline and focus of a Marine drill instructor.

The SUV pulled up behind her, and Janie waved as Ocean Rhodes and Paris Tuckwil emerged. Ocean was lanky, loose-limbed, with shoulder-length blond hair. A brown belt in Hapkido karate, he was counselor and camp sports director. Eight years her junior, Ocean was Janie's life partner, and had been since she first saw him dancing tai chi on a Mazatlan beach in 1993.

Paris was buxom, tanned, and hyper, with long brown hair and legs sufficiently Junoesque to resemble an R. Crumb cover girl. An A.A. in Graphic Design, Paris was Janie's arts and crafts director for the week.

Janie stretched, transforming the knots in her back and shoulders into little heat eddies. "Well," she said, "I figure the others will be along in a couple of hours. Our work's pretty well cut out for us."

Ocean wagged his shaggy blond hair. About five percent of the time, in the wrong light and at the wrong angle, he resembled Janie's older brother Tim. The other ninety-five percent of the time he triggered feelings that were dizzyingly unfraternal. "They'd better get up here. Hate to navigate a road that narrow at night."

"Oh, its alright." Janie sniffed deeply; the air was clear and cool. "Put that thought right out of your head. We're gonna have a great time." Excitement percolated inside her like a great hot bubble. Eight months of the year she worked as a bank teller, dreaming of summer. Now summer was here. "I had my doubts about this guy Park, but look at this place. It's *perfect,* and if you give me any lip, I'll brain ya."

Ocean grinned. "I have to admit, it's brown but beautiful."

"Sort of like me," Paris said, admiring her tan. "How'd you find this place?"

"I didn't," Janie said. "It was handed to me."

Paris wrinkled her nose. "A little dry for my taste. That's the lake?" She pointed north.

The camp was set on a bluff above an incline harsh enough to make their engines whine and grind for the last 300 meters. Steep ridges on either side gave a sense of compression, of nestling. Beyond the camp lay a shallow valley, and on the far side of that valley, another rise, leading to a higher bluff set in a densely wooded saddle.

Janie pointed up the rise. "That's Charisma Lake. We'll set the obstacle course up there. We have hiking trails—"

Camp owners Del and Diane Withers appeared from the direction of the mess hall, all smiles and greeting. Del wiped his flour-stained hands on an incongruous lace-frilled white apron. "Howdy!" Del said. "You must be Janie."

"And you must be Mr. Withers. Your land is beautiful." They shook hands.

"That it is," he said proudly. "Folks round here call it the Folly."

"Why's that?" Paris asked.

He gestured expansively. This was obviously a story he enjoyed telling. "Well, Old Moisha Weinstein put a lot of work into it back in '32. He was a big movie mucky-muck. His son couldn't get into a summer camp of some kind out in California 'cause of being a Jew. So daddy built him and some of his Hollywood friends their own camp. Pretty darned nice too."

"Well, our kids will love it."

"Expecting fifty?"

Janie scratched her neck, ending a small black fly's irritating dance. "That's the word. Haven't met 'em though."

"Just the gent you're working for?"

"Yep. I'm just a gun for hire."

"Done much of this kind of thing?"

Only when I'm not punching the clock. "Been a river guide, worked with Outward Bound and a couple of the county boot camp programs. Just love the kids."

"Amen to that," Withers said. "Say, will your boss be coming up today?"

"No. Later in the week, maybe." She paused. "He's not exactly my boss, but he's paying the bills. My crew and I get together every summer, bum from camp to camp across Arizona and New Mexico. Been doing it for four years."

"Sounds like fun. But don't the money people want to know what you're up to?"

She scratched a thread of blond hair away from her eyes. "I guess my reputation precedes me. I was just told to model this year's program on one I did last summer that got a little write-up in the *Tucson Daily News*." She shrugged. "Doesn't matter. Cash is in the bank, and the kids are on their way."

Some shadow of uncertainty flitted across Del's face, like a dark bird flying across the sun.

"Mite weird, but everybody spends their money a little different. Can't say I'm sorry."

Janie studied Withers for a minute, wondering if she could trust him. She decided she could. "You know what? Me neither."

They both laughed, enjoying that curious intimacy created by mutual antipathy for a third party.

"Y'all come on up to the house. We've got some cider, and we should orient you."

Janie waved the others to catch up.

In two hours Janie's crew had completed their basic inspection. Withers had toured them through the cabins, the showers, the archery field, the sports center, revealed the secret workings of the kitchen, the twin propane tanks, the trails and scenic spots, and the path up to the eponymous artificial lake.

Their entire camp was about three times the length of the regulation-sized soccer field, which lay north of the main complex. At the western edge of the field were a pair of basketball courts, a handball court, and the equipment hut and archery range. To the south lay the campfire pit, a cluster of bunkhouses, the mess hall, the activity hall and more shower rooms. Trails snaked off in all directions. North lay another incline, a shallow valley large enough to swallow the soccer field, and another rise.

"And up north there is the lake," he said. "Truck already delivered your equipment up the far side."

Janie smacked her hands together briskly. "Then I guess we should just get to work."

"I reckon so," Withers said. He was still in a great mood. It was night and day from the way he had responded to the mysterious Mr. Park.

During the day, Janie and her crew constructed or refurbished the obstacle course, which spread around the lake and extended off onto the hiking trails. They found a ten-foot climbing wall, a spider web of interlaced ropes, a balance beam and stumps, and other useful things left over from a Boy Scout jamboree. They adapted, dressed up, repaired and improvised. The sun lay dying on the west ridge when they finally trudged back down the narrow trail toward the main camp. Mr. and Mrs. Withers awaited them in the mess hall with meat loaf, corn bread and leafy green salad.

Mr. Withers's smile was warm and welcoming. "Looks like you soldiers put in a heck of a day today. Just a heck of a day."

Paris groaned, lying back on the bench with her head in Janie's lap, staring up at the ceiling. "Well, everything starts tomorrow, you know? Time and tide."

"And kids," Janie added, raising her water glass in a toast.

"And kids," the others echoed. The adrenaline was starting to run now. In her mind's eye, Janie saw a camp crowded with happy kids. Running, jumping, swimming . . .

It was going to be great.

East of the mess hall, up in the woods, two men were watching. Each, in a previous life, had been a combat NCO, used to hard living and stress. Each had, for decades, led a far more mundane existence: families, mortgages, wives, children, cholesterol counts, bad backs. They were Schott and a man named Silvestri, and for this week, these few terrible days, they were back down the rabbit hole, following another man's orders. Unlike Vietnam, this time they understood fully why their terrible actions were required. That understanding wasn't entirely palliative, but it quieted the nightmares.

Schott and Silvestri wore orange jackets identifying them as workers for a mythical central Arizona utility company. If anyone asked, they were merely surveying for underground cables, said cables to be laid in the fall.

They spoke little to each other, and so far had not activated the Bell Systems SatPhone representing their only link to the outside. With patience born of desperation, they watched, and waited.

Soon, now. Soon.

55

Wearing brown workmen's uniforms, two former Marines named Chuck and Hennings used a stolen key to admit themselves into the basement of Advanced Systems's research facility. Service records suggested that the basement hadn't been entered for three months, since the last inspection of the gas heating system.

Days of careful observation suggested that no one would enter for the next twelve hours. After that, it wouldn't matter.

The two men worked efficiently. Chuck shut off the gas while Hennings attached a specialized plastic splitting valve, allowing gas to travel through the system as usual while simultaneously siphoning off a few cubic feet a minute. A device very much like a weather balloon was attached to the left branch of the valve. Into that balloon Hennings bled a small metal cylinder's pressurized contents: pure oxygen.

The two men checked the connections, then left, taking the metal cylinder and locking the door behind them.

During the hours that followed, the balloon slowly inflated, the gas mixture pushing it around the contours of the room until it swelled to fill all available space. Gas continued to hiss into it until a pressure sensor shut the valve off. The black plastic sack now contained several thousand cubic feet of a highly volatile mixture of methane, ethane, and oxygen. Two remote detonators assembled from pieces available at any Radio Shack were taped to the inside of the balloon.

Silently, with that patience known only to the mechanical and the dead, the lethal device awaited its signal.

56

Vivian Emory drove at about eight miles per hour, her rented station wagon's springs and shocks jolting on the rutted dirt road. Beside her, Patrick felt a little deflated and tired, but beneath the fatigue lurked a low-level energetic buzz, a restless impatience that grew more intense with every passing mile.

He stared out the window at the internested web of spruce, fir and ponderosa pine. They had driven north through the desert, west through the foothills and then north again through the mountains. Since leaving Phoenix airport he had sensed they were entering alien territory, embarking on a great and mysterious journey.

"You act is if you've never seen a tree before, Pat."

Another layer of fatigue seemed to roll away. "It *feels* like I haven't. Look!"

Up ahead of them, an orange school bus was rolling to a halt, clouds of fine gray dust drifting about its wheels as excited kids piled out. Their car pulled up, and Patrick eased to his feet, favoring his sore right hip.

Three adult counselors were in sight, two male, one female. All held clipboards, and were calling out kids' names. It seemed a happy confusion.

"All right," bawled a lean, surfer-dude type with a name tag reading, appropriately enough, *Ocean*. "Check your enrollment sheets. In the top right corner you'll find a number. Evens come with me . . ."

"Odds with me." That one was named *Jason*. He was barrel-bodied but not fat, freckled, and decked out in a banana-yellow T-shirt. All he needed was a beanie with a propeller on top to complete the picture.

"That's appropriate," Ocean said. He reminded Pat of the gentle folks at the Inside Edge.

"Hey!" Jason said, and jostled him. It was corny, manufactured jollity, but funny nonetheless. The kids lined up quickly. Jason and Ocean passed out bunk assignments and information sheets. The campers snatched their packets and ran off, exploring.

A chunky kid with pink, punked-out hair and a badge reading: HI, MY NAME IS BUCKY! scooted past, chattering to a couple of friends. "This is *so* phat!"

Two of the busload were black, and carried themselves with a brittle inner-city wariness. Their badges read MATHIAS and HUGHIE. They were wiry, intense, as cautious as alley cats. They walked as if joined at the hip, gestures studiedly relaxed. They watched everything, reacted to nothing. Patrick's heart raced. Isolated in Claremont, he had known precious few black kids, and none possessing this level of sly physicality. Intimidation and fascination dueled in his mind. Fascination won out.

Mathias approached Patrick, looming a head taller and half again as wide across the shoulders. Despite his ogrelike stature, he seemed friendly enough. "Where you stay at, man?"

Wow. Just like rappers on MTV.

"Washington."

A nod. A black girl with three gold earrings and cornrowed hair approached. Her badge read *Aylana.* "Got cousins in D.C."

Patrick held up his hands. "No, not east coast. Washington state. Down around Portland."

Mathias looked at him suspiciously. "That's in Oregon." He pronounced it *ory-gone.*

"Yeah, but still just down the block." Patrick looked around for his mom, who was searching faces, scanning the group, kids and counselors alike, looking for someone in charge. She finally made eye contact with a short blond woman with a HI, MY NAME IS JANIE! name tag and a scarlet ASK ME T-shirt.

"Excuse me," Vivian said. "I'm Mrs. Emory. Who's in charge here?"

"I'm close enough," Janie said. She consulted a clipboard. "You must be the last-minute volunteer?"

Vivian nodded vigorously. "I don't know who I spoke to, but I'm going to need a place to put my things, and I need to check in. I guess I'm working in the kitchen."

"Did I hear 'volunteer'?" Diane Withers asked, coming up behind them.

"Sort of, I guess."

"Well," Diane said. "I'll show you, dear. It's no secret." She linked her arm with Vivian's and took her off toward a long, low, rust-brown building. Pat breathed a sigh of relief: the last thing he needed was Mom hovering over him. Sometimes, adults just needed something to make them feel useful.

There were four bunkhouses: Kiowa, Sioux, Apache and Comanche. Patrick was a Kiowa. He rubbed the walls with his palms as he entered. Real wood! It was crude, splintery, unfinished, but vastly preferable to the quarter–inch fake wood paneling in the trailer he called home. He loved it. Bubbling with contented energy, he threw his bedroll onto a top bunk nearest the door. "Dibs!" he cried.

"Hell it is—hey!" a beefy red-faced kid labeled CLINT said. "Are they already serving dinner?"

"Where?" Patrick asked, turning around.

Clint threw Patrick's gear out of the bunk, and his own bedroll in. "Should have read the guide," Clint sneered. "Dinner isn't for an hour. *'Pay attention even to little things.'* "

"Yeah, well, *'Do not think dishonestly,'* " Patrick answered automatically, and swept Clint's stuff off onto the floor. Then Patrick stopped and reconsidered the exchange. What the heck . . . ?

Clint glared at him, his face growing even redder. He balled his fists, puffing his chest out a bit. Then Clint's brow wrinkled quizzically, as if the same question had occurred to him. "Where'd you learn that?"

"What?"

" *'Do not think dishonestly.'* "

Was this guy pulling his chain? "*Five Rings,* man."

"Musashi," Clint said.

Another kid chimed in. *"The Way is in Training?"*

And another: *"Know the Ways of all professions?"*

There was a general babble of laughter, as they took turns rattling off their favorite epigrams. Patrick sat heavily on his bed, staring at them, dizzy with déjà vu. "Hey, guys," he finally ventured, "Do any of you hang in the Musashi chat room?"

Silence, and they craned their heads at him.

"Damned straight," Clint said. "I'm Ronin3."

Patrick jumped up, the throb in his hip forgotten. "No shit? I'm Marcus9!"

There was general chatter for another minute, the kids now babbling a mile a minute. Ocean appeared in the doorway, and they swamped him. "Guess what!" Clint said. "We know each other! We're all in the same AOL chat room!"

He blinked. "Are you all part of a club?"

"Not that we knew," Bucky chimed in. "I just got an e-mail one day, inviting me to join—"

"Me too!" several others chimed.

"Well," Ocean said thoughtfully, "I guess now we know how you guys were chosen for camp. You must have won some kind of Internet raffle or something."

Silence. They stared at each other, suddenly understanding the nature and intensity of their connection. "Well, hot damn," Clint drawled. "We're all a bunch of goddamn winners!"

Ocean protested, but the kids drowned him out, chanting, "Winners!"

They yelled and laughed and pumped their fists in the air, as if imitating an old *Rocky* movie.

"Winners!" Patrick shouted with them, and suddenly felt happier than he had in ages. Perhaps tonight he would be able to sleep without seeing the nightmare under the bridge. Or his father's dead face. Or hearing the sounds of the sirens as they drove along River View in their fruitless attempt to separate melted flesh from melted metal.

Perhaps.

"Winners!"

57

P A L O A L T O

A sh and fragments of glass and plaster covered the ground like August's first fall of dying leaves. The stench of scorched earth and flesh as a hot, wet cloud, hugging the ground in a sticky fog.

The four fire trucks stood at a safe distance. Exhausted firemen wound up their hoses like old men, displaying none of the urgency shown just two hours earlier. Then again, two hours ago there had been hope that survivors might still be trapped within the blazing ruins of the Advanced Systems building.

All that remained of A.S. were two charred walls, and a circular spray of gray-black powder projecting two hundred yards from the central building. The explosion had hurled fist-sized chunks of machinery three hundred yards. The charred and melted remains of a goose-necked lamp had shattered a U-Haul storage facility's office window a quarter mile away.

No one inside the building had had time to scream, or run. The blast had torn out two walls and blown off two-thirds of the roof. The fire that followed had done the rest.

The ambulances were carrying away zippered plastic bags. Their contents were lumpy, misshapen, only vaguely recognizable as anything human.

One of the firemen stopped and picked something up from the grass: a charred, half-melted computer disk. He shook his head, and leaned exhaustedly against the fire engine. "Man, oh man. What in the *hell* happened here?"

"I don't know," another said. "But at least it was quick."

*   *   *

A lime-green panel truck pulled up to the outskirts of the crowd. It parked, and a man in white overalls exited. He approached a police officer. He stumbled forward, staring at the crowd, the trucks, and the ruins of Advanced Systems.

"Shit fire, man," he said. "What happened here?"

"It just blew up," the officer said, still gawking at the ruins. He looked barely twenty, with bullish shoulders and slab-like forearms. Under other circumstances, the officer would have given a square-jawed, crew-cut, nothing-but-the-facts impression. Today he blinked too much, and had a vague, dazed, slack-muscled look about him. "Are you a vender or what?"

The delivery man nodded, ignoring the officer's unprofessional demeanor. Perhaps he was considering that if he hadn't stopped for an early lunch, he would have been *in* that building when the holocaust struck. Saved by a chiliburger. The delivery man's carefully cultivated tan paled, and his knees sagged.

The cop didn't notice. "Did they store explosives in there or something? Christ. It looks like a bomb went off."

"N-no. Not that I ever saw, b-but I was only there two or three times. They were just some kind of think tank. N-nice folks." He sagged, squatted down to catch his balance, then slowly stood again. "Oh, this is so fucked up I can't believe it."

Two firemen carrying a sagging plastic bag passed, and he shuddered again. "Did *anybody* make it out alive?"

"We're still trying to reckon that."

The delivery man blew a lungful of sour air and stood straight. He finally seemed to have cleared his head. "Well," he said, "what do I do with *that*?"

"With what?" the cop said.

He jerked a thumb back toward his delivery truck. "With their computer. They had a disk crash, and needed a recovery. Brought it to us. We saved their data all right, and the machine. But now . . . wow. What do I do?"

The cop looked around, as if trying to find a familiar face. "Listen," he said finally. "We're trying to figure out what went on here, and you might be some help . . ."

58

After a long day of orientation ("These are the rules: no fires, no stealing, no wandering off the campsite. These are called 'airport rules' because any violation and you go straight to the airport, and home") and activities (from the sublime—murder-ball—to the ridiculous—Mrs. Withers trying to teach them an achy-breaky line dance with moves like "the chicken" and "the Broadway"), the kids had piled into their bunks, talking the air blue (what movies rocked, what bands sucked, which camp girls looked "easy") until Ocean (who was taking first rotation sleeping with the boys) finally begged for mercy at three A.M.

When, too soon, morning arrived, the little angels were all asleep. Soft burring snores and the rustle of blankets were the only sounds as Ocean rose from his bunk and edged the front door open. Sunlight was just creeping across the central yard, and the morning air remained still and crisp. He savored the moment: this was the last bit of peace or quiet he was going to get for about ten days.

He sucked air and bellowed, "All right! Up and at 'em! First day at camp! No chowderheads allowed!"

With that call, the genie officially escaped the bottle, and chaos reigned.

Patrick rolled over. His eyes opened, and he was instantly awake. He was here, at Camp Charisma, and everything was just fine. He remembered no nightmares, had not awakened in the night thrashing in a clammy web of guilt. Maybe, just maybe, healing had begun.

Wonder of wonders, he actually felt *happy.*

He started to jump out of bed, remembering he was in the top bunk barely in time to avoid a skull fracture. The other kids emerged from their torpor like half-frozen nightcrawlers thawing in the sun.

A scramble to identify shoes and shirts and pants followed, then they blindly groped for the door, and prepared to greet the morning.

*   *   *

The shower room was a frenzy of scrubbed teeth and splashing, soapy naked male teenaged bodies. They groaned and shrieked as the water needled them, tiptoed through pools of liquid green soap, and in general dragged their way up to full consciousness kicking and screaming.

"God!" Clint said. "The water's freezing!"

Patrick shrugged, lathering his thin shoulders. "At least you're gonna wake up."

"Anybody got any toothpaste?" Bucky asked.

"Yeah," someone said from a closed toilet stall. "But not for you, numbnuts. Whattaya think?"

"Hey! Frankie!" Patrick called, grateful to hear a familiar voice. "When you get in?"

"Last night, on the airport bus." Frankie emerged to the accompaniment of a loud gurgling flush, tugging up his pants. In a graffito scrawl over the porcelain bowl, someone, perhaps Frankie, had immortalized that timeless and universal critique of camp cuisine: *Flush twice, it's a long way to the kitchen.* "God," he moaned, grimacing at Patrick. "First thing in the morning, I got to look at your ugly face? I'm goin' home."

"Your ma's already rented your room out." Patrick splashed him, and Frankie turned his head so that the water just dampened his collar.

"I'll get you later. When you least expect it, expect it."

Patrick chuckled, gaze falling to the tiled floor, where soapy, bubbled water swirled down the drain. For a moment that swirling reminded him of something. A dream. And what *was* that dream . . . ? Something about water? Nightmares of his dead father grasping at him, or of a screaming, flaming Cappy lumbering after him . . . those images had drowned out any subtler memories. But now, like a pattern in one of those Magic Eye books, something was struggling to emerge from the caverns of consciousness.

He wanted to grasp it, had a vague sense that it was something important. But the harder he fought to remember, the more it eluded him, and finally he gave up.

If it was important, he assured himself, it would return.

Boys and girls were clustered by gender in the mess hall. There were twice as many *he*'s as *she*'s. Patrick's eyes and ears scanned through a dozen different conversations and groupings, until he felt dizzy and overloaded. He looked out and saw Destiny, seated at a corner table with four new friends.

His attention focused on her, tunneling out the rest of the room. Then she turned and looked at him, and smiled. He felt the impact right down to his toes.

Frankie slapped his shoulder, breaking the moment of intense contact.

"You know what we've got this afternoon?"

Patrick wanted to slug him, but remained polite. "What?"

Frankie made rapid slashing hand gestures. "Kung fu!"

Clint grabbed himself. "Hey. I got your 'kung fu,' punk."

Frankie hissed at him, and the two of them indulged in a brief flurry of slap fighting before Janie shut them down.

"Hey," she said. "Hey, hey—save it. Guess it's easy to see who the fighters are." She raised her voice. "Now listen up! I'm going to read names. There will be colors attached to the names. When I finish, you will have three minutes to find everyone else of your color, form a group, and raise your hands. The last group to form has first cleanup."

With that last pronouncement, Janie suddenly had everyone's complete attention. She rattled the names off so quickly that a lot of people missed theirs and begged for a second read-through. Patrick and Destiny were both Greens when Janie finished. "Go!" she said.

The kids scrambled, and within forty seconds, everyone was in his proper place.

"All right. We have four tribes, and by the end of the day, you *will* have designed your tribal banners. Your tribes are important. You will compete in tribes, and go to activities in tribes."

One particularly ripe brunette said, "Do we *sleep* with our tribes?"

"Not likely, Courtney," Janie said primly. "So. Green team report to the rec room for martial arts, Blue team to the field for soccer, Red team to the craft center, and . . . White team—"

Hughie groaned aloud. "Why I gotta be in the white tribe?"

"Shut the fuck up," Clint said amicably.

"Watch the language," Janie said. "After this, teams will lose points for bad language or bad attitude. As I was saying, the white team will clean up the mess hall."

"Oh, sh—I mean, great!"

Grumbling, shoving, and stumbling into a gallop, the kids broke up into their tribes as the first full day of camp began.

59

I n the white quilted dome of the sports complex, the twelve members of the Greens were lined up. Seven boys, five girls, all heights and sizes, ages ranging from twelve to fifteen.

Ocean stood at the front of the room, cinching a frayed brown belt tightly around his waist. When he was finished he gave a sharp yapping shout, and began to bounce through a series of kicks and punches. He was lanky, loose-jointed. Patrick figured Ocean would probably do all right in a street fight, but wasn't exactly Jet Li. His long blond hair whipped in a dramatic spray as he twirled and leapt. His gyrations were rewarded by enthusiastic if not exactly worshipful applause.

"Hi, my name is Ocean," he panted.

A couple of campers smirked and Patrick whispered, "Yeah, all wet," just to hear his neighbors giggle.

Ocean looked at him suspiciously, wiping his forehead with a white hand towel. "And I'd like you to take your seats. Sit in a circle, would you?" They jostled and found places. "Good. We're going to practice karate every day, and at the end of the week, you're going to compete against the other tribes."

There were yells and high-fives of approval, as well as estimations of how much, how thoroughly and what variety of posterior was going to be kicked.

Mathias raised his hand and said: "Don't you have a black belt?"

"Not yet," Ocean said. "But I'm working on it."

Mathias nodded. *"The Way is—"*

And seven or eight of the other kids chimed in: *"in training!"*

Ocean looked at them, not fully computing, then finally just shrugged. "Ah, right. At any rate, at the end of the week, you are going to compete. But this competition is going to be a little unusual. You aren't going to be trying to hurt the other teams—you're going to be helping each other to learn."

"What does that mean?" Patrick asked.

"You'll find out pretty soon. So! Let's get to it. . . ."

He got them up, and began to put them through a stretching routine. Patrick was touching his toes, and looked up at Destiny, bending over on the row in front of him. She wore loose blue gym shorts. She grinned back between her bare legs.

Clint caught the interchange. "Watch it, Emory. You're gonna bust something."

Patrick flushed. "Like maybe your lip?"

In a bungalow across from the dining hall, the craft room looked more like a typical Claremont Junior High schoolroom than anything else. Drawings and sculptures from previous Charisma Lake campers dangled on the walls. There were photos of the surrounding forest, and maps of Arizona and the southwest.

"We have a special helper at camp this year," Janie said, addressing the Blues. "We didn't expect this, but she's extremely skilled with arts and crafts. Vivian Emory. Let's give her a hand."

The kids applauded. Vivian stepped forward nervously. "Well," she said, "what Janie asked me to help you do is to make banners for each of your tribes. I've looked into the craft larder, and we have some scraps of cloth, a few large pieces. I think that if you each make a contribution, of whatever kind—"

"Like what?" a delicate girl with a heart-shaped face asked.

"Sheets, towels, maybe a T-shirt. Whatever you can spare. We can do this if everyone chips in."

"Why do we want banners?" the girl asked.

Vivian searched for the camper's name badge, grateful for a moment's pause. Her confidence needed shoring up. "A flag pulls people together, ah . . . Jessica? By the end of the week, you will all be good friends. Right now you're still strangers. . . ."

And so it went the rest of the day, the kids playing, swimming, eating and bonding. Enjoying the kicks and punches and blocks in their martial arts classes, and occasionally outside of them as well. The counselors had to break up a few good-natured sparring sessions; warnings and Band-Aids were dispersed equally. The kids competed, joked and had a good time.

Frankie lounged on a bench outside the rec hall, waiting for his chance at the fountain, when he looked up in the hills and noticed a reflected flash, as if for an instant a mirror had caught the sun. It was only a glimmer at the corner of his eye. When he turned to search for it, it was gone.

He drank his water and then went to watch some of the kids play soccer out on the field, but for another hour the sense that someone was watching remained with him, like a bee crawling in endless circles between his shoulder blades.

60

Janie sat with her knees drawn up against her chest, hypnotized as Ocean capered and leaped and mimed before the campfire. It was story time, and the pile of flaming wood cooperated fabulously, burping smoke and casting fat, spiraling sparks up into the moonlit sky.

Ocean was winding up a spookily modernized version of Poe's "The Black Cat" rendered in a passable southern dialect. Hooting at first, the kids had finally quieted down, riveted by the tale of alcoholism, murder, madness and supernatural revenge. He concluded in a crouch by the fire: "—and that's why tomorrow dawn, they gonna strap me in that chair, pull that long lever, and run ten thousand volts up and down mah spine. An' I know I deserve to die, killin' the only woman I ever love like that. But could someone, anyone tell me—them cats, man, wuz them two cats the same cat? Was they two cats with one soul? I got to know, just got to, 'fore I go to glory. Can't anyone tell me? Please . . . ?"

He sagged, was silent for a long beat. Janie scanned the kids. Their eyes were riveted, not a sound, eyes wide. This was *great*! Then Ocean straightened and bowed as the kids applauded and screamed for another one.

"Tomorrow," he promised. After the kids finished cheering and giggling, Janie called them to order.

"I want to share something with you," she said. "It's what the Apache call a 'Horse Stealing' song. Different Native American tribes often considered it sport to grab each other's horses, and the young men of the tribe would compete to be the best thief. After a successful raid, they might celebrate by chanting something like this . . ."

She and Paris beat the drums and sang back in forth to each other, a repetitive, intoxicating chant sung at a gallop. *"Hey-yah hey-yah hey! Hey! Hey-yah hey-yah hey! Hey!"*

Haltingly at first, then with gradually increasing enthusiasm, the kids joined in. At first they were a bit rough. It was, after all, the first time that all of them had tried to create something together, in this case, a wall of sound.

They got the hang of it swiftly, beginning to compete with each other, and play off each other's voices. At every other camp she had attended, Janie had been forced to provide all the initial energy, carrying the kids on so that their natural shyness wouldn't dampen the spiral of song. Not now. This time, the teams competed with each other eagerly.

Blue chanted louder than White. Red, sweeter and wilder than Green. They stood, shouting at each other, and mimed riding horses. Although several of them couldn't sing a lick, their voices began to blend together as if a professional choir director had worked with them for weeks, the sour pitches somehow canceling each other out, the sweet voices guiding, the strong ones driving on.

Janie was first puzzled and then baffled, and finally boggled, just listening to the campers repeating that refrain: *"Hey-yah hey-yah hey! Hey! Hey-yah hey-yah hey! Hey!"*

They were dancing now, stamping their feet in imitation of countless television and movie Indians, faces screwed up in concentration. Janie barely had to squint to imagine them in headdresses and leather clothing, chanting and singing their joy and challenge to the sky, to the earth, to the elements.

These weren't just a bunch of kids, in four separate tribes demarked by color. They were a *single* tribe. If Janie didn't, couldn't understand how that had suddenly happened, it was still an indisputable fact.

She and her staff were the outsiders. She had the odd sense that if every adult vanished for the rest of the week, these kids would be just fine.

And instead of feeling relieved, ecstatic, admiring, she couldn't rid herself of a minuscule but growing sense of unease.

It was like a bizarre reworking of that old musical refrain:

Everything felt so damned right, something *had* to be wrong.

61

SATURDAY, JUNE 30

The high desert's afternoon heat baked the craft room, transforming each shallow breath into a labored chore. The Green tribe braved the biting black flies on the long, open patio, and only moved back inside when shadows swallowed the sun, and skeeters began their kamikaze dive-bombing runs.

Vivian was careful not to hover, but watched obliquely as Patrick struggled to render clay into an aerodynamic form. He couldn't seem to decide if it was a bird or a plane. It certainly wasn't Superman. Perhaps it was a big bug of some kind. . . .

He stopped, knuckled his fist against his temples, and looked down to the south, where a few dust devils were waltzing up the incline. In the free period after lunch she and Patrick had explored the terrain just below camp. It was a kilometer of dry grass, dead logs and brown, scrawny sad-looking scrub brush and stunted trees. It didn't get green until you came closer to the cabins, as if the caretakers had hoarded every drop of rainwater, using it where it would do the most good.

Almost on cue, Mr. Withers came trudging up the road, pushing a wheelbarrow stacked with red roofing tiles. He noted Patrick's expression, and looked back down to the south. The dust devils were whipping more intensely, dancing like little gray funnels. "That's the afternooner," Withers said. "Every day about this time, we get a stiff one blowing up the Folly toward Charisma Lake."

Patrick was working again, hunched over; then he straightened and seem to compare his efforts to that of his nearest neighbor, Bucky. Patrick had started adding an antenna to his model, which would certainly skew it in an insectile direction. Bucky was working with some pipe cleaners, making a skeletal outline of something resembling a soccer ball.

"What is that?" Patrick was instantly fascinated. Vivian drifted closer to listen.

Bucky shrugged. "I don't know. I saw it in a dream once, and started drawing it. See?"

His dusty brown nap sack was at the side of the table. He opened it and pulled out a gray vinyl sketchbook. Its pages were crammed with drawings, and Bucky was a good artist. Most intriguing were several images of those strange soccer-ball shapes.

Patrick studied them, then looked back at the pipe cleaner. Finally he said, "God, man. It's like I've seen that too." He looked at his own lumpy model, and then back at Bucky's drawings, and pushed his own model to the side. "I think I could build one of those."

One of the other kids was looking as well. Soon, all had gathered around to watch. Some of them began to take sticks and clay, forming their own balls.

Vivian shook her head. This was a familiar confusion, the odd sense of synchronization that had always existed around the Claremont preschool. Not regimentation, but as if the kids voluntarily, even instinctively, had aligned their thoughts and actions. She'd always thought the Claremont teachers were just brilliant disciplinarians, but what was she to make of *this*?

As they worked, she went to sit next to Mathias, who was working quietly. He seemed entirely pulled into the world of the wire sculpture.

"Hi," she said. He barely acknowledged her, but she had no sense that he was being rude, just completely and utterly absorbed in his project.

"Did you learn to make that in school?" she asked.

"Naw." His voice was quiet, far away.

"Why is it so interesting to you?"

He studied it. For a moment, his carefully cultivated inner-city toughness seemed to slough away. "It . . . it looks like the way I think," he said.

"What?"

"Well, when I got a problem, I try makin' a shape in my head."

"Something to hold the problem?"

"Naw. You wouldn't understand."

"I'm sorry. Try me."

He screwed up his square dark face, struggling to find a way to say it. Then he brightened. "I just did it."

"Did what?"

"I was trying to figure out how to explain it to you, you know?" His fingers traced shapes in the air, and he grew more animated. "And then *pow,* there was a shape in my head, like a pipe-cleaner soccer ball." He pronounced it *soccah bawl.* "And you see where the wires meet? Each of those points had a different picture, or feeling."

A different picture or feeling . . . ?

"All right . . ." Vivian agreed cautiously.

"And you were right here," he pointed to one of the interstices. "And I was here," he pointed to another. "And the idea, the shape idea thing, was over here—" he pointed to a third, so that the three points were evenly distributed around the surface of the ball. "Now if you're at my position, I go straight through the center of the ball to the idea, see?" He groped in his pocket, found a pencil and thrust it through the center, connecting the points. "But you don't understand, so you have to go around the outside, and it takes you a long time, because you don't see the connections. See?"

"Ah . . . sure," she lied. And then, without knowing why she asked, "How many different points . . . ideas . . . people, whatever, can you hold on that . . . ball, is it? At one time?"

"Usually only seven or so. The trick is to make a shape that fits any problem. Squares, pyramids, you know, stuff like that."

"And this soccer-ball shape?"

"It's just sittin' in my head, you know?"

"Where did you get it from?" *And where did the rest of them get theirs? And does Patrick have a set of mental tools like that too?* Suddenly, and fleetingly, she understood. The concept was similar to using a clothing dummy. A flat drawing of a costume revealed one set of needs and problems. Cutting the pattern and draping it on the form created an entirely new set of three-dimensional associations. And creating the first piece, and applying it to a living, breathing body, gave an entirely different view. More than once, she had asked herself how she would look at a problem if it were a costume commission. What materials? What effort? What time, skills and tools? What cost? What was it expected to do? What context would it be worn in, and how far away would the audience sit?

All of these things impacted the decisions and strategies that might take her from concept to finished product.

One darkly painful example: once upon a time, her marriage fit perfectly. As time went on, it seemed to shrink upon her, confining her spirit. She applied patches, let it out at every hem and seam, and still it strangled her. There had at last been an end to the devices at her command, a limit to the skill of her clever hands, her creative eye, her artist's heart. And if she hadn't had that costumer's perspective, that way of looking at a problem, a connection between heart and mind, between Patrick and Otis and a working woman named Vivian, between finance and love, responsibility and freedom, it might have taken more wasted years to see that the marriage had to end. That in the kingdom of her heart, the emperor wore no clothes.

Mathias watched her face, a clear question in his eyes. *Do you understand? Are you one of us? Or of them?*

And the truth was that she wasn't certain. Mathias (and how many of the others?) thought about his problems as if they were complex three-dimensional objects. Where in the world had he learned that trick? And how many other oddnesses remained to be found in their twelve-to-fifteen-year-old minds?

"I think I understand," she said uncertainly. And just maybe she did.

*   *   *

Six members of the Blue Team headed single file up to the lake, four boys and two girls. They trudged up the trail, across the little valley to the highest plateau, coarse white institutional towels draped over their shoulders.

The man-made lake was roughly teardrop-shaped. Mrs. Withers claimed it was a mile in circumference, but it looked larger. Other kids were already in the lake swimming, having fun, pushing each other in, diving from one of three boards. Denise Nicolas, a sturdy, twenty-something straw-haired lifeguard, oversaw them, ruling the pool with inflexible discipline. One kid sat over to the side, alone. He wore wire-rimmed glasses and was nearly swallowed by an oversized green Army surplus coat that he wore almost everywhere.

Frankie.

Denise's square jaw softened. "Hon, don't you want to swim?"

He wagged his head, gazing out at the water where the others were playing.

"Then why did you come up here?"

Frankie gazed out at the water. Something struggled in his eyes, something painful and private, a moment's glimpse, quickly buried, swiftly gone.

He got up and walked away. Denise looked after him, and then turned back to her charges. There were so many kids. Her heart was drawn to the boy, with his dense freckles and sun-peeled skin. He looked a little ungainly, but she was sure that if he'd just get in the water and mix with the others, he'd fit in fine.

But there was no time to concern herself with that now. There were so many kids, and only five counselors. It was easy for a boy like Frankie to get lost in the shuffle.

62

S UNDAY , J ULY 1

N ight had descended on Charisma Lake, and the crickets and night birds had awakened to sing their evening song. It had been a good day: the meals had been the traditional summer camp meld of canned vegetables, heavy starches and processed meats. The games were long and noisy and vigorous, the chance to bake in the Arizona high-desert sun intoxicating. As the day cooled, the boys and girls were separated by gender. The girls went to the white dome of the Sports center, the boys into the empty Arts room.

Now as the stars emerged, Janie spoke to the girls with quiet strength, the fine tiny wrinkles at the corners of her hazel eyes etched more deeply as she concentrated. "You are about to enter the circle of women." She paused, waiting for her words to sink in before she continued. "In most ancient cultures, there are ceremonies which draw a line between childhood and adulthood, but not in ours."

Some of the girls giggled, others shifted uncomfortably or looked confused. She expected that. The popular culture, movies and television and music, inundated the kids with images of adult rewards, adult sexuality, adult toys. But very little was said about the rigors of the passage between adolescence and full maturity. Heck, at thirty-nine she was still struggling with it herself.

"We're going to fix that," she continued. "Toward the end of the week you will have a chance to take part in a very special ceremony, something you'll remember for the rest of your lives. How many of you would like to hear more?" A moment's pause, and then about half the hands were raised. "Good. Good. Now, then. Building up to it we wanted to give you the opportunity to talk about anything you might have on your minds. Anything at all. Nothing said here gets back to your parents, or to anything or anyone on the outside. So. What would you like to talk about?"

There was a long pause. Then a girl named Heather said: "Boys?"

That was predictable. They giggled, and there was a little fast talk, some embarrassed chatter, all of which was perfectly normal. What rather surprised Janie was the way lovely Courtney's mouth twisted into a grimace, as if she had bitten down on something rotten. Her voice was an ugly rasp. "I'm not talking about what some *boy* wants. I know what boys want. Men want." Her hard expression grew harder, colder.

"How do you know that, Courtney?"

"Because I can get whatever I want from them," she said.

"And how do you do that?"

"You know," she said, her voice ugly. "You all know."

"You give them sex?" Janie tried to keep her voice neutral. Courtney was large, well developed, with full breasts and a woman's hips, but she was only fifteen.

Courtney shrugged noncommittally, but her slightly parted lips and half-lidded eyes gave all the answer she needed.

"What do you want out of life, Courtney?" Janie asked.

The girl shrugged. Janie tried another tactic. "Does that get you the kind of attention you really want?"

"I can get a man," she said. She looked at Janie challengingly. "I could get *your* man, if I really wanted to. Ocean's kind of cute. Don't believe me? Dare me." She wet her lips with her tongue.

What a brat, Janie thought, but that thought was almost instantly followed by, *No, not a brat. A little lost soul.* Janie listened to the disbelieving giggles tolerantly. "I doubt that, Courtney, but don't bother trying. I'm not interested in judging you, that's not why I'm here. I'll just say that 'getting' a man is different from holding one. Guys are easy to get in bed—"

"Ah heard that," Aylana said, and the girls giggled.

"But the ones they keep are the ones who they'd want to raise their daughters. Just remember that, no matter what they say to get your pants off. So these guys, the ones you sleep with. Do any of them look at you with the kind of love and respect that you think they'd feel toward their own daughters?"

"They love me," she said, but now she seemed less certain.

"Do you know the difference between love and lust? Would they still be there if you couldn't give them sex? What about if your pretty face burned off in a fire?"

Courtney physically recoiled from that. "No man would do that."

"My grandfather did," Janie said. "My grandmother was burned in an auto accident. He stayed with her for another thirty years, until she died. And he never married again."

Courtney opened her mouth, and then closed it. "You're lying," she said. Janie watched her without speaking. Courtney tried again. "Men aren't like that any more."

"They are, if the women are worth it," Janie said quietly. "Would you want a man to love you that much? Would all of you?"

At least half of the girls nodded their heads. "Good," Janie said. "We have honesty, and we need that. Now then. If that's what you want, what if you think about the idea that you'll never get anyone to love you more than you love yourself. This is a buy-low sell-high world, ladies. Guys will pay as little as they can to get what they want. What have you been trading your heart for, Courtney?"

"Fuck you," Courtney said. A single tear swelled from her left eye, and began its lonely way down her puffy red cheek.

Janie looked at her, a bit mystified now. "Courtney?"

"I know. I know . . ." Courtney wiped at her face and stared into the floor.

Janie looked at one of the other counselors, and sent her over to comfort the girl.

"Who else has had bad experiences with boys? Would anyone do us the honor of talking about it?"

Destiny shifted uncomfortably. "I . . ." she began, and then paused.

"Yes, Destiny?"

Destiny shook her head. "Not me," she said in a low voice. "My sister."

"What about your sister?" Janie asked.

"No," she said, shaking her head. "Not tonight. Maybe another night."

In the Arts and Crafts center, the boys sat sharing. Ocean and Jason were tag-teaming the discussion, and struggling with it. Having compared notes with Janie over the years, Ocean knew the boys would be far more reluctant to share emotions than the girls, but needed the release even more.

"No," Colin said. "The problem isn't that my father doesn't communicate. The problem is that the bastard won't leave me alone."

"Why would you say that?" Justin asked.

"Because he's in jail, and it's just embarrassin'. I wish he'd stop even trying to write me, call me."

A couple of the other kids nodded. Ocean blinked hard. Slowly, he asked, "How many of you have fathers who are incarcerated? In jail?"

About a third of the boys raised their hands. Ocean felt positively sick. He breathed deeply and plowed on. "Well . . . your fathers' path doesn't have to be yours."

Mathias stiffened defensively. "You're saying my dad did it. I don't think he did."

"Yeah," Colin said. "Everybody's innocent."

"Fuck you."

"Hey! Hey! That's a point off!" Ocean said.

Patrick sat, very quiet indeed. "My dad is dead."

"Dead?" Ocean's voice grew soft. "When did that happen?"

"A week ago."

The group went absolutely quiet.

"I killed him," Patrick said.

Ocean searched for something to say. Jason caught his eye, and his freckled face was baffled.

Before he could speak, Frankie jumped into the silence. "He means that he feels . . . I don't know. *Responsible.* Right?" He held Patrick's eyes. "But you didn't *actually* have anything to do with it. Right, Patrick?"

"Yeah. If he hadn't taken me shopping that night, nothing would have . . ." Patrick started to break down and cry. One of the other boys put his arms around Patrick. They formed a protective wall, pushing Ocean aside.

The two counselors shuffled around the outside of the knot, seeking entrance, and finally realized that the kids had closed ranks. For now, the adults were not wanted, or needed. Jason hunched his shoulders and crooked a finger at Ocean, calling him outside.

"This is weird, man." Ocean stared out across the camp, as if hoping there were answers hidden in the shadows.

Jason shrugged his massive shoulders again. "Yeah. And almost none of them have fathers in the home. Divorced, single moms, foster kids. I'd say the people backing this chose pretty carefully. Looking for at-risk kids. We've seen *that* before."

Ocean seemed vaguely troubled. "Yeah, but . . ."

"But what?"

He sighed. "Hell, man, I don't know." He peered back through the window. Back in the room, Frankie was on the outside of the hug. He looked out at Ocean and Jason, his eyes bright and tiny, like those of a small wild thing caught in the glare of oncoming headlights.

63

After the kitchen was clean, Vivian emerged into the waning daylight, sitting on a rude bench made from half a split log. She stared out at the woods filled with juniper, aspen and majestic blue spruce. The woods of her youth had teemed with pine, and she saw few of them here. Another loneliness.

North, on the athletic field, some of the kids were playing a quick pickup game of soccer, while others at the lake a half mile further north were getting in the last swim of a good, long day. The light was cool and fragmented, filtering through leaves and pine needles. The distant joyous sounds of happy children made this ending seem almost a new beginning.

"Hi, how are ya?" a voice said behind her. Vivian turned, startled, and saw Janie, who wore her customary wide, friendly grin.

She scooted over, making room. Janie sat. "I hear that you're doing great in the kitchen, and in the craft room. The kids like you."

Vivian smiled shyly.

"This is kind of a magical space," Janie said, breathing deeply and satisfied. "I hope you're enjoying yourself."

Vivian caught a distant flash of some kind, high in the western woods. Reflective metal, perhaps? Machinery or binoculars? "Are there people up in those hills?"

Janie shrugged. "I've seen people on the roads, some surveyors, whatever." She looked at Vivian curiously. "Why? What are you worried about? Everything is going fine."

After a hesitation, Vivian began to talk with Janie about her troubles, what had happened in Claremont. "After something like that happens, you are likely to start at ghosts."

Janie nodded. "You say that you and your ex-husband were separated?"

Vivian nodded. "There wasn't any way to heal. No way to get back to what we used to be, but we . . . I pretended that there was. For a little while."

She felt her face flush, and realized that she hadn't talked to anyone about this, not even Lolly Schmeer.

"I get the feeling that you don't talk to many people," Janie said.

"I watch the way you are with Ocean," Vivian said enviously, "like the song says: 'holding hands, making plans . . .'" She sighed. "It's too easy for me to remember the old days."

"You run your own business?"

She nodded. "Otis even tried to help. For a while. A big guy like that mousing around the fabric racks—it just didn't work out. But at least we were partners at home."

"Growing apart isn't a sin. Do you have anyone?"

Vivian paused, thinking. Did she? Was there? While realizing exactly how ridiculous it might sound, she said, "There is someone, but it's just a chance."

"A *chance*? Your whole face lit up when you said that."

"Well, I don't want to talk about it too much. If I talk about it, it might ruin everything. I'd like to think there's a chance." Her voice caught in her throat. "That I haven't run out of time. . . ."

She turned away from Janie, suddenly feeling dizzy and frightened.

Janie took both of her hands. "Honey, if you can even *pretend* to still feel like that, it's not too late."

With a smile, Janie went off about her business, but Vivian felt the warmth of the counselor's hands. Her own skin felt tissue-thin, and hot enough to blister.

Oh, Vivian, she thought wonderingly. *You are flat-out* sprung.

Janie found Ocean back at the main counselor's cabin. He was working on a map for the next day's scavenger hunt. "How's it going, big guy?"

"Pretty good. Kids are pretty coordinated—they pick up physical motion well, but are still a little closed." He paused, and reconsidered. "At least with us. With each other, they're like old friends."

"You have an admirer," Janie said, and threw herself into his lap. "Map later. Me now. I need kissy. Lots and lots of kissy." He hesitated for a moment, then surrendered to her affections for two steamy minutes, after which she nestled her head against his chest and pretended to swoon. "Sir," she murmured, "you undo me."

"Yeah," he whispered, combing his fingers through her short blond hair. "You tell that to all the counselors. That's how you get us so cheap." She kissed the point of his chin. "So," he said, "who's this admirer person?"

"The sex bomb."

"Oh, you must mean Courtney."

"Funny how you guessed that so quickly."

"So sue me, I'm male."

"We'll settle out of court." She licked his lower lip, and made contented cat sounds. Then she grew quiet and serious. "This is definitely the strangest camp I've ever chiefed."

"Oh? Why?"

"Don't tell me you don't feel it. There's something . . . I don't know. *Off-center* about this. I mean, who chose these kids? And why? And why aren't the money people here?"

"The cash is all in the bank, right?"

"Yep. It's just . . . I don't know. Something tells me that there are some surprises coming."

Ocean rubbed her nose with his. "The kids are great. They're bonding faster than I've ever seen."

Janie's eyes were closed. She was running over the faces, the places and the oddnesses. The absent boss. The number of apparently abused kids. Their uncanny ability to synchronize and bond. There was a pattern, she just knew it, but as yet it remained unclear. And no matter how she rearranged the pieces currently in hand, she was unable to find a way to feel good about them. Why?

Maybe it was just the shakes. There was a pattern, a flow to camps. You laid out the pattern, and you added the kids. The first few days you kept them busy enough not to notice that they were away from home. Kept them too busy to make enemies. You divided them into teams or "tribes," and set cabins against each other . . . all of that merely to distract them enough so they could relax and bond. But these kids didn't need *any* of that. In a strange way, it was as if they didn't need her at all. And that felt . . .

Oddly *lonely.*

Janie put her arms around Ocean and pulled him closer. This time, there was nothing sexual in the contact. She just needed to be held. In a month or so, she would be back at the bank in Santa Monica, and Ocean would be teaching American Lit at L.A.C.C., and their "real" lives would swallow them again. This was supposed to be their play-time, the emotional glue that held the rest of their lives together. Instead, she had a deep and pervasive sense of wrongness that gnawed at her sleep.

Eyes squeezed shut, she clinched her lower lip with her teeth and wondered what she would do with her thoughts if they didn't start to cheer up soon. This sort of thing could absolutely ruin a perfectly good week. Or month. Or summer.

Or . . .

64

The Green team captain was Colin, a tall, gangly Huck-Finnish kid who hailed from a place called Biloxi, Mississippi.

Colin's accent was as thick as oatmeal. He was quiet, and had a wounded look about him, something that told Patrick that he had been in too many fights without referees, too many scrapes without someone to wield mercurochrome and kisses. That even at fourteen, he was no one to be trifled with.

In another life, he thought that Colin might have made an excellent

Grizzly Adams type. It was weird to meet someone so obviously a loner, yet possessed of that strange animal magnetism that made him compelling even when silent and standing still.

They were on the second hour of the scavenger hunt, and had found four of the ten items: a tennis ball, a little plastic pig, a set of song lyrics from a musical called *Oklahoma* (!), and a paperback copy of a Louis L'amour western. He didn't know what was next, but there was a hint in the poem they found tucked into the back of the book:

The spider weaves its web to catch
The little flies that are its snacks
But if you look behind the fuel
You'll see three hints, two paths, one tool.

"Spiderweb?" one of the kids asked. "What in the world could that be?"

"Spiders're bugs," Colin said. "They have this sticky stuff comes out of their butts . . ."

"Hah hah," Destiny said. She looked at the note. "The fuel. Maybe the propane tanks?"

The twin yellow eight-foot 250-gallon tanks stood between the mess hall and the showers. The kids searched over, under and around. One of the smallest kids crawled behind it, finding three paper envelopes neatly taped to the back. The first was marked "one," the second "two," and the third "three."

They groaned, having previously encountered this very gambit. The one marked "three" had the best clue, but if you opened it, you got three points taken off your score. The one marked "one" had the lamest clue, but you only lost one point for using it. So you had to make a choice—maybe have to open all three, and lose six points, or just open the best clue and lose three, or just maybe open the first, and only lose one.

The seven kids huddled around, while Ocean watched them, curious as to what they would do.

Finally they decided to open the first.

The picture scrawled on it looked like a dancing Indian.

"What the hell is this?" Courtney asked.

"Maybe the dance hall?" Heather said. "You know, the rec center?"

"Yeah, but the dance isn't until day after tomorrow."

Patrick looked at it, and turned it around and upside down. "You know what this looks like to me? It looks kind of flattened out. I think it's a shadow, that's what I think."

"Shadow?" Courtney asked.

"Remember last night, doing shadow plays by the firelight?"

A light seemed to have gone on in their eyes, and without even looking at the other clues, they scrambled toward the fire pit.

The embers had long since cooled, but a cursory exploration showed two ten-inch cardboard arrows taped to benches around the fire pit. The arrows led them to saplings at the forest's edge, with yellow ribbons tied to their branches. Each seemed to indicate a path.

"Which one?"

They decided that the shadow indicated the left trail, and scampered along the path, which took them up the western rise. Ocean tagged along behind them.

They had gone halfway up when they ran into a thickset workman in an orange jacket. The man was tanned with a flat, weather-beaten face and shocks of gray shooting through his hair. He wore a khaki work shirt and faded blue jeans, and was crouching, apparently fiddling with a little tripod-mounted viewfinder. He nodded at them, smiling with his mouth but not his eyes. Patrick hailed him in return. "Have you seen a spiderwebby thing?"

"Hey!" said Ocean. "You can't ask that."

The big man chuckled. "Sorry kids." But when they ran past him, the little warmth in his eyes cooled, and then died to ashes.

Chuck tipped his hat back on his head, and made a spitting sound. "This is really screwed up," he said. "I got kids not much older than that. . . ." He tried not to think about those kids, or the life he had grown to love. He tried to think only of the mission that had begun with a midnight phone call, an intense, incredible conversation. With two hours of arguing, cajoling, commanding, and oblique blackmail. The conversation that had dropped him back down the rabbit hole and through a moral looking glass more frightening than anything he had survived in Southeast Asia.

Beside him, Hennings, a moon-faced man with small eyes and a tight, thin mouth, nodded meaninglessly. "We can't look at it that way," he said. Hennings was a grandfather. Sold real estate in Grand Rapids, doing pretty well if the rumors were right: the old team didn't stay in touch as much as they had promised to do. It was always that way. "I know if I did I'd go crazy. We know what the old man did. And now his poison is running in these damn kids. We let them go—they might kill one of my girl's kids, or one of yours." He was breathing heavy, and his color was bad. He was too old for this. Hell, they were *all* too old for this shit. But what the hell were they supposed to do? "Little Evelyn. Or Timmy," he murmured, looking off across the valley as if focusing on his little angels, maybe hoping their smiling, innocent faces would absolve him of guilt, save him from hell. "As hard as this is going to be, how the fuck would we live with *that*?"

Chuck's face was bleak. "I can do the job, but I'm not sure I can live with it. Either way."

"Two more days," Hennings said, "and it's over. And you'll live through it, and go back home."

The "spiderweb" was a rope netting with a dozen holes of different sizes—some easily large enough for an adult to slip through, others barely big enough to pass a butterfly.

The task, Ocean informed them, was to eel through without touching any of the ropes. And any particular hole could only be used one time. He didn't envy them the task: it still looked darned near impossible even to him, and he'd actually seen it done.

Green team wasted the first ten minutes just debating the task's impossibility, but as they argued Ocean noted that one of the kids, Mathias, walked around the web in slow circles, studying. Thinking, his lips pursed thoughtfully. *I think he's almost got it.*

"I think we can do this," Mathias said finally, calmly, and then laid out his plan. The kids fell in line behind him as if he had a divine right to rule.

Colin was the biggest of them, and they helped him through first. (Ocean had to fight the urge to help them: Colin's butt alone was wider than most of the gaps.) The Mississippian remained on the far side as they fed the others through one at a time. For the next twenty-two minutes there were few words, just focus, labored grunting, and a few squeals of dismay as someone accidentally touched a rope and had to begin anew.

Eventually they managed to complete their task without killing each other. Only then did they celebrate, and their cheers reverberated up and down the valley walls.

Cheryl O'Dey was a skinny redhead from Chicago. Beside catching endless grief for her last name, O'Dey made Colin look like Daniel

Boone. She had all the woodcraft of a cow with buckets strapped to her feet, but possessed limitless energy and enthusiasm.

She was only half the size of Mathias or Colin, but was as much a leader as either of them.

Her group, the Blues, was in the woods west of the athletic field. There stood a ten-foot wooden construct known simply as "The Wall." The object was to see how long it would take to get all team members up and over.

A little green-eyed Minnesotan fireball named Jessica Range received an enormous wedgie when her teammates grabbed her overalls in an effort to haul her over the top. Jessica shrieked, but bit her lip and just sucked it up, scrabbling until she got to the platform at the crest. Only then did she give vent to her feelings, crying and laughing as she shook her fists at the sky. Cruelly, (but also predictably,) the Wedgie Wall is what they called it for the remainder of the camp.

The lazy summer sun cooked the teams as they swam and played water games. When swim time was over they brought canoes and little motorized bumper-rafts out of the lakeside boat house, and played under Denise's watchful eye.

When the afternoon cooled, they retreated to their cabins and played spin-the-bottle, which the counselors found refreshingly retro. From one camp to the next, you were never sure whether you'd have to sweep the woods for lovers every half hour, or force the boys to dance at gunpoint. You just never knew.

65

Monday, July 2

Patrick awoke to the beep of his ten-dollar digital watch. Five o'clock, still dark, but time to get up. He stretched and yawned, the pain in his side and leg a dull, throbbing reminder of his brush with death. Lying in the darkness, it was hard to believe that he was actually free of Claremont, out of Washington, out of everything he recognized as his life. Here, guilt and pain and fear were increasingly distant memories, and there were whole hours at a time when he could forget the dead melon weight of his father's head in his hands.

He slipped on his pants and shoes, and awakened Frankie, who simply opened his eyes and sat up, going from dream to full alert with the speed of a combat veteran. They awakened Bucky and dressed, grabbed a blanket and slipped outside in time to meet Destiny, Jessica and Courtney. Courtney wore a green sweater, her shoulder-length blond hair ruffled by the cold morning wind. Her arms were crossed, pressing a folded green blanket against her chest. Destiny smiled at Patrick, and gave him a brief, sisterly hug.

Keeping silent, they walked up the path, moist stones turning beneath Patrick's feet, his flashlight beam reflecting from dew-spackled spiderwebs. It took fifteen minutes to climb to the top, and they had just settled onto their blankets, shoulders touching, as dawn's first pale fingers stretched up from the east.

Frankie seemed transfixed. "It's like I never saw a sunrise before," he whispered.

"Everything is special here," Destiny said. "Can you feel it?"

Frankie's thin shoulders trembled. "I felt like I'd lost something. Everything. That my friends and family were all gone. When you guys started that club and wouldn't let me in . . ."

Patrick felt a pang of remorse. The veterans of Claremont preschool were outcasts, but Frankie had been pushed even further from the light, denied even the company of his own kind. Patrick had to accept his share of responsibility for that. It made him feel like a small, mean thing. Before he could speak, Frankie shushed him.

"I know. It was Lee and Shermie. I don't blame you. But it hurt." His voice was low and sad, but not accusing. "But here, it's like there're fifty brothers and sisters that I've always had, but never met. Does that make sense?"

"It does to me, man," Bucky said. "And you're in *my* club. And you don't ever have to leave."

Maybe Frankie made a sound, but they couldn't tell. He turned his face away from them, gazing off into the woods, perhaps. Destiny reached out and touched his arm. Patrick watched as her fingers knotted around Frankie's, no slightest trace of jealousy in his heart.

Frankie gripped at her for a minute, then slipped his hand free. He let out a great sigh, and turned to watch the sunrise again. With that sigh, Patrick felt a weight lift from his own shoulders. *This is a healing place,* Patrick thought. *I wish I never had to leave.*

No further words were spoken as the sun made its ascent. And when it was time for them to gather their things and head back down the hillside, they still didn't speak, as if the very act of talking might somehow steal the magic from the moment.

*   *   *

Ten A.M.

Breakfast had been eaten and cleaned up, and the morning sports begun. The Whites were in art, the Reds were practicing kicks and punches, and the Greens were on the athletic field, cheering as three archers stood poised before their targets. The targets were set twenty yards from the line of kids, paper bull's-eyes pinned against bales of straw. Destiny stood tall and straight between Heather and Bucky, drawing her bow with two fingers and a long, slow intake of breath, maintaining single focus. Her bolts were truest, flew most often to the target's crimson center. Her tribe mates stamped their feet and whistled as she discovered a skill she had never known she possessed.

She didn't exactly *aim* at the bull's-eye. That was too direct. It had more to do with finding the right set of feelings. If her posture and her mind and feelings were all sort of lined up, everything went great. That was all it required. And of course, there was a need to use proper technique, to meld breathing and posture and alignment into a coherent whole. But there was something clean and basic about just viewing the target, projecting herself into the bull's-eye, drawing the bow with a single dynamic inhalation, pausing for a long sweet instant . . .

And then letting it go.

Ahhh . . .

There was no doubt about it any longer. In the camp's final archery competition, Destiny would be the Greens' representative.

66

After a long and eventful day, Patrick was up at Charisma Lake, enjoying the camp's first overnight expedition. The hike had been tiring and circuitous and his side ached as he marched along the nature trail up through the hills, looping around through the forest and then heading back south from north of the lake, just in time for sunset. Del and Diane Withers were waiting for them with hot dogs and foil-wrapped ears of corn. Marshmallows, graham crackers and squares of Nestlé's chocolate were melted into s'mores. It was the most delicious meal Patrick could ever remember eating.

The kids sang the Apache horse-stealing song back to the counselors. He had never particularly enjoyed singing in groups before, but now the twining harmonies were exciting. Their voices blended into an odd and mellifluous groove, altos and young baritones and contraltos flowing together as if they had practiced for months, producing a choral quality so excellent that it startled him. To Patrick's delight the teams no longer competed with each other, reaching beyond the boundaries of Blue, Red, Green and White to create a truly tribal sound.

There in the moonlight, they shared an unconcealed, unalloyed delight in their unexpected and newfound proficiency.

After the song Ocean rendered another spooky story, this one about a creature called "Pumpkinhead." It was perfect fireside fodder: a gory, oddly moral tale of Ozark vengeance. Patrick snuggled up between Bucky and Mathias, sleeping bags circled against night ghoulies as Ocean capered and pranced through the story. When he was finished he was rewarded by sleepy applause, and Pat had no strength to protest as Janie called it a night.

Vivian sat by herself, her back against a tree. She hadn't spoken three words in the last hour; she had been exhausted by the day's work, entranced by Ocean's story, and enraptured by the singing.

Now she allowed the first tiny threads of loneliness to creep into her mind. She watched as Janie and Ocean unrolled their sleeping bags side by side. *Please, God, don't let them zip those bags together.*

They didn't, but their easy companionship still gave her a jealous pang. The two sat five feet away from Vivian, and Janie produced a thermos of coffee. When she poured Ocean a cup, his hand shook a bit.

"Something wrong?" Janie asked quietly.

"Just nerves," he said.

"What do you make of all this?"

"It's like we've got twenty-five sets of twins," Ocean said. He turned to Vivian, who watched them, pulled deeply back inside herself. "Can I ask you a question, Mrs. Emory?"

"Vivian, please."

"O.K., Vivian. Was your husband ever in trouble with the law?"

Her shoulders tensed. "No." *Just a couple of drunk and disorderlies. I bailed him out before morning, and Patrick never even knew.* "Why?"

"Probably nothing," he said, and seemed somewhat embarrassed to have asked. "Patrick told me that he died a week ago. I'm terribly sorry."

Vivian's eyes stung, but she blinked hard. *I'm not going to cry.* "We were separated, but . . . I don't know. That doesn't make it any easier."

They were quiet for a time, Janie and Vivian sipping coffee in silence. Ocean turned away from them, as if he was embarrassed by the sudden revelation. Instead, he watched the kids, who were clustered in their bags, quiet now except for a few burring snores. He watched, glanced at his watch for a few moments, then watched again. "I think you better take a look at this, Janie," he said uneasily.

"What is it?

"Can't you *hear* it?"

"Hear what . . ."

And then she understood. All fifty kids were exhaling and inhaling to the same precise rhythm. Not a single one out of step, all blending together so that there were momentary hushes, followed by a rush of air. A hush, and then an inhalation . . .

"Shit," she said, nerves tingling.

She watched them, then stood carefully and walked around the periphery of the camp. Shook her head, then found herself a tree stump to stand on, so she could look down on them from above.

She immediately felt a sense of dislocation, as if she had stumbled directly from wakefulness into dream. What she was witnessing simply wasn't possible. Without apparent forethought or organization of any kind, the kids had arranged themselves into a pattern nearly as precise as a snowflake. As she watched, Colin rolled over in his sleeping bag. There was a brief interruption of the flow of breathing, a few sleepy grunts. Then as campers fell back into the groove, the entire pattern fluctuated like a kaleidoscope, and another pattern appeared. It was like a Busby Berkeley water ballet, or an aerial star created by a group of crack skydivers. Delicate. Complex.

Impossible.

Patrick dreamed. And in his dream, for the very first time, he was not alone. He couldn't exactly see the others, but knew they were there. He walked through the abandoned streets of the mobile home park, but it was more than that. This was a reservation, a barrio, a ghetto. It was the Bronx, it was Bedford-Stuyvesant, Cabrini Green, the slums of Honolulu. All at the same time, and all the faces were his face. He was running, and something was coming after him. The air swirled at his feet, lifting a scrap of paper which burst into flames as it swirled up, like a leaf in a spring wind.

He looked over his shoulder, and caught a glimpse, just a glimpse, of a flaming, churning tower. Without seeing them, he could hear other voices, frightened voices, but couldn't see them, couldn't see them—

Patrick awakened from the dream, beads of sweat burning at the corners of his eyes. The counselors were asleep, but three of the other kids were awake. Their eyes were wide, faces taut, shoulders hunched up. They trembled like small, frightened animals.

"Did you have a dream?" he asked.

The largest of them, a blond named Lizzy, nodded her head sharply, fear and uncertainty chopping five years off her age.

"Was there fire?" he asked.

She stared at him without speaking, exchanging glances with the other kids. She and one of the others lay back down quietly. The third was Aylana. She breathed shallowly, nervously, eyes too wide. Very slowly and carefully, she nodded her head. Then she sank back into her bag.

Hadn't Ocean's Pumpkinhead story contained a sequence of flame and death? Surely that image had invaded their dreams, had driven them all from the arms of sleep.

He just rolled back over, and stared up at the sky. He didn't want to sleep. He would wait to sleep . . .

But didn't. He was fast asleep in minutes, and had no disturbing visions for the rest of the night.

67

Over the last month, Renny Sand had checked his story a hundred different ways, seeking comment and verification without ever letting anyone know exactly what he was working on. It had been torture: he burst to tell *someone* what he now knew, was dying to crow to the heavens that he had within his hands the ability to destroy a cherished memory, to create his own new life.

So far, he had suppressed the urge, but the very pressure of that restraint had given him some kind of aura, some bizarre new attraction that had everyone at the office trying to be his friend. He had received more lunch invitations, more subliminally seductive conversations, more general meetings ("So, Renny—any ideas for a feature story? Anything interesting germinating in that mind of yours?") than at any other period of his life.

It felt *good.*

Because of the need for caution, it had taken weeks to trace down former secret service agent Kelly Kerrigan, finally locating her in a tiny tourist trap called Diablo, Arizona, where she owned a B&B called the Kerrigan House. He'd called the Diablo Chamber of Commerce and reserved a room, packed a light bag and left at four in the morning, driving out the I-10 to Arizona. He figured he'd have a better chance of getting her to talk to him if he was a face-to-face cash customer, and not just another voice on the phone.

Diablo was a hundred and fifty miles southeast of Phoenix, down a little turnoff road indicated by a single worn-out sign promising WESTERN SHOWS, WESTERN FOOD, AND GENUINE INDIAN CURIOS.

The heat was incredible, a hundred and twelve degrees as he passed the California/Arizona border, and hotter every minute. His air-conditioning was pumping double-time, but the sun was trying to claw its way through the windshield. He bet he could melt off his finger-prints just by touching his hands to the glass.

Finally reaching a faded WELCOME TO DIABLO sign, he drove the tourist drag searching for the Kerrigan House. It seemed that he'd driven through a time warp: cowboys swaggered the street, saloons with swinging double doors roared player piano music, and stage coaches rolled slowly past, blaring tourist spiels.

He pulled up to Kelly's white, two-story, trellised house at about three o'clock, and found parking shade beneath an ancient, spreading oak. When he opened the door, the dry, dusty air, skillet-hot, seared the oxygen from his lungs. It was like sticking his head into a kiln.

Sand reeled, then steeled himself. He grabbed his bags and hoisted them into the house, praying he wouldn't have a heat stroke along the way. The door was answered by a tall, tanned man in his seventies, his face weathered enough to hold a half cup of water. He wore a red NRA cap, and Sand had a feeling that he was bald beneath. In a voice that was pure Texas, the man introduced himself as Bobby Ray Kerrigan. His warm smile didn't entirely mask some deeper discomfort, a secret pain.

"I'm looking for a Mrs. Kerrigan?" Sand asked, praying to be invited inside before he died.

Bobby Ray's face lightened a bit at the mere mention. "Kelly's out and about. Home in maybe two hours." He pulled the door wider. "You Mr. Sand?"

"I'm almost too hot to remember."

"Come on in, sit a spell. You like lemonade?"

"By the bucket."

Bobby Ray chuckled. "Then take your bag upstairs and meet me in the kitchen. I believe I got a bucket with your name on it."

Renny did just that, taking his luggage to a room with a queen-sized bed with a white canopy. The room had an arched ceiling and pink floral decoration, with a leisurely rotating fan on the roof. Hot. He decided that he'd spend as little time as possible there during the day.

Down in the kitchen, Bobby Ray met him with a jelly jar filled with pale yellow lemonade. By the second swallow Renny was deliriously happy to realize that this was real lemonade, unadulterated by artificial flavors, colors or additives. Maybe it was just the excruciating drive, but he swore it was the best damned lemonade he had ever tasted in his life, and said so.

Bobby Ray chuckled. "Ain't it? That's Kelly's doing—and it's famous for miles. She wins every bake contest that I don't enter, too."

"You bake?"

The older man sipped deeply from his own glass. Renny caught a faintly alcoholic scent, and suspected that Bobby Ray had augmented his own drink before the reporter appeared. "Damned skippy. Helped my ma raise eight kids, all boys. Bake, sew, clean windows. Couldn't wait to get into the Navy."

Renny had a second glass, and half of a third, exchanging pleasantries as he did. Bobby Ray finally said it was time for his favorite game show, and invited Renny to join him in the living room. Renny declined, excused himself and went a-wandering through the tourist shops along Main Street, struggling to stay in shadows whenever he could find them. He bought a frozen cherry slushy from a chubby Pinal tribeswoman at a sidewalk stand, and took a stagecoach ride around town.

The gravel-voiced old coot of a driver pointed out the house of Diablo's first sheriff, a place where Wyatt Earp had supposedly nailed one of the Clanton lackeys responsible for his brother's death over in Tombstone, the former whorehouse turned restaurant ("where you can still get a hot piece of meat. I mean a damn fine steak, a' course!") and the boarded-up entrance to a long dead silver mine. Apparently, its collapse had taken four miners and half the town industry with it.

Renny finally parked himself under an awning at a show around the corner from Kelly's called Helldorado, where actors and part-time stuntmen ("Ol' Lupe here doubled for Emilio Estevez in *Young Guns II!*") entertained the crowds for tips. Most of Diablo was rather sad, a second-rate Tombstone, and from what he'd heard, Tombstone was no Universal City. But Helldorado was actually fairly elaborate for a tourist attraction. It was set back from the main street, sandbags stacked head-high outside the façade. Careful reading of the brochure revealed that the facility was also used in Western-style shooting competitions. Now *that* was something he'd like to see.

After a bit of over-amped range-rover music, the show began. Villains sneered and postured, leather-slapping cowboys bit the dust, bushwhackers appeared through trapdoors to menace fainting schoolmarms who transformed in a blur and a cloud of smoke into Annie Oakley clones. Their dialogue was looped into the music track and mouthed by the performers, cornier than a Republic two-reeler and comforting in its very ineptitude. It was more fun than he wanted to admit, and when it was over, when the gun smoke cleared and the cast brushed off the dust and took their bows, Sand was spanking his palms with the rest of the yokels.

He bought a bottle of warm water on the way out. The sun sucked the moisture out of his skin almost as fast as Diablo sucked the money out of tourists. Drugstores crammed with post cards and knickknacks, souvenir shops with carved topaz and wrought silver jewelry crowding their windows, coffee shops and sandwich vendors offering buffalo burgers and "sidewinder sodas" all vied with each other for the tourist dollar. Renny went deeply into observer mode, and watched the machine at work. Seen from one perspective, it was the same gentle swindle worked at carnies and amusement parks the world over. The Bermuda shorts and Hawaiian-shirt crowd was eating it up.

He maneuvered around an elderly Japanese couple walking a miniature boxer dog on a braided leash, and encountered a tall man with fine golden hair, dressed in black shirt, pants, shoes and hat, with a golden Sheriff's star over his heart. He carried himself as if the entire town was a Hollywood back lot, and everyone else merely a bit player.

Then the two of them stood face to face. He was Sand's height, and maybe fifteen years older. Renny had the sense that he'd seen this man before, and wondered where. After a moment he decided he was wrong. The sheriff was an archetype, familiar from a thousand Saturday morning reruns, that was all.

The sheriff tipped his hat and walked on.

Renny walked back to the boardinghouse, with the vague, and

vaguely discomforting, feeling that he had missed something. He also had the sense that eyes were boring into his back. Sand turned, and looked back down the street after him, but Black Bart was gone.

Renny returned to the Kerrigan House and his rented bed, and lay staring up at the slanted ceiling, hearing the fake gun-blasts from over at the Helldorado stage, wondering why he had been so spooked by a cartoon sheriff. It was as ridiculous as getting the willies because those damned portraits at Disneyland's Haunted Mansion kept staring at you.

When he came down for dinner, Kelly Kerrigan was busy straightening the living room. She was grayer than she had been in the video, her skin more weathered. But according to his research she was a sprightly sixty-eight, while her husband was, unfortunately, a completely used-up seventy-three. Sand had the impression that they had just finished an early supper.

"Evening," Sand said. "Am I the only guest right now?"

"Yep," she said. "We've got more coming in day after tomorrow, but July's just too darned hot for most out-of-staters. The real business is spring and winter."

She looked at him a few times as if some tiny alarm switch in her mind were triggering.

"Your name is Renny Sand?" Her voice was precise, polite, with a hidden strand of unbreakable wire within. "We've met before, haven't we?" She held up her hand as if anticipating a denial. "I'm rarely wrong."

"Oh, well . . ."

"Oh, come on." She leaned forward, eyes sparkling. "Indulge an old lady."

Damned sharp old lady, he thought. "It was years ago, ma'am. I was a reporter going through a reception line for Alexander Marcus."

She nodded, filing him away. He could tell she had dog-eared the corner of her mental Rolodex. *Renny Sand?* She wasn't buying his nonchalance. "Maybe that's it," she said. And then shrugged. "What brings you to Diablo?"

He considered a lie, and then realized, without any question, that she would see right through it. It was time to tell the truth. "You do," he said.

Sand and the Kerrigans sat on the front porch swing, gazing out on a street that was more dirt than pavement, toward a distant crop of blue-black mountains and somber desert.

"Mind if I smoke?" he asked.

Ray answered. "Go right ahead, young fella. I like the smell."

So he lit up, and told Kelly that he'd uncovered information about a San Francisco jaunt not listed on any of the official itineraries. He wondered if she would elucidate.

"I was assigned to Alexander between '86 and '87," she said. "He liked me. More importantly, his mother liked me. Even after he dropped out of the race in '87, there were still threats, and things just worked out for me to stay on. I liked it, most of the time. He said that if I wanted to take leave from the Service, he would pay my salary. I agreed."

"So . . . what was the San Francisco trip?"

She laughed. "It was all very hush-hush. He told me about it on the flight up. Some medical tests, I think."

The hair on the back of his neck tingled: reporter's instinct.

She continued, "Seems that maybe a year earlier, an old frat brother from Harvard introduced Alexander to a scientist of some kind. Educator. The man's name was . . . Dronet. Dr. Dronet."

He searched his mind, and no bell rang.

"Anyway, Alexander said this man had a great idea, and that he was financing it. He never said too much about it. Alexander was negotiating for a half-dozen midwestern radio stations at the time. I didn't see him much that trip, and tell you the truth I shopped while he took off with one of the goon squad for the day."

"A whole day? And do you know where he went?"

"No. He enjoyed teasing me about it, though."

Sand was very quiet, but then asked, "Mrs. Kerrigan?"

"Kelly, please."

"I want to be as honest as possible, but for reasons of discretion, I can't tell you everything I know, or think I know." It was strange, but he just couldn't imagine himself lying to this razor-sharp little woman.

She was very still. Her husband was watching them both, and dissecting Renny with an unnervingly piercing gaze.

"Let's say that I believed that Alexander Marcus was a complicated man, and that he might have had some dealings that were withheld from the public view." How in the hell could he phrase this? "In your time in his presence, did you ever have the sense that he was withholding secrets? I don't mean confidential business or political matters."

Her generous mouth thinned. "You're going to need to be a mite more specific. Everyone has secrets."

"I mean secrets that could have . . . destroyed him. Did he have an abnormal need for privacy?"

"He was surrounded by people, twenty-four hours a day, seven days a week."

"Yes, but . . ." Damn, damn damn.

Bobby Ray hadn't said anything at all through all of this, but finally he spoke, in a calm, direct voice. "You drove all the way out here to talk with Kelly, didn't you, young man?"

Renny nodded.

"You're a reporter, and you found something out about your former boss, and you're wondering about what to do with it." He paused. "You wrote that article about the cocaine, didn't you? I saw you on *Sixty Minutes*."

Oh, Jesus.

" 'Pears to me you're trying to be extra careful with your sources. Sorta got your fingers burned the last time, didn't you?"

His eyes, a watery but direct blue, seemed to go right through Sand. "Yes, sir, I am, and I did."

He nodded thoughtfully. "So the talk about San Francisco was more smoke screen than anything else?"

"No, sir. I have reason to wonder about San Francisco. But you got to see sides of him that he probably concealed from the rest of the world."

Sand felt a rush, a compulsion to lay out what he thought he knew, but just couldn't do it. "So . . . I guess I'll just ask you one question. And I pray you'll answer it for me. I think I'm on the verge of the biggest story of my life. It's so big that I barely know what to do with it, don't know what corner to pry up first. So far, it's all circumstantial. I need some verification that my wild suspicions might actually be correct before I dig any deeper."

Sand took a deep breath, and then went on. "Suppose I told you I thought that Alexander Marcus might have had a terrible, dark secret, something that kept him from running for the Presidency. Something bigger than race, or death threats, or his worried mother."

Her face might have been made of stone. Heart pounding, he went on.

"And suppose, just suppose I asked you what general area you believed that problem rested in. If you were to answer that question, what do you think you'd say?"

She was very quiet for so long that Sand wondered if he had insulted her, crossed over some invisible line. "I'd say that I couldn't answer that question," she said flatly. "The men and women of the Service are involved in the intimate lives of some of the wealthiest and most powerful people in the world, and we are sworn to maintain that veil of privacy."

He was at a dead end. This was miserable. "Please." He didn't want to beg, but could hear desperation creeping into his voice. "I'm trying to make sure that I don't accidentally tarnish the legacy of a great man." She remained unmoved. "If I ask you things, specific things, would you at least tell me if I'm off base?"

Another silence. "The first wrong question ends the conversation," she said finally.

Thank God. Under the circumstances, that was more than fair: it was a gift. "All right. All right. If there was one area that might have caused problems for Marcus in terms of the Presidency, that area was . . . a need for privacy."

She nodded slightly. "That would be safe to say."

"From time to time he would elude his bodyguards, and go off for some time by himself. . . ."

Her look was disapproving. "Half right," she said. "But not alone."

Shit! With a friend? Partner? "If there was a problem, it might have to do with women."

She looked at Bobby Ray, and his mouth flattened in what might have been an unpleasant little smile. She nodded.

"From time to time you had the sense he liked to play rough."

She stood. "I'm sorry, this discussion is over."

"Please . . ."

She held up her hand. "We made a deal, Mr. Sand."

He sighed. She was right. And he knew that he was right, too. She wouldn't talk about it, but there was something there. From time to time Alexander Marcus went off with a friend, and did things that she thought had something to do with women. He smiled. "All right. Thank you for what you were willing to say." He stretched, suddenly feeling the strain of the eight-hour drive. Kelly Kerrigan hadn't said much, but her eyes seemed to burn through him.

"You've found something you don't like," she said.

"I hate it."

"You admired him, didn't you?"

"Didn't you?"

"Yes, but I was also fascinated. Did you ever look at a tiger in a cage from a distance, watch it run, or climb, and think 'what an awesome machine,' then get close enough to see the muscles and bones working under the skin?"

He nodded, unsure of her newfound direction.

"I think I've always had a fondness for getting close to dangerous things," she said. "And Alexander Marcus, like most powerful men, was also dangerous. If you found something volatile, be very sure, Mr. Sand. Very sure. You could hurt a lot of people."

"I don't want to do that," he said.

"I believe you," she replied, and gave him a tight, bright, wary little smile.

He turned when he reached the doorway. "We made a deal, and you kept your part of it. Thank you. But if there is anything, any other information at all that you can give me, I would appreciate it more than I have words to say." She looked as if she were about to speak, and he raised his hand. "Please, don't make up your mind now. Think about it. Tell me in the morning." He tried to keep the plea out of his voice, but knew he hadn't succeeded.

Kelly gazed up at him, the calm in her eyes somehow communicating to him, banking the fire in his stomach. "I'll think on it, Renny Sand. Good night."

"G'night," he said, nodded to both of them, and disappeared inside.

Renny lay in bed that night, staring at the arched ceiling. What did he know? Everything, and nothing. Yet. He knew that Marcus had been born in poverty, a brilliant, athletic boy who had been tormented by neighborhood girls and then caught the eye of his high school history teacher. He knew their affair had been discovered, and Marcus mutilated, by her husband.

And that his mother had accepted money in a deal that allowed the husband to escape prosecution. How had Marcus felt about that? Did he both love and hate his mother for that? He certainly had reason to hate other women. The tall, rawboned, awkward genius he must have once been . . . the betrayal and fear . . .

And had he gone to other women, and been rebuffed? Marcus had never married, but obviously frequented prostitutes. Christ. If this horror show wasn't a breeding ground for monsters, he didn't know what was.

Renny saw the path before him. He needed to talk to someone, to lay the whole thing out to someone who could share it. This was just too much.

He was so used to lies, and half-truths, and expedient fabrications, and justifiable obfuscation. There was something refreshing about Kelly and her husband. He had wanted to speak nothing but truth before them, had known that the cost of dishonesty was dissolution of relationship. That was a breath of fresh air in his life. There were damned few people with whom honesty was more rewarding than ingenuity.

There was one other person who came to mind, who from the very beginning, from the very first contact, had provoked a similar response. Vivian. He had seen her, and known the reality of his own emotion so starkly that no lie could possibly have concealed his intent. Truth had gushed out of him like water from a turned spigot.

There was a problem with lying to others, one that had nothing to do with getting caught, or even the difficulty of keeping your lies straight. It was that lying to others inevitably led to lying to yourself. What he needed now was clarity. He needed to lay all his thoughts and feelings out before another human being, one he could trust to tell him what she thought, and felt, and saw.

Then he would know his next step.

There was only one person who fit that bill, and by sheerest coincidence, she too was in Arizona. Exactly where, he didn't know, but he would sure as hell find out in the morning.

Kelly and Bobby Ray sat out on the porch, gazing at the mountains, so dimly visible in the starlight. They spoke mostly of small things, Kelly carefully avoiding the subject Sand had broached. Bobby Ray knew his woman, knew that she was turning something over and over in her own mind, examining it like an archaeologist examining an ancient, mysterious artifact.

"You know," she finally said, "there are things from those days I don't look at. It was all sort of fun, and golden, and then he died. For a while I didn't even believe he was dead, that anyone so alive could *ever* die."

"Are you sure he did?"

She clucked. "I saw the body, and it was him, Bobby Ray. It was him. So the dream was over, and I came back to my senses a little. And when D'Angelo called and said he remembered I'd talked about wanting to run a B&B, and that there was one for sale here, and he could get us one hell of a bank loan, I remembered the old days, and . . . I jumped at it."

"*We* jumped."

She leaned her head against his shoulder, and was quiet again, for a long time. Then: "What if that reporter is right? What if there *is* something? *Was* something."

He turned her face until her hazel eyes met his. "Are you telling me you had suspicions?"

She broke contact. "Not exactly. But I knew he had secrets. Knew that there was a place inside him that he kept tight. To tell you honestly, I thought it was the race thing, that a Negro just wasn't going to open himself up to the white lady, no matter how much he liked her. But sometimes I wondered. He was always under such perfect control emotionally. Better than anyone I ever met. I wondered: What did he do with his anger? His pain? His fear?" She shook her head. "But that's awful, judging a man capable of evil things because he seemed so good." She turned to face Bobby Ray again. "Isn't it?"

He took his time thinking before he ventured a guess. "Was there ever a time that Marcus got away from the rest of you? Went off by himself?"

"Yes," she said quietly. "He slipped everyone except D'Angelo."

"Chasing a little tail?"

She sighed. "Maybe that's it. A string of little bastards up and down the coast?" *Alexander Marcus and D'Angelo sharing a little smile after a long night out? Wasn't there a Nike-tread print in sand, and a twisted sprig of evergreen, on the carpet outside the fire escape on Marcus's wing one of those late nights in San Francisco? How far would you have to drive to find soil like that, and plants like that? Just the local jogging track? Or further?*

"Strange about that," Bobby Ray said. "Angel never seemed the type. You ever get a sex vibe off 'im?"

"No," she said, and found that her throat was just a little constricted. It had to be the cold. "Not even once. But he did notice younger women a bit. He was extremely polite to them. Heavy-handedly polite. What seemed natural extravagance with Marcus was . . . well, almost mockery with Angel."

"Maybe homosexual?"

She considered. "That's another kind of secret, of course. D'Angelo and Marcus lovers?" She thought and sighed and finally shook her head. "You know, I don't think so. One of his executives was gay, and mooned over Angel, strange to say. Said he wished Angel was that way, but what he called his 'gaydar' said otherwise."

"Could have been wrong."

"True enough. But something tells me no."

"So . . . Marcus and D'Angelo had a secret. It might have involved women."

She shifted uncomfortably. "Something tells me it does. And now Sand's got my curiosity up, damn him."

Why have I never married? Alexander once replied on one of their numbing, innumerable coast-to-coast flights. *Because I'm married to my vision. It wouldn't be right to ask a woman to tolerate my schedule.* But there were the endless social engagements, the rumored relationships with actresses and congresswomen, executives and supermodels. Overlapping, short, no hint of intimacy with anyone but his mother, and the Praetorians. And Angel, with whom he disappeared at night. And returned with signs of exertion, and secretive smiles. Angel, who, she felt in her soul, loved nothing more than power. Political power (how much smaller a pond than Diablo could he have found?), physical power (his speed and marksmanship), financial power (exactly how much of this town did he own?). And of course, the power of life and death.

Especially death.

Kelly snuggled closer to Bobby Ray. Despite the warmth of the evening air, she suddenly felt very cold indeed.

68

TUESDAY, JULY 3

In the morning, Renny Sand packed his bags and went downstairs for breakfast. It was delicious. Fluffy eggs scrambled with sharp cheddar, crisp juicy bacon and sausage tender enough to cut with a spoon, mountains of homemade scones fresh from the oven, and pots of marmalade sweet and sharp and filled with little bits of fruit peel. It was all served on antique plateware with blue flowering vines winding around the rim, and accompanied by cups of strong, perfect French roast with thickened cream.

His hosts took their time serving, by their relaxed pace encouraging him to slow down, enjoy every bite, every sip. He couldn't remember when he had so relished a morning meal.

"That was just unbelievably good." He stifled a burp. They nodded happily. "Listen, have you heard of a place called Weinstein's Folly?"

Kelly shook her head.

"It's up someplace called Prescott. Do you know it?"

"Sure. About four hours, up the 17 from Phoenix."

He did some quick calculations in his head. "Great. I'm heading up there to see a friend."

Kelly smiled. "I thought over your request last night, Renny, and maybe I have something for you. You work for his company, and you're interested in how the man thought. Every few years Marcus would publish sections of his journals in-house. He gave copies to some of his intimates—myself included. Interested?"

"Am I?" he asked eagerly. "Lead me to it!"

"It's just a few chapters, but one of them deals with the whole business in San Francisco. Still interested?"

In a health exam? Marcus bending over for the rubber glove? Or something else, something very different. Could this be a smoking gun?

He kept his face calm, but his pulse raced.

She handed over the box. "I hadn't looked at this stuff in years. He asked me to check some facts for him, and I just held onto it. I'd forgotten: the whole exam thing was actually kind of interesting. It belongs in the archives, I think."

"I'll take a look at it. Thank you." He almost succumbed at that moment, almost told her the rest of it, nearly spilled his guts, placed the story of his life in her hands for her to affirm, deny, tear to pieces, cast to the winds.

But he couldn't, just couldn't. It wouldn't be right, or fair. First Vivian, and then, perhaps, he would return and talk to Kelly, tell her the truth. She and Bobby Ray deserved that.

So instead of confession, he packed his bags into his car, enjoyed a final glass of Kelly Kerrigan's famous lemonade, and drove on his way, leaving his hosts waving to him on the porch, arms around each other's waists.

But as he turned off their street and toward the highway, he was plagued by the thought: *You should have told her.*

69

As it happened, the package given to Renny Sand contained a relatively innocuous journal. However, in the months that followed Alexander Marcus's personal effects were scoured, and a more complete and unexpurgated version unearthed. If Renny had read that one, he might well have thought and behaved differently than he did over the next twenty-four hours. Of particular interest might have been an entry about five hundred pages into the six hundred page manuscript, an entry which ultimately found its way into the official record of what became known as the "Charisma Lake Incident."

That official document was reproduced in exactly forty-six copies, and was read by exactly that many people, no more, no less.

The most pertinent passage read as follows:

FROM THE JOURNAL OF ALEXANDER MARCUS

Drs. Jorgenson and Dronet made a simple observation, one I could agree with wholeheartedly: we are losing a generation of our best and brightest young men to poverty, racism, latchkey environments and a rigid, outmoded educational system.

On that day I had initially allotted half an hour for their presentation, but their proposal was a lightning bolt, electrifying my mind with possibilities. I cancelled the next two hour's appointments, and begged them to continue.

Dronet was impassioned. "Some people fail no matter what opportunities are available," he said. "Others will succeed regardless of the obstacles." I knew this. Everyone knows this, if they study history. The only question is how much of this capacity is inborn, how much learned in environment. Dronet theorized that whatever portion of this was environmental, that part could be taught, or literally implanted in a child's mind at the subconscious level. Hypnosis, somatropic drugs, neuromuscular re-patterning, subliminals and other disciplines perfected in the fields of psychology, psychological warfare and television advertising, promised to transfer ideas, concepts, values and beliefs more efficiently than at any previous point in human history. We could completely revolutionize education.

"We'll consider this 'teachable' component the software in the human biocomputer," he said.

I wasn't quite certain what he meant, and the two of them broke it down for me.

According to Jorgenson, the debate over intelligence generally centers around the question of testability or measurement separate from the cultural context. In other words, whether it is possible to create a completely unbiased aptitude test. Conservatism and liberality take opposite sides in this discussion: Conservatives tend to claim abilities are "hardware" dependent (genetics), liberals look to the "software," the child's environment and education.

All my life I have participated in such discussions, often instigated by social conservatives who think they flatter me by assuming that I am one of "them" and not one of "the others," the mass of humanity (often black humanity) which, in their opinion, functions at the level of mud. All my life I have watched the scientists and politicians debate these issues as if the very people they were debating were livestock instead of living, breathing human beings with hopes and dreams and emotions.

According to Jorgenson and Dronet (and I write this after reading the transcripts of our meeting), human beings operate on at least three levels of "programming"—their genetics, their early childhood environment, and their adolescent and adult education. Genetics were unchanging, and current thought said that between forty and sixty percent of innate potential in life simply depended upon choosing the right grandparents. By the time you are an adult, the childhood programming has set like cement. Getting down to that basic "stuff" requires the therapeutic equivalent of jackhammers and nitroglycerine. So the focus had to be early childhood.

Those core childhood programs were belief systems, value hierarchies, positive and negative emotional anchors, movement patterns, prejudices, interpretations of memories, unresolved traumas, and the thousand other things we absorb with our mother's milk, programming so deep it is rarely questioned later in life.

For instance, if a child grows up in a poor household, with parents who work hard, he can hardly believe that wealth is the result of hard work. If hard work produced money, why didn't his parents have any? He is most likely to adapt the belief that "money is the root of all evil," or "you have to have money to make money," or "it is easier for a camel to pass through the eye of a needle than for a rich man to enter the kingdom of heaven." I bless my mother for going out of her way, on a daily basis, to tell me that I could accomplish anything in the world, for whispering to me as I slept that I was a prince in exile, for showering me with a thousand different stories and fables of boys from humble beginnings who went on to win kingdoms.

Not that some people do not avoid the trap of poverty even without such a gloriously measured upbringing, but by definition alone, the average person behaves in an average fashion. Most people die in the social class into which they are born, be it high or low. Most people do *not* escape their environment unless they are extraordinary.

But it might be possible to teach ordinary, average children to think in extraordinary ways.

The key lay in reaching children at the preschool level, when the doors of perception were widest, and core behaviors most malleable. Instead of studying subjects, Jorgenson theorized that it would be more useful for children to study the people who have mastered their lives, contributed to society at the highest levels. Then convey the qualities that give these people unending passion and focus, as well as their specific problem-solving strategies. These two scientists believed that they had found a method suitable for extracting such qualities and imprinting them on a young child's mind, but had run into opposition from the educational establishment (imagine!), and failed to find government backing for such a project. They sought private funds.

After discussing their project at greater length, I came to the conclusion that this might be the answer to a question I had never dared fully formulate: how in hell do I help those trapped in the system my own obsessive energies had allowed me to escape? I knew I had more intelligence, more energy, more focus than any human being I had ever met. This had been tested on the battlefield, in the corporate world, in Olympic competition. I *knew* myself to be gifted, and longed to find a way for those less fortunate to escape the same traps that had almost ensnared me, despite all my advantages.

I urged Dronet and Jorgenson to apply for a grant from Mark-

One, one of my charitable foundations, and promised to ease the way for them. If their plans looked sound on paper, they would get their money.

The plan required a double-blind experiment, with one thousand children chosen from lower economic and social circles. The methodology was to be hidden among the children's normal daily activities. A national chain of daycare centers was actually looking for a new owner, and could be acquired for a bit over a million dollars. The equipment and apparatus required to stock them would require an additional three million, but these centers were already a money-making proposition. Once acquired, they could produce a substantial portion of operational capital.

To tell the truth, my mind already buzzed with a dozen ways the chain might actually turn a profit.

Months later, after we had concluded our third conversation on this issue, I noticed Dr. Dronet looking at me rather strangely. When prompted, he said that since the grant money had been approved, and he could no longer be considered guilty of pandering, he could finally convey his latest inspiration. . . .

That I be the initial experiment's primary role model.

Taken aback at first, I finally realized that I had conned myself, that I had known all along that I would be recruited. He reasoned that my military and political service, financial success and Olympic medal proved that I would make an ideal initial subject. Flattered, I needed only their assurance that my participation would remain secret: no need for this pilot program to seem more of an ego trip than it actually was!

And that is how I found myself in San Francisco, at a private health facility, subjected to an exhausting battery of examinations. From CAT to MRI, from batteries of lie-detector-type tests to computer scanning of my movement patterns, from voiceprints to eye movements, they extracted from me every conceivable attitude, belief, response, and value.

The tests were conducted over three grueling, sometimes painful days. Jorgenson and his crew then pored over the results for months, extracting what they called the "critical path" of my thoughts and behaviors, then devising a thousand ways to imprint my emotions and habit patterns onto children without their conscious knowledge. If it worked, so they told me, a thousand tiny Alexander Marcuses would grow to adulthood, programmed to operate at the very limits of their "hardware," self-motivated, clear in their goals and values, invulnerable to negative social programming, supremely confident and competitive. It was embarrassing to hear the expectations, but exciting as well.

For myself, I felt a hunger that had been long repressed within me. I had no children, had chosen a life of service and work. Now, there were a thousand children who carried, not my genes, but my *memes,* my inwardness. Who would spread the essence of what I have striven to be during my life.

Immortality, as no other man has ever known it.

My children, in spirit, if not in flesh.

Mine.

70

Sand followed his sketchy directions west on the 10 to the 17 and then north all the way to the Prescott turnoff. Thoughts, memories and questions swirled in his head, fighting for his attention.

Road signs warned him to switch off his air-conditioning as he climbed the grade. The sun burned with nightmarish intensity, but as the long miles passed and the elevation climbed into tan, sandy, mountainous terrain, the air mercifully began to cool.

As it did, his mind slipped back into a troubling groove. What to do? Sand couldn't blame Miss Kitty for her son's atrocities, but there was no way she would escape crucifixion by the press and public. And she wasn't the only one who would suffer: so would the stockholders, executives and employees at Marcus International. God, the whole thing could collapse. And to what end?

His head swam. He had Kelly's documents in his briefcase, and with any luck would find a few moments to go through them, to think about it, to puzzle through this mess. Until then, he would put it out of his mind, and allow himself to enjoy a treat.

She was here, very close. Even if by way of tragedy, Vivian was free, and in her e-mail she had invited him to visit her.

I would like very much to see you, he had typed.

So would I, Vivian had replied.

And for right now, today, that was enough.

*   *   *

His first impression of Charisma Lake was of a slow-mo explosion. His engine labored as he made it up the last stretch of grade, and he could see, but not hear, the children ahead. They scrambled in clusters, in groups more often than pairs or singles. Seemed like a bunch of fairly typical kids herded by a few Gilligan-hatted counselors. There was a "VISITORS" sign hung at one of the cabins, so he stopped off there.

A short blond emerged to meet him. She had improbably large blue eyes, and a face that was alternately sexy and homely depending on the angle and the light. "Hi," she said. "Can I help you?"

He exited the car, and spun out of the way as a couple of teenagers sprinted past. There was no real need for concern: without looking up, they veered around him like a pod of radar-equipped porpoises.

"Hi. My name is Renny Sand."

"I'm Janie."

They shook hands. "I'm looking for Vivian Emory. Can you point me in the right direction?"

"Just a minute." She disappeared back in her cabin for a minute, and emerged with a clipboard. She peeled back the top sheet and studied.

"I can't be sure," Janie said, "she's probably off duty. She was up late last night on the sleep-out, and up early this morning with breakfast . . . I bet she's taking a nap. Is she expecting you?" Then Janie suddenly paused, and took another careful look at him. "The reporter?" she asked, and *that* smile was suddenly on her face, the one that turned it from mischievously cute to something close to beautiful.

"That's the one."

"Counselor's Cabin 'B,' " Janie said, eyes sparkling. "Go get her, tiger."

Vivian couldn't sleep. She hovered just over that blessed place, hoping to enter and find rest. Again and again she approached slumber, only to find that there seemed a great weight, a massive center to her dreams that seemed to pull all imagery toward it, all of the darkness and the light, as if the very deepest parts of her mind were struggling to resolve some unknown conundrum.

No matter how long she slept, the puzzle never quite resolved, although her groggy mind kept trying to convince her that just a little more slumber, one more dream might give her answers. At odd times during the day she would remember snatches of dream, and be convinced that if she could just remember them, she would learn secrets and revelations beyond imagining. Worrying about that created a vicious cycle: hard to sleep, hard to awaken, distracted during the day.

Ordinarily, she would have just shucked it off, but it was almost impossible not to feel that there was something *real* here, and if she stretched out her arm completely, into the dark, her fingers could just brush the shape, and the shape was—

There was a knock at the door, and sleep's inky tides receded. "Damn," she moaned. "Damn, damn, damn."

She opened her eyes, squinted against the slanted daylight. For a fraction of a second she imagined that she was back in her Claremont trailer, but swiftly realized that wasn't the case. She was in Prescott, Arizona. She and Patrick were healthy and fine.

She heard the buzz of teen talk outside her windows, and also the woods murmurs, the bird sounds. They were a long way from whatever danger had threatened her tiny family of two, and everything was—

Another knock.

Vivian rolled out of bed. Her bare feet flinched at the rough, splintered wood floor, but otherwise she was dressed. Was it already time for lunch? But hadn't Janie said that she didn't have to work lunch today? Surely there was—

She opened the door, and there stood Renny Sand.

She gawked at him, sure for a moment that this was merely a particularly sadistic part of her dream. To her horror, she realized that he was actually framed in her doorway.

"Hi, Vivian. I was in the area—" he began brightly. She squawked, and slammed the door in his face. Jesus!

"How *could* you?" She braced her back against the door and screamed at him. "I didn't know you were coming!" Her mind raced. Makeup, shower, shampoo, oh, God—why hadn't he *told* her?

When he spoke again, his muffled voice sounded terribly embarrassed. "I'm sorry. I thought it would be a good surprise."

"Give me five minutes," she said. She must look a fright. There was no sink in the cabin, but she did have a sports bottle filled with water, which she used to dampen a face towel and scrub her face. She used the same water to moisten a toothbrush, and scrub her teeth. Finally she spit discreetly into the towel, hoping that she wouldn't need it again later. She found a hand mirror and brushed her hair, bunned it back, then smoothed down her shirt, sniffing under her arms. That perfume was not Revlon, but this was camp, and it was his fault for not giving her notice, and . . . oh, *shit.*

She opened the door again.

To his credit, Renny Sand had backed up several steps and was sitting on a low bench. He looked up at her sheepishly, his expression one of those *Gawd-have-I-screwed-up* puppy-dog specials, apology and explanation in one.

She wanted to be mad, but was too happy to see him. When their eyes met she understood *exactly* why he had come. He stood. He was shorter, thinner than she had remembered. Somehow, her imagination had ballooned him up to nearer Otis's mass. Sand was dressed in Nikes, faded jeans and a short-sleeved khaki work shirt. He was slender, fit, his body more runner than weightlifter or laborer. A blue Universal City baseball cap was pulled snugly over his short dark hair. His smile was softer than she remembered, his eyes ringed with fatigue. The air around him seemed to crackle with energy: excitement, expectation, hope? About her? This visit was to have been a surprise, a present. He had trusted their sense of connection, had just wanted to see her face when she saw his.

Why the deep creases at the corners of his eyes? The redness? Even scanning briefly, she counted five gray hairs. Could life have been as hard for him as it had for her? Merciful God, could they really be so compatible?

And if the joy in his eyes, and the abashed grin that suddenly made him look right at home with the rabbiting thirteen-year-olds told her nothing, then she could have looked into her own heart, and felt the last bad years melting away. A doorway to her heart was opening. Perhaps the midnight e-mails hadn't been the worst and most self-deluded kind of foolery. Just possibly they had been some sort of instinctive grasping toward an emotional safety line thrown to her from a thousand miles away. They were a whispered promise that her life was not over, that other possibilities existed, awaiting only her decision to live again.

"Hi, Vivian," he said humbly, and that was absolutely all that he had to say.

71

Patrick and the other campers sat crosslegged, ringing a cluster of blue mats.

Ocean stood at the center, barefoot and clad in gray sweats, his long blond hair knotted behind him in a pony tail. For the first time Patrick thought that Ocean seemed to really deserve the belt cinched around his waist. In fact, he could imagine a frayed, ancient black belt there, snug around his waist, a shadow of things to come.

"This is going to work in a very special way," Ocean said. "Everyone gets graded: for spirit, technique in attack, technique in defense, and the other teams will be graded for their spirit in cheering you on. This isn't about you competing with someone else. This is about you learning to defend yourself."

Patrick's stomach crawled with adrenaline. He felt slightly nauseated. He looked up into the nearly empty bleachers, and found his mother, sitting next to the Witherses and that reporter, Sand. Vivian gave him an encouraging little wave, and he waved back with three fingers.

She had introduced him to Sand, and told him they had met years ago. Patrick didn't remember, and didn't appreciate the way she sat next to the man. Too damned close for his liking. Patrick forced his attention back to the here-and-now. He'd deal with the reporter later.

"Red team first," Ocean said. "Two boys up. One does nothing but attack, the other nothing but defend." Clint and a chunky boy named Rory jumped up eagerly. Both wore twelve-ounce boxing gloves and protective head gear. Clint was designated "A" and Rory "B." Ocean said, "All right, B's go first."

Clint and Rory squared off with each other, and gave shallow bows. Rory blitzed in. Clint kept his hands high, catching punches on forearms and elbows and gloves. A few blows slipped through, snapping Clint's head back, but he kept his hands high and never lost his composure.

The entire sports dome transformed into a howling, stomping, shouting cacophony as the kids cheered both attacker and defender, spurring them on.

The air of sheer controlled violence mesmerized Patrick. By the clock the first match lasted only sixty seconds. Emotionally, it seemed an eternity. When it was finally over, Clint and Rory reversed roles and the clobbering began anew. The crowd roared approval.

Patrick searched the stands again. His mother's thigh was touching that damned reporter's leg. That thought brought up a startling burst of anger, one swiftly quelled.

Ocean called his name, and Patrick's anger fluxed into a burst of fear. He was shocked to feel how *afraid* he was. They had been practicing this exercise every day for the past four, but he still wasn't ready.

Maybe this was the kind of thing you *couldn't* get ready for. You just had to be ready for the fact that you weren't ready.

Heart leaping against his ribcage, he raised his thin arms, and waited as Colin got in front of him. Colin was one of the bigger boys, and had always carried himself as if he were the master of secret, awesome knowledge. But Colin wasn't smirking now. Instead, the boy held both gloves in front of his face and whispered, "Ah'm gonna kick yo natural ass," between them.

"Not a chance," Patrick said. The nervousness was transforming into something else. It was becoming eagerness. It was turning into *Let's get it on.*

Then came the signal to begin. Patrick flew at Colin, punching, trying not to swing too wildly, hammering in and feeling the meat of the Mississippian's forearms and elbows as he hammered, hammered, hammered.

On and on it went. Patrick was tiring rapidly, wondering when it would stop, but kept pounding away. When he reached the point of utter exhaustion, when his arms were as hot and heavy as flaming sausages, he used one of the tricks Ocean had taught. *If he gets past me, he'll hurt my mom,* he thought. Panic sent new strength pumping into his arms and lungs, and he kept going.

Then suddenly Ocean had jumped between them, yelling, "Time!" Patrick wiped sweat from his brow, panting. They were given a minute to rest, then reversed roles. The instant the command was given, Colin began to hammer at him.

Although he knew very well that Colin wasn't using his full strength (those big shoulders would have lifted him up and hurled him across the room!) he still felt the brute strength and weight of the blows as they smashed against his arms. But even muffled as they were, if he didn't keep focused, one of those haymakers would slip through and murder him.

Terror began to boil up again. *I can't take it,* he thought. *I'm not big enough, strong enough, tough enough—*

Then he glimpsed Colin's eyes. Focused, concentrated. But there was no anger there, just . . . *intensity.* When their eyes met, something like an e-mail flew between them. There were no words, just communication of intent. There was action here, force and fury, but no real violence. Nothing to fear. Just pressure, stress and the possibility of pain. Colin was not the enemy. The enemy was his own mind. Colin was like a mile waiting to be run on a track, a barbell waiting to be lifted. An obstacle, not an enemy. *Just keep your hands up. And move, don't blink, don't let the sweat running into your eyes blind you to the truth.*

And then suddenly, blessedly, it was over.

Colin's sweaty arms went around Patrick, hugging him tight. He felt the boy's racing heartbeat, smelled the sweat and heat rolling off his meaty chest, and thought: *he was scared too!* As the crowd cheered he reveled in the new understanding.

In sets of two, the other boys went through their ritual. There were split lips and one bloody nose, but no one quit, and no one cried. When the last boy had performed, applause rang like thunder.

And now it was the girls' turn.

Ocean addressed them again. "These rounds will be performed differently," he said. "On the street, very few of the girls will ever have to defend themselves against other girls. Most of the threats will be boys. Men. So now is the time to learn to face that energy."

Now he seemed almost imperious, as if he was attempting to call, by example, the very best from the young people in his charge.

"You are tribes! You are warriors! And these are your sisters, the women of the tribe. It is your job to protect them, and the way you can protect them today is by presenting them with your strength, your force, that they can experience the male energy, and prepare themselves emotionally.

"You may strike at them—but not with the intent to harm. It is only to strengthen them. Your job is to *protect.* The girls both block and attack. They must use everything they have, and they have to trust you, as brothers, to protect them in their efforts."

Somewhat surprisingly, the first called from the Blue team was Frankie. Opposite him was a small blond girl with the eyes of a frightened, intelligent animal.

Jessica. One of the youngest at camp, barely twelve, round and hyper, but right now she shook so hard she seemed like a little old woman. She was battling for each breath, and blinked at Frankie with wild, staring eyes.

Ocean helped her slow and deepen her breathing, but her hands were still trembling, and she gnawed at her underlip.

Ocean looked carefully into Frankie's eyes, as if searching to be sure that the only motivations there were clean and direct.

"What is your only job, Frankie?"

Patrick held his breath. Frankie, little awkward Frankie. Last chosen for any game except murderball, darling of the leadership class although, or perhaps because, they knew he would never win any office except mascot.

Frankie stared at Jessica, and he might not have heard Ocean's words. Ocean repeated them.

"Frankie," Ocean said, forcing the boy to tear his eyes away from his shuddering partner. "What is your only job?"

"To protect the women of my tribe," he whispered. There was no doubt in his eyes, no dissembling in his voice or manner. At that moment, Frankie was speaking the simple truth.

Jessica raised her arms, chubby forearms locked together, blocking her face. She was panting, but bent and braced her knees as Frankie came at her.

He punched with controlled ferocity, aiming at her arms. Jessica shielded herself, backing up one unsteady step after another, head hunched down as Frankie slid forward one precisely measured step after another. At first Patrick thought Jessica would remain totally defensive, but the instant Frankie tired and slacked off just a little, Jessica screamed and jumped at him.

She was all fire and spark, all small toothy animal ferocity, and if not for Frankie's helmet she might have torn his head off. He retreated two, three steps and then tumbled backwards. As he went down, she was right on top of him, swinging wildly, shouting, hammering with thin frantic arms. She had to be pulled off when Ocean called "Time."

Frankie staggered to his feet. Jessica stepped back and began to shake again. Then she burst into tears and fled from the room. After a glance at Ocean, Frankie followed.

Jessica stood by the water fountain, arms braced against the rock. Her limp, wet blond hair streamed down over her face, and her small rounded body shook.

Frankie came close to her, but had sense enough not to touch. "Are you all right?"

Her blue eyes were wide and frightened, and she made little catching sounds in the back of her throat. "Yes," she said. "Yes, I'm all right."

Janie emerged from the sports center and started to intervene, but Jessica waved the head counselor away.

For the moment she and Frankie seemed to be enmeshed in some kind of web, something that surrounded the two of them and no one else. Frankie felt very strange, whiplashed by a sensation he had never experienced. It was, simply, a sense of being in synch with a single human being. A single, very *female* human being.

"My stepfather went to jail last year for what he did to me," Jessica whispered. "They took me away from my mommy. She wouldn't believe me. Nobody did. An aunt turned him in, and ... and ..." She looked up at him, miserable. "I didn't ever fight. I just laid there. I didn't ever fight that motherfucker. And when I was hitting you, I was hitting him. I ..."

Jessica was crying again, quietly this time, her head against his chest. Then she shook herself out of it, and looked at Frankie with such a profoundly affectionate expression that he barely knew how to react. She darted forward and kissed his cheek. Then she disappeared back inside, leaving a stunned Frankie standing by the fountain.

He sat, looking out at the woods, not knowing what to say or think, or, in some ways, even really knowing who he was.

During a break, Ocean came outside. "Are you all right, Frankie?"

"I don't know," the boy replied. "I guess."

"You did a good thing in there," Ocean said.

"I did?" Frankie's voice was ragged.

Ocean nodded. "Listen. In my school we always acknowledge when people have made jumps, you know? Leaps forward." He opened his notebook, and pulled out a little pin-mounted plastic gold ribbon.

"This is a yellow stripe. You would have been given a white belt when you first came into the school. Then you'd get three yellow stripes, one after the other, tack 'em onto the end of your belt, and trade it in for a yellow belt. Start over again with green stripes, and so on. You understand?"

Frankie nodded, but didn't say anything.

"This is for you," Ocean said, and handed him the pin. "For what you did today. You gave Jessica exactly what she needed."

Frankie held it, looking at it, the precious yellow pin that represented his first step along a long and winding road. He could see himself. Yellow belt. Blue belt. Green. Then brown, and then ...

He could see it all, stretching out in front of him, a path to accomplishment, to healing, to reconciliation. To power and health and beauty. His heart beat wildly, and the world swirled around him.

"I don't understand," he said.

Ocean's voice was very kind, and soft, but somehow piercing. "What is your only obligation?" he said.

" 'To protect the women of my tribe,' " Frankie said.

"Did you do that?"

Frankie nodded again.

"Then, this day, you have become a warrior."

Frankie's eyes brimmed with tears. A great shuddering cry poured out of him and he threw his arms around Ocean, buried his face in the counselor's chest, and cried tears as if he had been saving them up for all his young life.

72

The girls were clustered in the shower room, crowded in front of the splotchy mirror, attempting to perfect clothing and makeup in the terrible incandescence of the naked overhead bulbs.

The room was all makeup and perfume, stockings and heels stuffed into the backs of duffle bags. The air boiled with excitement and expectation.

All week it had been skinned knees and scuffed elbows, dirt and sweat and competition. But tonight, something else entirely was emerging.

"This is gonna be great," Heather whispered. "There's three of them for every two of us. We get our pick."

"I always do," Courtney said. Heather elbowed her.

Destiny was hanging back, trying to find a way to get her jumper to look more feminine. She struggled with (in her opinion) achingly small success when Courtney managed to catch her eye. *What's wrong?* Courtney mouthed.

Again Destiny examined her mirror image, comparing herself to the other girls and not enjoying what she saw. She flushed, running out of the bathroom and back to her cabin.

When Courtney entered, Destiny was sitting motionless on the bed, staring miserably at the wall.

"What up?" Courtney asked.

Destiny wagged her head. "I can't do that. I can't wear makeup and stuff."

"Why are you tripping like that?"

"It's just not me."

Courtney clucked. "Bullshit. If you worked with that hair a little, just let yourself be pretty for a change, you'd be fine."

Destiny looked up at her doubtfully. "Would you help me?"

Courtney brightened and said, "Let's go back to the bathroom."

"I can't do that. I can't compete with you."

Heather had drifted in in time to overhear the last statement. Destiny flinched away, as if fearful of being struck. "Oh, come on, Dest. Didn't you help me with the archery?"

"Stuff like that just comes naturally to me," Destiny sniffed.

"Well, *this* comes naturally to us," Heather said. She pursed her lips like a biologist examining the contents of a petri dish. "We need to bring out her eyes, and I don't have the right shade of eye color."

Courtney dug into her purse, bringing out a tube of lipstick. "This will work."

"Lipstick? For eye color?"

"Become acquainted with every art." she said. "A *real* artist knows how to improvise."

By the time Destiny made her entrance into the rec hall, the dance was hopping. D. J. Jason was demonstrating a musical sensibility that ranged acrobatically from Aerosmith to Limp Bizkit to Snoop Dog.

A nervous Patrick finally crossed the crowded floor, unable to take his eyes from Destiny. He had to stand very close to her in order to be heard above the lyrics of *Love in an Elevator.*

"I . . . I've never seen you looking like this before," he said. Her hair hung in a cascade of ringlets. Instead of her customary jumper, she wore a black dress that showcased her legs and the firmness of her waist. She was almost perfectly proportioned, something far less evident in her customary jeans and T-shirts.

"Is it all right?" she asked anxiously. "I wanted you to like it."

Struck temporarily mute, he could only nod. Destiny reached out her hand and took his, leading him out onto the dance floor.

Frankie stood alone in a corner of the dance floor, watching, as he always did. Perhaps he was guarding the punch bowl. He stood as if doing something of terrible importance, as if he hadn't noticed that he was one of the very few not thrashing in search of a beat.

Little Jessica emerged from the crowd, stood beside him through the entire length of Hammer's *U Can't Touch This.* She looking up at him wistfully, and then impatiently. He glanced at her and then away, at her and away again. She wore a blue dress with pink frills, and black high-heel shoes that made her look like a heftier version of Prom

Night Barbie. Finally she grabbed Frankie's arm, twisted him toward her, looked him right in the eye and said: "Are you going to ask me to dance, or do I have to punch you again?"

He stared at her for a moment, and if she hadn't held out her small hand, he might have run away. He took it, and managed to guide them both to an empty spot on the dance floor.

He gyrated to the beat, surprised that he was able to find it. Next to him, Patrick grinned and gave Frankie a thumbs-up.

When the song changed, Colin began to move in a way Patrick recognized instantly, arms and legs sliding in smooth synchronicity with the rhythm line. That was the Claremont Groove! He and his friends had created that, and somehow, it had spread all the way to Mississippi!

"Yeah!" Mathias said. The Chicagoan was dancing with Cheryl, and it looked as if they had a little of that special wait-till-lights-out energy cooking. "Now *that's* what I'm talking 'bout!" He pulled Cheryl over with him until they stood next to Colin, dancing in concert, flipping and dipping in a kind of hip-hop line dance. Soon the entire room was in synch, all fifty of them, lined up and kneeling, turning, spinning to the music, whooping and cheering as Courtney or Hughie improvised a move and then flowed back into the repetitive ten-step cycle.

Outside, Vivian and Sand stood watching. The kids were doing some kind of variation on the Electric Slide that he'd never seen before, and from their grace, he assumed that they'd been practicing it every day. They moved like the gears of a big clock.

His toes tapped along to the beat. Vivian seemed glued to the scene before them, but he knew she was aware of him, knew that her breathing was a little shallower, her heart beating a little faster, because he was there. It had been like that all day, a thin membrane of propriety limiting the amount of touch. It was obvious to him that they both wondered what that touch would be like. Wondered when it would eventually happen.

From time to time she drifted closer and her hand brushed his, fingers beginning to intertwine. Then she would catch Patrick's accusing eye, his *my father isn't even cold yet* stare, and she wilted away from him again.

God, he thought. *Have I got the world's worst timing, or what?*

After the song was over, another fast one played, and the kids did their little slide-step dance again, hooting and hollering as if they'd just discovered pirate treasure. After that they returned to the kind of stylized gyrations that have passed for partner dancing ever since the cha-cha was outlawed.

Vivian hummed, watching appreciatively, her hips swaying hypnotically to the music without quite breaking into steps. Sand waited while one fast song after another played. That wasn't what he wanted or needed. If he and Vivian had any chance at all he was going to have to create a window of opportunity, and soon.

He excused himself and entered the sweat-steamed rec room, heading over to the turntable. Jason listened to his proposition with a knowing grin. "I'll slip you a five if I have to," Renny said.

"Not necessary," Jason replied. "Go for it."

He went back outside. Vivian pretended not to notice that he had gone, or what he had done. But when the tempo of the music changed, slowed from *The Thong Song* to a sultry remix of *Didn't I Blow Your Mind This Time,* she looked at him with eyes that were luminous and wise and afraid.

"May I have this dance?" he whispered.

She lowered her eyes and hesitated. He took her hands, and Vivian flowed into his arms. He held her loosely, felt her close the gap between them by another inch, each of them afraid of the heat, but weary of the cold.

And they turned in slow, dreamy circles that didn't stop even when the music itself finally did.

Inside the hall, Patrick and Destiny moved together as slowly as melting ice cream.

"This is a *great* fucking week," Patrick whispered into her hair.

Destiny nodded silently, her cheek buried against his chest.

"Destiny," Patrick said. Her footwork was marginally better than his, so she was very subtly leading him.

"Shermie and Lee . . . I know that when summer is over, we're not going to be what we were. Everything changed." He hesitated. "I changed everything."

"You didn't change anything," she said, her lips close to his ear.

"What I did . . ."

"You had to do." Her eyes locked with his. They still swayed gently, but he was startled by the ferocity of her expression. "I don't ever want to hear you say that again. I don't want you to talk about it again, to anyone but me, and maybe Frankie. Do you hear me?"

He shook his head numbly. His senses were spinning. Patrick fought to bring himself back to reality, and remembered her basketball hero boyfriend. "Destiny. What about Billy Kumer? When we get back—"

The music was sweet, intoxicating. It, and the motion, and the evening were all blending together seamlessly.

"Already over," she said.

"Because you wouldn't kiss him?" he asked.

"No," she whispered. "Because I wanted to kiss you."

And there, in the shadows, she touched her lips to his. They were slightly parted, and her breath was like a spring wind rolling across an ocean of honey. She touched her tongue against his upper lip and then closed her mouth again, the touch of her lips firm and cool and a comfort beyond anything he had ever known.

Then she pulled back, still leaving him in his startlement. Destiny laid her head upon his shoulder. "There," she said, as if she had settled something. And perhaps she had.

"Well . . . ah . . ." he searched wildly for something to say. "That kind of screws up the whole friendship thing, doesn't it?"

"I hope so," she said, and snuggled against him, innocent and trusting as a baby. Patrick closed his eyes, and was lost.

And found.

73

Kelly and Bobby Ray were watching Morey Amsterdam and Rose Marie trade lightning repartee on an episode of *The Dick Van Dyke Show.* An old and beloved game between them was pretending they had watched the original sixties-era shows together, pretending that they had shared these laughs before, snuggling beneath quilted blankets, her leg over his, munching butter-flavored popcorn and stealing kisses like a pair of teenagers.

There was genuine comfort in the ritual. After Dick and Laura Petrie said good-night, Kelly and Bobby Ray would watch *Happy Days,* which they actually *had* watched in first run, when initially courting. When there were no guests enjoying the hospitality of Kerrigan House they might stay awake until three in the morning, enjoying *Good Times* and *Bob Newhart* and *M*A*S*H* reruns until they were too exhausted to keep their eyes open, then fall asleep snuggling right there on the couch.

Bob's fingers scraped the bottom of the popcorn bowl, and he stuck out his lower lip. "Dry again," he announced, and sighed. "Shall I go one more?"

"Only if you love me," Kelly said, and he brushed her lips with his.

There was a knock at the front door.

She pushed herself up out of the couch, mindful of her back, and answered the door.

A tall lean black man in his fifties stood smiling at her. He doffed his cowboy hat, revealing a head of startlingly white hair. "Evening, Kelly," he said.

"Evening, Charlie," she replied, surprised to see him at eleven o'clock at night. "What can I do for you?"

"May I come in?" She pulled the door wider. Charlie Wisher and Deputy Woodcock entered. Black man and raw-boned Okie, two ex-military peas in a civilian pod. What was *this* all about?

Bob looked up at them, nodded without smiling. "Charlie. Nice long leave you had. When'd you get back?"

"Just today," Wisher said.

"Where've you been?"

"All over," he said calmly, scanning the room. "New Mexico, Illinois. California."

Just like the old days, when you trotted behind Marcus like the beta wolf you always were. "Business or pleasure?"

"Business," he said.

"So, what brings you here tonight?"

Wisher scratched his white hair, a gesture she instantly considered a deliberate attempt at aw-shuckishness. He wasn't Barney Fife, and this wasn't *Mayberry RFD*. At the back of her neck a little internal alarm bell triggered.

"According to Woodcock, you had a guest who drove a white Toyota. That right?"

"Yes. Renny Sand, out of Los Angeles." *Why is this your business?*

"Well, a car of that description was seen leaving the site of a burglary over in Sierra Vista."

"When was this?"

"Oh, last week. Friday."

"That's right," Woodcock said. "Friday."

"Well," Kelly said. "I couldn't say about that. He arrived yesterday, and left this morning."

"Do you have his address and phone number?"

"Surely do," she said, and went into the hall to fetch the guest book.

Wisher studied the television screen. On it, Carl Reiner was trying on wigs, and Mary Tyler Moore was industriously stuffing both feet into her lovely mouth. The audience roared. "Like that show," Wisher said.

Bobby Ray grunted agreement. He was pretending to watch the show, but was actually studying their guests. From long experience Kelly knew Bobby Ray was not at all happy with this intrusion.

Truth be told, neither was she.

"Here it is," Kelly said, and handed Wisher the book.

"Did he say where he was going?"

"Someplace called Charisma Lake," she said. Both men suddenly became very still, very tense.

"Charisma Lake?" Wisher whispered.

"Yes. Does that mean something?"

Wisher regained his composure. "Pretty filled up this evening, Kelly?" The question was asked casually, but Kelly Kerrigan's veins burned with adrenaline. Woodcock and Wisher had separated, stood seven feet apart now. In a very casual way, they now bracketed her and Bobby.

"Nope," Bobby said, finally looking Wisher dead in the eye. "Next guests due in tomorrow."

No point in a lie: Wisher knew there were no cars parked outside, no new names in the guest book. *But oh, Bobby,* she thought. *What kind of trouble is this?*

Wisher nodded again. He whispered something to Woodcock, and the junior deputy stepped outside. Through the window, she could see him speaking on a cell phone, but couldn't hear anything. She tried to watch the television set, but her nerves wouldn't stop prickling.

When Woodcock came back in, he nodded once to Wisher.

"Is that all, Charlie?" she asked, hoping they might leave.

"One more thing," Charlie Wisher said. "What did the three of you talk about out on the porch?"

"What?" Bobby Ray stood up.

Wisher's fingers rested lightly on his sidearm. "We know he was asking about Alexander. But once you went outside, we couldn't hear you." His voice was low, regretful.

"What the hell is this?" Bobby balled his hands into big red knobby fists.

"What did you talk about?" Wisher asked softly. Woodcock closed the door.

"I think you'd better leave," Kelly said, more certain by the moment that they would do no such thing.

"I'm afraid I can't do that. And don't touch that phone." He wagged his head. "If you'll just tell me what you talked about, this will all be over."

"I don't understand," Kelly said, afraid now that she did. "I don't understand one damn bit."

"We tried to keep you out of it, Kelly. We actually like you. You were one of us. So we brought you here to Diablo, where we could watch you. And listen to you."

He tapped the telephone. "Anytime we wanted, we could turn on the mic in your phone and listen. The whole house is bugged, Kelly." Dear God. Every laugh, every sound of passion, every tearful conversation recorded by these bastards? How *dare* they. Sheer corrosive anger clouded her vision.

Wisher leaned forward. "I'm giving you a chance to live through this, Kelly. I don't want to hurt you. Just tell me: what the fuck were you talking about? Why did he go up to Charisma Lake?"

"I don't—" she began. Wisher stepped forward, and slapped her, very quickly and quite hard.

Bobby Ray moved far more swiftly than anyone his age had any right to move. He swept the lamp up off the table, and with a single sweeping move brought it down on Woodcock's head. It crunched, and Woodcock sagged to his knees.

"No!" Kelly screamed, too late.

Wisher pivoted, drew his service revolver and shot Bobby Ray precisely in the center of his chest. Kelly screamed and threw herself at Wisher's legs. Clinching her fist, she dug a short hooking punch into his groin. He groaned and fired down at her as his knees sagged. She felt a hot flash, and pain exploded as the bullet tore a groove above her left temple. Kelly swung wildly, once again sinking her fist into Wisher's crotch. Wisher groaned again and fell to the floor, the gun spilling from his hand.

Time froze. Bobby's eyes were open and staring. The wound in his chest welled with blood. His mouth worked silently, eyes filled with love and tears as he whispered, *"Run!"*

Call the hospital. Head still ringing from Wisher's service revolver, Kelly turned to the phone. From the corner of her eye she saw that the gun was mere inches from Wisher's hand, and he was even now clawing toward it. She'd never make it. Mind dulled by shock and fear, operating on pure instinct, she dashed for the door, and through it.

Not that way.

Stumbling through the shadows, Kelly moved in the other direction. She sobbed as she ran, her head wound twinning the world.

She lurched into a shadow, fighting for a moment's calm thought. How many damned Praetorians were in the Sheriff's department?

Three. D'Angelo, Wisher, Woodcock. They'd said that Diablo was a great place to retire.

Bobby Ray. She hated to say it, even think it, but judging by the placement of the chest wound, Bobby Ray was gone. He would want her to live, had died to give her a chance. If she had remained in that house another moment she would be dead now, without ever knowing why.

It all had something to do with the reporter. With Alexander Marcus. With Charisma Lake. With the Praetorians. With those secretive night-time excursions.

Bob, honey, oh God . . .

She scrambled through the back of a clapboard fence, and was out on Main Street. There she froze, and thought. Where could she go? It was near midnight, and Diablo was mostly closed down. They would expect her to head for Excellent Mary's, the saloon on the east end of the street. There were still people at Mary's, but even now she saw the cruiser gliding around the corner. Without thought, she headed directly across the street to Helldorado. She ran down the aisle through the spectator seats to the stage.

The Helldorado's stage was flanked by western-style house shells. Kelly crept through the shadows and up onto the stage, hunkering down in the left wing as the two deputies came looking. From her hiding spot, she could see little save shadowy figures and flashlights, and the occasional glimpse of a gun.

Kelly hunched down more deeply. She could see one of the deputies, Wisher probably, creeping toward the center of the stage.

"Come on out, Kelly. We can talk about this. We get this sorted out, and we can get Bob to the hospital. . . ." Even in her confusion, she recognized her surge of crazy hope as nothing more than desperation. She needed to seal it away, for now. Maybe forever.

There was the tiniest creak. Wisher pivoted, very professional now, not at all the Deputy Dawg Diablo's officers usually pretended to be.

He crept closer. "This isn't doing anyone any good. You know we can't let the reporter go. But you're one of us, Kelly. You understand how things work. . . ."

Kelly was shivering, muscles in her belly knotting painfully with the adrenaline surge. *Breathe. Get it under control, you silly bitch—*

And then she saw the stage levers. Clearly. How many times had she watched the show? Watched the bandits and the Indians pop up from the trap doors?

Her hands fumbled at the levers, trying to sense them, understand them. Soon after first moving to Diablo, Rowdy Hawthorne, the retired western stuntman who owned Helldorado, had demonstrated their operation.

Pretty simple, Kelly, but you got to get it right. This lever operates the safety rods locking the traps. Four traps up there, and you have to get the right one right, or somebody's going to have a nasty spill. We use movable scaffolding down here to get the actors up topside, usually after setting off a flash bomb to distract the audience. . . .

The entire rig had been designed by an old vaudevillian stagehand, a gnome named Chucky who had died last year at the age of ninety-seven. Chucky swore that Helldorado's stage was as good as anything at Hollywood's Pantages Theater, and for all she knew, he was right.

Now, all that was required was an accurate memory of the machinery's operation. The four ring-pins were intersected by a two-foot red metal rod, locking them tight into a safety bar. She tugged at the rod helplessly. It wouldn't move. She set her feet, pushed with her legs, and one inch at a time, the rod slid out, leaving the row of ring-pins armed and ready.

Wisher had reached the center of the stage, then stopped and looked almost precisely at her hiding place.

"Why don't you just come on out?"

Then he glanced away. He'd been bluffing. He turned around, uncertain, and took a step backward—

He stepped on the square. She pulled the *#4 Center Stage* ring, and the floor opened beneath him. Wisher gave a single despairing wail, flailed his arms and fell.

Stairs. The stairs to the basement were only a dozen paces behind her. Kelly ran for them. Without seeing him, she heard Woodcock run for the other side. *There are more stairs on the other side.*

Her old legs seemed to be moving in slow motion as she rushed down.

The basement was fourteen feet below the stage. Wisher was sprawled with arms and legs splayed at swastika angles.

The gun wasn't in his hand. She searched desperately, hearing Woodcock's footsteps as he charged down his side of the stairs—

Kelly, frantic, saw Wisher's gun, lying just in a shadow. She dove and landed on a feed bag, the breath slamming from her body.

Woodcock dropped into a single-knee shooting position. Kelly rolled once to get a clear shot. Upside down, she fired twice, the revolver's roar deafening in the basement's confined space. Woodcock toppled over, mouth sagging in surprise, left eye socket a bleeding pulp.

She rolled off the bag, ribs aching, eyes cold, and limped over to Wisher. He was sprawled in partial shadow, twisted like a broken pretzel.

His face oozed perspiration in the dim light. Absurdly, she had a sudden, vivid memory of their first meeting, in New York, almost two decades ago. Clean, erect, alert at Marcus's side. Marine Lieutenant Charles Wisher at your service *ma'am*! "I think . . . I think something's busted," he gasped.

She cocked her head a bit sideways. "Let's find out." Very deliberately, she ground her heel into his knee.

He stared at her without making a sound. No pain. Too bad.

"Not your leg, Charlie. Your back."

"Help me. . . ."

"First you're going to tell me what it's all about."

He hesitated, but she raised her foot, and set it on his hip, rocking gently. This time he screamed.

"It was Marcus," he gasped. "He went bad, Kelly. We just did what we had to do."

"Bad how?"

"He was killing women. We didn't know how many. But it had to stop. We had to stop him."

"How many women?"

"We don't know. Angel guessed more than ten."

"Angel guessed more than ten." Did you really have to guess, *Angel? Was Alex alone those nights? Somehow I think you had a very damn exact count. And when someone tumbled wise you knew the game was up, and it was time to cut losses. You son of a bitch.*

"So . . . you killed Marcus?"

He blinked. "You know what he meant to people. If it had ever come out . . . so we sabotaged the plane. And now this reporter is stir-ring it up." Charlie Wisher bit his lip. "Sweet goddamn, it hurts."

"Just a little longer now," Kelly said. "What did you think I told the reporter?"

"The kids. Those fucking kids."

She could hardly stand. Her anger was so intense it was a physical weight, bowing and bending her, slowing thought and action. It felt as if her nerves were frying.

"What about the kids? I don't know what the hell you're talking about."

Wisher gazed up at her. "I can't feel any . . . any . . ."

But before he could finish, Charlie Wisher's eyes glazed, becoming as still and expressionless as ice cubes.

Feeling a million years old, Kelly climbed up out of the basement.

Diablo's streets were dark and empty. If anyone had heard the gun-fire, well, that was just some of the deputies practicing on the Hel-ldorado stage, don't you know. She felt dislocated, floating above herself as she hobbled back to her house.

There she found Bobby Ray on the floor, his spilt blood congealing around him. She crawled up next to him, lay his head in her lap. The entire world seemed a little dark and unfocused. The wound on her head hurt horribly, and in a distant way, she realized that she was probably going into shock.

"What do I do, Bobby Ray?" Her whisper seemed to echo in the dead, cold house.

She had just killed two deputies. What was the conspiracy? How far did it go, and who else was involved? D'Angelo had set this up, all of it. If she called the police, exactly who would she call? And what would they do?

Why hadn't that bastard Angel come personally?

Because he has other business. With the reporter. With "those fuck-ing kids" at Charisma Lake.

That's where she would find Angel, before the police found her, and Bobby Ray. Before everything else, anything else, there was some-thing she had to do.

Still moving like a sleepwalker, Kelly levered herself up. "Sleep easy, honey," she said. "I swear I'll kill him. I'll kill that son of a bitch."

She went out the back door to Bobby Ray's shed. She dialed the combination and opened it very quietly.

No light. No sound. There, on the bench, stock ready for refitting, sat Bobby Ray's Sharps rifle. She removed it from the vise, and grabbed a box of cartridges.

She kissed her fingertips, still moist with her husband's blood, and brushed them across the gold framed portrait of the two of them: a Western-style shoot outside of Fort Worth. They bore wide smiles and first prize medals. . . .

And then she was gone.

74

By one in the morning, the music had died.

In safety-minded pairs and bunches the kids drifted off to their cabins, waving sleepy good-byes.

Vivian walked hand in hand with Renny, feeling more than ever like just another dreamy, love-struck camper.

She dropped his hand with awkward speed as Patrick and Frankie approached. Patrick had his arm around Destiny (as if she couldn't see *that* coming!). Frankie Darling stood as tall as she'd ever seen him, Jessica the blue-eyed firebomb superglued to his side.

"Hey, Mom," Patrick said, and managed a smile. Vivian guessed that he would have hugged her if that wouldn't have seemed terminally uncool.

"Can I talk to you for just a moment?" she said.

"Sure. I'll catch up, guys."

"G'night, Mrs. Emory."

She turned to Renny. "This will just take a second." She walked a dozen paces with Patrick, so that they stood by the stone-walled water fountain beneath an arching vine-wreathed trellis.

"You saw me dancing with Mr. Sand, didn't you?"

Patrick nodded. "Umm-hmm." His eyes were studiedly neutral.

"I don't want you to be mad with me," she said.

Patrick closed his eyes, and Vivian had the sense that he was playing mental tapes, arranging thoughts, centering himself before speaking. Finally, and in a very controlled voice, he began. "You and Dad . . . had been pretending for a long time." Vivian's eyes watered. He had paraphrased her own thoughts, so precisely that he might as well have read her mind.

"You took him back, for one night. You tried to save his . . ." he bit down hard on the words. "You tried to keep him from fighting. It didn't work."

Vivian looked down at her boy child, speechless.

"Not everything works out like we hope, Mom."

"You don't hate me?"

"Mom," Patrick said, as if she were the child. "Don't trip, okay?"

He looked over at Renny, who was carefully studying something in the opposite direction. "He really likes you," Patrick said doubtfully. "Hope he's not an asshole."

Vivian was speechless now. Patrick gave her a quick, ultra-uncool hug, and then rabbited after his friends.

Vivian rejoined Renny, who walked her to her cabin. She sagged against the door. "I had a *great* evening," she said.

"Me too. Janie's letting me bunk with the guys."

"The counselors?"

"No, the boys. Sioux cabin."

"Oh, the *boys*!" she giggled. "That should be an experience."

Her giggle quieted, and something shut behind her eyes, leaving only the great and aching sweetness of her face, the clarity of her smile. "Let's take it slow, all right?" She inhaled deeply, turned her face up toward the stars. "This is like some kind of fantasy. It isn't my world. Nothing but strangers, except for the kids. I don't know who I am up here."

"Did you know who you were down there?"

She smiled. Sand felt a great, aching flame growing within him. He longed to touch her, to taste her smile, an urge so strong it was almost a physical pain.

Instead, he lifted and kissed the tips of her fingers.

"Thank you," he said, "for the best night of my life." He took her chin, very slightly turned it until one cheek faced him, and brushed it with his lips. Then before he could say or do anything that he might regret later, he turned and joined the Sioux.

75

Kelly Kerrigan drove hard, taking poorly-lit back roads north and west to Prescott. She didn't know where she was, or what she was doing. She had wrapped a scarf around her head, wadding tissue against her wound in a makeshift bandage, but blood still ran into her eyes. She wiped at it without conscious thought. It took all of her concentration to keep her attention on the road, which continued to flicker in and out in front of her, like a twisted yellow ribbon blowing in the night wind. Her headlights pierced that darkness, showed the drop-off to the left down to the valley floor. One part of her wearied of weaving through those mountains, moving in and out, back and forth, seeking to find her way.

She knew a way to find swift and certain peace: just turn the wheel sharply to the left, plunging through the low metal guard railing. She would sail out into space, plummet into a well of darkness. In the depths of that well waited her beloved Bobby Ray, his arms out-stretched. But she couldn't do that yet. Not yet—there remained a terrible task to complete. She couldn't quite remember what it was. She knew that she had a concussion. She knew that there was some-thing wrong with her, but she couldn't stop. Not now, not until she had confronted Angel, and wrung the truth from him.

Her hands clutched the steering wheel as if they were holding onto a life line. Another mile rolled up on the odometer, and then another. Further and deeper into her private hell she plunged. She had no il-lusions about where she was: some place beyond herself, beyond le-gality. She only knew that there was something to be done, that the spirit of her dead husband would never rest until she had accomplished that goal.

Then Bobby Ray could rest, and if necessary, she could join him.

76

Silent shadows slipped among the cabins that night.

The shadow-makers were noiseless, purposeful. They signaled to each other with hand gestures. When one pair moved forward, the others covered.

They positioned themselves around the boys' cabin, and then ex-ploded through the front doors, banging pans in a hellish cacophony.

They turned the lights on. Janie, Ocean and Denise looked at the empty room, baffled—

And then were struck from behind by a dozen balloons filled with water and shaving cream.

They'd been outflanked! The boys had enlisted Renny in their efforts, sworn him to secrecy, and made stealthy preparations in the dead of night.

The first wave of counselors recoiled, but Janie burst out with the most dreaded secret weapon known to man or child: a Super-Soaker charged with ice water. The battle cry went up, counselors versus kids, an ambush that got ambushed. The kids, not at all the innocent, help-less victims that the counselors had anticipated, fought back savagely. The cabin war raged into the night.

Renny couldn't *believe* how much fun it was.

Up in the western hills, Tristan D'Angelo was peering through a sniper scope, laughing himself sick. He had to admit the water balloon am-bush had been fun to watch. In another world, another life, he wouldn't have minded being down there with them, or for that matter having some of these kids watching his back in a hot zone.

Have a good night, little soldiers, he thought. *It's the last one.*

Kelly Kerrigan parked her car down on an overgrown utility access road north of the lake. She had studied three different maps before finding one with the information she needed.

Obtaining the maps had been almost as great a challenge as the eight-hour drive. She had only fingers to comb her hair, and a rest-stop paper towel to mop crusted blood from her face. Despite her efforts, she must have looked like day-old death when she limped into the Arco station in a micro-town called Dewey. The station attendants stared at her as she fumbled through the map rack, asking if she needed any assistance.

She tried to reassure them, but they frowned as she smoothed her crumpled five dollar bill on the counter. She collected her change, and left without a backward glance.

Kelly checked herself in the car mirror, and saw the reason for their consternation: her scalp wound was oozing blood again, and she hadn't even felt it. The left side of her face was numb. She wiped the blood away with the side of her hand, climbed back in her jeep, and drove away.

The attendant had watched her as she left, perhaps wondering if she would weave in an alcoholic haze. His breath fogged the window.

She'd had sufficient presence of mind to travel the last quarter mile toward Charisma Lake without headlights, creeping at a walking pace, trusting to starlight and moonlight. She parked off the road, and waited there in the darkness, listening. What was out there? Who? Her head hurt abominably, ached and pulsed like the worst headache in history. She chewed another Tylenol, the bitter, powdery taste somehow making the pounding even worse before it began to improve.

It had taken her an hour to climb up a road barely delineated on the map, lugging her dead husband's rifle case every inch of the way.

She felt like a ghost. Her wounds clouded logic, masked her fatigue and smeared her sense of loss into a gray blur that colored everything, disconnecting Kelly from her emotions. Tomorrow, perhaps, she would feel the pain, the fatigue, the loss. Today she barely felt the cold.

Every step was a grueling effort. What would have been fifteen minutes of brisk hiking for any healthy young person had taken her over an hour. But then she followed the thin, distant, delighted sounds drifting from south of the lake. Her senses were dulled to any sensation within herself, but seemed unnaturally responsive to the external world.

She finally reached the lake, paused to rest her shaking legs, then began to trace her way around the periphery. She saw something in the distance that she thought might have been a lit cigarette. She only saw it once, briefly, but that was enough. Kelly backed up, found deep shadows where two trees grew close enough to lean one upon another, and burrowed into the bushes. She wrapped herself in the blanket that had covered the backseat of her car.

She wanted D'Angelo. He was here, or here she would find men who could lead her to him. Then she would see what happened.

Then they would *all* see.

77

Sand was heading back to the cabins with the rest of the campers when it happened.

Wet, cold, shivering but delighted, some kids had gone to the showers to clean off before popping back into bed. Renny was coming back from those showers, towel draped over his shoulders, when he almost bumped into Vivian going the other way. She wore a white terrycloth robe, a big fluffy thing that made her look about fifteen years old.

She smiled at him shyly, said "Good night," then glanced around—went up on tiptoe, and pressed her lips quickly and firmly against his. A promise of a promise. Then, fleet as a fawn, she was gone.

Renny awakened four hours later, feeling utterly rested, ready for the day. He wondered what had awakened him, and realized that two of the other Sioux boys were awake as well.

"What are you doing?" he whispered.

"The lake," they said. "Watching the sunset."

He was a lifelong city rat, but something inside him itched to find out what this was about. He donned shirt and pants and shoes and followed them.

Their flashlight beams stabbed the early morning air as they went. By the time they got up to the lake, he was perspiring a bit, just enough to make the cold more piercing.

The sunrise. Occasionally when he was wrung out from exercise, food garnered an extra sharpness, an extra edge of flavor that transported the taste buds into a realm far beyond the reach of spices and sauces, however delicate or carefully applied. Those states were always memorable, and never predictable. And he had entered into one now.

Something had shifted inside him, he was sure, because this sunrise seemed so much more than the one he had seen just yesterday, driving up over the mountains.

Perhaps *he* was just a little different now. Sand had his story, he knew it, and he could run with it, and it would make him. And there was a woman he had waited for six years to kiss, and her taste still lingered on his lips.

There had been no lies, no manipulation, no calculation. He had been honest, and everything was just fine.

It was a new day. He swore to make it a memorable one. He thought of the journal given him by Kelly Kerrigan, and laughed to himself. All thoughts of murder and conspiracy and Pulitzers seemed very far away now, vanquished by the power in one small woman's dark eyes. He would get to it soon—perhaps by lunchtime he could begin.

FROM THE JOURNAL OF ALEXANDER MARCUS

I spent a week in San Francisco, during which I was subjected to every non-invasive indignity imaginable. I answered thousands of questions, while leashed to EEGs, lie-detector-type

devices, CAT scans and machines that, I was told, measured my brain waves from beta to theta.

I performed the Chen style tai chi form, two sword forms and a Shotokan *sanchin* form I learned decades ago in a Chicago YMCA. My knees, elbows, shoulders, head, hips, knees, and ankles were marked with reflective tape. They said that computers were making a thorough model of my movement patterns and coordinating them with my breathing, heartbeat rates, and blood pressure.

For dozens of hours I engaged in spontaneous discourse on subjects from economics to Bobby Fischer to Buckminster Fuller, while lights measured my eye motion and pupillary dilation. I cannot remember all of the things that were done during that time, but I ended every day exhausted.

I knew only that they were attempting to gain as precise a picture as possible of my every thought and feeling. In future, they said, they would perform the same series of tests on a variety of people, and collate the results to determine which factors were consistent to successful types, and never or rarely found in those who have not experienced high-level success in multiple areas of their lives. The discovery of these core motion patterns, emotional sets and mental stratagems would allow Advanced Systems to transfer excellence from one individual to another "without simultaneously transferring non-essential, peripheral or undesirable traits."

Luckily, they said (and there was a great deal of good-natured jollity at this) in their initial role model they had found someone who needed very little of this filtering to insure a clean and positive transference to the proposed targets.

78

WEDNESDAY, JULY 4

At approximately 1 P.M., a small fire in the Mingus Mountain area attracted the attention of the Prescott National Forest's fire company. Their trucks traversed the narrow wooded trails and deployed effectively against a blaze that seemed to have been triggered by a common road flare, ignited and left in a tangle of brush, perhaps as some kind of sick prank.

There was no emergency, no need to call units from further away. It might take an hour or two to get things under control, but everything was just fine.

The identity of the person reporting the fire was never determined.

79

For the past hour the Whites and Greens had expended gigawatts of energy, playing a good, tough, fair game of touch football out on the soccer field. Sand found the spectacle intoxicating, enough to make his heart beat faster and trigger a longing to find some pretext to get into the game himself. Only the spectacle of a middle-aged man huffing and puffing and crumbling from a heart attack kept him on a leash.

Vivian seemed to sense his thoughts. "Youth is wasted on the young," she said.

"Yeah," he replied. "And wisdom is wasted on the old." There followed a brief string of free-associations, and he found himself ruminating about Marcus. He had read two hundred pages into Marcus's autobiography during the night, and while it had been fascinating, the pages had concealed no earthshaking revelations. This seemed like a good time to stretch out, watch the game, enjoy Vivian's company, and maybe get some more pages under his belt. "Come on," he said. "I want to show you something."

As they walked back toward the cabins, the camp's single public phone, an unsheltered General Telephone hookup next to the craft center, bleated in mechanical irritation.

"Excuse me," Vivian said. "I have to get this." She lifted the receiver. "Hello?"

In five seconds, her expression went from jovial to puzzled. She handed the receiver to Renny. "It's for you."

That caught him completely off guard. Who the devil knew he was here? He could only think of one person. "Hello? Kelly?"

"No, not Kelly, Mr. Sand." The voice was a man's, one he had never heard before. "Kelly is probably dead by now. You, on the other hand, have an opportunity to live."

Sand heard his own breath reverberating in the receiver. "Is this some kind of sick joke?"

"Your apartment? Already cleaned out. Computer? Gone."

Sand felt frozen in place. "Who is this?"

"Come now, Renny," the voice chided. "You know who this is."

Did he know? Did this have to do with the story? It must. Then Marcus had shared his secret with at least one confidant.

But not alone, Mr. Sand.

"What do you want from me?"

Cold eyes in a long-ago reception line. Cold eyes on the street of Diablo, set within a black parody of a sheriff's garb.

I think D'Angelo is sheriffing out west somewhere.

"D'Angelo?"

"Excellent. You really are quite intelligent, and have made a good beginning. Don't squander it with stupidity. None of the children have to get hurt, if you answer my question: What is the password for your computer files?"

"What?"

"I need to know who you talked to. If you haven't shared your suspicions with anyone else, it can end now. But for me to know that, I have to place those lovely children at risk. Do you know what a high-powered rifle would do to, say, the little blond girl in red playing football right now?"

He saw the girl in red. He'd met Jessica last night, a darling possessed of boundless energy, idolized by a stubby kid named Frankie. "You wouldn't," he said. Then, despising the note of desperation in his voice, he said, "You can't."

"Watch the stump to your right," D'Angelo said.

Not ten yards away, a can of Diet Coke sat on a severed pine stump. Without warning of any kind, the can exploded, flew into the air spraying soda, and bounced against the ground, leaking.

Not one of the kids noticed. The game continued.

"Tell me the code word, Mr. Sand. I will check. If it's correct, our business is complete. You, and that lovely lady at your side? And the children? None of them will be hurt. I need an answer. Now."

Vivian was talking to the chunky kid named Bucky, and had noticed none of this. Sand scanned the woods, sick with fury that he had brought danger to these innocents.

"I'm not a patient man, Mr. Sand."

"You helped him kill those women, didn't you?"

"As a matter of fact, I did."

"Why?"

"Reporter's curiosity?"

"Human curiosity. I see a creature like you, and I want to understand."

A soft chuckle. "Some times you learn things about yourself you didn't know. Alexander and I discovered that soon after we first met."

"In Vietnam?"

"You have a decent memory. Yes. We were both involved in prisoner interrogation. A female prisoner. We found we liked it very much. The war ended, but our games didn't have to."

Sand's head was starting to pound. "Oh, God."

"Yes," said the voice on the other end of the phone. "Very much like that."

"And when the other Praetorians discovered Marcus, you convinced them that it was just him, and they helped you kill him."

"I've satisfied your curiosity, Mr. Sand. Satisfy mine. Or I'll turn the little girl's head into a piñata."

"Wait—"

"Five seconds, Mr. Sand. Four, three, two—"

"Mijenix."

"What?"

"M.I.J.E.N.I.X. It's the name of the utility software I use to maintain the computer."

Soft laughter on the other end. "Please wait."

Sand's blood roared in his ears. He looked out at the field, wondering if it would be the last thing he would ever see. Certainly they would kill him. They had his computer, but the information in his head wouldn't just go away. Or would they attempt murder in front of so many witnesses?

After a gut-wrenching delay, the voice came back on line.

"Very good, Mr. Sand. Our business is now complete."

He gritted his teeth, waiting for the spine-smashing blow. "And now?"

"Have a warm day, Mr. Sand."

The phone clicked dead. He exited the booth, looking around, wondering if a bullet was going to shatter his spine. If a clear blue sky, a soccer game, the concerned and beautiful face of Vivian Emory would be the last things he ever saw in this world.

He waited. Nothing.

Vivian said, "What was that?"

"I'm not sure," he said. Sand desperately needed time to think. What the hell was going on? A bluff?

Fresh from the game and perspiring prettily, Courtney ran to the phone. She picked up the receiver, started to dial, and then held it away from her as if it were a snake. The youngster looked up with disappointment.

"Hey," she said. "It's dead!"

For the rest of his life, the next few moments would be indelibly inscribed on the inside of Renny's skull. Everything seemed sharper, more vital. The kids on the sports field, the shingle-roofed cabins, the wisp of smoke drifting up from the kitchen. The walls of the hillsides, which now, almost irrationally, seemed like a trap.

He detected a distant whizzing sound. Afterwards, he savagely castigated himself for not recognizing it.

Vivian placed it first. "A little early for fireworks, isn't it?" she said.

And then the gates of hell opened.

80

Clearly now, Renny could hear the whirling and sputtering of sky-rockets and pinwheels, some two hundred meters below the camp.

Mr. Withers ran out of one of the Kiowa bunkhouses, where he had been making ceiling repairs. "What the hell . . . ?" His tanned face reddened, and his jaw clinched tightly. He was so enraged that he seemed almost to have entered a state of wonderment. "What kind of goddamn idiot!?"

As it did every day at two o'clock, the afternoon wind was blowing up the Folly's south face. Although the wind was moving swiftly, in the landscape of Renny's mind, the leaves and bits of grass tumbled in almost grotesquely slow motion.

He stood, rooted in place with alarm. Renny heard the fireworks whistle and buzz, his mind still grappling with the implications of Withers's anger. What kind of homicidal idiot would set off fireworks during the day? In a mass of shredded tinder? At a bone-dry children's summer camp?

What kind of idiot, indeed?

*   *   *

The afternooner swept the sparks up into the dry, waist-high grass below the camp.

Several of the kids took halting steps down toward the fire, but Denise and Jason held them back.

His marathoner's legs pumping madly, Ocean sprinted to the road, seeking and gaining a better vantage point. The grass below them churned with white smoke. Red at the roots, it clawed steadily towards them. In the two minutes since smoke first began to curl skyward, the fire had grown to a front almost thirty feet deep and a hundred feet long, accelerating even as they watched, a few sparks transformed in mere seconds into a mindless, eyeless, flaming amoeba.

Ocean ran closer, trotting this way and that, searching for a route back down the access road. Coughing violently, he was finally driven back by smoke that chewed at his eyes and lungs with burning teeth. Nowhere was the grass more than three feet high, but that actually worsened the situation: the fire raced along the blade-tips. It roared at them with its ravenous, unliving laughter.

The brush fire fed the bone-dry knotted and snarled timber, each layer of fire pre-heating the fuel above it, transforming the scrub grass into a crawling, twisting, blazing maze. Superheated air rose and was funneled by the ridges to east and west, driven by the wind like steam channeled through a whistling teakettle's narrow spout. The fire accelerated up the twenty-five percent grade as the air compressed and then exploded out again, sealing the narrow dirt road with a blistering wall of heat. Again Ocean attempted to brave it, and was driven back by what felt like a demonic, flaming hand.

Del Withers fished the keys to his dusty old Dodge Dart from his pocket, and rounded up five of the closest kids, including Rory and Bucky. Bucky's pink punk-spiked head swiveled back and forth frantically as he watched the fire approach. Withers herded them into his car, yelling, "Come on! Pile in!" He threw his wife the keys, and said: "You get them out of here, Diane. Get some help. The phones are dead."

She gave him a swift, solid kiss. "You take care of yourself, and get these kids up to the lake."

"Just get the hell out of here!"

Without another word Diane backed the car up, and made a Y-turn, heading back down the narrow road, directly into the fire. Bucky stared back at them through the rear window, his pink hair no longer defiant or outrageous, merely a pitiful contrast to his whey-pale complexion.

Renny watched carefully, holding his breath. Success for Diane would bode well for the rest of the camp. The car rolled on, apparently unaffected by the fire, and his hopes swelled. *They were going to make it!*

The car rolled fifteen feet through the flames, then there was an odd sound, something completely, terribly out of place. A *chuk*-ing sound like rock hitting glass.

The Dart slewed sideways into a ditch, instantly swathed by flames. He heard the screams of the trapped children as the flames closed in from all sides.

The soccer game had long since ended. All the campers now gathered, staring down the hill into the fire, sniffing the smoke, their eyes tearing less from irritation than fear.

Courtney sheltered her eyes against the gusts, gazing down at the blazing car. "Oh God," she mouthed, but no sound passed her lips.

The trapped children's screams escalated until they barely seemed human at all. They uttered animal sounds, now, crying and cursing and begging, all intertwined in a pain-wracked cacophony. The smoke shifted for an instant, and they could see Bucky pounding his clenched fists madly against the glass.

"Diane!" Withers screamed, and stumbled down the grade after her. Ocean tried to stop him, but Withers shook his hands off and picked his way down into the fire, staggering on unsteady legs. At first he seemed able to avoid the pockets of fire, reading the wind shifts and holding the tail of his shirt to his face, filtering enough breathable air to keep moving.

Renny watched leaves swirl as the wind shifted, watched the fire close in around him, heard Del Withers scream and stagger but not fall, heard the desolate wail of the trapped children. Withers reeled back, hands protecting his eyes from flare and heat as the Dart's gas tank detonated with a deafening roar. He was briefly, horribly outlined in flame, then he disappeared as flaming fuel showered everywhere and curled into a fireball.

Burning bits of glass and steel showered around them, spreading the fire even further and faster. Smoke gushed toward the camp as the bleeding, smoking, starving thing crawled toward them.

For a few seconds no one spoke, and then one of the boys whimpered. "Julie . . . ?" he called questioningly. Then he screamed it. *"Julie!!"*

The kids broke, and ran scrambling and screaming in three directions: to their cabins, toward the valley walls, toward the distant, hoped-for safety of Charisma Lake.

Janie grabbed at Clint's arm, but the boy twisted himself free. "Gotta get my stuff!"

Behind Renny, Vivian screamed, "Patrick! Patrick! Come here *now!*" When there was no reply, she ran toward the cabins.

Paris struggled to herd the kids into a manageable formation, fought to keep them calm and alert, but for once the campers' odd bond of discipline seemed to have gone completely to hell.

Renny was forced to grab two of the smaller kids by the waist. Screaming and struggling, they fought him until he screamed *"shut up!"*, which finally bought him a moment's peace. Which way? Toward the lake seemed most reasonable, but did that make it safest? They had to move, that was certain: the heat was so intense that his shirt was starting to smoke. *Move! Move!* His mind screamed at him, instincts older than conscious thought warring with higher brain functions.

The lizard-mind won. Dragging the pair, he headed north, across the soccer field.

Gagging on smoke, Courtney tried to unwrap a garden hose from the side of the mess hall and play it out on the fire as it licked its way around the wooden panels. It had already crept around the other side, and was now tonguing the propane tanks behind her.

She seemed frozen there on the spot, waving a long wavering finger of water at the approaching flame as if making some kind of mystical gesture, not seeing that the fire, craftier than she and sensing helpless prey, had almost completely encircled her.

Ocean tried to pull her away, and she fought with him, struggled with him as if *he* were the enemy, not the faceless, armless horror between Courtney and the only route of escape.

"Come on, damn it!" he screamed. Courtney clawed at his face, strained against him, then convulsed and ceased resistance to lay panting in his grasp like a panicked woodland creature.

"Someone has to try. I think that—"

Those words, and a metallic screech that raised the hair on the back of his neck, were the last sounds Ocean ever heard.

Due to faulty thinking during the original set-up procedures, the twin propane tanks shared by kitchen and shower rooms were positioned to vent *against* each other. The valves screamed in protest, and then one of them ruptured, triggering the reaction known as a Boiling Liquid Expanding Vapor Explosion. The BLEVE gushed a seething wall of flaming gas, which rolled out and caught Ocean like a scrap of driftwood in a tidal wave. His flayed body cushioned Courtney from the blast. She was tumbled into the bushes surrounding the fire pit, but Ocean, hair and clothing aflame, was hurled thirty feet against the wall of the craft center.

Frankie Darling was there within moments, beating out Ocean's smoldering clothes with his navy jacket. Patrick arrived a moment later, stripped off his own shirt and beat at the flames as well. Frantically, the boys rolled Ocean over once, twice, muffling fire in dirt. Ocean lay broken, eyes open and staring, twisted like a burned, broken puppet. Frankie's face went blank, as if someone had turned off the light behind his eyes.

"Frankie . . . ?" Patrick called, but his friend was already standing, dusting his hands on his pants, his entire body shivering as if he stood naked in a blizzard.

There Vivian found them. She tried to shelter Patrick's eyes from the sight of Ocean's singed body, but he twisted away from her. "Mom—we've got to help the others!" He didn't seem frightened at that moment—he was all purpose and concern for his friends.

"All right," she said. "But together. Stay with me." The fire continued to devour the bunkhouses and other standing buildings. Vivian yanked one kid after another out of the cabins, where they had scrambled in an attempt to save their belongings. "Leave it!" she screamed. "Leave everything!"

Heather stared at her uncomprehendingly. "But my *clothes*!" She tried to gather an armful of jeans and shirts.

Vivian tore them out of her hands and pushed her toward the door, ignoring wails of protests. "Are you crazy? It's just cloth!" Smoke was already seeping through the window, and the wall outside was aflame. "Now move!"

81

The winds were peaking now, whipping dirt and leaves, grass and burning needles into a flaming dust devil. The mini-twister grew almost magically, climbing toward the brooding, cloudless sky, swirling and churning until it formed a thirty-foot tornado of fire. It capered impossibly in the commons between the buildings, like a creature escaped from the very pits of hell.

The campers stared at the apparition, hypnotically fascinated, temporarily beyond the capacity for reason or flight. The blazing funnel seemed more than merely some lethal but natural phenomenon. It was an omen, a savage portent, and they viewed it with almost superstitious awe.

In blind flight, Janie almost stumbled over Ocean's smoldering body, knew he was dead and heard the sob break in her throat. She hardened her heart and pulled at two of the transfixed children. "Damn it, *move!*"

The tornado moved south to brush the edge of the mess hall. Flaming shingles exploded from the roof, scattering embers like grenade fragments. The kids cried, and batted at the burns, but still seemed almost petrified, unable to move, to think, as if the twister had triggered some deep and atavistic death wish.

Then Vivian and Patrick emerged from Heather's cabin, the teenager struggling helplessly in their grasp. When she saw the kids staring at the twister she followed their gaze, and for a moment was equally transfixed. Then she sucked a blistering lungful of hot air and screamed: "Damn you all—MOVE IT!!"

At first they just stood, staring at her and then at the tornado. Then Heather began stumbling north. In another few seconds all of the kids were running, leaving the dancing swirling tower of flame to lurch among the smoldering ruins of Camp Charisma Lake.

Renny Sands was exhausted. The two kids had fought with him at first, made him carry them, and he had tried it for the first few hundred feet. Then he set them down and stared at them. "What are your names?" he asked.

"Clint."

"Trey."

"All right," Renny said. "Clint, Trey—do you want to live?" Two small faces bobbed emphatically. "Then we're going to run, all right? I can't carry you, but I can get you there safely if you run, all right?"

More nods. He grabbed their hands and they all began to flee toward the northern plateau, dreaming of water, of the lake. The lake. Certainly, there would be safety at the lake. *Please, God,* he prayed. *Let there be safety.*

The thick-bodied counselor named Jason was ahead of all of them. Displaying surprising speed, he'd made it across the plateau and was heading up the final rise to the lake when he stiffened, screamed, and fell back down, tumbling down the incline, crashing against brush and rocks, his fingers clutching at his leg. He slid to a stop at the bottom, moaning and trying to crawl. He collapsed, and fainted.

"Jesus," Schott said, wiping his head. From his position on the western ridge, he could see the entire valley: the dancing fire-twister, the smoking ruin of the car, the twisted corpses and the screaming, milling children, scattering like ants. "God amighty." The custom-made slugs were blunt moldings of specialized acrylic and lead shot, traveling at subsonic velocities with sufficient power to bruise and break bone without piercing the skin. They made little noise, and the plastic binder would burn in the fire, reduce to ash and a scattering of melted lead pellets indistinguishable from the debris around them.

From his vantage point he had targeted Jason, as one of the other men had taken out the camp owner's wife as she attempted to drive to safety. As they would cripple anyone who threatened to escape from the trap.

He fed another plastic slug into his rifle, and began to aim. He swore he could actually *feel* his soul shriveling as he did, but it was too late now. Too late for any of them, below or above, to escape hell.

With a silent prayer, his finger tightened on the trigger once again.

Renny realized something was horribly wrong. The first of the counselors should have made it to the top of the ridge, but instead Jason slid back down the hill, clutching at his leg. Was it his imagination? Or had he heard a gunshot?

Have a warm day.

For some reason he could not even imagine, D'Angelo had decided to kill him, and the counselors, and every child in the camp.

But . . . this was so obscenely elaborate, so incredibly organized . . . how in the world could anyone possibly have planned it all in twenty-four hours? Or less?

The only answer was that he couldn't. And that meant that he had planned this before he knew Renny was coming.

Which meant that *Renny Sand wasn't the target.*

Then who . . . ?

That question might never be answered. And if he did manage to riddle it out, the solution might be buried with his charred and broken bones.

*   *   *

Whatever small amount of discipline the children had retained was dissolving completely. A general walla of crying and screaming and wailing rose up as they slid into a collective malaise. The anguish and fear was communicable, jumping from camper to camper like a virus, overwhelming, shutting down the capacity for individual thought and action. As fire licked up from below, the heat rolled up the side of the mountain like a tide, the air itself rose, funneling, swirling back in a heated cycle, driving the campers north toward the lake. Its imagined safety was their only hope. When the first of the plastic slugs knocked Jason back down, even that tiny hope evaporated.

They were very close to utter, mindless panic, to a reversion from the logical human to the animal, mortal terror chewing away thought and discipline and education, leaving only a blind rush for survival. Frustrate that urge as well and all that was left was the glandular response, and that meant no more than milling and stampeding in a circle, then finally huddling in pockets and waiting for the devouring flames to deliver them from despair.

Kelly Kerrigan's scalp wound was a driving torment, but with that odd, unpredictable anomaly that sometimes occurs during moments of great stress, her senses seemed almost supernaturally acute.

She had heard the sniper rifle's first muffled crack, had watched and listened for another *pop* and a puff of smoke to find the assassin.

There he was. Two hundred yards away, neatly nestled on the ridge above the valley. That distance was simplicity itself, on a range. She had occasionally hit the mark at three-fifty with the Sharps. But those shots were on good days, under perfect conditions, without the handicap of a throbbing head wound.

Her limbs were weak as she took the first shot. Eight pounds of steel and wood smashed back into her shoulder, and she grunted with pain and effort.

The .44 hand-loaded slug flew at just under 1100 feet per second, traveled for a fraction more than one-fifth of a heartbeat. It transferred all of its energy to the bone and soft tissue of Chuck's head, detonating his skull like a grenade. The sniper dropped like a stone, bereft of the slightest suspicion that he had been killed.

*   *   *

Destiny heard the .44's roar. And then another. Every plastic slug had been carefully underpowered to diminish the report, but the Sharps could be mistaken for nothing but a high-powered hunting rifle.

A *shot.*

Around her, the sniffling and screaming stopped. Something else, something deeper triggered within them. There were enemies about. Human enemies.

They were *hunted.*

The representations, values and philosophies transferred from Alexander Marcus had failed them when it came to dealing with a natural disaster, but human foes were a different matter. However strange the environment, however bizarre and indirect the weapons, this was *war.*

And war Alexander Marcus had understood.

Destiny's eyes found the red and white sports hut, and her mind remembered what it contained.

Denise, Mathias and Heather died in the valley north of the camp, as a foehn wind downdraft met the rising hot air. The air blended and churned upwards into a vertical column, sucking the oxygen out of the entire pocket. They suffocated in the open, two campers and one counselor, gasping and clawing at the ground, crawling toward the lake.

The surviving children weren't operating on logic now. What moved them was older, and colder. The wind moved in pulses, driving the fire and smoke up. They pulled T-shirts up around their mouths and noses to protect their lungs, and began to climb.

"Which way?" Vivian panted.

Patrick studied the route to the lake. And then the valley walls. The fire was coming from the south, driving toward the north. Certainly that was the way to run. Wasn't it?

"Patrick, do you hear me?"

Suddenly he wasn't in the valley. Patrick was standing far above himself, as if suspended from a zeppelin. And from there he saw everything: the valley, the lake, the camp, the fire. The campers. He saw the fire sweeping north, and knew, *knew* that if they ran north the fire would outrun them. They hadn't a prayer.

But east, or west, running perpendicular to the breeze . . .

Yes. It was just insane enough to work.

He grabbed his mother's hands. "Listen to me," he yelled above the screaming wind. "You have to trust me."

"What are you talking about? We have to run!"

"If you don't listen to me, we're going to die." His voice was calm, and cold, and older than his years, and in spite of her terror, Vivian's expression went from one of tension to bafflement.

"Mom," her son said, "I know what we have to do. . . ."

Hennings swept the ridge with his binoculars, looking for Chuck. He had heard a *boom,* a sound deeper than the reverberations of the .32 plastic slugs, something alien and somehow alarming. And now he couldn't find Chuck.

He peered between shoals of drifting smoke, studying the valley floor. As he did, the wind shifted, diffusing the smoke, obscuring his view. Dammit: so much smoke! D'Angelo hadn't really taken that into account, but it wasn't necessarily fatal. It might mean that the children were suffocating, that this horrendous, mind-numbing job was almost over.

Although D'Angelo's brutal plan was apparently working, Hennings couldn't ignore the fact that Wisher and Woodcock had never returned from Diablo. And now Chuck was gone.

Hennings took a deep breath, calming himself. Even if something had happened to Chuck (what?), Schott, Silvestri, and the deadly D'Angelo remained. Together, they would get it done.

The alternative was unthinkable.

If Hennings could have seen through the smoke he would have been less optimistic. Concealed by the shifting, impenetrable haze, Vivian and a dozen of the surviving kids, led by Patrick in a spontaneous act of counterintuitive perception, had climbed the ridges to the east and west. Once there, panting and choking, they clambered down to safety on the far side. Once safe, they would be able to rest. And once rested, they would have time to think.

Hennings continued to scan his binoculars north and south, slow steady sweeps that covered the length and breadth of the killing zone. During the brief moments when the wind shifted sufficiently to give him a view across the valley, he spotted another of the kids climbing up the incline, and gritted his teeth. Time to get back to work. He picked up his rifle, checked the sights, and raised it to his shoulder.

Twenty yards south of Hennings, Destiny had clambered up the ridge. She crouched, hidden from the killer by an overhanging bush. Struggling not to make a sound, she pulled her bow off her shoulder, and without pause positioned it carefully, nocked an arrow, and drew.

Smoke drifted up from the valley, obscuring her target. Choking back a cough, Destiny waited. She dared not blink, or swallow, or give in to fatigue. Instinct told her that she would have only a moment, only a second in which to act. Her eyes burned, and she blinked them one at a time, praying that the same clouds of ash that blinded her would prevent her unknown enemy from acting.

For a moment the smoke parted, giving her the barest view. She saw the rifleman, crouched, aiming down at her friends. She whispered that briefest and sincerest of prayers: *Please God,* then released and watched the arrow fly twenty-four feet to strike Hennings in the throat.

He reared back, eyes mad with agony, unable to scream, hands fumbling for the shaft. He struggled his way up to standing, and tugged at the arrow, but couldn't extract it. Blood gushed from his mouth. He staggered, crazed now. Destiny could not move from his line of sight, even when Hennings finally spied her.

All strength in Destiny's arms and legs and mind drained to nothing as Hennings raised his rifle and sighted at her. He managed to get the rifle halfway up, and still Destiny could not move, the roar of her own blood a deafening wall of sound.

Hennings fired, but the slug went wild and short. He crumpled to his knees, his eyes already filming over, his mouth set in an odd, crimsoned mask of resignation. He fell over onto his side, kicked his legs a few times, and made an aimless crawling gesture. Then he collapsed and was still.

Spread by explosion and convection, the fire blazed out of control now. Smoke had been sighted by helicopters and picnickers with cell phones. Fire units from as far away as Prescott roared toward the Folly, the good men and women who drove them counting the minutes and seconds, knowing the time lag between alarm and response, knowing the distances involved, and fearing for the lives of the children trapped in that valley.

Even without the threat of the riflemen, the firefighters' fears were justified. The afternooner whirled a constellation of sparks up out of the saddle, away from the Folly and into the forest beyond, sweeping a wall of flame that the kids were lucky to have beaten to the crest. The fortunate ones fled through the forest, seeking the road on the far side of the lake, and safety.

*   *   *

Kelly sighted again, blinking hard. Her vision doubled and then cleared as she sighted down the slot at Silvestri, who crouched on the western ridge. *Wait for it.* She took a deep breath, let it out, and fired. Sighted again, this time at Schott, and fired a second time. Unfortunately this time Kelly had unseated the Sharps just a bit, allowed just a hair of space between the butt and her shoulder, but it was enough. At recoil, the rifle's stock slammed back into her shoulder, shattering it.

The bullets traveled for just over half a second. The first took Silvestri in the body. He stumbled forward, dropped to his knees, and was still.

The second shot went wild. Schott stared at his partner, disbelieving, not realizing that death had passed less than two feet from his head.

The echo of the shots still rang across the valley, a rolling *boom* completely unlike the crack of the rifles carried by his team. As the haze cleared he glimpsed the kids climbing up the valley's east and west faces. With Woodcock and Wisher missing, Silvestri and maybe Chuck shot by someone unknown, it was over. There was no way to keep the trap sealed. All he could do was run for it.

And he did, making it along the ridge south. The wind blew northwest now, and he figured that the fire would follow it. With a little luck . . .

Schott felt the branches slapping against his leg, and at first thought that the pain in his ankle was a deep, ugly thorn scratch.

He looked down at his calf, and saw the blood oozing through the rip in his pant leg. Someone scuttled back into the bushes, and he couldn't see who or what it was.

Schott pivoted to the right. He didn't have time to register the blur, never saw the arrow before it drove into his gut. Even with most of the energy absorbed by his heavy shirt, the head penetrated two inches. He screamed, grabbed the shaft and wrenched it out, just in time to feel another pain in his back. He pivoted and reached around to wrench an X-acto craft knife from the hand of a skinny black girl who was even now creeping back into the brush. He stared at the blade in his hand, his own blood leaking from it, and felt momentarily disconnected from reality. This was all a dream. It had to be.

Something very like a whimper escaped his throat. He took another hobbling step, then a big hick-looking kid stepped out, his face set as serious as Death.

The kid walked right up to him. The world was spinning, and now there were other kids, appearing out of the brush, seared, dirty, smudged, their eyes hollow and cold, carrying screwdrivers and folding knifes, kitchen cutlery and even a garden rake.

Schott took another step back. The big kid put his palms flat against Schott's chest, and pushed hard.

Schott slid backwards down the incline, into the burning underbrush, screaming all the way.

Silvestri was still alive when the children found him. He lay on his back, blood bubbling from a hole in his chest. He watched it with fascination, each breath bringing new seepage. Silvestri touched it with his fingers.

Blood was warm, wasn't it? Then why did this feel cold? He couldn't wrap his mind around that, couldn't puzzle it out. When the children appeared, he hoped that perhaps they could help resolve the conundrum.

"Help me," he said, voice thick, wet, and somehow infantile. They said nothing, just gathered around, watching him very carefully. A Hispanic girl's cheeks were scratched, smudged with soot and tears. Silvestri held his bloodstained hands out to her. "Help . . ."

"All right," Destiny Valdez replied coldly, and raised her bow.

D'Angelo was on the run. It was over, everything was ruined, and he wasn't even sure why, or how it had all come apart.

Then like an apparition from hell, Kelly Kerrigan rose up from behind the stump of a shattered tree, an ungodly huge rifle propped on the stump. Christ, was that Bob's Buffalo rifle? D'Angelo had a quick, sickening thought of the damage the .44 slug would do ripping through his body, then shut that horrific thought from his mind.

She looked like a scarecrow, clothing smudged and torn, her golden eyes the only things alive in her face. Even eighteen feet away he could see that her hands were shaking. If he could only distract her for a few seconds, he knew he could draw and fire before she could pull the trigger. He knew her reaction time, knew he could beat it, even if she had him dead to rights.

Then he saw something in her eyes, and realized that she was *already squeezing.* D'Angelo threw himself sideways as the Sharps roared. He gasped, bowled sideways as if someone had taken a sledgehammer to his ribs. D'Angelo hit the ground hard enough to see stars, rolled, then realized that the slug had only grazed him. Incredible.

He rolled to his feet. Kelly was done, exhausted. She was having trouble moving her right arm. She had fallen backwards, and the Sharps was on the ground. She fumbled for the rifle with fingers that would no longer obey her. D'Angelo walked over and set his foot squarely on the rifle. She glared up at him, eyes seething with hate.

"Don't blame me, Kelly. And when these kids start killing people, you'll have only yourself to thank."

"Damn you to hell," she gasped. "You don't give a damn about anything in this world."

Tough old broad, even at the last. He grinned, wincing at the pain in his side, and drew his gun. "You're right about that," he said.

He squeezed the trigger, but at the exact same moment blinding pain flashed in his head, a moment of exquisite void that tore a moment free from the continuum of thought.

D'Angelo stumbled sideways, jerked around, realizing that he had been hit, he had been attacked, but by who . . . ?

And saw the boy facing him, armed with a bow and arrow. D'Angelo looked down, realizing that a feathered shaft jutted from his own shoulder. He felt the strength draining from it, and fought to keep a sudden surge of panic from engulfing him.

The boy was black, skinny, scared. "Who the fuck are you, mister?" the kid said.

"Arizona Marshal," D'Angelo said. "This woman is under arrest. Arson and attempted murder. And you're under arrest for assault." He gripped at the arrow, yanked at it. It wasn't deep, only a flesh wound.

"Don't believe him, son," Kelly gasped. "He set this fire. He wants to kill all of you."

The corners of D'Angelo's mouth twitched upward. "Don't believe it, boy." He brought his pistol to the level, squared it on the boy's chest. "Are you alone?" he asked quietly.

A Hispanic girl stepped out from behind a tree. She carried a bow and arrow as well. Her hands weren't shaking at all.

And then a small blond boy appeared. And a taller redhead, carrying fist-sized rocks, eyes narrowed.

"We travel in packs," Destiny Valdez said coldly.

"This is a gun," D'Angelo said, and hated the squeak that had crept into his voice. More footfalls. God. Four, five, eight more children. All armed with rocks, or sticks. Or arrows. His arm ached.

D'Angelo whirled in response to a sound behind him. A blond boy was with Kelly, had helped her prop that big ugly rifle up. Now its bore was centered on D'Angelo's chest.

Exhausted, Kelly managed to smile. "Well, Angel," she said. "Do you think you can kill us all?"

His mouth worked silently, then stopped moving. His gun-hand sagged to his side, and the pistol fell from nerveless fingers.

The wind carried sparks and burning brands into the forest around Charisma Lake, and it boiled with hot spots. It took almost forty minutes for the first fire unit to arrive. It seemed that several trees had mysteriously fallen on the road leading up Mingus Mountain to the Folly.

In another hour, additional units began to arrive, by which time fully eight hundred acres were smoldering.

All forty-three surviving children had collected at the lake, where they were loath to stray from the safety of water. From there, they could see the fire as it encircled them. Still threatening, but not deadly.

There were enough kids to drag D'Angelo, and carry Kelly, back up to the lakeside boathouse. D'Angelo's hands and feet were tied with belts and rope and twisted wire. Destiny stood over him, an arrow nocked and pointed at his right eye.

"I can watch him," Kelly said. She sat on the ground with her back against the wall, holding D'Angelo's Colt in her left hand,

"Are you sure?" Destiny said. Kelly nodded. Despite her evident pain, she seemed completely alert. "Good," she said. "I need to find Patrick."

When Destiny left, Kelly Kerrigan sagged back against the wall of the equipment room, pistol pointed unwaveringly at D'Angelo. "Why, you bastard?" she whispered. "And for God's sake . . . how did you get those men to agree to kill these children? The Praetorians were never saints, but they weren't *monsters.*"

D'Angelo's tongue snaked out to lick his lips. He watched her craftily, perhaps waiting for her fatigue and injuries to numb her, increasing her vulnerability.

"How?" he said. "Not as hard as you think. Those six killed Alexander. They thought they were protecting his legacy, that he'd gone crazy. Once they stepped across *that* line, I had them. I had leverage, you see.

"Why? Simple, you silly bitch. The imprinting was working. The kids were turning into a thousand little Alexander Marcuses. What do *you* think will happen when they hit puberty? Do you honestly believe that some of the children you saved won't take up Alexander's special little pleasures?" His laugh was like a punch in the gut. Kelly longed to pull the trigger, but decades of discipline stopped her. Bobby's memory stopped her. The fear of becoming like D'Angelo stopped her.

He seemed almost to know her thoughts, and gauged his words to damage. "Your cheap heroics have probably killed a thousand innocent people."

Kelly shook her head. "You already tried that one," she said. "You don't give a damn about those children, or about innocent victims. Maybe you care about the truth being traced back to you—" she watched him carefully, saw the calm in his face.

"No," she said. "That's not it, is it, Angel? You've already got a cut-out. Already severed the connection between you and those kids, if I know you." She leaned closer, squinting against the pain in her shoulder. "And I do. No. You did it because you *could*." His lips curled. "Because you had your hooks in those five. Once you talked them into killing the man they admired most in the world, you had your hands in their souls. And you twisted."

His smile was impenetrable as a glacier.

"God," she said. The fatigue suddenly hit her like an avalanche, and her vision washed into black and red waves. "I wish I was strong enough to pull this trigger."

"I wish you were, too," D'Angelo said, his eyes shifting away from her.

"Finally," Kelly murmured in disgust. "The truth." Then exhaustion, pain and blood loss finally overcame her. Kelly slumped back against the wall, then slid sideways to the ground.

D'Angelo waited three frantic breaths, and then began struggling with his bonds. There was still hope. If he could just get his arms free, and then get his hands on that gun . . .

Before he could shuck even the first layer of wire and rope, a small pale boy in a sooty T-shirt entered the boathouse.

His face was smudged, and one lens of his wire-rimmed glasses was broken. He stared at D'Angelo as if he were a specimen of some kind, but didn't seem hostile.

"Hey, kid," D'Angelo said. "Your friends got it all wrong."

"Did they?" Frankie asked. He examined Kelly briefly, saw that she was breathing, and then straightened. He seemed to be searching for something.

"Listen," D'Angelo said. "If you'd just loosen my arms I'll show you my identification. I'm a U.S. Marshal, and if you can help me get this all sorted out, there's a reward in it for you."

"Is there?" Frankie asked. He was peering into a shadowed heap of equipment. D'Angelo couldn't see what the boy was looking at, and the kid's expression never changed, but he seemed to make a small, satisfied sound deep in his throat. He reached into the equipment pile.

"Yeah. Big reward. Maybe a medal. This woman is conning your friends. She's dangerous." Frankie withdrew his hand, and D'Angelo saw what he now held.

It was two feet long, and curved like a question mark, rusted steel with a wooden handle. The point looked wickedly sharp. Boat hook. Frankie's eyes roamed over D'Angelo's bound body, as if trying to decide where to begin. A sudden, electric current of raw terror seized D'Angelo's mind, dampening logical thought. "Wait!" He babbled as the boy halved the distance between them, hook raised. "I'm a U.S. Marshall—"

"Were you?" Frankie said, and then the hook descended.

Frankie emerged into the waning daylight, his hands smeared crimson, his face alight with a fire that burned everything, warmed nothing.

The children were waiting for him as he emerged, faces tense and accepting. He stared at them as if his eyes had lost the ability to focus.

Behind them the raging fires began to yield as planes and helicopters dropped their loads of retardant, and the firefighters coordinated their own lines of engagement. Fire companies from as far away as Phoenix had traveled at breakneck pace to the struggle.

But Frankie, looking down on the burning forest, the sky above him gone black with ash, saw none of it, nothing at all.

He brushed past the others and then kept walking, out into the lake, a strange, inarticulate cry winding its way from deep in his chest. At first the others thought that he was trying to wash the blood off, and then, when he kept going, they waded after him, and dragged him back, fighting and thrashing and sobbing.

Jessica held him, his head in her ample lap. The others gathered around but gave them room, exchanging glances. No words were said.

None were needed.

*   *   *

"What happened here? *What happened here?*" Sand screamed at the dozen children around the boathouse. Their utterly calm expressions were an unspoken answer. The door hung wide, and he saw it all, or as much as his shell-shocked mind would allow him to absorb.

Frankie lay in the middle of the kids, coddled by Jessica and Courtney. The bigger girl stroked Frankie's head, but she watched Sand carefully as she did.

"I said, what happened here?"

Renny entered the boathouse, right hand clapped over his mouth. Kelly still lay unconscious, overcome by shock and exhaustion and exposure.

D'Angelo was another matter. What remained looked like something caught in the gears of a machine, something too raw for the slaughterhouse.

Renny staggered back out.

The survivors watched him, an unspoken question in their eyes. Vivian was right behind him, and she looked in the boathouse, and then ran back out, gagging. For almost two minutes she made sick, wet sounds without actually voiding anything.

When she straightened up, she saw Renny's sooty, frightened face. For that moment, their nonverbal communication was almost like the strange bond shared by the children.

Without a word, they went back to the boathouse, and moved Kelly out to where the children could care for her. Renny searched until he found a half-filled gas can, then sloshed the pale pink fluid over D'Angelo's corpse.

Vivian lit the match.

82

WASHINGTON, D.C.,
FRIDAY, OCTOBER 5

Centered in a pitiless cone of incandescent light, Kelly sat tall in her wheelchair, her unfrilled blue smock starched and pressed until it seemed almost military in function. Beside her, Sand wore a carmine sweatshirt and the same blue slacks that had carried him through the last two hideously fatiguing days. The room was very plain, with no windows and only a single door. In that room, six men and women had asked endless questions. Renny knew that the children and two surviving counselors, Janie Summers and Paris Tuckwil, had been similarly quizzed. But now, finally, it had come down to just Renny and Kelly Kerrigan.

The chairman of the meeting was Shannon McGuire, senior Senator from Indiana, a woman of iron hair and strong, sloping shoulders who seemed to have aged five years since the hearings began. "We have documents," she said, "recovered from Advanced Systems in Palo Alto. Those in combination with deathbed testimony from a Sergeant Schott and Mrs. Kerrigan's statement, give evidence of a conspiracy without precedent in our experience."

And so the pieces were fitted together, and a lethal mosaic it was.

In 1988 serial killer Alexander Marcus had finally made a mistake, leaving clues that Martin Schott and Orren Silvestri followed to the gnawed corpse of his latest victim. Horrified, Schott and Silvestri took the information to D'Angelo, who pretended innocence. A decision was made. To save the reputation of the man they all admired, an accident was arranged, using a small fuel-air explosion, a method that would later be employed to destroy a Northern California research facility.

The Palo Alto research lab known as Advanced Systems had attempted to extract from Alexander Marcus the secret of his success, and implant it in children known to be at risk using repetition, physical patterning, and advanced hypnotic techniques. Initial success gave way to panic when a small group of them began to exhibit pathology, specifically the violent, sexually-charged dreams of the Columbia Daycare kids. Advanced Systems had called a halt to the programming, but continued to cautiously collate results.

When years had passed, and no further negative behaviors were reported, and the positive results became obvious, Advanced Systems prepared to go public with the results of what they called the Aristotle Project.

Unfortunately, the first person they contacted was the man who Marcus had listed as his closest friend and confidant: Tristan D'Angelo. D'Angelo listened to Advanced Systems's description of the actual nature of their tests, and realized the danger of his situation. D'Angelo sent Wisher and Schott as representatives and liaisons to A.S., while he plotted and planned and worried: What could be done?

D'Angelo believed that if these children reached puberty and began to follow their role model's darker side, that the pattern of death would eventually lead back to the preschools, and then to the Aristotle Project, and eventually to Alexander Marcus and Tristan D'Angelo.

Once the decision was made to destroy Aristotle, the next and most logical question followed: what of the children themselves? How many of the approximately one thousand kids might go over the edge? Two percent? Five percent? Between twenty and fifty kids, each capable of killing dozens of people?

D'Angelo might not have cared, but apparently his men did. They had fought and killed for their country, had destroyed their hero in order to save him. The children constituted an absolute nightmare: at least a dozen women had died at Marcus's hand. What might a thousand Marcuses do?

So the Praetorians conspired to kill the five percent of the children who would be considered greatest risk. Those from broken homes, with criminal parents, crack babies, those who might be on police blotters as young arsonists or animal torturers. God only knew their precise criteria, or how they had twisted Advanced Systems's research to their own perverted end. But they had found those children, and cast their net, and drawn them in. Children unable to attend the death-trap summer camp were simply singled out and murdered by mobile hit teams.

And if not for a sixty-eight-year-old former Secret Service agent, D'Angelo and the six men who killed Alexander Marcus would have murdered every living thing at Charisma Lake.

The six senators comprising the special investigative committee looked as tired as Renny felt. Just possibly, the previous few days had been horrible for them as well. "Mr. Sand," Senator McGuire asked, her gray hair seemingly whiter and more brittle than it had been just forty-eight hours earlier, "what do think we should do with these children?"

"Let them grow," Sand said wearily.

Beside her, the junior senator from Arizona leaned forward. "According to F.B.I reports, Master Sergeant D'Angelo was found to have wounds inconsistent with death by fire. Can you explain those?"

The reporter looked directly at them. "Some of his own men must have killed him," he said. "Before the fire began."

Kelly Kerrigan spoke slowly. "There's an expression about birds coming home to roost," she said. "Beyond that, there's really nothing we can say."

*   *   *

Renny rode the limousine with Kelly to Dulles International. He pushed her wheelchair through the ticket lines, and then to her departure gate. She could have walked, but the doctors had been adamant that another week off her feet would greatly speed her healing.

They waited in the lounge, watching the clock creep along, listening to the faint echo of the announcer as she detailed the arrival of flights from New York, London, Los Angeles. He felt numb, and hardly felt it when her hand found his.

Renny sighed heavily. "So," he said. "What now for you, Kelly?"

"I can't stay in Diablo," she said. "There just isn't enough there for me. Not any more."

"What then?"

"Bobby Ray was born in Texas. That's where we met. He was a Ranger, Renny. He was tall and proud and beautiful when we met. I guess if he had a choice he'd die the way he did. He was afraid of turning into some kind of vegetable. Of being a burden on me until I wouldn't remember the good times any more." Her hands gripped at the wheelchair's leather armrests. "That idiot. Couldn't have ever happened, until the day I don't remember my own name any more." She sighed. "I think I'm taking him home, Renny. I think that's what I'll do."

A single tear brimmed at the inside edge of her left eye, and brimmed over, leaving a glistening track on her cheek. "Aw, hell," she said, and the tears were glimmering just beyond her control. He still couldn't believe it: Because of this one little woman, forty-three children and four adults were still alive. Twelve innocent people had died, plus six weak, evil men, and one creature of fantastic virulence.

Kelly seemed so small, so helpless. Renny would always remember that he owed her his life.

And that because of him, her beloved husband was dead.

Might Kelly and Bobby Ray have had more good months, watching the warm Arizona sky together? Holding each other? Speaking of the good times? All of that was now gone, gone forever.

Renny didn't realize how it had happened, but suddenly he was kneeling by the side of her wheelchair, Kelly Kerrigan was holding his hand, and he was crying.

"Renny Sand," she said. She stroked his head as his mother might have, had she lived. "In life, things just happen sometimes. The Lord makes those decisions. We all have things we regret. Most of the time it doesn't matter what we try to do, or what we want. It's *His* will that's done. Not ours."

All the strength he had felt facing the Senate committee, the men and women who might decide the fate of a thousand innocent children drained away, and with it any sense of who or what he was.

She seemed to sense that he was a man who had no words, but desperately needed to communicate. "Renny," she said. "There's a good woman who needs a husband, and a good boy who needs a father. There is nothing more cleansing in this world than building a home. Put your past behind you. Life is too damned short."

A blue-uniformed flight attendant touched her shoulder. "Excuse me, Mrs. Kerrigan. We're ready to begin pre-boarding. Would you like to come along now?"

Renny took a deep breath and hugged her. "God, Bobby Ray was one lucky man."

Kelly kissed his cheek gently. "You go on now," she said. And the flight attendant wheeled her away from him, and down the tunnel to her waiting plane.

He never saw Kelly Kerrigan again.

83

MARCH 2002

Renny Sand drove north on the I-5 freeway, heading out of Portland toward Claremont. It was a cold gray day. Water beaded against his windscreen, turning the road into a rain-streaked watercolor. He was growing accustomed to the weather, and no longer felt deprived for lack of sunlight and blue sky. If he was going to live here, he reckoned he had better get used to real winters, and real weather.

He had been a Portlander for two months now, had carted his stuff north after resigning from Marcus Communications and finding work at the *Oregonian.*

For the first months following Charisma Lake he still smoked half a pack a day, but eventually Renny couldn't strike a match without remembering a dancing cone of fire. In time the urge to swallow smoke recreationally weakened to a dull ache.

As he drove, his mind wandered to his notes on the Marcus affair.

After all this time he still hadn't decided what to do, or even what to think.

In the final analysis what *was* Alexander Marcus? War hero? Entrepreneur? Political figure? Olympic medalist? Faithful son?

Serial killer?

There were no hints in any of Marcus's writings. Not journals or papers, memos or articles. Nor in public speeches. Every single word that might eventually come under public scrutiny had been sanitized. It might well be impossible to determine who and what Alexander Marcus had really been beneath his mask.

In desperation, Renny had read Marcus's favorite tome, *A Book of Five Rings,* six times, praying that the words of a sixteenth century killing machine might provide some explanation of the man. But Musashi, who the Japanese called the Sword Saint, also urged his students to "exist for the good of mankind." Musashi killed men who were trying to kill him. A killer, but not a murderer. Not a monster.

What of Marcus's early childhood, the abuse at the hands of boys and girls in the streets of Harlem? The mutilation? The betrayal by both his mother and the agent of his (possibly) first sexual experience? Could that explain it? Too damned simplistic. If Renny tried to blame Marcus's environment, then what to make of the thousands of abused boys and girls who never become twisted things, who live with their dark memories, and struggle to be good and moral beings.

Vietnam? Korea? The horrors of combat, and the greater horror of meeting some secret part of yourself behind the closed door of an interrogation room? That was the hoariest cliché of all, and one that insulted every veteran who has returned to his family, picked up the plow or the school book on his return, reintegrated with society. Over the last months he had researched further, almost obsessively, and found so many conflicting opinions that he decided one could theorize, but never truly understand, why human beings took one path or another. The ultimate answer, he decided, lay not within the range of human analytical capacity, but in the mind or domain of whatever creative force had molded the essential force . . . the soul, if you will, that gave a being will and consciousness.

Whatever had molded Alexander Marcus, be it nature or nurture, had also formed his beliefs and values, and many of those were now buried so deep, rooted so firmly in the children, that there might be no psychic surgery capable of removing the shards. All the Charisma Lake campers had undergone therapy or counseling in the months fol-

lowing the incident in Arizona. Other children on the list were evaluated and interviewed using a variety of ruses. The counselors quietly
reported their findings back to a certain Senate subcommittee.

So far, the conclusions were almost unanimous: the children were
brilliantly focused and abnormally creative, with self-esteem indices
far above the norm. Even the survivors of Charisma Lake seemed to
have suffered far less trauma than expected.

The words *sociopathic* or *psychopathic* had not, as yet, been mentioned.

As yet.

Sand knew that in cloistered academic halls, very secretive discussions were in process. Every scrap of Charisma Lake information was
being evaluated, debates about nature and nurture given new life.

The children were a thousand walking, talking, breathing lab rats,
locked in a maze without walls.

Outside of a dozen people in D.C., Kelly Kerrigan, Renny Sand
and Vivian Emory were the only living people who knew that the
children carried Marcus's spiritual seed. If Renny decided to go public,
it would be the scoop of the century.

But whom would it benefit? Thousands of people would lose jobs.
Hundreds might lose fortunes as Marcus Communications stock plum-
meted. And if, God help him, the truth about the children ever saw
the cover of *Newsweek*, each and every one of them would carry that
stigma to their graves.

What was right? What was wrong? Kelly and Vivian had said they
would not judge him, but Renny just wasn't sure anymore. He suspected that he would never publish these notes, and that was the final
irony. He had prayed for a story that would save his career, make the
public forget a certain terrible mistake. This *was* that story, that career
miracle that comes once in a lifetime.

But he couldn't run with it, and was in an odd way happy that he
couldn't, because the old Renny Sand could have. He would have
justified it, rationalized it: *Someone else would stumble across it. Penelope Costanza would tell her story to someone else. A policeman
somewhere would tie two threads together. A computer disk from Advanced Systems would turn up at a girlfriend's house, and prove to
contain a list of children . . .*

Or that old, reliable standby: *The public has a right to know.*

No, they didn't.

If disaster struck, in any form, he would be able to stand with

Vivian and Patrick, and the boy would know that he, Renny Sand, had not betrayed their trust. Had done everything he could to protect them all. When Renny looked at Patrick Emory he saw only the clear brown eyes, and the open heart of a boy who had lost a father, and needed a friend.

Renny wanted to be that friend so badly that it hurt to think of it.

He reached the Claremont turnoff (there was only one), and turned east to corkscrew west, drove two miles through familiar twisting streets, and found Costumes, Period. Vivian's battered blue car was parked in front, along with a bicycle that he now knew belonged to her son.

He reached through the door and quieted the bell before entering: one of his greatest pleasures in life was simply observing Vivian when she was off guard.

And now, she was in the back of the shop, working with a heavyset female customer trying on a Wonder Woman outfit, gold tiara and all.

Vivian was dressed for dinner and a Lionel Richie concert at the Portland Rose Garden: a dark blue pullover that hugged her torso like a dream, and an ankle-length saffron skirt so perfectly tailored that it couldn't possibly have fit any other human being on the planet as sublimely. Her hair was a fall of relaxed ringlets that kissed her shoulders with every move she made.

Patrick was working the cash register, and peered out at Renny from behind the counter, allowing a smile of recognition before returning to inventorying a box of monster teeth. "Hey, Renny," he said casually.

At that, Vivian looked up from her customer, and her face lit up. *One minute,* she mouthed silently, and then went back to pinning up the hem on a dress that looked like something from a Star Wars tarot deck.

Renny leaned against the counter, waiting. "How's school?" he asked.

"Fine," Patrick said. He didn't follow that up with any additional probing. The rules had been established early on. *Don't try to be my father. If you're dating my mother, fine, but just because I trust you, just because you helped to save my life, don't try to be what you can't be. I get one father. One. And he's gone.*

But maybe, just maybe, we can be friends.

Vivian shunted the customer off to the dressing room and came to Renny, depositing a kiss on his cheek. Despite his reserve, Patrick didn't turn away fast enough for Renny to miss the grin.

The peck had been conservative, considerate of Patrick's feelings, but Renny knew how much more of her there was, knew the miracle that had been granted him. He treasured the memory of every night they had shared. Tonight, Patrick would be staying at Frankie's house, and Vivian would come to Renny's apartment. There, after dinner and music and perhaps dancing, she would share with him all that he had ever dreamed of, and despaired of ever experiencing.

They were both torn, both lost, but in the depths of night, one blessed evening following another like pearls on a golden strand, they were slowly but surely healing each other's wounds.

"Hi," she said, and took his hand in hers. Her fingers were strong and warm.

"Hi back," he said, and wanted to kiss her right there, in front of her son. The urge was almost overwhelming. He didn't. Not quite yet. But soon.

She seemed to sense his thoughts. "So . . ." she said. "Ready to go?"

"Absolutely."

She turned to Patrick. The boy had grown two inches in the past year, and was starting to fill out a bit. A bit more of the bearish Otis was manifesting in Patrick's youthful body. "Do you have cash for tonight?"

"You paid us already," Patrick said, but she reached into the register, pulled out another twenty, and handed it to him.

"Just a little something," she said. "What time will you be back tomorrow?"

"Maybe I should ask you that," he said, and she ruffled his hair.

"Give me a hug," she said.

"Aw, Mom . . ." he protested, a reply more ceremonial than heartfelt. She pulled him from behind the counter and squeezed him, scanned her store one more time and then tugged Renny toward the door.

"I've got energy tonight," she said, "and I want to burn it."

"My very thought," he said, letting her into his car. "There's a little jazz club called Annie Pearl's I keep hearing about from our entertainment editor, and we have a table at midnight."

"Ooh, Mr. Sand. Food, music, alcohol. Are you sure you can handle the consequences?"

In answer, he leaned toward her, and she toward him. Their lips met, and opened, and for half an eternal minute they spoke to each other wordlessly. When she finally pulled back, he felt dazed.

"Are you sure?" she whispered.

"Hope to God," he said. Before he could get in on his side two more bicycles came speeding along the alley behind the costume shop, bearing Destiny and Frankie. They seemed to be having some kind of race, careering into the parking lot with hair-raising speed before dual squealing brakes brought them to a halt.

"Hey Mrs. Emory, Mr. Sand," Destiny said. Frankie just waved, quiet within the folds of his new navy jacket. Renny always winced to see it. He remembered his last sight of the old one, left covering Ocean's smoking body.

"Just in time," Vivian said. "Help Patrick on the inventory, would you? What time is your movie?"

"Eight-twenty," Frankie said, chaining his bike to the fence. Every motion was controlled. No wasted words. Even this small amount was, Renny knew, more than Frankie gave to most people. There were those who had been at Charisma Lake, and then there was the rest of the world.

Renny Sand had been there, and despite the pain and the nightmares, despite what he had seen and done, was glad. Not that it had happened, but that for once in his life he had been in the right place, at the right time, and had done the right thing.

Sometimes, that was enough.

84

Patrick's head came up as Destiny and Frankie entered the shop, and he breathed a sigh of relief. "Hey, dudes," he said.

Frankie waved, scanning the shelves as if looking for spiders. Destiny glared at Patrick and kissed his nose. "I am not a 'dude.' "

"Dudette, then."

"Try again."

"I guess 'bitch' is out of the question—" He ducked back to avoid her swinging palm, and she was after him, had chased him halfway around the shop and yanked his arm up behind his back in a punishing hold before he could escape. She leaned her head close as she pinned him against a pile of fabric. "Ow! Ow!" he protested.

"Take it back—"

"All right, I take it back. And I buy popcorn tonight."

She released him, and he rubbed his shoulder in protest. "You get no sympathy," she said.

"It was just a question—" She balled her fist, and he relented. "Okay. I'm a shit."

"Yep, but a cute shit."

"Head's up, guys," Frankie called. "Customers."

Patrick ran back to the front of the store as the front bell tingled, and three teenagers in leather pants entered. They looked like some odd cross-breeding of goth and leather punk, with pierced cheeks and belly buttons, leather vests open to the belt, spiked hair, pale skin and bad teeth. Two guys, one girl, and all thin as concentration camp inmates.

Patrick took his place behind the counter, continuing to inventory, watching them in the security mirrors. He'd seen these three around town. They'd even come into the store, asked a lot of questions, but ultimately purchased nothing. His mom was polite to them. Then again, she was polite to everyone.

Frankie was just trolling the aisles, maybe pretending to be another shopper. Patrick found himself immensely relieved that his friends were there, but that thought made him think of Shermie and Lee, and the distance that had grown between them. As he'd suspected, his friendship with them was irreparably strained by the events of the last year. The sudden flurry of media attention around Patrick, Destiny and Frankie hadn't helped at all.

One of the three "customers" was looking at leather studs in the glass case under the register, then looked up at Patrick. A gleam of recognition flashed in his eyes. "Hey, man," he said. His breath was like curdled milk. "Weren't you in the paper or something? That deal with the summer camp?"

Patrick said nothing. Destiny appeared beside him, her arm brushing his.

"That was like so fucked up!" the tall one crowed. "Did they ever find out what those assholes wanted?"

Patrick just shrugged. The media blitz had been intense, but brief. The killers were said to be veterans of an elite unit known as the Praetorians, who had followed Alexander Marcus, and subsequent to his death had gone bizarrely crazy. No motivations. Just the awful irony that the followers of a man Patrick admired had tried to kill fifty kids. The kids had all met in AOL's Musashi chat room. Marcus had admired Musashi, but there seemed no direct connection. Patrick believed that the FBI or the CIA or *somebody* knew more than they were saying. Maybe even his mom, or Renny.

The pierced guy studied Patrick as if he were a goldfish in a bowl, then laughed. "Snap, crackle, pop, man." He brayed as if he'd said the funniest thing in the world. His two friends were chortling now too, and picking up and putting down things in an accelerated, agitated fashion. Patrick could feel his stomach tightening. These assholes meant no good. Their blood was up, and they wanted trouble.

"Can we help you?" Destiny asked, a voice of reason in the growing storm.

Pierce-face looked at her incredulously. "Another one! And the other kid, too! What is it? This place specialize in fire sales?" The three of them were absolutely dissolving now.

Frankie had drifted up close to the cash register. His eyes were narrowed. He peered up at the tallest of the intruders, his face utterly calm. A touch of alarm squirmed along Patrick's scalp. He knew, Destiny knew, his mom and Renny and all the kids at Charisma Lake knew what Frankie had done, what he was capable of. Pray to God that no outsider would ever be privy to that terrible knowledge.

There was a brisk click at the back of the store, and his mother's most recent customer emerged from the dressing room, wearing a Storm costume from the *X-Men* movie. It was too tight for her, but in reality, his mother's magic hands would have found a way to make the costume work, if the customer really wanted it.

"Hello?" she called. "Do you think this is my size?"

Pierce-face looked back along the aisle, stared, and then hooted in disbelief. "Sure don't *look* like Halle Berry, lady."

Another one laughed until he was red in the face. "Beautiful skin, baby, but just too much of it." They were almost collapsing with mirth.

Frankie seemed almost unnaturally calm. *God, Frankie, please don't—*

The customer was red-faced, and just a little frightened by the hooting apparitions. At the moment when she seemed on the verge of tears, about to turn and flee to the safety of the dressing room, Frankie turned to her and said, "No, ma'am, that's probably not quite right, but I'm sure we have your size." His face was utterly sweet and sincere, his voice calming. "And I'm sure it will look fine." He paused for a moment, his head tilted at an angle. "Excuse me, but do you have relatives in Minnesota?"

She seemed confused, glancing back and forth between this pale, earnest boy and the three intruders, who had quieted, baffled by his line of conversation.

"No," she finally answered. "No, I don't think so."

"Do you know the Ranges? Jessica Range is my girlfriend. I'm going to visit her over spring break. You remind me of her."

For a moment she stared, as if wondering if he was teasing her. Frankie's face shone with sincerity, and her shoulders relaxed. "No, I don't think so," she said, a tiny smile curving her lips. "But I think she's a very lucky girl." She brushed her fingers along his cheek. Then she glared at the three dark-clad apparitions, and returned to the dressing room.

Frankie returned to the front desk. The three so-called "customers" pretended to shop for another minute or so, but their mood was broken, the fun over. Grumbling, they left the store.

Patrick high-fived Frankie. "Does she really remind you of Jessica?" he asked.

"Whattaya think?" Frankie grinned, then his expression went shy as Destiny gave him a tight, long hug. Frankie's eyes closed, and he gripped her for dear life. Patrick found something to keep himself busy until that hug ended, then the three of them began the work of closing the shop down for the evening. As they did, Patrick had time to think.

He should have trusted Frankie more, known that the *capacity* for violence is not the same thing as a *tendency* toward it.

All three of them had dreams, nightmares, night sweats too awful to share with anyone who didn't already know who they were, and what they had done.

His urges were there. But he had the other Charisma Lake kids now. They were scattered across the country, but they were a tribe, bonded by blood and heart. A tribe. Every day he was learning more, understanding more. He knew that there was something that no one would tell him, something that might help explain everything that had happened.

He sensed that there was a deeper truth, one connecting Patrick and Destiny, Lee and Shermie, Frankie Darling, and at least fifty other brothers and sisters. A pattern he couldn't understand, but would. He saw it in the eyes of the therapists sent by the government after that terrible time in Arizona. He saw it in Renny Sand's face.

Frankie still rolled the streets, but his parents were at least trying now. He had seen Reverend Darling's tears when he first hugged his son after the fire, and if it had taken Frankie a few seconds for his thin arms to twine around his father's waist, at least it had happened. A long road lay before the Darlings, but at least they had taken the first tiny steps.

That was, Patrick supposed, a small miracle. It was good to know that miracles actually happened from time to time. Miracles like life, and love.

Love. His mom was falling in love with Renny Sand. Despite being a reporter, Renny was actually pretty cool. The guy usually talked pretty straight with Patrick, despite hiding at least one secret.

Patrick knew he'd ferret it out one day. He, and the other kids. They had phones, and e-mail, and they all enjoyed games. The kids were sure they were being observed, but that was a game, too.

Sometimes he woke up in the middle of the night, with one of the bad dreams working its way up through the corridors of his mind. Occasionally when one of his mom's customers was rude in the shop, he imagined how it would be to show the bastards what *pain* really was. When the customer left, he would go to Destiny, or his mother, and they would hold him for a while. He would feel their warmth, and he would be all right. Sometimes Destiny needed to talk, or be held, and he was always there for her.

Sometimes the three of them went off on long walks in the woods with his mom and Renny, and they would talk of life, and play, and the seasons, or sports . . . anything but the dark red thing burrowing within him. And he knew that as long as he had friends and family like these, he was safe. Safe from the world, and from himself.

There was something in him, something with fangs and claws. Something that remembered the violence of the past year and said that it was *right,* it was *good,* and that the evil men who died had deserved their deaths, deserved *more* than death. In fact, they had been fortunate to have perished so easily.

The voices went no further than that before running into a wall composed of love, and morality, and sheer living will.

That thing, the thing within him and Frankie and Destiny that could kill, *had* killed, wasn't the greater part of them. It wasn't who they chose to be.

It wasn't who he chose to be.

A choice, once made, creates its own path. Truer words were never spoken.

We decide, he said to himself. *I decide. No matter what the world throws at me. I have people who love and understand me, and the future is waiting.*

And if every goddamned day he had to remind himself who and what he was, then so be it. Every successful person Patrick had ever read about had been constantly forced to remind himself who he was, what he was committed to. They all had urges and compulsions. What had Marcus said? *The mark of greatness was to master desire, rather than allowing desire to master you.*

Patrick knew he would be great, could feel it in his blood and in his bones. He had survived the tempering flames, and emerged stronger, purer. He would remind himself of that bright hot passage, of the flaming, lethal tornado of Charisma Lake that had swept all before it. Every day and every night for the rest of his life he would remember.

When he closed his eyes, that cone of fire roared. It danced in his dreams, purifying thought.

Exist for the good of mankind.

I decide, he thought.

I decide.